You Started It

You Started It

JACKIE KHALILIEH

tundra

Text copyright © 2025 by Jackie Khalilieh
Cover art copyright © 2025 by Leni Kauffman

Tundra Books, an imprint of Tundra Book Group,
a division of Penguin Random House Canada Ltd.,
320 Front Street West, Suite 1400, Toronto, Ontario, M5V 3B6, Canada
penguinrandomhouse.ca

Published simultaneously in the United States of America by Tundra Books of Northern New York, an imprint of Tundra Book Group, a division of Penguin Random House Canada Ltd., P.O. Box 2040, Plattsburgh, NY 12901, USA

Tundra with colophon is a registered trademark of Penguin Random House Canada Ltd.

All rights reserved. No part of this book may be reproduced, scanned, transmitted, or distributed in any form or by any electronic or mechanical means, including information storage and retrieval systems, without permission in writing from the publisher, except by a reviewer, who may quote brief passages in a review. No part of this book may be used or reproduced in any manner for the purpose of training artificial intelligence technologies or systems.

The authorized representative in the EU for product safety and compliance is Penguin Random House Ireland, Morrison Chambers, 32 Nassau Street, Dublin D02 YH68, Ireland, https://eu-contact.penguin.ie

Publisher's note: This book is a work of fiction. Names, characters, places and incidents either are the product of the author's imagination or are used fictitiously, and any resemblance to actual persons living or dead, events, or locales is entirely coincidental.

Library and Archives Canada Cataloguing in Publication

Title: You started it / Jackie Khalilieh.
Names: Khalilieh, Jackie, author.
Identifiers: Canadiana (print) 20240412079 | Canadiana (ebook) 20240413350 | ISBN 9781774884751 (hardcover) | ISBN 9781774884768 (EPUB)
Subjects: LCGFT: Romance fiction. | LCGFT: Novels.
Classification: LCC PS8621.H3365 Y68 2025 | DDC jC813/.6—dc23

Library of Congress Control Number: 2024940850

Edited by Lynne Missen
Designed by Lisa Jager
Production edited by Bharti Bedi
Typeset by Terra Page
The text was set in Arno Pro.

Printed in the United States of America

1st Printing

Dear Reader,

This novel contains the following:

- Discussions of anxiety disorder.
- Physical symptoms of anxiety on page, including irritable bowel syndrome (IBS) symptoms.
- Multiple panic attacks.
- Character with claustrophobia.
- Divorce. Absent parent.
- References to a past teenage pregnancy and birth.
- References to alcoholism.

If any of these topics are sensitive for you, I hope you will be comforted in knowing that much of the story celebrates love, in all forms, as well as joy. If you decide to continue on the ride, I promise that you will find a very happy ending.

With love,
Jackie

For Dad,
the best man I ever knew.
I miss your lectures (I will always try to make sure my gas tank is full);
I miss your laugh (especially when it was at my expense);
and most of all, I miss you (every second of every day).
This one is for you.
The one with the Arab hero.
Because that's what you were to me.

♥ Jacko

"The question isn't, 'What are we going to do?'
The question is, 'What aren't we going to do?'"

Ferris Bueller's Day Off

CHAPTER ONE

I can look at a picture of myself, even one I don't remember posing for, and know exactly how I was feeling when it was taken. It's in the eyes. What is it that people say? They're the window to the soul? It is one hundred percent a cheesy cliché but also, in my experience, one hundred percent true.

When I look at this picture of me and Ben taken the summer before ninth grade, every thought and emotion I harbored in that moment was captured. Not for the world to see. To anyone else, it's merely a photo of two kids smiling for the camera. But for me, it's like a time capsule of the girl I was when Ben Cameron entered my life.

Mom told us to pose for the photo in front of Ben's large maple tree. My stomach fluttered as if a thousand tiny butterflies were performing a choreographed dance when he placed his arm around me. We'd known each other for almost two months by then. We both had huge crushes but hadn't admitted them yet. It's so obvious though. My smile is embarrassingly wide in the picture. And not only because Ben's fingers were on my bare shoulder. I was on the precipice of something big: high school was a week away and I'd be the new girl. But I wasn't going in alone. I had Ben, and for the first time in a long time, I was excited about my future.

Despite the bright smile and butterflies, my eyes do a poor job of hiding the grief. I hadn't learned to live with it yet. I still (foolishly) held out hope Dad would come back for us. That was three years ago, and I haven't seen my father since.

"Jamie, Ben's here to see you," Mom calls from downstairs. She has her sweet-but-fake voice on. The one that matches her non-intimidating stature, but I know better. I tuck the photo back in my memory box and shove it under my bed before glancing at my phone. Four thirty. Great. I lost two hours browsing through old photos and mementos when I was supposed to be looking for my left Converse. My time management skills need work. So do my organizational skills.

"Looking for this?" Amo Eli stands in the doorframe of my room holding up my missing shoe, a sourpuss expression on his squishy face. Makes it hard to take him seriously.

"Yas queen," I say, practically leaping to grab it. He grimaces as I reunite it with my other shoe.

"Don't 'yas queen' me. I tripped on this thing walking up the stairs." He sighs as he takes in my bedroom. "Why is it every time I come in here it looks like your room has just given birth to fifty more books? The mess I can almost tolerate, and there are worse things to be than a book nerd, but I can't deal with the rest of my house looking as if a teenaged tornado has swept through. Capiche?"

"Did you know the word 'capiche' derives from the Italian word 'capire,' which means 'to understand,' and from the Latin 'capere,' which translates to 'to grasp or to seize'?" I ask my uncle, while holding back a grin.

"Jamie..."

"And," I continue while slipping on my shoes, "in formal Italian, 'capiche' is pronounced 'cah-PEE-sheh,' but in Italian slang and

English it's 'cah-PEESH.' I bet you thought it started with a *K* but, fun fact, there's no *K* in the Italian alphabet."

"What is your point?" He folds his arms while very obviously trying not to look impressed, even though I know he is.

"My point, Amo, is that no one uses the word 'capiche' anymore, unless maybe they're an Italian nonno. Capiche?"

"Jamie!" Mom calls again.

"I'm coming." I try to exit my room but my uncle is still blocking the door. I have four inches on him, but he has girth. "I'm sorry," I finally say, giving him my best puppy dog eyes.

"I don't get how someone who is such a stick-in-the-mud type A could also be such a hot mess."

"Ask yourself that," I say, squeezing past him and smacking him on the butt before racing down the steps.

"You're lucky I love you so much," he shouts from above.

"Ben." I can't fight back my smile as I reach the bottom of the stairs where Mom has Ben captive in the foyer. I wrap my arms around his neck and pull his body to mine for a long overdue hug, but he's stiff as a board. He's always trying to be respectful in front of my mom.

"Ben was filling me in on his summer adventures," Mom says as I release Ben. "Maybe I *should* have let you tag along. Sounds like he learned a lot." Mom elbows Ben's side and grins at me. She can't actually be serious. I begged and pleaded with her to join Ben at camp and now she acts as if she made a small mistake by making me stay behind, like buying the salt-reduced bacon. "Ben, let me know if you need me to cut your hair before school starts."

Ben runs a hand though his dark locks and nods. He's tanned. Looks a little more muscular. His hair is longer than it's ever been. But he's still perfect. I try to make eye contact with him, hoping he'll read my mind and say something to appease my mother so she'll leave, but he's not meeting my gaze.

"Jamie, did you clean your room?" Mom asks.

"I'll do it later," I say, locking my arm through Ben's. I just want to be alone with my boyfriend. Is that too much to ask?

"Jamie," my mother says, like it's the only word in her vocabulary.

"Yes, Mother," I reply, clenching my jaw and wrapping my fingers around Ben's wrist.

"Would it hurt you to try to at least exhibit a show of gratitude? This is your uncle's home. All he asks is that you clean up after yourself."

"I'm not the one who got hair dye on his Persian rug," I say, clasping on tighter to Ben. He finally looks at me and his eyes are telling me to let it go, but how can I? This is so embarrassing. She always picks a fight whenever he's around.

"That was an unfortunate accident, which occurred because I had to race upstairs to answer the door mid-client since *someone* had their headphones on. And I paid to have it cleaned. It's important that we show Eli we respect him and his home."

"Okay."

"Okay?" she repeats.

I unspool my arm from Ben's, stepping up to my mother. Ben remains by the door, probably planning our escape. Can't blame him. My mother ruins everything. This was supposed to be a romantic reunion, but she won't get the hint and scurry off to her basement salon.

"What else do you want me to say?" I raise my hands, then quickly lower them once I realize it looks like I'm about to choke her.

Mom puffs air out of her nostrils and places one hand on her hip. "I want you to say, 'Sure, Mom. I'll keep my crap out of the rest of the house and maybe I'll even clean my room once in a while. I might even cut the attitude and show some appreciation to my uncle who has sacrificed his privacy for us.'"

"If this is not a good time . . ." Ben begins, his hand on the doorknob.

"It's a great time. Mom," I say, glaring at her, "I haven't seen Ben in two months. TWO. MONTHS. Can you save this lecture for later?" Ben's been away working as a counselor at an overnight camp up north. The goal was to go together, but Mom wasn't cool with the idea. Even though I'm seventeen, going on eighteen, and even though she's pretty chill for an Arab mom, it was still a hard no. But if she knew me as well as she claims, she'd know Ben and I would never do *that* . . . at least not yet.

We're waiting until winter formal.

"Fine. Amo is going out with Eric tonight. He wants to bring him back here after. Just make yourself scarce," she says.

"All good. We'll hang out at Ben's," I say, nodding at him for approval.

He opens his mouth and looks back and forth between us. "Actually, that might not work."

"Why not?" I ask, trying to read his adorable but slightly distanced face. We've been together since our ninth grade winter formal. That's when we made it official, but we were destined to happen. Our moms were best friends in high school. They grew apart when my mom married my father and moved to the middle of nowhere. Okay, not the middle of nowhere, but two hours north of Toronto. One of the few benefits of my dad leaving us has been getting to live closer to the city.

Ben's mom, Lucy, and my uncle remained close through the years and even live in the same neighborhood. So, when Mom and I came to stay with my uncle three years ago, it was only a matter of time before Ben and I would have our magical meet-cute.

It happened about a week after we'd settled in. Mom, Eli, and I were invited to Ben's house for a barbecue to welcome us to the neighborhood. I'd heard about Ben. Was told he'd show me around and make my transition easier. I wanted to tell my mom that I didn't need someone to make things easier for me, but that would have required an open and honest conversation, and we weren't always so good at that. Especially back then when things were still so raw.

Growing up as an only child with parents who sometimes suffered from a state of arrested development, I'd gotten used to being independent. Over the years, there were kids who tried to befriend me, and I sometimes tried, despite being a shy and anxious child. But my parents were so inconsistent. They'd agree to bring me to a birthday party and then cancel last minute when they forgot to buy a gift. Mom would arrange playdates, but after one of my friends told her parents that my mom and dad screamed at each other the whole time she was over, word got out and people stopped accepting *and* extending invitations. That's when books became a lifeline. As long as I had a good story to keep me company at recess and on weekends, I could block out the rest of the world.

When I saw Ben for the first time, reading on a hammock, it instantly put me at ease. He was my kind of people. Back then, he wasn't as tall as he is now, or as filled out, but I could see the potential.

"What're you reading?" I asked, deciding to skip all pleasantries. He was dressed in khaki shorts and a short-sleeved button-up shirt, like he was about to attend an all-day golf tournament.

Ben looked up from his book, his hazel eyes locking in on mine. The breadth of his smile reached almost across his face, and it made his eyes disappear into little slits. He had this one tiny dimple on his left cheek, and the sight of it melted me. *Maybe being an independent woman is slightly overrated*, I thought.

"It's just . . . um . . ." He struggled to get out of the hammock, stumbling slightly and dropping his book. "You're Jamie?"

"I'm Jamie," I said as he bent down to retrieve the book. He seemed a little awkward, but to me, it was endearing.

"My mom—" He cleared his throat. "She didn't tell me you were so . . ."

"So . . . tall?"

"No." Ben looked down at the ground, trying to hide his blush. He cleared his throat again, finally looking me in the eye. "Pretty."

I couldn't help but smile. Puberty had been quick and kind to me, but being pretty isn't enough. It doesn't fix the messy parts of your life. It doesn't keep your parents together. It doesn't stop you from doing or saying or thinking things you shouldn't. "Thanks. My mother probably thinks warning people about the words that may come out of my mouth is more important than giving them a heads-up about my supposed above-average looks."

And then something unusual happened: Ben laughed, the sound like a song I wanted to play on repeat. The tingles that pulsed through my body in response told me everything I needed to know: this guy would be my first—everything.

"You're funny too," he said, standing straighter.

"My mother doesn't seem to think so."

Ben glanced over my shoulder and sucked in a smile. I turned to find the adults gathered by the barbecue, pretending not to watch us. Ben waved politely at my mom and uncle before returning his gaze to me.

"There must be some sort of microchip that reprograms a person's DNA once they have kids, which sets off as soon as we turn thirteen. That's when they seem to stop understanding us," he said.

"Yes. Oh my god, YES! Although"—I paused and spoke more quietly—"my mother and I made it to fourteen before that fully happened."

"Aren't you fourteen now?" he asked. I nodded, and Ben studied me for a moment before asking, "What happened this year?"

I twisted my heel into the grass, deciding whether I was going to open up to this person or not. My heart told me I could, but my brain said *Be careful*. I'd carried around a heaviness, this all-consuming dread, ever since . . . ever since.

"Things with my parents kind of went downhill," I responded with a level stare.

"Right," Ben said. "I heard your dad isn't really in the picture anymore."

"No. It's why we're here."

Ben's eyes slowly met mine, causing my heart to thump, thump, thump into my throat. "Is it wrong for me to admit I'm kind of glad you're here?"

"No." I smiled. "I'm kind of glad I'm here too." And in that moment, I really meant it. "So, the book?" I asked, nodding to it.

"It's a . . . um . . . it's stupid," he said, holding it up.

"*How to Kill It in Life: A Guide to Achieving Everything You Want (and More)*," I read aloud. "Kind of intense."

"Yeah, well, I'm kind of an intense guy." He rolled his shoulders back, and it was like he was letting his guard down slightly, just for me.

"I've also been told I can be quite intense." By my former classmates. My father. My mother. Basically, anyone who has ever met me.

I haven't quite found the balance between feeling *too much* and *not enough*. It's like I was born on high alert or something. Always waiting for the other shoe to drop. *What now? What more can life throw at me?* I'm either aware of every single thing surrounding me or I disassociate, watching the world unfold and I'm just an invisible character taking it all in.

"As far as I'm concerned, intensity equals passion, and who wants to live a life without passion?" Ben asked.

"My mom apparently," I quipped, and Ben chuckled. Up until this point, I hadn't found my match—not in friendship or in love. I'd been searching for that person, *my* person, for my whole life. I couldn't help but wonder if there was something inherently wrong with me, something that made me unfriendable—besides my messy parents. But it became clear that day: all this time, the person I'd been searching for was Ben. Moving here was my fresh start, and Ben was my endgame.

"You can't come over because I already have plans," Ben says to me now. He swallows and his eyes dart away from my stare.

"I should go—I have a client," Mom says, tossing Ben a strained yet polite smile. It's like she's finally clued in that she's being a gigantic third wheel.

"Plans?" I ask Ben, as Mom heads to her salon. "Why would you make plans without me on a Friday night? I thought we could discuss our Kill-It List before school starts. Make sure our goals for the year sync up. I've added a few since we last spoke. I was thinking of taking calculus instead of statistics. Figured it would open more doors when university applications come around. What do you think?"

Ben reaches a hand behind his head and scratches his neck. "Maybe we could just stay here for a bit."

So that's what this is all about. Ben wants to be alone with me. A smile spreads across my face as I grab his hand and lead him past the foyer.

Amo Eli comes down the stairs. "Na-ah! No shoes on my new runner," he says, pointing at my feet.

"Hi, Mr. Taher," Ben says, nodding a cordial hello at my uncle. *Mr. Taher?*

"Benjamin. You too. Shoes off."

I roll my eyes before removing my shoes and kicking them to the front door entrance. What is up everyone's butt? Today is a great day! The sun is shining. Ben is back. And school starts in less than a week.

"And you wonder why you lose your shoes," Amo says as one shoe ends up behind his bench.

"Do you mind?" I ask my uncle, who is barricading access to the stairs. "We kind of want to be alone."

"Why would I mind? This only happens to be my home." Eli steps aside and heads to the foyer where he proceeds to arrange my shoes neatly, side by side, next to Ben's.

"Let's go to my room," I say, pulling on Ben's arm.

"Leave the door open," Eli shouts as we walk up the steps, two at a time.

"Finally," I say, slamming the bedroom door shut and basically tackling Ben to my bed. "I missed you so much." I bring my lips to his but he turns his cheek and crawls out from underneath me.

"Let's talk."

"Ugh," I say, tipping my head back. "All we've done this summer is talk. When I said I missed you, I meant I missed your bod." I try to untuck his polo from his shorts but he pulls away.

"I can't do this right now." He gets up and walks to the other side of my room.

"Can't do what? Kiss me? I'm your girlfriend." A sudden rush of nausea swirls through me. Usually, when we're alone, Ben can't keep his hands off me. We've been counting down to our senior winter formal for two years. We decided it would be the perfect night and setting for our first time. It's just over a hundred days away (not that I'm counting). I wasn't always so obsessed with making goals and lists and checking things off. It's Ben's influence. He said it would help with my nerves and he was right. Ben makes me better.

"Jamie, we need to talk."

"Okay," I say, perched on the edge of my bed. Maybe Ben requires more time to ease himself in. He's kind of thoughtful like that. He needs to feel a connection before getting physical. Unlike me, who is basically raring to go 24/7.

Ben tosses the dirty clothes piled on my desk chair to the floor and sits across from me. "I've been thinking a lot about senior year."

"Me too." I reach for the notebook on my nightstand atop a stack of overdue library books and open it up to the purple tab, labeled *Senior Year*. "I've got it all planned out. Check this out," I say, as the nausea is replaced with excitement. "We've spent three years talking about how we live in this great city and never go to any of the tourist traps, so I made a list of all the dates we can go on, leading up to winter formal. Sort of like an extracurricular branch to our Kill-It List."

I place the notebook in Ben's lap, and his eyes move through the list I've curated with accompanying photos. "Ripley's Aquarium . . . Royal Ontario Museum . . . CN Tower?" he asks, looking up at me. "I thought you were afraid of heights."

"I'm not afraid of heights. I'm afraid of elevators. I'm claustrophobic. How don't you know that?" It's been eight weeks. Not eight months.

Ben puts the notebook back on my nightstand and tips his head down. "Here's the thing . . ."

Oh no. Not the thing. That's how my dad started his sentence before he told me he was leaving.

"Here's the thing, James," Dad said, using his nickname for me. "I'm feeling a bit stifled here. I'm getting older and my life is slipping away from me. This isn't what I saw for myself. I just need some distance to figure things out. But I promise I'll be back."

I was such a fool for believing him.

"This is our last year of high school," Ben goes on, "and I don't know, I kind of want to loosen the reins." He runs a hand through his shaggy hair. "We've been in our own bubble for three years, just you and me, checking things off our lists. Like, don't you think it's a little pathetic that we have to plan our dates in advance?" he asks, nodding to my notebook. "Why didn't we ever just hop on the subway and go to the ROM or the aquarium?"

"I thought you liked lists. And plans. And setting goals." My cheeks flush as my voice grows higher and squeakier with each word. It's like I'm fourteen again.

"I thought I did too, but then, this summer was . . ." He laughs and there's a far-off look in his eyes. Ben Cameron doesn't do far-off looks. "Everything went off the rails. The kids were monsters and it rained almost every day. The itinerary had to change from second to second, and you know what happened?"

Words don't come to me as a piercing cramp stabs through my lower abdomen. I bring my hand to my stomach and exhale, trying to hide the pain while squeezing my eyes shut.

"We had so much fun. Being forced to switch things up. Trying and failing and trying again. I got to know people on a really deep level." My eyes blink open to find that the color has come back to Ben's cheeks. He's speaking so fast, I don't recognize the person in front of me. "People I never would have spoken to before. Something that wouldn't have happened if I'd stuck to the plan."

People? In the three years Ben and I have been together, we've never needed other people. It's always just been us.

"Okay, so fine." I nod, trying to keep my cool, playing along with this new version of Ben. "We won't do lists this year. We'll just fly by the seat of our pants. I can do that." I grab a pen and the notebook, flipping to a new page. I write in all caps *BE SPONTANEOUS*.

"No." Ben shakes his head. "Not we. Me. I'm sorry, Jamie, but I think we should break up."

"Wait, what? Are you serious?" I straighten in my seat, the notebook sliding off my lap and onto the floor. All those dancing butterflies fall to the pit of my stomach and I'm seconds away from throwing them up. "I'll play along. I'll be whatever you want me to be." My voice cracks. I can't let him walk out that door. If he does, it'll be just like my father. And I regret not trying harder to convince him to stay. I won't make that mistake again.

"Do you even hear yourself?"

No. All I hear is the sound of my heart breaking.

"Jamie, you're just clinging to me because it's comfortable, because I'm all you know, but this would be good for you too," he says, like he's trying to convince me to try a new vegetable.

"What's wrong with being comfortable?"

"Do you really want to go through life making safe choices? It doesn't leave room for us to make mistakes and grow."

"So, let's grow together," I say, grabbing his hands.

"You're not getting it," Ben says, ripping his hands away from mine and standing. "I need to strike out on my own. See what else is out there. Being with you is holding me back. It's holding both of us back."

"No." I shake my head and bolt up, my hands balled into fists. "You're wrong."

"I'm sorry, Jamie. It's over."

"What about winter formal?" I know it's pathetic of me to ask, to even use sex to get him back, but I'm desperate. He's slipping away. My anchor. My everything.

"The winter formal plan is off." Ben pauses and takes one last look at me and my room, like this is the final picture of me he'll have in his head. "Hopefully we can be friends someday." He forces out the world's phoniest smile before opening my door and leaving.

Friends? Someday? This isn't Ben. This isn't the way it's supposed to be. For the last three years it's been Ben Cameron and Jamie Taher-Foster. Why do the men in my life keep leaving me? What am I doing wrong? Not only am I unfriendable, but apparently, I'm unlovable too.

CHAPTER TWO

It's been just over twenty-four hours since Ben dumped me. I haven't left my room or bed since it happened, except to use the bathroom. A lot. I've decided to torture myself by scrolling through three years' worth of pictures, zooming in on Ben's face, trying to determine if he was ever happy or just faking it all this time. But all it's doing is making me feel worse. Am I supposed to delete all my photos of us?

Wait, what if Ben has already erased me from his socials?

"Are you decent?" Amo Eli asks from outside my door.

"Yeah," I respond from bed, forcing myself to put my phone down as my uncle enters my den of heartbreak.

"Where's Benjamin?" Amo Eli asks, his eyes darting around my room. "I was worried I'd come in here to find the two of you macking."

"Amo, if you're going to insist on speaking like you've stepped out of a sitcom from the nineties, could you at least get the terms right?"

"What? Mackin' the ladies—it's, like, kissing and . . . other things."

"No. Mackin' is like flirting, obnoxiously, trying to *get* with the ladies."

"And what else?" he asks, now seated on the edge of my bed.

"What else, what?" My face scrunches up as I try to both read my uncle's expression and find a polite way to get rid of him.

"What are the other meanings of the word 'macking'? You know you want to tell me." He places a hand on my leg, shaking it. Just like that, I lose my cool, bursting into a fit of tears. "Habibi, what's wrong?" he asks, scooching closer. He lays his bear paw hands on my arm, which I'm using to mask the tears.

"Nothing. Except everything. My life as I know it is over!"

"It can't be that bad," he says, moving my arm away from my face. And there it is—a pitying look. I guess I'd better get used to receiving those now that I've been dumped.

I sit up and draw my knees to my chest, wrapping my arms around them. "Ben broke up with me."

"Hmar," my uncle says, his upper lip raised like he's a matador trying to intimidate a bull. As much as I appreciate him taking my side, calling Ben a donkey isn't all that helpful. And even if he is a donkey, he's my donkey. Or at least he was. "Do you want to tell me why?"

"Not really." I size Amo Eli up and, unfortunately, am unable to stop my face from reacting. "Going somewhere?"

"You don't like my outfit?" He pulls on his bright pink polo and runs a hand over his teal shorts.

"It's just a little casual." It's loud is what it is. Doesn't quite go with the pickle-up-his-butt persona and minimalist home decor.

"We're going to a clambake. Sort of a 'goodbye to summer' party. You want to come?" he asks, his brown eyes open wide.

I can think of a million things I'd rather be doing than hanging out with my uncle and his boyfriend. They're in the lovestruck phase, where everything they do or say is adorable to one another. I hate it. Ben and I were never that mushy. Well, Ben wasn't. I tried to suppress those giddy feelings. He didn't really believe in public displays of affection, which made the few times he held my hand in public special.

"I'll pass. But thanks." Wouldn't want to get in the middle of someone else's flourishing relationship.

First, it'll be overnight visits. Then Eric will start moving his things in gradually. Next thing you know, my uncle will be sitting Mom and me down before saying, "Here's the thing . . ." It won't be long before we're left to figure out a new plan.

"What about Mom?" I ask. "What's she doing tonight?"

"She's giving the salon a deep clean and restock for fall." He leans in. "Between you and me, your mother needs to get a life. So back to Benjamin. What happened?"

I get up and start picking all my discarded clothes off the floor. "He wants to break free. Experience senior year without ties or binds to me." I aggressively collect my clothes until there's a huge pile against my chest. "As if three years together, planning and building up to this moment, means nothing to him. He got a taste of what it's like to be 'one of them.' A person who goes through life without goals and a 'let's see what happens' mentality. He's not cut out for that lifestyle. He needs grounding. He needs structure. He *needs* me," I say, standing in front of my uncle and dropping the pile while pointing to my chest.

"Sit." Amo pats my bed and I grudgingly sit next to him. "You remind me a lot of your mother, you know?"

"You're supposed to be trying to make me feel better," I say.

He shifts to face me and I match his pose, humoring him. It's not like I have anyone else to confide in. My whole world has been Ben for the last thirty-seven months. I never bothered to nurture any other friendships because I didn't need to. It was me and Ben against the world. Or at least, it was supposed to be.

"Your mother is a stubborn mule like you are. And there's a time and place for that. But other times you have to step back and listen to what the universe is telling you. What Benjamin is telling you. Jamie, my little firecracker, this boy has made it clear he doesn't want to be with you. Why spend another second wasted on him?"

"Because he's wrong. He doesn't know what he wants. He's confused. He hasn't acclimated yet back to real life. His head is still in the clouds."

"Khalas," my uncle says, his voice rising slightly. "Stop making excuses for Benjamin. I don't even see what's so great about him anyway." Eli clicks his tongue and rolls his eyes like the drama queen he is. "He's what my generation called a wannabe. Let him go. You, my love, will find someone deserving of your attention. Someone who loves the real you."

Love the real me? How could someone love the real me when I'm not even sure who that is without Ben?

"He is right about something though," my uncle continues. "This is your last year of high school. A great opportunity for you to live a little, make new friends, see what the world has to offer." He eyes my notebook, then me. "Without a plan. Or lists."

"I can't believe you compared me to my mother at a time like this."

"Did you hear *anything* I said?" he asks. "Ya Allah." He checks his phone. "I have to go. What're you doing tonight?"

"You're asking me, a recently dumped seventeen-year-old, what my plans for tonight are? Are you trying to make me cry again?"

"No. I'm trying to make sure you do something other than sulk in your room while looking at pictures of you and Benjamin. The guy has no style. No sense of humor. He did you a favor. Look around, Jamie." Whenever my Canadian-born uncle gets passionate about something, which is often, a random Arabic accent surfaces and he starts pronouncing my name Jam-e, dragging out the *J*.

"I'm looking."

"The person you turned into for Benjamin wasn't the real you. The real you is spunky. Messy. Chaotic. Loud. Brilliant. You tried to be something you weren't for him. But you couldn't keep up the charade. That's why your room looks like this. It's your safe space. Where you let it all out. A reflection of the real Jamie."

"What are you even saying?" I fold my arms over my chest, trying hard not to roll my eyes.

"I'm saying you watered yourself down to be the version of Jamie that Benjamin wanted. He took all your best qualities and put them in a box. You're free of that now. All of it."

"But you hate that I'm messy. You called me a tornado yesterday."

"So? You remember everything I've ever said?" His lips set in a hard line. "You are who you are and you need to find people who get you."

"Sure. You make it sound so easy."

"Hey," he says, his thick brows furrowing. "I know more than anyone else how hard it is to find yourself. I grew up with Arab parents in the nineties. 'Gay' wasn't and still isn't a word in their vernacular. But," he says, his expression softening, "you don't have to deal with that bullshit."

No. I just have an absent father and a mother who I constantly butt heads with—probably because I look just like the man who left her.

"You'll see, with some time and distance, this is probably the best thing to ever happen to you. And when that moment comes, I expect you to find me and say 'You were right, Amo.'" He points to his face for a kiss. I oblige, giving him a peck on his scruffy cheek. He places a kiss on my forehead before standing.

"For what it's worth, in the UK, 'macking' is slang for surfing a large, powerful wave."

"Sounds like a mack daddy of a ride." My uncle smirks before tripping on a shoe and shooting me a look full of wrath. "Clean this room."

"I am who I am!" I shout back as he exits.

And what I am is someone who makes the rules, so sorry, Ben Cameron, you don't get to decide when things are over. That's not how this works. This is my life you're messing with.

He's the one who turned me into this person. Someone who had to set goals and meet them. It's like a drug. I can't stop now. If the plan falls apart, it'll have a domino effect on the rest of our future together—and my own. Matching undergrads at University of Toronto to go with our matching law degrees from McGill University. You're not getting the win on this one, Ben. You started it. Now, I'm going to finish it.

I grab my notebook and open it to a new page with a new tab.

Goal: Get Ben Cameron back in time for winter formal.

CHAPTER THREE

Step one in getting Ben back: a plan. I need to come at this logically, logistically and without emotion. I have to make it so he sees what a major mistake he's made. I will *not* grovel. I might want Ben Cameron back with every inch of my body (and loins), but I know enough about guys to know thirsting after them isn't a good look.

But first, food! That's what I need to temporarily fill the emptiness inside me. Everything is fixable. Well, almost everything.

I poke around my uncle's immaculate kitchen in search of something to eat. I skipped dinner last night and all three meals today. I've gone from hunger strike to ravenous. But it's Saturday night, which means the kitchen is closed and we're expected to fend for ourselves. My mother popped her head into my room only once since my ass got dumped, to see why I was hibernating, and didn't push when I'd blamed it on an "engrossing book." She's one of those people who eats only to fuel herself. Nadia Taher (no longer hyphen Foster) doesn't derive any pleasure in biting into a juicy cheeseburger or forking a gravy-filled bowl of poutine.

I slam the cabinets, unable to find anything appetizing. Usually there's leftovers from my uncle's shawarma restaurant in the fridge, but tonight it's bare.

"Jamie, is that you up there?" Mom calls from the basement.

A long, annoyed breath escapes me. "Yes."

"Come down here, would you?" she asks.

I shove a couple crackers in my mouth before heading down. Mom has her dark, curly hair up in a messy topknot with a thick chartreuse headband keeping back the baby hairs. All her products are spread out on the shiny white tiled floor, in groups.

What was supposed to be a temporary stay three years ago has become permanent. Mom built her salon, In the Hair Tonight, in Amo Eli's basement and does well, despite its terrible name (big Phil Collins fan). Mom's a savvy businesswoman. She's better at social media than I am. Her salon Insta has over five thousand followers and she's constantly enlisting my help with creating reels. Most of the girls from my high school come here. Sometimes Mom forces me to help when a classmate is getting their hair done, hoping we'll, like, bond over hair dye or something. Even after I started dating Ben, she wouldn't let up about making friends. Like it's so easy. Like baking a cake or something.

"Could you dust the top shelves for me?" she says, handing me the Swiffer. "Make sure you get the corners."

As I'm dusting, Mom hits Play on her terrible playlist, which is overrun with songs by Phil Collins—or "Uncle Phil," which is what I used to call him when I was a child with no discernable musical taste of my own.

"Why aren't you and Ben out?" she asks, wiping the mirrors.

That's shocking. Amo Eli didn't run straight to Mom to spill the tea. I pause, debating whether to tell her the truth. Mom likes Ben but has made it clear that she a) doesn't think he's the one for me, and b) believes I'm way too serious about him. "Learn from my mistakes," she likes to say.

"We're taking a break," I respond, avoiding eye contact. Maybe it's better if Mom believes this was my choice too. That way, when we get back together, she won't hold it against Ben for breaking my heart.

"Oh, Jamie, I'm sorry. How did you both arrive at this decision?"

I turn and face her, biting back the tirade of angry words I want to shout for both her lackluster attempt at empathy and her therapist-like question. "It's fine." I raise my shoulders and return to the shelves, dusting with vigor. "He's just going through a phase. Those camp kids got into his head. Something that wouldn't have happened if I'd been allowed to go with him."

Mom comes up behind me and places her hand on my arm, forcing me to stop my aggressive dusting and face her. "Jamie," she says, her head tilted at me like I'm three. "Are you two really on a break or did you break up?"

"Ben may have been the one to suggest it."

"Suggest the break?"

"No," I say through gritted teeth. "Suggest we break up, okay? Is that what you want to hear?"

Mom's face falls at my tone. I'd almost feel bad if I didn't feel so sad for myself. She brings up a hand and strokes my cheek. "Sweetie."

"It's fine," I say, shrugging her off. "I'm giving him space. He'll change his mind."

"And if he doesn't?" Mom asks. I can tell by how she's looking at me that alarm bells are going off inside her head. Whenever I snap or refuse to listen to her, she instantly jumps to the conclusion that my anxiety is taking over. God forbid she'd see my moodiness as a rightful result of being dumped and not assume the worst.

"He will," I respond with indignant determination.

"Just don't pretend you're not hurting, like your father does. Ethan Foster would rather bury his head in the sand than admit to having feelings. Emotions are completely natural."

"I know that," I reply, taking a step back.

"Even still, it might not be a terrible idea for you to book an appointment with Dr. Mueller again. I know you're not interested in seeing a therapist on a regular basis, but seasonal check-ins might be helpful for managing your anxiety," Mom says, hope brimming in her voice.

And there it is. The suggestion I knew was lurking around the corner. "It's not that serious," I say, a forced laugh escaping. "Truly. I'm fine."

Mom nods and walks back to her chair, wiping the table under the mirror. "This is probably for the best," she says. "You've been with Ben since you were fourteen. All your high school experiences are attached to him. This will give you time to get to know yourself before you go off to university. Figure out what Jamie wants."

Jamie wants a cheeseburger and not to hear her mother spew terrible advice. Mom wouldn't know good advice if it landed on the tip of her nose. Her life has been a series of bad decisions. Dating my father against her parents' wishes. Getting pregnant at eighteen. Eloping and moving far away from everyone. Cutting her parents out of her life. Then turning the only person on her side—my dad—against her by constantly nagging him to be someone he was never meant to be. She makes me so angry, but sometimes I just feel sorry for her.

This isn't the life she wanted. And I just serve as a giant, five-foot-ten reminder of that. But hey, at least I can reach the top shelves.

"Do you need me for anything else?" I ask once I'm done dusting.

Mom stares at me, her eyebrows knitted together, like she's trying to figure me out. "No. You're free to go. I won't even ask you to clean your room." She cracks a smile and for a split second, I see the mom who held my hand on my first day of kindergarten. The one who endured my weird crush on SpongeBob SquarePants by watching it alongside me, on repeat. The mom who slept next to me in bed every night for a month after Dad walked out on us.

And then swiftly made me get fitted for a night guard because, apparently, I grind my teeth in my sleep.

"Good. Because I wasn't planning on it," I say, cracking my own miniscule smile. I stall, trying to melt some of the ice between us. "I'm going to grab something to eat. Want anything?"

"I'm fine. Drive safe," she says before crouching down and polishing the stainless steel base of her chair.

I nod and head back upstairs.

Just as I'm about to walk out the front door, I catch my reflection in the hallway mirror. What's so wrong with me that Ben had to end our relationship days before senior year? I'm a solid 8.5 and stand out in that mixed-race kind of way. My dad and his family have been here for multiple generations by way of England. Mom's a first-generation child of Palestinian immigrants. Together they had me: a tall, dark-haired, olive-skinned girl with light-brown eyes. Aside from that, I'm highly intelligent. What more could Ben want?

So maybe I don't really have any talents outside of being able to read fast and ace tests. I just never spent much time focusing on other things. As early as I can remember, Mom lamented how much she wished she had gone to university and how her life would be different (a.k.a. better) if she'd had a "proper" education. That's the one thing I've taken from her: the drive to be successful. Ben saw that drive and encouraged it even more.

I close the front door behind me. It's barely eight but it's already dark, another sign summer is almost over. This is usually my favorite time of year. A fresh start looming, the promise of great things, but tonight the violet-tinged sky just makes me want to lay flat on the grass and cry. But I'm tired of crying over men.

Parked outside the drive-thru, I down my cheeseburger, medium fries, and water (because health). I'm not ready to go back home. *Home.* Even saying that feels like a cheat. It's not the home I grew up in. Sometimes I feel like a squatter, especially when Eli rags on me for my messy room. What did he even mean by saying my room was a reflection of my true self?

I'll just drive around listening to sad music until I'm ready to go hide in my room, and if I happen to pass Ben's house and if his lights happen to be on, then maybe I'll walk myself up to his front door. He may find it hard to resist me under the night sky and in the late summer breeze.

I turn the corner onto Varley Crescent, mentally preparing what I'm going to say when I ring Ben's doorbell, and a baby-blue BMW convertible catches my eye. It's parked in front of Ben's house. I don't recognize that car as belonging to anyone in Ben's family or extended family. I would know. Ben's house is like my second home. What's more annoying is that this baby-blue eyesore is parked where I usually park my car.

I slow down to study the BMW. As my car crawls past Ben's house, his front door opens and a girl steps outside. Her face is covered by a dark shadow, but her shoulder-length black hair is shiny even at night. She's a tiny little thing with a snatched waist. *Who is this?* Probably the owner of the obnoxiously colored car. Ben joins her a second later, shutting the front door.

I lower my music and open the window, hoping to hear something, anything, to help me figure out who this is. I'd like to believe this is some sort of door-to-door evangelist or Girl Scout, but my heart tells me it's something else. The ease between Ben and this person. Their proximity. I've studied Ben for years. This girl is more than just some random person or friend. She's standing in my spot, in front of my boyfriend, tilting her head in the same flirtatious way I used to.

I flick off my headlights so as not to draw any attention to me or my car. Laughter travels from Ben's porch into my front seat, and my stomach sinks like a million bricks. That's a laugh I've never heard come out of Ben's mouth before. With my foot on the brake, I crank my neck to get a better view as Ben dips his head down to kiss the girl. Ben Cameron is kissing another girl. I slam my hand into the steering wheel and the horn sounds. *Damn it!* Ben and the girl turn their heads in my direction. I lay my foot on the gas pedal, heart pounding out of my chest as my car surges forward.

About three seconds into my great getaway, and not even three houses down, I come into contact with something that causes my car to bump up and down. *Shit.* The loud thump has me crossing my fingers I didn't hit a person . . . or worse, an animal. With my heart up in my throat, I put my car into park and swallow. *Please don't be a dog. Please don't be a dog.*

I step out slowly, pulse pounding as I will myself to look in front of my car.

A bike.

I ran over a stupid bike. Thank god!

"Hey!" a voice calls from the driveway. "You ran over my bike."

"I'm sorry. I didn't see it," I say, studying the wreckage.

"No shit. Your lights were off."

I turn back to check if Ben saw me run over this person's bike, then whip my head toward the silhouette on the driveway. "Would you keep your voice down?"

"What for?" he asks, his voice rising. The person, who appears to be around my age, crouches. "Aww man. You destroyed Betty White."

"You named your bike Betty White?"

"First you run over Betty White, then you make fun of her name?"

Is this guy for real?

"Why is it parked on the road anyway?" I ask.

"It wasn't. It was on my lawn."

I squat to study my car more closely and find the right front wheel perched atop the curb in front of this person's house.

"Are you high?" he asks. I stop staring at the carnage and turn my attention back to the person attached to the annoying voice. Huh. Not what I expected. I figured it would be some scrawny skater boy but he's . . . well, he's not scrawny. He looks like the kind of guy who'd be in a Netflix teen romance. Not the guy the main character falls in love with, but that guy's obnoxious best friend.

"Hi," he says curtly. "Could you get your car off my curb so I can pull my bike out from underneath your beast?"

"Beast? I'll have you know this is a 2007 Dodge Charger."

"I stand corrected. An *old* beast. And what're you doing driving around without your headlights on?" He rises and runs a hand through his curls. The hair on the sides of his head are tapered. It's a ridiculous cut. Not at all practical. How is one supposed to wear a hat with hair like that?

"Jamie? Is that you?" Ben calls from the end of his driveway across the street.

No, no, no. This is all wrong. I stand quickly, taking a step so I'm face-to-face with Mr. Betty White. "If I promise to fix your bike, will you play along? Please?"

"Play along? What're you—?"

"Jamie, are you alright?" Ben approaches the scene of the accident. His eyes assess the wreck as his "new" friend joins us.

Olivia Chen. *Her?* She's one of those types everyone loves. Popular. Involved in any school committee that has to do with hosting "fun" events. Average intelligence. Basically, my complete opposite.

"I'm fine," I say, walking over to the driver's side. "I was just parking here and didn't see his bike." *Smart, Jamie. Enlist a person's help when you don't even know their name.*

"Were you coming to see me?" Ben asks. Olivia eyes me up and I eye her right back.

"No. Why would I come see you? We're broken up," I say matter-of-factly.

"She came to see me," curly top says as he approaches us. "Axel. Jamie's boyfriend." He places a hand around my waist, pulling me in, and it feels weird, foreign, but I don't fight it. The look of confusion on Ben's face is worth having this strange person's fingers on me. But *boyfriend*? "I moved in a month ago."

Ben's eyes zero in on mine. "Boyfriend? Already?"

"That's right," I say, staring back at Ben. "I guess we both recovered quickly."

Ben swallows before his eyes size up Axel. He extends a hand, in typical Ben fashion. "I just got back from being away this summer, so I didn't notice someone had moved into the Khans' old house."

Axel shakes Ben's hand. It's civil at first but then Ben shakes harder, almost aggressively. Axel matches his energy and my body vibrates alongside his. "That would be us."

"You going to Maple View?" Ben asks, withdrawing his hand and rolling back his shoulders.

"Yep. Eleventh grade."

Oh my god, he's younger than me.

"So how did you and Jamie meet?" Ben asks, his eyes back on me. "Jamie never mentioned you."

I interject to control the narrative. "I was on a run and . . ."

"A run? You don't run," Ben says, looking me square in the eye.

"Okay, I was on a brisk walk," I say, gritting my teeth, "and I happened upon Axel's house the day he was moving in and, you know, we started talking."

"And how did it go from talking to this?" Ben asks, waving an accusatory finger between us. The nerve he has considering only moments ago he was kissing OLIVIA EFFING CHEN!

We got paired up in geography last year to do a project on earth's nonrenewable depleting resources and she thought it would be "cute" if we staged a fundraiser with props, but each prop would represent a step everyday citizens could take to help. Ironically, she ordered balloons for this presentation/fake fundraiser, completely missing the mark on the helium shortage. Despite that, we got an A because of how "accessible" the lesson was. Another win for mediocrity.

Axel clears his throat and tightens his grip around my waist. He's not as tall as Ben, but he's pretty built and I can tell Ben is slightly intimidated. Olivia smiles a nervous smile at me and I squint my eyes in response. Maybe it wouldn't be so bad to have Ben believing, at least for a little longer, that this Axel person and I are together.

"I've been waiting for Jamie to finally cut you loose," Axel says. "Sounds like you did me a favor. But don't worry. It was all above board until you set her free. Can *you* say the same?"

Axel leans in and Ben takes a step forward. I kind of want to pull Axel back, but I also kind of want to see what might happen. Will Ben take the bait? Will he fight for me?

"Ben." Olivia locks her arm through Ben's, stroking her fingers along his wrist. He looks down at her and then across at me.

"Well, I guess there's no point hiding that I've also started seeing someone. Jamie, you know Olivia from school, right?"

"Yeah. I know Olivia," I say, placing my arm around Axel's waist. "We go way back. But I didn't realize the two of you did."

"Ben and I got to know each other at camp," she says, as if she doesn't realize she's incriminating herself alongside Ben. "We were both counselors."

Ben's jaw clenches at Olivia's admission.

"Yeah. I figured you weren't one of the campers." Ben gives me the look he always gives me when I've just said something rude. Shaking off his disapproval, I continue. "Is Olivia the reason you so badly wanted to 'strike out on your own'? 'Cause, hate to break it to you, Ben, immediately coupling up with another girl kind of negates the whole 'doing senior year alone' thing. But then again, I guess it makes sense seeing as you connected with people on a 'deeper level' this summer. Clearly."

Ben shakes his head, and his shaggy locks move with him. "Jamie."

"It's all good. No bad blood here," I say, trying my best to play off that I'm not seconds away from pummeling both of them. I don't buy them as a couple. In my wildest dreams I'd never pair the two of them. Which should make it easier to break them apart.

An awkward silence descends between the four of us as literal crickets sing a chorus in the background.

"Do you need help with your car?" Ben finally asks, his question slicing into the quiet like a knife.

Axel squeezes me closer while waving Ben off with his other hand. "We got this. Jamie isn't your problem to fix anymore."

Smooth.

"Okay, well, try not to run over anything else tonight," Ben says. A smile stretches over his teeth before he and Olivia head to her car.

"You're welcome," Axel whispers in my ear. His hot breath tickles the back of my neck. I wait until Ben and Olivia have driven off before I squirm away.

"Boyfriend? I said play along, not write your own fantasy."

"You needed to make the guy jealous, and that did the job."

"I was thinking more along the lines of hanging out, or something less serious, but boyfriend? I don't even know you. And you're younger. And Axel? Is that seriously your name?"

"Hold up," Axel says. He bites on his lower lip while shaking his head. "You ran over my bike. You asked me to play along with two seconds' notice, and when I do manage to save your ass, you complain about the logistics behind it?"

"I just . . . I needed an excuse to be here."

"An excuse for stalking your ex?"

"All I needed was for you to play along long enough for . . ." I stall, trying to keep my breathing steady. Now is not the time to lose it. Especially in front of a stranger. "It was supposed to be, you know, a short-term excuse. Me being here . . . with you. Dropping off cookies or handing out flyers for my mom's salon. Anything! But now he thinks you're my boyfriend. And you're in eleventh grade."

"Yes, we've already established that."

"How am I supposed to make Ben jealous dating a younger guy?" I ask, placing my hands on my hips.

"First of all, we're not really dating, so don't get ahead of yourself. Secondly, that guy is a dork. Younger or not, I'm an upgrade."

"You think pretty highly of yourself," I say, sizing him up in his gray sweats, hiked-up socks, rubber slides, and band tee.

"At least I don't expect people to read my mind." He folds his arms over his chest.

"What're we going to do?"

"First, we're going to rescue my bike and then you're going to pay to fix it."

"Yeah, about that . . . I don't have a lot of money. The thing is, I kind of have a book-buying problem."

"Then I guess we have ourselves a predicament. What else have you got to offer me?"

I fold my arms across my chest, matching his pose. "What do you want?"

The corners of his lips turn up. "Glad you asked." He rubs his hands together, his shoulders bouncing, and it looks like he's about to break into dance. "Seeing as you destroyed my wheels, I'm going to need a way to get to and from school every day."

"You want me to be your own personal Uber?"

"Look at it this way. Picking me up means having to drive by your boy Ben's house, every morning. It'll keep him thinking you and I are together. That's what you want, right?"

I don't know what I want. All of this has happened so quickly. I haven't even had time to process the fact that Ben has moved on with Olivia Chen.

"Okay, fine. If I drive you to and from school until your bike is fixed, we're square."

Axel laughs. "Not even one corner of the square are we."

"What's that supposed to mean?"

"We'll discuss it later. But first," he says, stepping closer so we're nose to nose. "Would you please get your car off Betty White?"

CHAPTER FOUR

The house is dark when I pull into the driveway. My heart continues to race above its regular rhythm, and it feels as if my intestines are twisting into themselves. This night was an epic disaster. This is why having a plan is so important.

The front door is unlocked. Jazz music streams inside from the back deck along with laughter from Eli and Eric. I guess they've returned from their clambake date. I lock the door and kick off my shoes before tiptoeing up to my room. I don't want to interrupt, but mostly I don't want to be on the receiving end of another lecture.

I've had enough of people talking at me for the day. There's only so much one person can take.

I plop down on my bed and open Instagram, typing Olivia's name into the search bar. There's nothing quite like the high of looking someone up and finding their profile set to public. Her feed is perfectly curated. Each photo uses the same dreamy filter. There's a healthy mix of nature and food photos—to balance out how shallow she is, no doubt. Speaking of, the obligatory bikini shots that show off her even proportions and perfect skin are also present. So, she's attractive. So what? I am too. I don't need to post pictures of myself in a tiny bikini to prove it.

Not that there's anything wrong with that, I remind myself. The path to living a life free of internalized misogyny is a bit more challenging when the broken-hearted version of you feels justified in hating the girl who stole your boyfriend.

Stick to the facts. Follower count: 1,579. Makes my seventeen followers look pathetic. She definitely goes hard on hashtags and the very millennial phrase "Nevertheless, she persisted," which she's used for a photo of her posing in front of a butterfly mural, laughing with friends on a boat, and drinking an iced coffee amid fall foliage. Gee. Talk about persistence in the eye of the storm.

I scroll back up to the top and see a link in place of her bio.

vsco.co/livvychen

I click on it and it sends to me to a separate photo-sharing site. God. How many photos does one person need to post of themselves online? I continue to scroll (and roll my eyes), trying to figure out what about this person drew Ben to her, and that's when I see it: a picture from July 28 of the two of them. He has his arm over her shoulders. There's no caption, just one hashtag: #bolivia

Bolivia?

Like the country in South America or . . . wait. Ben + Olivia = Bolivia.

I think I'm going to be sick.

I bolt out of bed and pace around my room as anger pulses through my veins. In all the calls and texts we exchanged throughout the summer, Ben never once mentioned Olivia or gave me any indication that something had shifted between us. Okay, the distance made our calls sometimes a little awkward, but we'd eventually find our groove. However, our calls did get shorter as time went on. July 28 would have been about four weeks into his job, enough time for him to meet and get to know Olivia on a "deeper level." I stop in my tracks, my racing heart causing a burning in my chest. *Inhale. Exhale. Inhale. Exhale.*

This isn't a matter of our relationship just fizzling out. Nor is it about Ben wanting to branch out. It should have been obvious by how quickly he coupled up with Olivia, but this photo cements it. Ben betrayed me.

And I'm sorry, #bolivia?

Before I know it, I'm back in bed typing the letters A-X-E-L into my Instagram search bar, trying to find curly top. I left immediately after backing off his curb and releasing his precious Betty White from underneath my car. Driving him to and from school will definitely make Ben believe something is going on between us, but I'm not sure what Axel and I are going to talk about on these rides. We seemingly have nothing in common. And what if he suggests we eat lunch together? All I know is, I wasn't in the headspace to discuss (or agree) to anything else in that moment.

Someone like Axel definitely has his Insta set to public. He should be easy enough to find, but as I scroll through the multiple profiles with the same name, I'm proven wrong, once again. Just as I'm about to give up on finding "my" Axel, a profile picture of a guy on his bike with the username AX catches my eye. I click on the name and, lo and behold, there he is, wild curls and a smirk that rivals King Tut's.

Yikes. Pretty much every third picture is of him and Betty White. If his bike was so important, why did he just leave it on his front lawn? At night? If I didn't run over it, someone else may have stolen it.

Look at this guy. He's shirtless in half his posts. Dancing in the other half. I didn't realize I'd agreed to fake-date Baryshnikov (or someone my generation actually knows).

Axel has a few reels of himself dancing, and while I know nothing about dancing, I can't deny this kid knows how to move. It's a bit hypnotic watching his body flow in one continuous motion, his hips gyrating way more freely than most guys my age. Okay, so he has a nice body. But I'm not that easily impressed by a six-pack.

I zoom in. Correction: eight-pack. *Brains.* Brains turn me on. Not slick dance moves.

(Even if the tingles pulsing through my body beg to differ.)

I boldly hit Follow so I can message him. We need to sort things out. We need to talk. We need—*AX requested to follow you.* That was fast. My finger hovers over the Accept button. If I do this, it's like I'm agreeing to keep up with this charade, and I'm not sure if that's what I want to do, but also, I kind of feel like I have no other choice. I accept his request. Almost instantly, a DM from "AX" comes through.

> Axel: I see you found me.
>
> Me: Took a minute. Why AX?
>
> Axel: Axel. Ax. You don't get it?
>
> Me: Are you American?
>
> Axel: No. Y?
>
> Me: Technically speaking, ax and axe are both correct, but usually British-English-speaking countries, like Canada, prefer to spell it a-x-e.

The three dots appear and disappear, on and off, for a few minutes.

> Axel: Sorry. Your last message put me to sleep.
>
> Me: Just be happy I didn't use this as an opportunity to school you on all the axe idioms.
>
> Axel: Maybe another time. So when do you want to meet up?
>
> Me: Meet up?
>
> Axel: If we want to make this thing believable, there should be a picture on the gram of the both of us. A couple selfie. And a hashtag.

Me: I have a question.

Axel: Yaaaas?

Me: Why are you so down to do this for me? For all you know, I could be a miscreant.

The three dots appear and disappear again.

Me: Corrupt. Evil.

Axel: A low-down dirty scoundrel?

Me: Yes. Wait. Are you mocking me? It's hard to tell over text. I also don't know you well enough to know if this is how you tell jokes or if maybe you're just being oppugnant.

Axel: ???

Me: It means combative or antagonistic.

Axel: I'm sorry. When did this become an English lesson?

Me: Words are kind of my thing. Especially homographs. They're words that are spelled the same but have multiple meanings.

Axel: Is this how you won Ben over?

Me: No. My dad and I used to quiz each other on them. I guess it's just a habit I've picked up and haven't let go of yet.

Axel: Your dad doesn't play along anymore?

Me: Kind of hard to since he's not in the picture.

Axel: Sorry.

Me: It's fine. Are you going to answer my question now?

Axel: 😊 I'm new. I don't know anyone. But I don't see how it could hurt to show up hand in hand with a senior babe on the first day of school.

Babe? I *should* be offended, but I'm kind of flattered in a way that feels like I'm betraying the feminist sisterhood. Again.

Me: I didn't agree to holding hands.

Axel: Do you want this to be believable? What's the end goal here? Get Benji back?

Me: Ben. And yeah.

Axel: #jAX

Me: ???

Axel: It's our couple name.

Me: Why is the j lower case? It makes the eye go right to the AX.

Axel: Fine. #Jax. Is that better?

It's definitely better than #bolivia.

Axel: Come by tomorrow. We'll discuss the terms and conditions of this "relationship."

Me: I can't. Working at my uncle's restaurant.

Axel: What's his restaurant?

Me: Shawarma Sitty.

Axel: Let me guess: Sitty is a play on City and Grandmother in Arabic.

Me: How did you know that?

Axel: I'm Lebanese.

Me: Oh. That's cool. I'm half Arab.

Axel: I don't believe in that.

Me: In what?

Axel: Being half of something. It trivializes your identity.

Me: I never thought of it that way.

But maybe subconsciously I have, since my mother pretty much likes to pretend our Arab heritage doesn't exist.

Axel: So is it your mom or dad who's Arab?

Me: Mom. She was also born here but her parents, my grandparents, are Palestinian.

Axel: #freepalestine

Well that just earned him a couple points.

Me: Why's your bike named Betty White?

Axel: This is classified information.

Me: Meaning?

Axel: Meaning you'll have to work a little harder to earn that bit of Axel trivia.

I let out a heavy exhale. Before I can think of a response, another message from Axel pops up.

Axel: When's your shift over?

Me: Four.

Axel: I'll see you then!

But I didn't even agree... This guy is full of something. The polar opposite of Ben. How can I expect anything to go smoothly with such a loose cannon? Is it too soon to regret this decision? It feels too late to back out of it. Just as I'm about to put my phone down, a text comes in from Ben.

Ben: Wasn't expecting you to move on so quickly.

Ooh. My plan seems to be working already. I sit up and grin as I type my reply.

Me: Like you did?

Ben: You seem to have landed on your feet. Kind of fast if you ask me.

Me: I didn't ask you. But that's what I do, Ben. One man leaves and there's another, around the corner.

Ben: That's not how you operate.

I'm so tempted to fire off a round of questions, starting with when he and Olivia became more than just co-workers, but resist the urge.

Me: Well, like you said, senior year and all. Can't expect me to spend it moping around in my room. I have places to see. People to get to know.

Ben: I guess I'm just surprised not only by the speed at which you moved on but with who you chose to move on with.

Me: What's wrong with Axel?

Ben: He isn't exactly your type.

Me: Clearly, my type hasn't been working for me.

Ben: That's kind of hurtful. We spent three years together.

Me: What's your point, Ben?

Ben: No point. I'm happy for you.

Me: I'm happy for me too. Night!

Always leave them wanting more.

My uncle's shawarma restaurant closes early on Sundays, which means around three all the neighborhood moms come in to pick up their dinner order and repeatedly ask Eli for proper reheating instructions, giggling and fawning over how cute he is. Calling Shawarma Sitty a restaurant is kind of a stretch. It's more like a diner, but not even really that. The food is way better than regular fast food, but there's only eight tables and we don't wait on patrons.

Amo Eli has been looking to hire a student for months but he can't find anyone who will stay on longer than a few weeks. I agreed to help fill in the gaps this summer, seeing as I didn't have anything better to do with Ben gone. Mom won't let me accept payment for my labor since we've already taken so much from my uncle, but Eli pays me "under the table." About a hundred bucks a week, which is probably less than I would have earned as an official employee. But this way there's no taxes and no guilt trips from Mom. I also get paid in free shawarma sandwiches and indigestion.

As I'm sweeping the floors, Axel appears behind the locked glass door with a big, dopey smile on his face. He's boyishly cute, I'll give him that. Which is fine, but I'm about to be a twelfth grader, and Ben could easily pass for twenty-one. Ben passed boyish about halfway through tenth grade.

Axel pretends to knock on the door, then twists his foot around his other and ends up doing a spin while waddling like a penguin. What's up with this guy?

I unlock the door and he basically glides in.

"Are you always this obnoxious?" I ask.

He swipes the broom from me and takes over sweeping, swaying his hips with it.

"Most people find me charming." He smiles, but I don't reciprocate. "It smells so good in here. Please tell me there are leftovers." His eyebrows wiggle and I let out an exasperated sigh.

"Keep sweeping." I head behind the counter and assemble a plate of leftover beef and chicken shawarma with pickled turnips, pickles, raw onions, hummus, tahini, and a pita. "Hot sauce?"

"Are the popes Catholic?"

I grit my teeth and squirt extra hot sauce over his plate before bringing it to the table. "It's on the house," I say, as he reaches into his back pocket. Axel actually finishes sweeping before he sits. He immediately rips the pita in half and assembles his own sandwich.

I nod to the plate. "I got you a fork."

"Don't need it," he says before inhaling a gigantic bite. I pass him a napkin and lean back in my seat.

"So," I start, not really knowing what to say next.

"So." Axel nods before taking another bite.

"School starts Tuesday."

"For real? I thought it was next week."

"Right. Tuesday is next week."

"Is it already Labor Day tomorrow?"

"Do you wear a watch? Or a fitness device? How do you keep track of dates?" I ask.

"It's summer. Who's keeping track of dates?"

I run my hands through my hair and sigh. "Maybe this was a mistake. How about I just pay you the money to fix Betty White and then we can pretend none of this ever happened?"

He sits up and wipes his face. "You've got four hundred and fifty dollars?"

"Four hundred and fifty dollars?" My eyes bug out of my head as Axel passes me a folded-up piece of paper from his back pocket. "That's ridiculous!"

"It's the third quote I got," he says, taking another bite. "And the cheapest."

"No," I say, sliding the estimate across the table. "I don't have that kind of money."

"You don't get paid working here?"

"It's complicated. Plus, I have a thing for special edition hardcovers and those are kind of pricey." Not to mention gas money for when my tiny allowance runs out and then there's my penchant for cheeseburgers.

"I have an idea," Axel says. He pushes the plate aside and leans his elbows on the table. "I'll cover half of this bill if you agree to help *me* out."

"Umm . . . am I not already providing you with rides?"

"That deal is mutually beneficial. And since the two of us are going to be hanging out anyway . . ."

"I am not agreeing to sexual favors," I say, sitting up straight.

"Don't flatter yourself," he retorts, eyeing me up and down. "My parents, Dad in particular, aren't really on board with my dancing. That's where you come in."

I nod as I try to follow along. "So, you want me to pretend I'm your girlfriend because you're gay?"

"No. God, Jamie, stereotypical much?"

If Axel *were* gay, this whole fake-dating thing would probably be easier. I wouldn't have to worry about him getting mixed messages or falling in love with me.

"Okay. Go on," I say.

"Now that I live outside the city, I'm on my own. I used to dance with my buddies Finn and Diesel."

Do people give their kids normal names anymore?

He continues. "I need to basically start from scratch and rebuild my platform as a solo act. Which takes time and interesting locations to serve as a backdrop for my TikToks. If I tell my parents I'm out with my girlfriend—a nice Arab girl with a car, they won't question where I am all the time and I won't have to get any lectures about how I'm too serious about dancing and that it won't get me anywhere."

"I'm sorry, I must have missed the memo that gas was free now."

"I'll chip in." His lips curve up in a closed-mouth smile. It's less of a smirk and a tiny bit more playful but genuine.

"So, if I agree to extend the fake-girlfriend farce to your family, as well as being your occasional driver, you'll knock the repair price by half?" That's two hundred and twenty-five dollars. It's still going to take me at least a couple months to come up with that. Bye-bye pretty books.

"Farce? You do realize you're not a seventy-five-year-old man, right?"

"That's not a very nice way to speak to your girlfriend," I say, resisting the urge to smile.

"Then you'll pretend to be a nice Arab girl in front of my parents?"

"Hey!" I sit up and slam my hands on the table. "I am a nice Arab girl."

Axel leans back in his seat. "We'll see about that." His eyes scan the restaurant. "How often do you work here?"

"I just help my uncle out when he needs it."

"So he's looking for help?"

Before I can respond, Amo Eli comes out of the backroom carrying a case of drinks. Axel shoots up and offers to carry the load for my uncle.

"Who's this?" Eli asks, his eyebrow raised.

"Alexander Dahini," Axel says. "A friend of Jamie's."

Alexander?

"Jamie doesn't have any friends," Eli says, his glance darting in my direction.

"He's a new friend," I say, rising from my seat as my cheeks burn. "We met yesterday."

"Okay." Amo Eli smirks. "I see you." He nods his head slowly and deliberately, clearly believing his pep talk got through to me. I'll let him believe it, for now anyway.

"Jamie says you're looking to hire. Good news, because I'm looking to work." Axel smiles and his brown eyes twinkle, like his plan is coming together perfectly.

I walk to where Axel and my uncle are. "Technically I never said..."

Amo Eli cuts me off. "You have any experience in the service industry?"

"I worked at Harvey's all of last year," Axel replies.

"Why'd you leave?"

"May I?" Axel asks, placing the case of drinks onto the floor. My uncle nods and Axel opens the fridge, lining the drinks up, one by one, making sure to put the older drinks in front. "I just moved here."

Eli twists his mouth while apparently sizing up Axel. "If you can provide me with a résumé and two references, the job is yours."

"I can do that. Does Jamie count as a reference?"

Both of them look at me and it's all I can do not to scream. What is even happening here? This guy is taking over my life. First, he moves onto Ben's street. Then he gets me to agree to fake-date him (okay, part of the onus of that is on me), and now he's managed to weasel his way into a job with my uncle. If I'm not careful, in a few months I'll have to slap a restraining order on... Alexander Dahini.

Who knew my savior's last name would rhyme with *tahini*? A sauce that I love but sends me straight to the toilet every time I ingest it. Just like this entire interaction is about to. With quick feet, I grab my things and disappear into the bathroom. One problem at a time.

CHAPTER FIVE

It's Tuesday, the first day of school, and for the first time since starting Maple View High, I won't be walking through the front doors with Ben. I'm seated at the kitchen table with Mom and Amo Eli. Not wanting to draw any attention to my current state, I have my phone opened to my favorite book. Rereading it helps ease some of my nerves. At least I know how this story ends.

"I like your friend," Amo Eli says as he pushes the bowl of cereal Mom put out for me closer. But I can't risk another stomachache. I'm anxious enough as it is. I don't need lactose aiding me.

"He's a hard worker," Amo Eli goes on.

I look up from my phone to find both my mother and uncle staring at me. "How could you possibly know that already? You spent one day with him, training in an empty restaurant."

"What friend?" Mom asks. She takes a slow, controlled sip of her coffee.

"Jamie didn't tell you? She made a friend." Eli tilts his head and smiles at me.

"Jamie tells me nothing," my mother says, as if I'm not literally sitting across from her.

I exhale and take a big gulp of my orange juice before wiping my mouth with the back of my hand. "He's new. And I just agreed to show him around."

"He's cute," Eli says to my mother with a knowing grin.

"He's in eleventh grade. And boys mature at a slower rate than girls. That's not me being sexist. It's science."

"So?" My uncle stands and glares down at me before collecting the dishes. "Eric is three years younger than me. Anyway, this kid has more style in his pinky than Benjamin could ever dream of."

"I don't think we should be coming down on Ben," Mom says, also rising from the table. "Lucy is one of our closest friends."

"Yes, but Jamie is my favorite niece." My uncle winks at me, but I'm too riled up at Mom's response to appreciate his kind words.

"Then you're taking Ben's side?" I ask her. "Did you know that he's dating someone else?"

"No," Mom says, her shoulders dropping.

"Already?" Amo Eli replies, turning from the sink.

"Yes. Already. So I really don't care about protecting his feelings, since he clearly didn't care about protecting mine when he blindsided me."

Mom lowers her head, shaking it slightly before pouring the rest of her coffee into the sink. My uncle playfully shoves her away while he does the dishes. She turns to face me again. "Hey," she says, her voice oozing fake cheerfulness. "It's the first day of your senior year and you've already made a new friend. Things are looking up."

"Right. And with that encouraging pep talk, I've got to run." Leaving behind my soggy, uneaten breakfast, I head to the front door, backpack in hand. I slide into my Converse sneakers, which Amo Eli has lined up for me, and make my way to my car. If I can just go through the motions and not ruminate over everything that's happened, I may be able to get through today without completely breaking down. Once in the driver's seat, I take a deep breath and release it slowly as I turn the engine on.

You're fine. You're not going to get a stomach attack. You didn't even have breakfast. It's all in your head.

I've got this. I've got this. I've got... nothing. I don't even have a plan. I'm basically heading into a war zone without any weapons, just some curly-haired kid with fancy feet.

A few minutes later, I turn onto Ben's street. Olivia's car is parked out front of his house again. She's waiting in her car, filming something on her phone. She posts something like five hundred stories a day and they're all fifteen-second glimpses into her superficial life. Yesterday she chronicled her Labor Day at the beach with Ben. Can't lie: seeing Ben in his trunks lying on the sand next to Olivia made me feel some kind of way. Like a wanting-to-punch-a-wall kind of way.

I squeeze my eyes shut as a stomach cramp zaps through my lower abdomen. The beach would be a nightmare location for someone like me. It's probably why we never went together. Ben must find it refreshing to be dating a girl who doesn't need to take inventory of the nearest toilet every time they go somewhere new.

When I pull up to Axel's house, his twisted-up bike is perched against the garage. It looks worse than I remember. He comes out just as I'm about to text him. We exchanged numbers over DMs last night. His mom follows him out the door, like the two of them have just stepped out of some family sitcom from the eighties.

Axel opens the car door and he widens his eyes as he forces a smile. "Mom, this is Jamie."

His mom bends down to catch a glimpse of me through the open passenger door. Should I get out of the car? Shake her hand? Before I can decide what to do, Axel slides into the front seat. His mom is still bent over, staring at me with a wide grin.

"Hi," I finally say. "I'm Jamie."

"I already said that," Axel says as he buckles his seatbelt.

His mother slaps his shoulder. "Don't be rude. She's beautiful," Axel's mom says, as if I'm not sitting right here. I must have some sort of cloak of invisibility on me today or something.

"She's not bad," Axel says as he reaches for the radio knobs. "We've got to go."

"Fine, fine. Have a good day. Make sure to thank Jamie for the drive," she whispers loud enough for me to hear before tossing another smile my way and closing the door.

"I'm okay?" I repeat, once his mother's out of earshot. "I thought we were supposed to convince your parents I was your girlfriend."

"We are."

A mix between a laugh and a sigh escapes me. "Very convincing."

"I'm not the kind of guy to fawn all over a girl. They know that. Especially my mother. She's got like a sixth sense or something."

"Whatever you say."

Just as I'm about to drive away, Axel places his hand on top of mine and stops me from shifting gears. He leans in; his warm breath is minty. "Ben's getting into Olivia's car but he's looking over here. Pretend you know how to flirt and touch my hair."

"Your hair?"

"Just do it. He's watching." His lips tickle my ear and I swallow, resisting the urge to pull away (or lean in farther).

I bring my left hand up and run it through Axel's light-brown curls. They're soft. Really soft. And he smells nice. Like clean laundry and maple syrup.

"That's good," he says, nuzzling his face into my neck. He's not actually doing anything, aside from pretending to . . . I don't know, smell under my earlobe, but it's been over two months since I had any real interaction with a guy and, well, it's kind of nice being close to someone. A car passes and Axel leans back in his seat. "He totally fell for it. Couldn't keep his eyes off you," he says, as he fingers his curls back into place.

I sit with my body still slightly angled toward his, frozen. "Oh. Good. Good." Shaking it off, I face forward and shift gears.

"Mind if I reprogram your stations?" he asks as I begin the short drive to school, still in a bit of a daze.

"Yeah, whatever."

He settles on some obnoxious pop song that I recognize only because my mother made me set one of her reels to it.

"We need to figure things out," I blurt, letting the nerves take hold of me. "Eli assumes something's going on, and I presume your mother does as well based on how much she was cheesing at the sight of us. I think we should come up with a contract or something so that neither of us gets screwed."

"A contract?" he asks.

"You have just as much at stake as I do. Possibly even more. You wouldn't want me to scam you out of your money or rides to school or fake-girlfriend-ing in front of your parents."

Axel sighs. "How about you draw it up and I'll just sign it."

"No." I pull into the school parking lot. "That's not going to work. If we're going to pretend to be in a relationship, we have to learn to work as a team."

"Partnership."

"Fine. Partnership." I put my car into park and unbuckle my seatbelt before reaching into the backseat and grabbing my notebook and pen. I open the book to a fresh page and jot down the word CONTRACT in upper-case letters.

"Do we have to do this now? I was kind of hoping you'd show me around." There's a softness to Axel's voice. Vulnerability maybe? He's nervous, which makes sense since it's his first day at a new school. I'm nervous too. Nervous this will blow up in my face.

"Fine, but let's set some major ground rules first. Orally," I say, closing the notebook.

He twists in his seat to face me. "Lay it on me."

"Okay, first rule, we don't tell anyone about this fake relationship. All it takes is one set of loose lips and the whole plan falls apart."

"Got it. What else?"

I bite on my lip, trying to figure out what the most important rules are. It's not like I'm well-versed in faking relationships. "Rule number two: limit your flirting with other people while we're doing this thing."

He shakes his head. "That might be a challenge. People kind of flock to me."

Holding back an exasperated sigh, I force myself to speak in a nonthreatening tone. "I really need your cooperation. At least until I can win back Ben. And fix your bike."

"How long do you think it'll take to get him back?"

"I figure a few days. A couple weeks tops. Once the fog of his camp-induced haze lifts and he sees Olivia in her natural habitat, he'll come crawling back. The ultimate goal is to go to winter formal together."

"Shouldn't the ultimate goal be getting back together? Wait," he says before I can respond. "Winter formal... as in December?" Axel wiggles in his seat like it pains him to have to sit still for more than two minutes.

"Yeah."

"That's four months away," he says, studying me. "This is kind of a long commitment."

"Don't worry. It won't take that long." He stares at me, not quite believing my words as much as I am. "Worst-case scenario, and we need the full four months, I'll make it worth your time."

"How? This is a business arrangement, correct? Not a friends with benefits relationship."

"We're not friends," I say, narrowing my eyes at him. "And like you said, it's a partnership."

"Rule three," he interjects. "You need to pretend to like me in front of other people. That means being nice and not recoiling every time I touch you."

"I don't recoil, and I don't not like you. It's just..."

"Just what?"

"It's nothing personal." It's just... he's not Ben.

"You did play along really well back at my house," he says. "For a second there, I thought you may have enjoyed yourself. It was my hair, right? Reeled you in? Or maybe the smell of maple syrup left over from breakfast." He grins and all his perfect white teeth show.

"You're incorrigible."

"Incorrigible?"

"It means beyond hope."

"Rule four: no big words." Axel smirks. "And from where I sit, I'm the only hope you have, so I wouldn't bite the hand that feeds."

"That's not even..." Before I can finish, Axel has stepped out of the car. He appears at my door and opens it for me.

"M'lady."

I suck in a sharp breath and grab my bag from the backseat before slamming both doors shut. Axel takes my hand in his as I shoulder my backpack. I debate pulling away, but we're surrounded by people and, to be honest, walking into the building with someone next to me beats the alternative.

"It's time we hard launch this... partnership," he says, pausing at the end of the parking lot. He grabs his phone and holds it out in front of us before whispering, "Pretend I'm Benji."

"It's Ben! Just Ben." I grit my teeth and tilt my head to his, giving off the biggest smile I can muster.

"Ooh, nice teeth," he says, staring at the picture. "Now let's do another, a little poutier this time. I know you can do that." Just as I'm about to flip off the camera, Axel nuzzles my neck and it catches me off guard. He takes another picture and shows it to me. My eyes are wide. My mouth opened slightly. I look like I'm in heat.

"That's the one," I say. "Tag me."

Once he's done, I take his hand and head into the building with my secret weapon. Axel's right. He's all I've got right now so I'd better play nice.

After I showed Axel around the school before morning bell, we parted ways and agreed to meet in front of the cafeteria at lunch. It was weird walking the halls with someone else. When I was with Ben, I didn't notice other people and, surely, they didn't notice us. But this morning, it felt like me and Axel were at the premiere of a movie or something. All eyes were on us. There was whispering too. I used to whisper to Ben. That's when everything felt like an inside joke.

By second period, there are over a hundred likes on the picture Axel posted. I've never received a hundred likes on anything. I made my Instagram profile public yesterday, like Axel's. It was a strategic decision. Even if Ben were forced to unfollow me because of Olivia, he'd still be able to keep track of what I'm doing and who I'm doing it with. It's kind of comforting that he hasn't unfollowed me. Maybe he still cares. He must. You don't just forget about someone you were with for three years that easily. At least, I couldn't, even though I tried to convince Ben otherwise.

Before meeting Axel for lunch, I stop at my locker to unload my calculus and chemistry textbooks. The hall is empty and it feels like I can finally turn off the act for a second. The day isn't even half over and I've had more than ten people come up to me to ask about Axel, like he's some sort of celebrity. A few of them recognized him from the TikToks he used to do with his friends. It's preposterous. I dated the most intelligent, handsome person in all of Maple View and no one ever thought to congratulate me on my choice in partner. They'd rather celebrate someone with "sick moves" and a big following.

Ben appears from around the corner. "Hey," he says, casually strolling up to me, like he's done a hundred times before. He leans on the locker next to mine. "How's the first day back?"

"Fine." I shrug half-heartedly and continue organizing my belongings, fighting my smile and reminding myself to stay cool.

"Hashtag Jax?" he says, scratching at his jaw.

"Sorry?" I ask as I shut my locker.

"You and that new kid have a hashtag."

"Yeah, so? I seem to remember seeing a #bolivia post from all the way back in July."

Ben clears his throat and swallows. "I'm not sure what you're talking about."

"I went on your girlfriend's VSCO account. Right there, for the world to see, was a photo of the two of you, your arm around her shoulders—#bolivia, and it was dated July 28."

Ben rakes his fingers through his hair and raises his shoulders. "That's just what the camp kids called us. We were counselors for the same age group so we did a lot of activities together. Her girls with my boys. They're the ones who came up with the hashtag," he rambles.

"And the reason for your arm around her shoulders?"

"We were just posing for a picture, Jamie. You're blowing this up into something it's not."

"What do you expect me to think when you return home from camp, break up with me, and then I see you out with Olivia the next night? How am I not supposed to think something happened between you two over the summer?"

"I never crossed any physical lines with Olivia. Not until after we broke up."

"We," I say, moving a finger between my chest and Ben's, "didn't break up. You dumped me. Which makes it very hard for me to believe anything that comes out of your mouth."

"Jamie, come on." He sighs, and I'm annoyed. I'm no longer excited that he's standing in front of me. That he's made the effort to come and speak to me. Like I should be grateful. Because I'm not.

"Come on, what?"

He leans in and says in a quiet but stern tone, "You don't expect me to believe you're dating this Axel guy, do you?"

"I don't care what you believe," I reply, and in this moment, I actually buy what I'm saying.

"I spent a few minutes on his Insta. He's not your type. It's almost laughable." He lowers his head. "You can drop the lie," he says. "I didn't tell my mom or dad about seeing you guys together."

"Do you even hear yourself? How condescending you sound?"

Ben squares his shoulders. "I'm not being condescending. I'm being honest. This is how I always sound. He's just . . . not right for you."

"And you get to decide that?"

"I *do* know you better than anyone else. You hate dancing, you hate social media, and you hate when guys are obsessed with their hair."

I cross my arms over my chest. "You used to know me better than anyone else. But I've changed."

"In four days?" Ben raises a brow and one side of his mouth goes up with it.

"You were away all summer."

"Are you saying you cheated on me?"

"No." I shake my head. "I didn't. I *wouldn't*."

This entire interaction is going south. Fast. I have to stop letting my anger get in the way of the big-picture goal. Get Ben back. But how am I supposed to do that when it's still so new and there are so many unanswered questions? Do I want to be with Ben? Yes. Am I angry with Ben? Yes. Both things can be true. I just need to learn how to play it cooler like . . .

"James," Axel calls from behind.

I turn around and relief flows through me. "Axel."

"What's going on? I was waiting for you outside the caf."

I shift my eyes back. He does a slight nod and grin as he walks toward me and Ben. "Benji, right?"

"Ben."

"Right, right. Benji, I'm going to steal Jamie for lunch."

"We were in the middle of a conversation," Ben says, slightly stepping to Axel. Despite Ben's towering height, Axel doesn't flinch.

"The thing is, you don't really get to occupy her time anymore. That's my privilege." He turns to me and smiles. "As long as you're okay with that?" he asks, waiting for my approval.

"I'm more than okay with it." I smile back.

Axel grabs my hand and nuzzles my nose with his before tipping his forehead to mine. He winks and I can feel my cheeks flushing.

Maybe there are benefits to fake-dating someone the same height as you.

"Then off we go, James."

"She hates when people call her that," Ben says, an edge to his voice.

"That may have been true in the past," I reply, my eyes moving from Ben's to Axel's. "But I like when he does it."

Axel raises a shoulder at Ben and cocks an arrogant grin. "She likes when I do it."

We turn and make our way down the hall. I can almost feel Ben's eyes searing onto the backs of our heads.

Axel's good.

He's really, really good.

~

"Don't," I say, as Axel reaches for the chicken breast. "You'd be better off eating rubber. Go with the burger. Trust me."

"Noted." After we fill our lunch trays with barely edible food from the caf, we sit at an empty table by the stage. "Is this your regular spot?"

"I don't have a regular spot. Ben and I used to eat lunch in my car or in a quiet hallway."

"Is that why . . ." He stalls, opening his can of pop.

"Why what?" I ask, with a mouthful of burger. My body is weird. When I'm anxious in the morning, I can't eat because it will mean a trip to the toilet. But for some reason, it's not the same for me later in the day. I do tend to be more anxious in the mornings. And before bed. My mom likes to remind me that a lot of this is "in my head" and that I have the tools to manage it. As if I would choose to live my life this way.

She keeps pushing me about talking to my therapist again, but like I've told her a million times before, I've gotten everything I can out of Dr. Mueller. Anxiety is something I have to learn to live with. I've accepted that. Talking about my triggers or breathing exercises is not going to make it go away. What *does* help is crafting a life and future that not only meets my goals but gives me a sense of control. It's what I had with Ben and it's what I need to get back.

"It's just, I've noticed that you don't really, you know . . ."

"Have any friends?" I finish Axel's sentence so he doesn't have to. "You're right. I don't."

"What do you do when you want to go somewhere?" he asks in earnest.

"I always went places with Ben. Actually, over the summer, I created this sort of bucket list of dates that he and I could go on together when he got back. Mostly, like, cheesy tourist attractions. I don't know," I say, picking sesame seeds off my burger bun. "I guess I thought it would be fun AND help rebuild some of what was lost."

"What was lost?"

I swallow and press my finger into some crumbs on the table. "Well, he was away for two months."

"Did distance make the heart grow fonder?" Axel asks, straight-faced.

I glance up to see Ben taking a seat at a table a few rows away. It's filled with Olivia's followers . . . I mean friends. Olivia sits on Ben's lap and I know he must be cringing inside with such an overt PDA. Except on the outside, he looks just fine.

"Not for him clearly."

Every now and then, people pass our table and wave or say hi to Axel. A few even invite him to sit with them. Once again, it's like I'm not even here.

"Why do you go by Axel?" I ask as he takes the last bite of his burger. "I heard you tell my uncle your name is Alexander."

"Would you buy it if I told you it's because I used to play the guitar?"

"Not when you phrase it like that." I wipe my face with a napkin and slide away my tray, sneaking another glance at Ben and Olivia. They don't even make a cute couple. Their sizing is all wrong.

"I didn't learn how to spell my name correctly until second grade. I kept getting the 'X' and 'E' mixed up. Eventually, it stuck. Besides, I think it kind of suits me."

"What do your parents call you?"

He lets out a laugh as he leans back in his chair. "I can't repeat those words in front of you."

"Your mom seems nice."

"My mom's great. My dad on the other hand . . . we don't really see eye to eye on things. You'd get along with him though. He's a real stick-in-the-mud."

"That's how my uncle describes me."

"I know." He laughs. "Eli's your mom's brother, right?"

Olivia and Ben get up. I reach across the table and hold Axel's hand, stroking his skin. "Yeah. My mom's younger brother. By one year." I keep my eyes on #bolivia as they walk, fingers interlocked. It's like Ben has transformed into someone I don't even recognize. "And my mom is nothing like him. She's like a fish that's been plucked out of the water in the dead of winter and left to die on the ice. But doesn't. It just flops around, making everyone feel sorry for it."

"Damn, girl," Axel says, eyes wide. "That's harsh."

"What's harsh?" Ben asks as he and Olivia stand by our table. Instinctively, I pull my hand away from Axel's.

"That hairstyle, bro. What's going on with it? Is it coming or going?" Axel asks before shoveling a spoonful of chocolate pudding into his mouth.

Ben runs a hand through his overgrown locks. Axel's right. Ben looks like one of those emo kids from the 2000s.

"It's growing out," Olivia says as I take a sip of my water. "We're going for a nineties grunge look but with a Gen Z twist meets hipster revival."

I just about choke on my drink and end up spitting water across the table at Axel, who cracks up. We both laugh as he passes me some napkins to wipe my face and the table.

"Anyways," Olivia continues.

"It's 'anyway.' Grammatically speaking." I blink excessively, holding in a grin.

"Are you going to Wonderland for Seniors' Night?" Olivia asks, ignoring my grammar tip. "I'm in charge of selling tickets and I need to get a rough estimate."

"Jamie would never go to Wonderland," Ben pipes in. "She hates roller coasters."

"You," I say, looking up at Ben, "no longer get to speak for me." I glance across the table at Axel, who seems to be enjoying himself a little too much. "Do you want to go?"

"When is it?" Axel asks.

"A week Saturday," Olivia responds.

"The event is for seniors," Ben says.

"He'd be my plus-one," I state.

"Ignore Ben. You can bring whoever you want," Olivia says, almost sincerely. "Cutoff to buy tickets is this Friday. They're fifty dollars each and include transportation. I hope to see you there."

"Yeah. I'm sure," I reply dryly.

Olivia offers me a strained smile before walking away.

"Did I upset her?" I fake-whisper to Axel.

"You could try being a little nicer," Ben says, looking down at me. "She's working overtime organizing this event."

"It's kind of hard being nice to the girl my boyfriend cheated on me with."

"We've been over this already," Ben begins but stops himself. He looks around, unable to make eye contact with me. "I've got to go."

I watch Ben walk away and that twisty feeling in my stomach returns. It's like every time we interact, things get more strained. But I can't seem to control my temper, especially whenever he's with *her*.

"Hey," Axel says, pulling me out of my thoughts. "You handled that great. Ben is clearly second-guessing his decision to dump you."

"You think?" I can almost hear hope spring into my voice.

"Totally. The opposite of love is indifference. Him getting riled up shows he still has feelings for you. So, Wonderland, eh?" He pauses, his eyes on mine. "That'll be a great place to film more content. I've been working on one set to the new SZA song. I just need someone to hit Record." He winks, and I can't help but smile.

"I *am* my mother's creative director for her salon reels. So I got you," I say, sucking in my cheeks.

"And I've got you. See? We're good at this partnership thing." Axel takes a sip of his drink. "So, your mom, what's her story?"

"You don't have to do this," I say.

"Do what?" Axel shakes his head.

"Ask me questions about my life. It's not part of the deal."

"What if I want it to be?" he says, a kind smile sneaking out.

"Okay." I sit up straight. "Let's trauma bond. My mom grew up with strict Arab parents. Rebelled by dating and, subsequently, sleeping with my father as a teen. Which resulted in me."

"Did her parents disown her? I have older sisters and to be honest, I have no idea how my parents would have reacted to something like that."

"I don't think my mom gave them the chance to. She took off with my dad right after telling them about me."

"Did your parents end up getting married?"

"Oh yeah. They did the whole domesticated thing until my father had an early mid-life crisis and walked out on us three years ago. But I don't fault him, entirely. Living with my mother isn't easy. She blames everyone for everything that's ever gone wrong in her life. But she does it in a way where you don't even know she's doing it until after the fact. She's got skills, I'll give her that."

"If it makes you feel any better, my father doesn't support my love of the arts. He thinks anyone who doesn't get a degree as a doctor, engineer, or lawyer is wasting away their potential for greatness."

His father's not wrong, I think, but I know enough not to say it aloud. Axel's so young and immature. He still has stars in his eyes. No need to pop that bubble just yet. The world will do it for him one day.

Happened to me when I was fourteen.

"Is there anything outside of the arts you're interested in?" I ask.

Axel looks around dramatically, then leans in. "Who sent you?"

"Excuse me?" The bell rings and people rise from the tables and begin to make their way out of the caf.

He runs a hand through his curls. "Just thought for a second my dad put you up to talking me out of pursuing my passions."

"I would never do that." Mostly because I don't care enough about this person to worry about what he chooses to do with his life. "But if you ever need someone to help you make a plan or a list of life goals, I'm your girl."

"Noted." He stands. "Meet you in the parking lot after school?"

"No." I rise and smile. "Meet me at my locker. We'll walk out together."

"Sounds good."

Despite the caf being almost empty, Axel leans over the table and places a kiss on my cheek. His warm lips press against my skin and, reflexively, I place a hand over my face.

"I'm sorry," he says. "Was that not okay?"

I remove my hand and think on his question before answering. I wasn't expecting that. I also wasn't expecting it to make me feel so . . . safe? Cared for? Valued. Instead of unleashing my current

Russian doll of emotions onto Axel, I lean over and kiss him on his cheek.

"It's fine."

He looks down, burying a smile. I think I just made him blush. Wasn't sure that was possible, considering how cocky he is. Maybe there's more to Axel than I initially thought. He's nothing like Ben and, I don't know, that doesn't seem to be such a terrible thing.

CHAPTER SIX

Axel and I have technically been fake-dating for almost two weeks, since the night I ran over his bike. We made it official on the first day of school—that's when we had our public debut as a couple—and still, we have yet to come up with a contract. Every time I bring up the subject, he finds a way to deflect. He's too focused on choreographing his next TikTok while balancing a new school and job.

"You don't need to drop me off," Axel says as we pull out of the school parking lot, his hands playing a drum solo on his knees. "Your uncle wants to meet at your place. I'm working a shift tonight."

"He's making you work on a Friday night?"

"I asked for more shifts."

"Is this about Betty? Because I'm trying to scrounge up the money to pay you back. I've been on a book-buying ban for six days, and I've only purchased three books."

"That's great self-control." He chuckles while adjusting his baseball hat. "It's not for Betty, though. I need the money for my cousin's wedding party. I have to buy a suit."

"Your parents won't cover the cost?" I ask as we reach a stoplight. "I thought Arab parents spoiled their children."

"They spoil my sisters, probably a little too much." He pulls the insides of his empty pockets out. "They both got married last summer. You know Arab weddings. They're very showy and lavish. And lately my dad is all about me being a 'responsible man' and learning to pay for things myself. I think it's his roundabout way of forcing me out of dancing."

"Actually, I *don't* know Arab weddings," I say as the light turns green. "I've never been. My mom doesn't talk to her parents. Amo Eli rarely does. I was raised without any culture, basically." As I say the words out loud, I'm surprised to hear the disappointment in my voice. I never really give much thought to the Arab side of my family. I've only met my grandparents a dozen times or so. Eli sometimes has discussions with me about Palestine, and, out of all of us, he's the most in tune with his roots, but Mom is completely detached. Those visits with my grandparents? Chaperoned by Eli while Mom stayed home and stewed.

"Everyone should experience an Arab wedding at least once. Come with me to my cousin's."

We hit another stoplight, and before I can say no—my innate response when I'm invited to do something fun—I pause and think about it for a second. "When is it?"

"October 12. Thanksgiving weekend. The Sunday."

"Oh." I stare ahead, not really at anything. I spent last Thanksgiving at Ben's. His dad let him carve the turkey for the first time. Mom and Eli were there too. Come to think of it, we've spent every Thanksgiving with Ben's family since we moved here. This will be the first one I'm not invited to. Guess that means Mom and Eli aren't invited anymore either. Good job, Jamie.

"The light changed," Axel says.

"Right, sorry." I shake my head and force an awkward smile as we continue.

"You okay?" He turns the volume down on the radio, his tone laced with concern.

"I'm good. Thanks for the invite, but I'll probably be back together with Ben by then."

"Right." Axel nods.

"So tomorrow night is Wonderland," I say, pulling into my driveway and shifting gear into park. "It's a big day for us and this whole fake-dating thing. We need to make sure we're on the same page. And speaking of pages..."

Before I can reach into the backseat for my notebook, Axel stops me by placing his hand on my arm.

"Hey, we've been at this for two weeks and have I let you down?" Axel's eyes meet mine. I've never noticed how light they are. They're definitely brown, not hazel, but they're almost crystal clear in the sun.

"No, but," I continue, "an entire evening at an amusement park surrounded by classmates, where we have to be *on* the whole time, is a completely different beast than sharing lunch and meeting up between classes."

Axel removes his hand from my arm as one side of his mouth rises. "That won't be a problem for me. Will it be for you?"

Holding Axel's hand, eating meals with him, going on rides together, I can handle. But how am I supposed to get Ben to believe Axel and I are serious when anytime I see Ben and Olivia together, I crumble into little, pathetic pieces? I've never been very good at disguising my emotions. Good or bad.

"Jamie?"

"Yeah?"

"You spaced out again. What's going on with you?"

"What's our goal for tomorrow?" I say, turning to face him.

Axel shrugs. "To have fun."

"Can you be more specific?"

"Okay. I've decided on two dances that I'll need you to film, but aside from that, I'm all yours. Which means, my other goal is to make Ben regret ever letting you go."

"And how are we going to do that?" I ask, releasing a deep sigh.

"We're going to start by not overthinking it. You just follow my lead and I, in turn, will make sure that by the end of the night, Ben will find an excuse to speak to you. Mark my words. I know guys."

"You don't know Ben."

"Ben is like all the other straight, white Bens. I got this. Okay?" he asks, his eyes wide as he grins. His confidence is so annoying, but also kind of annoyingly reassuring.

"Okay." I smile back.

We get out of my car and collect our things. On our way to the front door, I grab Axel's wrist. "Wait."

He turns to face me. "Now what?"

"Are we . . ." I stall, chewing on my lower lip. "I think we should be consistent."

"What's that mean?" he asks, turning his baseball hat around. My stomach flips at the sight of Axel in a backward cap. It makes his jawline more pronounced. His lips stand out. His eyes . . .

"Girl, did you smoke some reefer in the school bathroom today?" He laughs while pretending to smoke a joint. "Not judging."

I slap his arm. "This is serious. If even one person knows the truth, it could blow our cover. Did you tell Eli anything?"

"He didn't ask. I assume he thinks we're friends."

I suck in my lips, thinking. "He teased me about liking you on the first day of school and I shot down those accusations."

"Well, that's before you had a chance to get to know me," he says, his overt confidence oozing out once again.

"Right. An easy enough response if he asks. Okay. I guess we're doing this in front of my mom and Eli. After all, an experiment is only fully effective if we go all the way with it." Axel opens his mouth to reply with what I know will be a smart-ass sexual innuendo. "Shut up."

"I'm at your service," he says, placing an arm around me.

We step through the threshold, and I shrug Axel's arm off my shoulders. "We don't have to overdo it." Axel drops his backpack to the ground and slips off his shoes. He tucks them under the front bench and removes his hat.

"How do I look?" he asks, but he doesn't really care what I think. Even I know I have zero personal style. You could place me in any decade after 1940 and I'd blend right in. Nothing flashy about me. But Axel? He defines Gen Z. Even if he were in gray dress pants and a white tee, he'd still be the poster boy for today's youth. God, I sound like a boomer.

"You look fine. Amo? Mom?" I call out.

"Jamie?" Mom walks around the corner, in her smock and signature headband. "In between clients," she says, an unfamiliar grin painting her face as she sizes up Axel. "Hello."

"Hi." Axel reaches out his hand.

"You must be Axel," Mom says, shaking his hand. "Eli won't stop talking about you. Says you're a dream employee."

"Oh yeah?" He smirks. "And what does Jamie say?"

"Jamie hasn't told me anything. But she never does. So don't take it personally." Mom crosses her arms over her chest as she studies Axel more closely. "Where are you from, Axel?"

"Mom," I say, trying to stop the interrogation.

"Relax, Jamie. I'm just trying to get to know your new friend."

"Boyfriend," I state.

Her mouth falls open. "Oh. Well. You don't waste any time, do you?"

"I'm Canadian born," Axel interjects. "But my parents emigrated from Lebanon. My mom is Jordanian though."

Mom nods her head slowly. "Thought you looked Middle Eastern."

"Jamie tells me you're Palestinian."

Mom clears her throat. "Parents are, yeah."

"Then that means you are as well," he says.

"I know what I am." There's an edge to Mom's voice. No, it's more than that. She's being straight-up rude. My pulse races, wanting to defend Axel, but for what? Being proud of where he comes from?

Axel shifts from foot to foot, like he's a puppy who's been berated.

"Amo told Axel to meet him here," I say, but what I really want to do is grab Axel's face and kiss him right in front of my mother just to spite her.

"He's out getting drinks for the weekend." She studies the hair dye stains on her smock, as silence lingers in the air between the three of us. "We're having Eric, Lucy, and Jared over tomorrow," she blurts.

"Excuse me," I say, trying to process this latest bomb. "You're inviting my ex-boyfriend's parents to our house?"

"Your uncle's house, and they're our friends. Just because you and Ben are no longer together doesn't mean we have to cut off our relationship with Lucy and Jared."

"Uh, I think it does. He dumped me. For another girl. A girl he met over the summer. So he probably cheated on me. And let's not pretend we don't know who's to blame for that."

Axel clears his throat, his eyes begging me to stop, but I am so mad. At my mom. At Ben. At my mom.

"You can't possibly think any of this is because of me," Mom says, all big doe eyes. Like she's played no role in the destruction of my life.

"If I'd gotten to work at the camp, like I'd wanted to, none of this would be happening."

"I'm sorry you feel that way, Jamie, but this is not my fault. It's not your fault. It's not even Ben's fault. Your relationship just ran its course. It happens."

My mouth opens to speak but no words come out. A relationship doesn't just "run its course" when one person leaves the other for someone else. Why can't she understand that? There's no point in even trying with her. She doesn't get it. She never has. Instead, I shake my head and race up the steps to my bedroom. Axel follows and I slam the door once he's inside.

"Do you believe her? She never takes responsibility for anything. She got knocked up and it was my dad's fault. Her crappy relationship with her parents, their fault. Dad leaving us, my fault."

"She doesn't think that." Axel approaches so we're nearly nose to nose. His close proximity stops me from pacing.

"Really? You're taking her side?"

"I'm not taking sides. Relationships are complicated, but divorces are almost never about the kids. Your mom doesn't blame you for your dad leaving."

"And what about the way she treated you?" I ask. "Rude!"

"It's fine. She has her own baggage. You don't have to let it be yours. Do I need to remind you that we're pretending to be together? Bringing up how much Ben hurt you isn't going to sell her on our relationship. And," he says, before exhaling, "it's a good thing that the lines of communication are still open between your mom and Ben's parents."

"How is that a good thing?"

"You're still in one another's lives even if Ben is temporarily dating someone else. Their ongoing connection will benefit you. It's an advantage you have over Olivia."

I sigh. "You're right. It sucks and I hate to admit it, but you're right. How are you so zen?"

"It's the dancing." He grins and it has a mirroring effect on me, but I try to hide it. "Too late. I saw that smile. Come on, try it."

"Try what?"

"Dancing." Axel pulls out his phone and messes with it for a second before a song begins to play.

"I can't dance."

"I can teach you."

"Okay," I say, releasing a nervous laugh. "Let me make this clearer. I *don't* dance."

Axel places his phone atop a stack of books on my desk and then shoves the piles of clothes on my floor aside with his feet. "This should be enough space. Just throw your arms over my shoulders. Trust me."

Trust him? I don't trust anyone. "I seriously have two left feet."

"Your feet don't need to do anything they're not already doing. Come on, arms over my shoulders."

I grit my teeth and glance around my room. It's a complete disaster and Axel didn't even flinch. Nothing about me seems to faze him.

"Fine." I swallow before lifting my arms to his broad shoulders. "Now what?"

Axel places his hands around my waist. "You a fan of Dua Lipa?"

"Is that some kind of trendy food?"

He laughs, just short of a snort. "No. She's a singer. It's her song we're dancing to."

"You call this dancing?" I look at him and down at our feet.

Axel eases in a bit closer and his hands move lower, guiding my hips to sway left and right. "Look at that. They move. I thought we were going to have to bust out some lube."

I freeze in place. "Uh . . . what?!"

"I meant like oil, to grease your hips. Sorry." He removes his hands, his cheeks flaming red. "I'm a little nervous."

"Why?"

"You know, for a smart girl, you're really clueless."

"How so?" I take a step back, crossing my arms over my chest.

"Jamie, we're in your bedroom. I'm a guy, you're a girl, we're standing close, music is playing, you're coming off a fight with your mom—there's a palpable heat," he says, waving a hand in the space between us.

I bark out a laugh and stare up at the ceiling. Who does this kid think he is?

"There is no heat. This is . . ." I say, flailing my hands in front of me. "We're not . . . it's fake."

"Yet we're alone in your room and I'm teaching you how to dance."

"You're forcing me to dance. This is exactly why we need a contract."

"Fine. Whatever. Draw up your contract. I'll have my lawyer go over it." He picks up his phone and turns off the music. "I'll wait for your uncle outside."

"You don't need to do that," I say as he heads to my bedroom door with his things. Regret and shame collide in my stomach. *Why am I like this?*

"It's all good. I'll see you tomorrow." He places his hand on my doorknob and for some reason I don't want him to leave.

"Axel."

He turns to face me.

"I'm sorry. I'm just pissed at my mom and took it out on you." I take a few steps so we're face-to-face again. "That was kind of fun. But don't expect me to ever do that in public," I say, holding my finger to his nose. He brings up a hand and grabs my finger before leaning in. Our eyes lock and I move my gaze down to the small beauty mark below his left eye.

"I'd never expect you to do anything that made you uncomfortable," he says, releasing my finger.

I nod, and just as I'm about to ask him to stay, Amo Eli calls from below.

"We're good, okay?" he reassures me, his eyes softening as they meet mine again.

"Okay," I say.

As I watch Axel race down the steps, an indescribable longing pulses through my chest. Every interaction with Axel comes with a multitude of emotions that leave me feeling both breathless and at a loss for words.

And, lately, confused.

CHAPTER SEVEN

Saturday, and it's Seniors' Night at Wonderland. I tossed and turned last night in bed, unable to get any sleep. My mind raced with thoughts of Ben and Olivia and what happened between them over the summer, imagining the moment when Ben decided he'd stopped loving me and wanted to be with her. Then my disagreement with Mom played out over and over in my head, making me angrier each time. And if all that wasn't bad enough, there's the weird physical reactions I've been experiencing around Axel.

His lips are curves and peaks like a roller coaster. I bet his kisses feel like one too.

Stop it!

Axel is basically everything I'm not. He's also kind of annoying. But I'd be lying to myself if I didn't admit that sometimes I like spending time with him. What's even more worrisome is that I occasionally miss Axel when he's not around, and even find myself looking for excuses to text him.

What Axel is is a distraction, and that's not always a bad thing. When I'm around him I'm less sad about Ben. He talked me off the ledge yesterday with Mom. And, most important of all, he's helping me get Ben back. Even if he always manages to change the subject when I bring up a contract. Which is why I've spent all morning in my room typing one up. I'm going to bring it with me to Wonderland and have him sign it tonight. On our first official fake-date.

Working on the contract has also been a good way to avoid my mother. We haven't spoken since yesterday's tiff, but Saturdays are her busiest days, which means it's probably safe for me to come out of my room and make lunch.

I bring my laptop with me, figuring I can finalize the details of the contract while enjoying my meal. Eli's at work and the house is mostly quiet, except for the music from Mom's salon thumping through the floor.

Phil Collins really loves a dramatic musical transition.

Eli's kitchen is pretty small, but quaint. There's a round table by the sliding glass door that leads to his deck and backyard. A bunch of fresh groceries are laid out on the small island in preparation for tonight's dinner with the Camerons. It almost looks as if the kitchen has been staged for a photoshoot or something, with the bright produce contrasting against the black granite counters. Eli has an eye for design, and his dark wood cabinets and black-and-white tiled floors give the space sort of a homey yet stylish feel.

The home I grew up in was a bungalow. We had a big piece of land, since the farther north you go, the less expensive housing is. The layout was pretty spaced out, so when Mom and Dad fought, I'd just go to my room at the other end of the house and hide. Made their shouts more of a whisper. But they still felt like a sharp stab to my heart.

At first, they used to fight about little things, like dividing up tasks and blaming each other for not doing their share. But then the subject matter got more serious. Dad felt stifled. Mom felt underappreciated. Dad said Mom didn't acknowledge how hard it was for him to work a corporate job when his heart wasn't in it. Mom said he refused to grow up and accept his responsibilities.

As I got older, I started to see that the reasons for their arguments ran deeper. Dad felt trapped by fatherhood. Mom felt like I didn't love her enough. Dad was unhappy, and Mom regretted ever marrying Dad and having me.

"Jamie?" Mom's voice sounds from the kitchen entry. I grip my butter knife while spreading Nutella on my bread. "Is that what you're having for lunch? Not very healthy."

I exhale and use my knife to collect more Nutella to spread on a second slice before slapping the pieces together. I turn and lick my finger. "If you don't want me to eat Nutella, then don't buy it."

"I don't buy it. Eli does." She enters the kitchen and cleans up after me while I bring my sandwich to the table.

"Don't you have clients?" I ask, while waking my laptop up. She pours a glass of water and places it next to me.

"At least stay hydrated. And no, I'm done for the day. Took the afternoon off to prep dinner. I'm making steak Neptune and need time to get it ready."

"What's the special occasion?" Their son finally getting rid of that annoying girlfriend? I bite into my sandwich in an effort to keep my angry words at bay.

"Eli wants to put his new dining table to use," she says while washing her hands.

"This was his idea?"

"Hey, Jamie, we're not conspiring against you." Mom wipes her hands dry on her jeans before opening the fridge. She grabs some ingredients and places them on the island, moving the fresh produce to the counter by the sink. Back at the island, Mom pulls out a huge piece of red meat from the butcher paper. "I know all of this can't be easy on you, but the Camerons are our friends, and we can't dictate who Eli invites into his own home." The doorbell rings and Mom shrugs, holding up her dirty hands. "Would you get that?"

I rise from my seat and head to the front door. As soon as I'm done with lunch I'm going back to my room and finishing this contract so I can focus on making myself look as irresistible as possible tonight. I turn the knob and open the door to find Ben on the other side, carrying a silver platter.

"Hey," he says, as my stomach somersaults onto itself. His floppy hair partially covers his eyes. I kind of want to brush it away but fight the urge. "My mom told me to bring this over."

I take the platter from him and swallow, unsure of what to say or how to act. "Thanks."

We stand there, quiet, both seemingly studying the grains in Eli's wood floor.

"You have a little . . ." He points to the space next to his lips.

"Oh." I feel around my face before wiping off the Nutella residue.

"Looking forward to tonight?" he asks.

"Yeah. Can't wait to ride some . . . rides," I say, fully aware of how foolish I sound.

He laughs. "I never thought I'd see Jamie T-F on a roller coaster. You don't even go one number over the speed limit while driving."

"That's because I adhere to the laws of our town. Besides, Axel's adventurous and he's influenced me to break out of my old and stiff ways."

"I didn't think your ways were old and stiff," he says, a small smile edging its way onto his perfect lips. God, I miss kissing those lips. The lips he now uses to kiss Olivia Chen. I want so badly to make a smart remark about how if he truly felt those things about me, he wouldn't have dumped me for someone else, but less is more. I need to remind him of all the good parts of me.

A car horn beeps in the near distance. I glance over Ben's shoulder to see that obnoxious baby-blue BMW. "I've got to go. Olivia's waiting," he says. "See you later."

I raise my hand to wave but instead bring the platter up and almost smack him in the face with it. I clear my throat as I bring it down. A poor attempt to distract him from my loser move. "Later."

After watching him get into Olivia's car, I stop short of slamming the door and make my way back to the kitchen. I place the platter on the island and toss the second half of my sandwich in the compost, having completely lost my appetite.

"Was that Ben?" Mom asks, slicing the meat slab into steaks.

"Yes. It was Ben."

"Judging by the fact that I didn't hear a screaming match, I take it you and he are now cordial?"

"Glad to see you think so highly of me," I say.

"I didn't want to say anything last night, since you were already upset," Mom says, moving Eli's sharp knife through the meat, "but I think you're moving on a tad too quickly from Ben."

"No. You've made yourself pretty clear." I stand on the other side of the island, leering down at her.

"So then you're serious about this boy?"

My eyes flit to the floor. It's harder to lie to someone when you look directly at them. "Yeah."

"It isn't healthy to jump from one relationship to the next. And I don't like that you brought him into your bedroom."

"You let Ben come into my room."

She gathers up the scraps of meat and tosses them into the compost before looking up at me. "No. I didn't. But you don't listen. And I trust Ben a heck of a lot more than I trust this Axel person. To be honest, I have a hard time seeing what you like about him."

"You don't even know him." The truth is, I don't really know him either, but I feel myself growing defensive regardless.

She turns on the faucet with her elbow and begins washing her hands. "I know enough. His parents are Arabs. That means he's probably a mama's boy who has never picked a dirty sock up off the floor. I wouldn't be surprised if his mother still cuts his steak up for him into tiny little pieces."

"Where is this coming from?" I ask. Her hands have now formed a soapy lather while my heart pounds against my chest in fast, heavy beats.

"I just don't think you should get involved with an Arab boy. They're chauvinistic and old-school."

"I'm an Arab."

"You're half," she says as she dries her hands with a paper towel.

"Don't diminish my identity," I respond, taking Axel's words from the first night we DM'd to heart. "Are you telling me that you don't want me to date Axel because he's an Arab?"

"You don't know Arab guys. Look at my father. He was furious with me when I got pregnant. He wouldn't know what a feminist was if I smacked him in the face with Gloria Steinem and her fabulous hair."

"What about Amo Eli? He's an Arab man."

"That's different. He's my brother and he's gay, and," she says, her voice rising slightly, "he barely has a relationship with our parents."

"I don't choose who I'm going to date based on their background. That's racist, Mother."

"It's not racist. I just want you to be informed about what you're getting yourself into."

"Maybe I *want* to be informed," I say, my hands gripping the ledge of the island. "Maybe I want to surround myself with Axel's big, loud, Arab family and connect with my roots. Maybe I don't want to grow up to be a self-hating Arab."

"Jamie." My mom's face hardens. I went low and definitely hit a nerve while I was down there.

"What?"

"I am not . . . I just wanted to . . ." She picks up her knife and begins chopping vegetables. "I was trying to spare you from having to learn the hard way like me."

A sharp pang twists through my lower abdomen. *Not again.* I'm already stressed enough about tonight as it is. I don't need to add another fight with Mom to the list of stressors. Or another stomach attack. Instead of snapping back with the harsh words I want to say, I'm going to be the bigger person here and let this go.

"I have to get ready," I say, running a hand over my stomach. Mom nods in understanding as some of the tension leaves the room like a slow-leaking balloon.

"Make sure to use the bathroom before you go tonight. And try not to eat anything too greasy. You know how your body reacts." Her eyes flit to my hand, still absentmindedly rubbing my stomach. "And Jamie," she starts.

"Yeah," I say, exhaling a deep breath.

"Promise me you'll think about what I've said."

"I always do," I say as I pick up my laptop and make my way to my room.

If Amo Eli and Mom thought my room was a disaster before, they'd have an aneurysm at the sight of it now. But the stakes are high. If I'm going to get Ben's attention, I need to stand out. I'd never admit to this juvenile/typical teenaged-girl behavior to another living soul, but I studied Olivia's Insta trying to figure out her style. Not to copy it but to elevate it. Tonight, I'm going to do everything I can to make sure I stay within Ben's sight line. With one last satisfied look in my bedroom mirror, I head downstairs.

My hope for a swift getaway is derailed by Amo Eli, who comes out of his dining room with napkin rings.

"Gold or silver?" he asks, holding them up.

"Silver. To match the Camerons' platter Ben dropped off earlier."

"Ooh, do I hear some snarky undertones in your response?"

I glance around. Mom's in the kitchen and the Camerons haven't arrived yet. I lean in and say in a quiet but disappointed tone, "How could you invite Ben's parents over?"

"Because they're our friends." He responds as if I asked both the simplest and stupidest question ever.

"Blood is thicker than neighbors," I say, placing my hands on my hips.

"And I've known Benjamin's mom since before you were born, so you can see how this complicates things. Listen, Jam-e," he says, with that fake Arab accent again. "Benjamin's mom was there for me in high school. She was also there for me after your mom took off to marry your dad. Her son breaking up with my niece isn't going to destroy a decades-old friendship. Sorry, babe."

"Doesn't mean I have to like it."

"No. It doesn't. And I can respect that. But I hope you can return that respect to me. So," he says, releasing a breath, "you and your mom fighting again?" He cocks his head to the kitchen. "She's been in a mood all afternoon."

"She's always in a mood," I say, looking away from my uncle's discerning brows. "She's racist against Axel."

"Oh." Eli's shoulders slump. "She doesn't like that he's an Arab?"

"Nope."

"She has some messed-up stuff she needs to work through, but then again, don't we all?" He runs a hand over his freshly shaved face as he looks past me at the front door. "Is Axel meeting you here?"

"His bike is kind of broken so I'm going to pick him up."

Amo nods as I slip on my shoes.

"I see Axel's having an effect not only on removing those permanent scowls but also on your fashion sense. Don't worry. Axel told me that you two are together, but I called it the first time I saw you with him at Shawarma Sitty."

"Called what?"

"That you'd end up together. It's cute. You're like a million tropes balled into one fiery couple."

"Anyway," I reply, breathing in and exhaling out slowly. "Axel and I are just seeing what happens." Again, my gaze falls to the ground. I didn't realize how much lying would be involved in fake-dating. "And by the way," I say, pointing to my clothes. "This isn't Axel's influence. I drove myself to the mall and bought these boxy jeans and crop top." Putting yet another dent in my bank account, along with the fifty-dollar entry fee to Wonderland. I grab a cardigan and throw it over my top.

"Well, I think you look dope. Hey." He grins. "Did you know dope means 'very cool' and 'marijuana'?"

I cross my arms over my chest. "Did you know it also means to smear or cover a surface with a thick liquid-like varnish?" I ask, with an exaggerated smile.

"I did *not* know that."

"My title of Homographs Queen remains intact," I say with an assertive nod. "Have fun tonight."

"You too," Amo Eli calls as I walk out the front door.

Fun. Not many homographs for that word, but tonight I plan to create my own version of it.

CHAPTER EIGHT

Axel's crumpled-up bike was still on display when I picked him up. I can't help but wonder if he leaves it there to make me feel bad or to remind me how much I owe him. When I arrived, he basically ran into my car to avoid any conversations with his, according to him, "overbearing mother," who waved pleasantly from the front door. We were running a bit late, so I didn't have time to show him the contract, and the bus ride full of our classmates, including #bolivia, was definitely not the place to bust it out.

"Have you ever been here before?" Axel asks as the bus turns into the massive parking lot.

"No." I shake my head and gawk out the window at all the colorful structures. "It's on my Kill-It List though."

"Kill-It List?"

I face him. "My list of goals. I told you about them. The tourist-trap dates." My eyes dart to the back of the bus where Ben and Olivia are seated. I run my hands up and down my thighs. A little stimming never hurt anyone.

Axel shimmies himself closer. "What exactly is on this list?"

I sigh and sit back as the bus pulls up to the curb. "I wanted to go to an outdoor concert at Budweiser Stage and watch a hockey game at Scotiabank Arena. I wanted to kiss under the Rainbow Tunnel. Walk hand in hand at Ripley's Aquarium. Pretend we were highbrow at the ROM. Face my claustrophobia and fear of elevators with Ben by my side, at the CN Tower. Most of all, I wanted to make memories."

Axel studies me but the eye contact is too intense, so I look down at my intertwined fingers on my lap, sore from all the rubbing and squeezing. I guess I'm a bit more nervous about tonight than I thought.

The bus doors open and the aisle fills up quickly. I remain seated, grinding my teeth, frozen in place.

"Well," Axel says as he rises, extending his hand. "Let's go make some memories."

I exhale and take his hand, not for show but because I want to. Because in this moment I want to make memories with Axel. It also strangely puts me at ease and stops me from walking around with two tightly clenched fists.

We head inside the park, and Ms. Weaver and Mr. Pine, a couple of teachers well past retirement age, remind us to meet by the fountains at 10:50 p.m. and not a second later. Axel lifts my wrist to read the time.

"That gives us five hours," he says. "What do you want to do first?"

Ben and Olivia walk by. Ben offers me a polite nod and smile before Olivia guides him past the fountains and farther into the amusement park.

"Um . . . well . . . we, um, maybe we could . . . it's unseasonably warm tonight, right?" I ask, fanning my hand in front of me.

"They're gone," Axel says, his tone a bit dry. "You can act like yourself again."

"Sorry." I shake it off. "It's just weird, you know? To see them outside of school as a couple doing couple things."

"I'm sure Ben thought the same thing about seeing you with me. It's why he looked back at us before Olivia yanked him away."

"You think?" I ask, hearing the desperation in my voice.

"I know." He smiles and my shoulders lower, just ever so slightly. "Should we discreetly follow them?"

"No," I say assertively. "Let's film one of your dances, eat, film another dance, play a couple games . . ."

"Wasn't the plan to make Ben jealous?" Axel asks, his brows pinched.

"It is, but he's already seen us here together. I think a little distance will make it less obvious. I also really don't want to see them right now," I admit, studying the interlocked paving stones.

"Fair enough. Are you hungry already? We could eat first."

I look down at my left hand, which is unconsciously rubbing my stomach.

"No." I blush. "Just nervous butterflies." A group of people run past us, shouting about the newest roller coaster.

"Planning on riding any coasters while we're here?"

"Do *you* want to?" I ask. My heart is thumping faster and faster as this awkward interaction with Axel grows even more awkward.

"Only if you'll go with me."

"Why would anyone want to ride a roller coaster with me?" I ask.

"Because you're smart, fun, easy to trigger. Need I go on?"

"Fun?" I feel my face scrunch up at the accusation.

"In your own way," he says with a smile that reaches his eyes. The shrill squeals of riders as the roller coaster above us passes causes a chill to trickle up and down my spine.

"Let's go to the kid's section first," he says, clearly reading the fear on my face. Axel takes my hand in his and gives it a gentle squeeze. "We'll ease you in with the less intimidating rides. Work our way up."

"That's a very sensical plan, Mr. Dahini."

"Mr. Amil Dahini is my father." He shivers. "What's your dad's name?" he asks as we begin walking.

"Ethan... Foster."

"What's he like?"

I blow air out of my mouth as I try to think of a suitable response. It's been so long since I've seen him, he's almost become like a character in a book I read a long, long time ago. "You know how in every marriage there's the fun parent and the serious parent? Dad was the fun parent." I smile to myself. "He's really into music. When he was in high school, he was in a band. He played guitar and was the lead singer. But he was also a really talented hockey player. And smart. And he gave the best hugs."

"You speak pretty fondly of a guy who walked out three years ago and hasn't visited since."

My smile falls at Axel's truth bomb.

"Sorry," he says, probably sensing my discomfort. "I'm just surprised. I thought you'd be angrier."

"I'm angry with my mother. She's the reason he left."

"I'm sure there's more to it. More that you don't know. Probably more than any one of you knows. Sometimes it takes people a while to figure their shit out."

"Says the guy with the perfect home life."

He shrugs. "Maybe on the outside. It's like my parents have put me in this box, one I had no say in creating, and it's a nice box, but it's less nice because I'm being forced to stay inside it. For them. It's all for them. They don't really care about the things I love. The things I'm passionate about. They're so focused on my future. They want me to be something bragworthy."

"They're not impressed by your large online following?" I smirk, already knowing the answer.

Axel shakes his head. "When my first TikTok blew up, back when I was with Finn and Diesel, I showed it to my parents. Mom liked it. My dad, not so much. Said if I put that energy into my studies, I'd be further along."

"Maybe with time you'll find a balance that you'll all be okay with. But it is your life, Axel, and ultimately, you should do what makes you happy. Even if I tend to agree with your father about the prospects of a career in the arts."

He laughs. "Come on. Planet Snoopy is around the corner."

We arrive at the kids' section of the park. The entrance is marked by a rainbow over a bridge with pastel-colored cobblestones. The park stays open until Halloween, and they've already started to decorate for fall and spooky season, even though it's only September. But that's life, right? Always ten steps ahead and never in the moment.

"This would be the perfect place to film a TikTok," Axel says, arms outstretched under the Planet Snoopy sign. The park is closed off to the public tonight and open only to senior classes from all over the city, which means this part of the park is pretty quiet at the moment. "And there's a rainbow," he says, pointing up. "Is this where we have our first kiss?"

"No." The answer comes out a bit more briskly than I'd intended. I clear my throat, my heart racing. I've only ever kissed Ben, and I only ever want to kiss Ben. I can hold Axel's hand, touch his hair, even "dance" with him, but I am not sharing my lips with his.

"It was just a joke," he says. "I know this isn't the rainbow you were talking about, and I also know I'm not Ben." He places his backpack on the ground and removes his hoodie to reveal a black T-shirt. Axel stretches his arms and then legs before opening his backpack.

"What's that?" I ask as he pulls out a black rod.

"It's a Steadicam. I stick my phone inside and you hold it up to film me. Makes the shot . . . steady."

Axel sets it up and then shows me what to do. I didn't realize how much work went into making one of his dance videos.

With my mom, I just hold up her phone and press Record. He busts out a portable Bluetooth speaker and props it on the ledge of the bridge.

"Wait. Are you going to do this *here*?" I ask as people walk past us.

"Yeah. That's kind of the point."

"But aren't you afraid of people judging you? What if you screw up?"

"That's what edits are for. Besides, people will judge you no matter what you do." He smiles and little crinkles form around his eyes. "Plus, it's a rush. And fun."

"I guess we have different ideas of what equals fun. I'd sooner die than have to dance in front of an audience."

Axel strolls over to me. "I think by the end of tonight, your idea of fun will change."

"To be honest, it already kind of has since meeting you." I glance up to find Axel's eyes on mine. The intensity of his stare makes goosebumps break through my skin. He's usually so goofy, but once in a while this other side of him comes through, and I haven't quite figured out what to do with it. Backtracking, I laugh and say, "Running over bikes, pretending to make out in cars, cracking jokes about Ben's terrible hair."

"And we're just getting started." He tips his forehead to mine before sliding his feet backward as if he's moonwalking. I think that's the term. I don't know. I don't know anything about dancing and yet I somehow got roped into standing on the other side of this rainbow holding a Steadicam and waiting for Axel to perform despite other people existing around us. "Ignore everyone else. Just keep that camera focused on me."

"How much do I film?"

"Just hit Record and I'll take care of the rest. A lot gets done in post-production."

He hits Play on his speaker and gets into place. "Baby" by Justin Bieber begins. Why he's chosen a slightly immature, retro song is a mystery to me, but I do my job and hold up the phone.

Axel starts dancing like it's the most natural thing in the world. He has this uncanny ability to move in a fluid motion along to music, as if he can feel it inside him. And it's not just his body; his facial expressions are almost as big a part of it. God, even when I tap my feet along to the beat of a song, it feels forced. This is a real talent. He puffs out his chest a lot, in this sort of primal yet confident way. It's definitely cocky. It's also kind of hot.

A few people continue walking past, and a decent-sized crowd has formed behind me to watch his performance. For some odd reason, I feel proud. His dance makes people smile and encourages them to do their own (sometimes awful) standing-in-place dancing.

As the song comes to an end, Axel lifts his face to the camera, a bit breathy, and smiles widely. He nods for me to turn off the music and stop filming. People clap and begin to swarm around him, building a wall—a wall that I had finally started to let down.

Instead of going to him, like I want to, I gather his things and place them inside his backpack, waiting for his fan club to disperse. I prepare myself for the speech where Axel tells me he's going to take off with some new friends and leave me behind.

Axel eases his way out of the crowd and comes to where I am, on the other side of the bridge.

"Ready?" he asks.

"Sorry, what?"

"To go on some rides."

"But what about them?" I motion to the group of people under the rainbow. "Don't you want to hang out with your groupies?"

"Nah." He smiles. "You're the only groupie I plan on hanging out with tonight." Relief flows through me as Axel shoulders his backpack. I think about telling him that he doesn't have to, that he's free to do as he pleases. But I actually believe that he wants to hang out with me. We walk past the group and make our way into the kid's section of the theme park—together.

After sharing a meal of chicken fingers and fries, Axel's treat, he eases me in by riding the kiddie roller coaster three times. Once I've gotten used to the feeling of bars pressed down against my thighs, he suggests we try another lap-bar roller coaster—this time adult-sized. It's kind of nice how he acknowledges my apprehensiveness about the chest bars because of my claustrophobia. I didn't even have to say anything. He just gets it.

Aside from the chewed-up chicken fingers tumbling around my stomach, the two wooden roller coasters we ride are fun, if not a little frightening. He asks if I want to try any that loop and I suggest we play some games first—my treat. I win Axel a small Garfield stuffie that thankfully fits inside his backpack and we take a break with cherry ICEE's while sitting on a grassy knoll, observing the people below us.

"You dance really well. I mean, I knew you could dance from your TikToks, but seeing it in person—the way you draw people in. It's magical."

Axel's cheeks flush and he leans his shoulder into mine. "Aww shucks."

"Maybe if your dad saw you perform in person, he'd get it. Your passion radiates, and it's pretty contagious."

He slurps his ICEE, then nods. "A passion that will get me nowhere in life, according to my dad."

"What you have needs to be shared with others," I say with a bit more gusto than I'd intended. "It's special. You even managed to change my mind and I bet your dad isn't nearly as tough a critic as I am."

"Maybe one day," he says, his brown eyes shimmering in the night. "It's getting late and we still have to film the second dance. What do you say we try Dragon Fyre? It's pretty tame but it has a couple loops."

"Sure. But if I barf my ICEE all over you, I'm not buying you a new shirt. I'm already in the hole two hundred and twenty-five dollars for Betty White."

"Ahh, sweet Betty. How many books did you buy this week on your book ban?" he asks with a grin.

"Only two. I'm getting better." No need to mention one of them was a special edition with stenciled and sprayed edges and that the only reason I didn't buy more was because I had to buy an outfit for this "date."

Axel helps me up and because of the uneven ground, holds onto both my arms to steady me. It's dark and there's music playing in far-off speakers and riders screaming in the background. A cool, brisk wind passes between us, but all I can feel are Axel's fingers gripping my arms. I wish I could freeze this moment. Study him a bit longer. Figure out why I sometimes feel so drawn to him while other times all I can think about is Ben.

I shiver as another cool breeze passes.

"Here," he says. I watch his fingers move up my cardigan as he delicately secures each button. When he reaches the last one, he leaves it open and then rubs my arms up and down to warm me up. "Better?"

"Better." I smile.

The lines so far tonight have moved quickly, but I guess since Dragon Fyre is close to the exit people are trying to squeeze one last ride in before departing. It's finally almost our turn, and that's when I notice Ben and Olivia two rows over.

"Ben and Olivia are synced up to ride the same time as us," I say quietly.

"I see that," Axel says, glancing over my shoulder.

"We haven't done the best job at rubbing our relationship in his face tonight. I haven't gotten a chance to speak to Ben yet or show off how great I look."

Axel laughs. "You do look great. But you always look great," he says with one of his signature flirtatious smiles I know he shells out easily. "I've got an idea."

"What's that?"

"Do you trust me?"

"Um, kind of?"

"Better than what I thought you'd say." He chuckles.

When the metal gate squeals open, signaling our turn to get on the ride, Axel tosses his bag to the other side before cutting off Ben and slipping in beside Olivia.

"Sorry," he says, looking up at a confused Ben. "This seat's taken. There's a free spot next to Jamie."

Ben stands there, at a loss for words. Not one to draw attention to himself in a public place, Ben sits in the empty seat next to me and pulls the bars over his head. Olivia glances back at us, peeved. Or maybe that's just her face.

"Did you put him up to this?" Ben asks.

"No. He just thinks he's being funny, I guess."

Ben lets out a small smile. "So, you're really going to do this?"

"Yeah." I wiggle a bit in my seat. "I went on two roller coasters already. This will be my third. Axel really pushes me outside my comfort zone, but not in an aggressive way," I backtrack. Come to think of it, I haven't had any stomachaches tonight and my palms aren't aching with fingernail indentations. But Ben's face falls slightly at my admission. "This is my first roller coaster with loops though."

The dimple on his left cheek appears and I bite down on my lip at the sight of it. "I'm honored to be sharing this first with you."

A muffled voice comes out over the speaker, warning us to keep our hands inside at all times. I grip the metal handles on the chest bar and try to breathe.

"Hey," Ben says, his voice filled with warmth. "If you get scared, I'm right here." He opens his hand and I take it before nodding. *Sweet victory.* Axel looks back at us and I raise my brows. His eyes go right to my hand in Ben's and instead of wiggling his brows at me like I'd expected, he faces forward.

The chest bar pressed against my lungs makes taking deep breaths feel almost impossible as we climb the first lift hill. The rattling noise of our car as it makes its ascent does not settle my nerves. I know it will soon be followed by a fast drop and then my first-ever loop.

"It'll be over before you know it. It's easier if you close your eyes," Ben says.

I nod slightly, because that's all I can manage with this suffocating chest guard, and grip his hand even tighter once we reach the top of the hill. After a sudden drop we descend quickly into our first loop, then a second, and that's when I open my eyes. It's dark but the lights from the park make me feel like I'm on another planet. Lost somewhere between space and time. I release Ben's hand and raise my arms to the sky for the banked turns, allowing myself to scream and laugh with the wind.

The ride comes to an abrupt stop and I catch my breath. I want so badly for Axel to turn around and see the look of pure elation on my face, but he remains focused up front.

"You did it," Ben says. "I don't think I've ever heard you scream that loud before."

"I don't think I have screamed that loud before. It was kind of freeing." Excitement continues to pulse through me. I can't wait to tell Axel all about it.

"Hey, Jamie," Ben says as we pull into our stop.

"Yeah," I say, slightly distracted, my eyes on Axel's head.

Our chest bars release and we lift them off. I unbuckle the seatbelt and Ben's fingers trace over my hand, still resting between us.

I freeze up at the sudden touch, words unable to form at my lips. Olivia clears her throat to get Ben's attention. He jolts his hand away. We both bolt up, parting ways, acting as if we're just two strangers who sat next to one another on a ride. I race down the ramp, leaving Ben and Olivia behind, to find Axel.

"That was amazing," I say, grabbing Axel's arms and jumping up and down when I spot him at the bottom of the exit ramp. "It kind of felt like having a panic attack but in a good way."

His tight-lipped grin turns into a smile and I pull him in for a hug. It's weird, but even though Axel isn't tall like Ben, which I love(d), our bodies kind of fit together perfectly. I don't feel small with him like I thought I would. I feel safe.

"He's gone," Axel says, leaning back as Ben and Olivia pass. "You don't have to hug me anymore."

"That's not why . . . I mean . . . it must have been the adrenaline or something." I shrug it off. "So, ready to film that last TikTok?"

He lifts his shoulders slightly. "It's fine. We can forget about it."

"No way, Tahini. The deal was you'd accompany me to Wonderland and I would film two TikToks for you. See? This is why a contract is so important. Makes sure neither of us gets screwed. Let's go," I say, grabbing his hand.

"*Dah*-ini," he corrects me, softening ever so slightly.

"Fun fact: tahini gives me stomachaches."

"And what do I give you?" he asks.

"The jury is still out on that one." I manage to make him smile again. It's kind of like winning a prize every time I do. "So . . . 'Baby'?" I ask, as we make our way to the front of the park.

"Yes, darling?" Axel responds, eyebrows pinched together.

"No." I laugh. "The song you danced to. 'Baby' by Bieber. It's *old*. Even I know that."

"Good music transcends time. I don't chase trends when I post on TikTok. At least not always. I choose songs that make me feel something. 'Baby' captures the innocence of first love."

"Do you think there's only innocence to be found in firsts?" I ask. Axel raises an acknowledging hello at a group of kids from our school who walk in a pack next to us. "Do you think we become hardened after our first loves break our hearts?"

"Yes. No. I mean, the right person will always give you those first-love flutters. I think. I've never actually been in love before."

"Huh," I say, trying to hide my surprise.

"Speaking of first loves, did something happen with you and Romeo on the ride?" Axel asks. The smell of funnel cake tickles my nostrils but my stomach is already full of so much crap. And maybe a few butterflies. The source of those butterflies is yet to be determined. Tonight has been a lot.

"I held his hand—just until the second loop was over. And then," I say as we come to the front of the fountain.

"Then?" he asks. Most of our classmates are gathered by the front, with both teachers doing a rough head count.

"He stroked my hand with his finger when the ride was over. Clearly, he isn't as committed to Olivia as he would have me believe." I suck in my lips as my eyes flit to the sky. "While I think we're making good progress, we *are* at the end of week two of school and they're still together, which means we're going to have to keep this going." I remove Axel's bag from his shoulders and fetch the Steadicam and speaker. "Are you okay with that?"

"Yeah." His tone is hard to read, but his eyes are focused on mine.

"We don't have a lot of time," I say as I notice most of the class has reunited and our teachers look ready to leave.

"Right. I want to change the song though."

"Can you do that?"

He smirks. "I can do whatever I want."

Axel hits his mark and I press Record once the music starts. Another older, familiar song by yet another Canadian artist plays: "Treat You Better" by Shawn Mendes. He's really laying it on thick with the cheesy love songs tonight.

But there's something different about this performance. For one, Axel mouths the words along to the song as he dances, and second, he keeps making eye contact with me, not the camera. His moves are deliberate. Whereas his last performance was kind of sweet, there's an edginess to this one. Sharp angles and aggressive stomps.

His eyes never leave mine. His curls move in sync with his body. His gait goes from wide to narrow. Axel pounds his chest as he gets down on his knees and back up with ease, twisting his feet and turning. He somehow knows exactly how much to move to stay within the frame.

Our entire class and others stop what they're doing to watch Axel dance in front of the lit-up fountains. Even Ben seems mesmerized by Axel's performance. He's a star. He belongs in front of the camera. He's more than I could have ever expected. And then some.

The song comes to an end, and instead of remaining still until I finish filming, Axel walks right up to me, stopping inches from my face. I can feel all eyes on us, waiting to see what he does next.

My heart pounds in my chest. Is this the moment . . . ? Is he going to . . . ? His breath is warm. His scent a bit musky from dancing.

Axel leans in and murmurs, his lips grazing my ears, "How's that for adrenaline?" He pulls back before taking the Steadicam from my shaky hands.

"Time to go," Ms. Weaver shouts.

As the class heads to the exit, Axel included, I remain frozen, watching everyone leave. My knees are weak and I'm finding it hard to stand upright, much less walk. And now, even though I met all my goals for tonight, I'm left with this overwhelming sense of disappointment.

CHAPTER NINE

Axel Dahini is a *CEO*. A *boss*. A *main character*. Apparently he's also a *snack*. Basically, and in layman's terms, what my classmates are trying to tell me when I pass them in the halls, when I'm trying my best to follow along with my lessons, and even in the bathroom stalls, is that he's a catch. "How did you and Axel meet?" (a.k.a., how did *you* land him?) is the most popular question, followed closely by "Does he move as well *off* the dance floor?"

I shrug off their questions and comments because, unlike Axel, I'm not comfortable with attention, and besides, that's so not the point. The point is to make Ben jealous, and I can't quite tell if he is.

Since that finger-stroking moment at the amusement park a couple weeks back, he seems to be avoiding me. *Avoiding* is putting it lightly. I haven't even crossed paths with Ben since Wonderland. I wonder if he regrets it. Maybe he doesn't remember it. Or possibly, and this is the explanation I find most feasible, Olivia is keeping him locked in a dungeon in her basement. But it's not like other dungeons, because this one is painted baby blue and filled with balloons.

Ben stroking my hand on the roller coaster isn't the only thing that's been occupying space in my mind. I had a ... um ... dream about Axel. I bury my head in my pillow even though I'm alone in my room. Ever since I dreamt of him and me doing *things*, I can barely look him in the eye. Probably because my eyes are so focused on his lips, his strong forearms, and his chest, which he really needs to cover up. It's like the buttons on his shirts don't work.

There's this raw animallike attraction building on my side, and if I don't get it under control I'm bound to slip up and pounce on him one day—maybe soon (but only if it's consensual, because I'm a respectful queen).

It's the last weekend of September and Axel still hasn't signed the contract. I asked him to come over after his shift but didn't realize it was Saturday night when I asked him that and now it kind of looks like I invited him over for a date or, worse, a booty call. And that wasn't my intention. (I don't think.)

I sit up in bed and grab my notebook, staring at the contract I drew up for Axel and this whole arrangement. I don't know why he's so reluctant to sign it; it benefits him too. There are certain things I have agreed to for this partnership to be fair and equal, aside from the things we discussed in my car on the first day of school. Such as items one through five.

1. Provide $225 cash by winter formal to help pay for the damage I <u>accidentally</u> inflicted on Betty White.
2. Drive you to and from school until Christmas break.
3. Occasionally, provided I've been given ample warning, drive you to locations within the GTA to help you film TikToks (gas money to be provided).
4. Pretend to be your girlfriend in front of your family.
5. Help you get a job to pay for the other half of Betty's damages—Check!

As per item number one, I keep running into difficulty. Now that I'm no longer helping Amo Eli out at Shawarma Sitty, he's no longer slipping me hundred-dollar bills at the end of the week. Between gas for my car and my book-buying ban failing miserably (oops, I've purchased five more books since I last stepped into the bookstore—paperbacks though, because I'm on a budget), I currently only have one hundred and thirty-five dollars left in my bank account and half a tank of gas. I could try borrowing money from Mom but she'd probably ask too many questions. As it stands, she expects me to make my hundred-dollar-a-month gas budget actually stretch for the entire month. The woman is delulu. I flip to my green to-do list tab and add: *find another way to make money!!!*

Just as I'm about to reread the part of the contract that goes over what I agreed to do for Axel, Mom's voice screeches from below, telling me there's someone at the door. I glance at my phone. Axel still has another ten minutes left in his shift. I'm not even dressed yet. Oh well, it's probably best he sees me in sweats. It may encourage my silly hormones to behave.

Mom's eyebrows are knitted together when I reach the bottom of the stairs.

"What's going on?" I ask, looking around the empty foyer. "You said someone was here to see me."

She clears her throat as she leans up against the front door. "Ben is outside. I asked him to wait on the porch. I wasn't sure if you'd want to speak to him."

Ben is here? Why? And why now, when I look like a total schlump? I swallow and try to play it cool. "Yeah, it's fine. I'll go see what he wants." I slip into my uncle's too-small slides and step onto the porch. Ben's seated on the porch swing. He's in jeans and a black hoodie. His hair is still shaggy but he looks good. Then again, I'd probably think he looked good with a bag over his head.

"Hey." I lean against the railing across from Ben, keeping a healthy distance between us.

"Hey." He runs his hands up and down his thighs. "How are you?"

"Fine." I say it almost like a question. He's clearly nervous and I can't help but revel in it. For once, he's the one who's anxious. Unsure. There's a part of me that wants to ask him where he's been. Call him out on why he's been avoiding me. Tell him he can't just stroke my hand and then disappear. Ben's gaze meets mine briefly and his jaw clenches.

"I'm kind of struggling," he begins, and immediately my mind starts to fill in the blanks. He misses me. He can't live without me. Breathing is harder when I'm not around. "I had a bad stomach flu and missed a bunch of school. I'm so far gone that I got a sixty-seven on my last calculus test. You have Mr. Hanna, right?"

He wasn't avoiding me. He was sick.

"Yeah? Second period."

"How are you doing in his class?"

"I got a ninety-eight on the last test," I say proudly.

"You and I both know math has never been my strongest subject, but when we were together, I was able to scrape by with high B's," he says. "I've been trying to catch up on what I missed but it's like reading a different language. It also doesn't help that Olivia is such a big distraction."

I hold out my hand like a shield. "Spare me the details."

"I can't get a C in calculus."

"Then work harder," I say.

Ben rises and walks toward me. "Could you help me? Just a couple times a week until I bring my grades up."

"You're here because you want me to tutor you?" I know I'm making a disgusted face but I can't seem to stop myself.

"Well, yeah. You're the smartest person I know." He smiles and my facial muscles relax, slightly. Ben Cameron knows exactly what to say to weasel his way into my heart and I hate him for it. Unless . . . this *could* be an excuse to get closer to me. First, he strokes my hand on the ride. Next, we're bumping shoulders in the library as we work side by side. It almost seems too good to be true. Too perfect.

"I don't know," I say, turning to face the street and sucking in my cheeks to hide a smile. "I'm kind of busy."

"I'll pay you," he says.

I face him again, the wheels in my head spinning overtime. This could be the answer to all my problems. If I tutor Ben, it means spending one-on-one time with him, which will remind him of our strong connection. And if he pays me, I can use that money to put toward paying Axel back. It's like God is smiling down at me, for once in my pathetic existence.

"I won't accept any less than thirty dollars an hour," I say, squaring my shoulders. "Twice a week, to make it worth my time."

"Whatever it takes."

"Does Olivia know you've come to me for help?"

"I didn't think it was worth mentioning until you agreed." He runs a hand through his hair and I swear he's trying to flirt. Ben never flirted with me before, but I recognize this gesture because Axel does it all the time to annoy me. He loves to get under my skin. (Dream Axel likes to get under my clothes.)

"Jamie?"

"Yeah?" I say, shaking off those confusing thoughts.

"I asked you how Monday after school works?"

"Monday? I think it's fine."

"Great. I'll meet you at the library." Ben heads to the steps and turns back. "I'm looking forward to it."

"Looking forward to what?" Axel says, coming out of Eli's car. I didn't notice them pull up. He doesn't waste a second slipping into his role of fake boyfriend as he makes his way past Ben and up the steps to where I'm standing, placing a kiss on my cheek. I lock eyes with Axel and then dart them to Ben.

"Remember to bring a calculator and your textbook. Don't be late."

"I won't. Axel." Ben nods.

"Benji." Axel nods back.

Ben stops to speak to Eli and I pull Axel into the house, dragging him to my bedroom.

"Sit," I say, and he sits on the edge of my bed. I close the bedroom door and pull up my desk chair so we're face-to-face. "Ben asked me to tutor him."

"Isn't he supposed to be a genius?" Axel asks, leaning back on his elbows.

"He's been sick and he's fallen behind. He also blamed Olivia for being a distraction. Now he's completely lost in calculus and needs me!"

"Do you believe him?" Axel has one eyebrow raised and it's clear he doesn't.

"Does it matter? Our plan is working. He's come to me when he could have gone to anyone else. And he's paying me, which means I'll have your money sooner than I thought."

"Nice." Axel leans fully back onto my bed, resting his head against his hands like he's marking his territory or something. This is just like in my dream. Axel was in my room, acting like his cocky self, and then I tripped and landed on him, making us both fall into my bed and then . . .

"Jamie?"

"Yeah?"

"You zoned out again. Were you picturing me naked?"

"What?" I bark out a laugh that even sounds fake to me.

"It's okay if you were. I am a bit of a TikTok star. I'm almost at one million views for the dance in front of the fountain," he says with an annoying smirk that's a little bit sexy.

"Thanks to my amazing filming abilities. Which you didn't credit me for."

"Yes," he says flatly. "It had nothing at all to do with the routine I spent hours perfecting."

"Actually," I say, noticing my open notebook just inches away from Axel, and remembering why I asked him to come over in the first place, "let's go over the contract."

"You and this contract. Is my word not enough for you?" he asks, shifting onto his side and propping his head up with this hand.

"It's absolutely not enough for me. Move over," I say, grabbing the notebook. Axel sits up and leans against my headboard. I join him. "These are the terms and agreements," I say, placing the notebook in his lap.

"You typed this on the computer, then pasted it into the notebook?"

"Yes. This notebook is my lifeline. Don't worry, I'll make you a copy of the contract."

"Oh good," he says, deadpan, before cracking a warm smile. He makes his way through the document. "I'm surprised you included everything you said you'd do."

"My word is gold."

"I see that." He clears his throat, then reads his side of the contract:

"1. Pretend to be Jamie's boyfriend leading up to winter formal.
2. Agree to waive half the cost of the repairs for Betty White to $225. Final payment to be received no later than the eve of winter formal.
3. Find ways to make Ben jealous. Bonus points for orchestrating situations for him to speak to Jamie."

He stops reading and glances up at me. "Is this it?"

I shrug.

"It's just there are five items for you to complete on my behalf and I'm only looking at three on my list to do for you."

"I guess I'm just not as demanding as you are." I smile.

He smiles back, and once again I'm suddenly very aware that Axel and I are sitting on my bed, alone, together.

"Can I flip through the rest of this notebook or is it private?" he asks.

"Go ahead. I have no secrets."

Axel flips through the pages, laughing and asking me questions about some of my past goals and marveling about how, up until this year, I've managed to check each and every one of them off. Easy enough to do when they're all mostly academically based.

"Ah, the infamous bucket list branch of the Kill-It List," he says when he lands on the collage. "You've really never been to the aquarium?"

"No."

"Not the ROM either? Or a hockey game? You're telling me you never went to the CN Tower, even in grade school?"

"My class did," I say. "But I begged my mom to let me stay home that day."

"Because you're claustrophobic?"

"Yeah. Anyway, we went over this already."

"Where's your red pen?" Axel asks.

I reach for it on my nightstand. "Here. Why?"

"We went to Wonderland. Give yourself a check mark. You know you want to."

"But I was supposed to go with Ben."

He takes the pen from me and crosses Ben's name out of the title, changing it from *Ben and Jamie's Bucket List* to *Axel and Jamie's*. "I'm going to take you to all these places," he says. Before I can protest, he flips back to the contract and adds a fourth item: *Take Jamie to all the locations on ~~her~~ our bucket list.*

"Axel." I shake my head. "That's going way above and beyond."

"Nah. These dates will benefit me too. Some of them would be the perfect backdrop for TikToks. And you agreed to film me, so it works out for both of us. We'll pick a place, post pictures to the gram, which will drive Ben crazy—item number three on *my* list—and then you'll film TikToks for me, item number three on *your* list."

"I put a lot of places on the bucket list. There's no way we can do them all before the formal. Plus, some of them are seasonal. Like an outdoor concert at Budweiser Stage. They're probably closing soon."

Axel pulls out his phone and googles the concert venue. "We're in luck. Next weekend is their last concert. Some band called Blue Rodeo."

"Who's that? Country singers? Anyway," I say, pointing to the screen, "the show is sold out."

"Minor details. Next Saturday don't make any plans. I am taking you to an outdoor concert at Budweiser Stage to watch Blue Rainbow."

"Rodeo," I correct him.

"Whatever. Now go ahead and give yourself a check mark for the Wonderland date. You earned it."

I did earn it. I take the pen from Axel and give myself a nice red check mark next to the photo of Wonderland. My heart aches slightly seeing Ben's name crossed out, but when my eyes land on Axel's name in its place, I'm filled with a rush of excitement and anticipation.

"No CN Tower though," I say. "I'm not ready for that." I go to mark a giant red X over the photo but Axel grabs my hand before I can.

"Let's work our way through the list first. Then we can revisit."

"Fine. Does this mean you'll finally sign the contract?"

Axel flips through my notebook in search of the contract. He reaches for the pen in my hand, his fingers grazing mine. We both freeze up at the unexpected contact as our eyes lock. "Does signing this make you legally bound to me?" he asks.

"Would it be so bad if it did?" Clearly, my inner flirt escaped and betrayed me.

Axel tips his forehead to mine. "Sometimes being bad feels good." He licks his lips and my heart pulses against my rib cage. I want to throw the notebook on the floor and kiss him while running my hands through his curls and . . .

A knock at my door.

"I'm opening this door in three seconds, so you better be decent," Mom says.

I bolt up and clumsily sit on my desk chair while Axel chuckles to himself.

Mom opens the door. "I said no boys in your room, Jamie."

"We were just doing homework," I say.

"Then leave the door open."

"Hi, Mrs. Foster," Axel says, waving from his spot on my bed.

"It's Ms. Taher." Mom turns and walks away, leaving an icy chill in her wake.

"Sorry about her," I say.

"No worries. I better get going," he says, sitting up. "Got my cousin's bachelor party tonight."

"The wedding is soon, right?"

"Two weekends from now."

"I'll do it," I blurt, as Axel rises from my bed.

"Do what?" he asks, rolling his sleeves to reveal his tanned forearms.

"I'll be your date to your cousin's wedding," I say, standing across from him now.

"What about Thanksgiving with Ben?"

I suck in my lips and swallow. "Realistically speaking, I don't think Ben and I will be back together by then. This has admittedly been a bigger challenge than I'd anticipated."

"I mean, I'd love for you to come to my cousin's wedding, but it's kind of a big ask."

"Nah." I grin. "It's what any good partner would do in this situation. Besides, going could give me an excuse to add another item to my—sorry, *our*—bucket list. Attend an Arab wedding—bonus event."

"Yeah?" A wide smile lights up his face.

"Yeah."

"Awesome. I can't wait to show you off."

Before I can reply, Axel is already halfway down the stairs.

After I hear the front door close, I open my laptop and print off calendars. Between tutoring Ben twice a week and going on elaborate dates with Axel and filming TikToks for him, my calendar is filling up faster than Eli does at Armstrong & Wong's Chinese Canadian buffet.

I'm going to need to keep track of all these social engagements and commitments if I want to pull this off and continue to keep my grades up.

As the calendar pages print, I find a blank page in my notebook and write a note to myself. A little reminder. *Stop fantasizing about kissing Axel. Ben is endgame.* I skim through my notebook to find Axel's signature still missing from the contract. Biting back a smile, I tell myself I'll get him to sign it the next time we're together.

CHAPTER TEN

It's Thursday afternoon and I'm waiting at the library for Ben to show up for our second tutoring session. Technically, I'm breaking one of the contractual agreements by not driving Axel home twice this week, but to be fair, he still hasn't signed the damn thing, so I figure there's some wiggle room. I even slid a copy of the contract into his locker on Monday and it somehow ended up back in my notebook by lunch—unsigned. It's like trying to nail down a worm.

"Hey." Ben greets me at the table, slightly out of breath. We've started to say hi to one another in the halls again, but only when he's not with *her*, which is sus since I say hi to him when Axel's by my side.

"You're late," I say as he pulls up the chair next to mine. A musky scent trails from his body.

I must be making a face because he asks, "Do I smell? I had to run here."

"Where were you?"

"Over on the football field watching Olivia's cheer practice."

Of course he was. I find it so odd that he talks to me about Olivia because, one, he dumped me for her and, two, if he *is* using this tutoring as an excuse to get closer, why remind me about the girl he left me for? "Does your girlfriend still not know I'm tutoring you?"

"I'll tell her next week after I ace the quiz. That way I'll have proof that I'm working with you because I need to and not . . ."

"Not what?" I turn my head swiftly, locking my eyes on his with deep intensity. "Because you want to?"

"I didn't say that." Ben looks away and unzips his backpack.

"You were about to."

"But I stopped myself because I knew it sounded . . ." His voice trails off and he sighs before his eyes meet mine again. "I need your help. That's true. I just don't want her to think it's an excuse to spend time with you."

"Why would she think that? You dumped my ass for her," I say, whipping the math textbook open. I am having deep regrets about agreeing to this. I wish Axel were here so he could make fun of Ben's hair and make me laugh and forget for a moment why I so badly want to get back together with this guy who unabashedly broke my heart.

"You make it sound like I kicked you to the curb. I didn't."

"Felt like you did," I say as I flip through the pages. "You weaseled your way out of my room pretty quickly the night you ended things."

Ben shuffles in his seat. "I've never broken up with someone before. I guess I didn't know how to do it, and you're pretty convincing when you want to be so I figured I had to say what I needed to say and get out of there before you could change my mind."

I huff out a laugh. "Whatever. You couldn't wait to get out of my room and out of my life."

"Not true, Jamie." He places his hand on the textbook to stop my aggressive page-flipping. "I miss being around you."

"Well, I don't want you to get the wrong message," I say, burying a slightly victorious smile. *He misses me.* I sit up straight and open my pencil case. "This is not me forgiving you. This is me tutoring you until you can crawl out of the hole you've dug for yourself. Plus, I need the money."

"Okay." Ben nods and I exhale the breath I'd been failing to swallow. I'm proud of myself for not taking the bait. For not trying to tease out a confession about how unfulfilling his relationship with Olivia is. This is not how I want to get him back. It needs to be more than this. Bigger than him just saying "Oops, I made a mistake."

Besides, I'm not done torturing him yet.

"What do you guys do for fun?" Ben asks as I review the answers to the practice questions I assigned him last session.

"Axel and me?"

"Yeah. You and Axel. And what kind of name is that anyway?" He chuckles obnoxiously.

"His given name is Alexander. Axel's just a nickname." A smile escapes me as I recall the moment Axel introduced himself to Eli. He's quite charming when he wants to be. The only people he hasn't seemed to win over yet are my mom and Ben. I'm still undecided.

I correct one of Ben's responses by showing him the proper formula in red pen before finally answering his question. "He's actually teaching me how to dance." The white lie slips out, but I needed something better than "we hang out and plot different ways to make you jealous."

"You?" Ben turns his face to bury a laugh.

I jab him with my elbow. "Yes, me. Is that so hard to believe?"

"Sorry. I'm just picturing the time Eli tried to get you to do the Macarena at our Labor Day barbecue and—" He holds up a finger to allow himself a moment to catch his breath from laughing so hard. It's contagious, and I end up laughing too.

"It's true." I shake my head. "I am the most uncoordinated person ever." I clear my throat. "But dancing is important to Axel, so

I try. *For him.*" I really want to drive home the last two words because that's the kind of girlfriend I am. It's the kind of girlfriend I was to Ben. I'll step outside my comfort zone for someone I love. Despite what some people might think, it's not weak to do things for others. It's how I show love. But I guess with some distance, I can see that maybe I tried to push my love language onto Ben a little too hard when things started to feel strained between us. And if I'm being honest with myself, it started even before he left for camp.

The first two years with Ben were perfect, at least from my perspective. Ben was pretty much the reason I didn't crawl into a hole and hide after Dad left. He helped me get through the pain of losing my dad. The anxiety of never knowing when I'd speak to him next. He asked me about my sessions with my therapist and reminded me of the coping mechanisms she taught me when I felt a panic attack coming on. It made me grow even more attached to him, to the point where I didn't think I needed to see her anymore. When Ben started distancing himself slightly, I clung on even tighter because I was afraid. I'd already lost my dad. I couldn't lose Ben, too.

"Hey, I didn't do so bad," Ben says, looking over his work. "Only got one wrong, and you even gave me partial marks." He brings up his hand for a fist bump. I ignore it.

"Let's get to work."

Trying to catch Ben up on the last few weeks of calculus is pretty painless. He's picking up on the lessons quickly. I still can't figure out if this is all a ruse to get me alone. But Ben must know he doesn't need to make up an excuse to be with me.

He starts on another practice worksheet I made for him, and I can't help but ask the question that's been nagging at me.

"Before you left for camp, were you happy? I mean . . . did you think we were in a good place?"

Ben looks up from his notebook. He swallows and the grip on his pencil tightens. "Sure."

"Ben." I tilt my head. "If things were so good between us, then you and Olivia would never have happened."

He exhales as his eyes move around the library. "I didn't want to admit to you or myself that part of the reason I took the job at the camp, even after you learned you weren't allowed to come, was because I needed space."

"Space from me?" I ask.

He turns to look at me and heat rises through my body. I know I'm not going to like what he says next, but even so, I need to hear him say it.

Ben sighs and runs a hand through his hair as he puts his pencil down. "There's this energy that surrounds you, Jamie, and I don't . . ." His voice trails off again, as he searches for the right words. "I don't blame you for being the way you are. I know with your dad leaving and your mom being your mom, it's not easy for you. But a heaviness was starting to seep into our relationship, and once I was at camp I was surprised by how much lighter I felt."

I face forward in my seat, my body sliding down ever so slightly. "I see."

"Hey. It all worked out, right? You've got Axel and I'm with Olivia." Every time he says her name, I envision myself grabbing a pair of rusty scissors and chopping off his long, greasy hair. "The fact that Axel's teaching you to dance and you're allowing him to is proof that he's able to reach a part of you I never was." Ben's voice sounds almost sad as he delivers the end of that sentence. His phone buzzes before I can come up with a reply. He picks it up and types a message before turning to me. "Any chance I can catch a ride home with you?"

I agree without questioning why, too defeated by this entire conversation. Besides, after I drop Ben off, I can go to Axel's and get him to finally sign our contract. And as a show of good faith, I'll even play the doting girlfriend in front of his family.

The drive back to Ben's is short but weird. It's like every romantic song in the history of romantic songs plays during the seven-minute ride. My fingers can't seem to change the stations fast enough.

"Since when did you start listening to pop music?" he asks as I pull up to his house and park.

"Axel programmed all those stations."

"He's really into music, eh?"

"Yeah well, it's pretty much part and parcel of his job."

"Job." Ben laughs. "I've watched a couple of his TikToks. The one in front of the fountains at Wonderland was intense. It's like he performed that one just for you. You must have hated the painfully overt display of affection."

"Why do you say that?" I ask, twisting in my seat to face him.

"Because that stuff makes us cringe."

"Does it?" I ask, furrowing my brows. "Because whenever I see you with Olivia, all of her is draped over all of you. And I only stopped myself from PDAs when we were together because you made it clear you weren't into it."

"So you like how showy Axel is?"

I think on his question for a moment before answering. "Yeah. I do. It doesn't make me uncomfortable. It never did."

"Oh." Ben nods, like I've just told him those vegan breakfast bars he's been consuming since ninth grade are made of pork. But this can't be news to him. I followed his lead. I was like a little puppy, trying to do whatever I could to get a treat from my master. Looking back, I can see how pathetic it was. How pathetic I was. Especially since I wasn't like that in the beginning.

"You want to come in?" he asks. "Mom would love to see you."

I ponder his offer. Mostly I think about how my gut response to his invite is "Nah, bro. I'm good." It's not that I don't want to get back together with Ben anymore, it's just not as simple a solution as it once felt. While I never thought things were perfect, I thought maybe I was the only one feeling the disconnect. I can't fault Ben for having doubts or even wanting space, because there were times that I had doubts and wanted space. I also still can't help worry that maybe something did happen between him and Olivia at camp. They just looked way too comfortable together that night I ran over Axel's bike.

And here comes the anger again.

"Thanks for the invite but I have plans," I respond.

"Right. You're probably going to Axel's," he says, the tone in his voice a mix between disappointment and desperation.

"Remember how you said you hoped we could be friends someday?" I ask.

Ben's eyebrows rise as he leans in.

"I'm not there yet," I say. "I'm not sure when or if I'll ever be."

"Are you even trying?" he asks, slinking back.

"Why should I? No, seriously." I shift to face him. "Why should I bother trying to be your friend when you can't be honest with me about how you and Olivia came to be."

"Is that what this is about? I thought we went over this. Nothing happened with Olivia until you and I broke up." He looks away, and in that moment, I know for sure he isn't telling me something.

"Physically maybe. But I don't buy emotionally. See, the thing is, Ben, you were never really emotionally available to me that last year we were together, so in a way, it hurts more that you were busy forming this deep connection with Olivia over the summer while I stared at my phone, waiting for you to call or text."

"What about you and Axel?" Ben says, an accusatory tone to his voice. "Were you really just staring at your phone all summer or were you hanging out with him?"

"That is neither here nor there," I say, trying to divert attention from Axel's and my origin story. We've been too busy building our current timeline to come up with a detailed backstory.

"How come you get to be pissed at how quickly I moved on with Olivia, but less than twenty-four hours after we were broken up, you were already dating him? That's never sat right with me."

"This is such... do you even hear yourself? How hypocritical... I mean, I can't even with you. I only got together with Axel because, well, because I was single. You put the wheels in motion for that to happen. You started it."

"Real mature, Jamie. Sorry for thinking we could possibly be friends."

"That's just it. We never really were friends. I had just conflated our romantic relationship with a friendship. Ergo, I don't think there's a way we can be friends now, since the foundation was never there."

"Why does everything have to be all or nothing with you?" he asks, his voice rising slightly.

"Because, Ben, it does."

Ben studies my face. Perhaps he's hopeful I'll falter at his puppy dog eyes, but they don't seem to affect me as much as they used to.

"I'm sorry you feel that way." He reaches for the door handle.

"Wait," I say. He turns back to look at me, a glimmer of hope forming in his eyes. "I don't think I should tutor you anymore. It doesn't feel right."

"Whatever you say." His shoulders slump before he exits my car.

I reverse out of Ben's driveway and make the short trek to Axel's. After parking, I grab the contract, stuffing it into my back pocket. I basically run to his front door and knock aggressively, a rush of energy coursing through my body.

A man with a beard, sprinkled with gray and trimmed to perfection, answers. "Hello," he says, his Arab accent thick like molasses.

"Hi." I try to catch my breath. "Is Axel here?"

"No. But Alexander is."

"Right." I laugh but his father doesn't reciprocate. Time to lay on the charm. "I think Axel is a ridiculous nickname too. Especially since he has such a strong, classic name."

Despite the thick beard, a miniscule smile becomes visible. I reach out my hand. "I'm Jamie Taher-Foster."

"Taher," he repeats as he shakes my hand. "Arabi?"

"Yes."

"Hal tatahadath alearabia?" he asks.

"No. But I understand it a little." *A little* might be an extreme inflation of the truth.

"Come in," he says, waving me in from outside. "Do you want to learn?"

"I've always wanted to but no one in my house speaks it. Sometimes my uncle does, but mostly just when he's angry." And those aren't words I can repeat to my fake boyfriend's father.

Mr. Dahini chuckles. "Your mother, she's an Arab?"

"Yes. Her parents are Palestinian."

"Christian or Muslim?"

I don't know why Arabs always ask me this.

"Greek Orthodox, but we're not very religious."

I feel like I'm being interrogated and failing, badly. From what I've seen and heard of Axel's parents, their culture is extremely important to them and so is religion—in his foyer alone there are three crucifixes. I can't imagine what his father is thinking right now, speaking to this half-Arab girl who can't even answer simple questions without stumbling.

"Ah. You either are religious or you're an atheist. No middle."

"Baba." Axel comes down the stairs, shirtless, to find me and his father discussing faith and religion. Totally normal conversation for someone you've only just met.

"Alexander," his father says, his voice low. "Is this your girlfriend?"

"Jamie? Sure."

Real convincing, Axel.

His father nods and smiles. Axel mouths "what're you doing here?" Did I do something wrong by showing up unannounced? I thought I was supposed to play the girlfriend role. My stomach twists at Axel's lackluster response to my presence. He's usually happy to see me.

"Easha'i?" his father asks. Axel shakes his head.

"Um, no?"

His father grins. "Do you know what I asked you?"

Axel, who remains on the bottom step, behind his father, pretends to eat something out of a bowl. I didn't realize coming here would mean a spontaneous game of charades.

"My mom is expecting me home for dinner. But thank you," I say, trying to recover. "I just wanted to give Ax—Alexander something."

Just when I didn't think things could get any more awkward, the front door swings open and Axel's mom walks through with two other women, who look a bit like Axel. Must be his older sisters. All three of them pause when they see us standing in the foyer. One by one, smiles grow on their faces, each telling a different story.

"Ahlan, Jamie," his mother says, greeting me. She says my name the same way Eli does when he pulls out his fake accent. Only hers is real. "Are you here for dinner?"

I shake my head again. "No, thank you. I just have something to give Axel."

"Is it a shirt?" she asks, eyeing her son. "Here." She places her shopping bags on the floor and pulls out a T-shirt. "Put this on."

Axel takes the shirt and smirks before throwing it on. His mom comes up behind him, pulling off the tag.

"Mama, Baba, leave them alone," one of his older sisters says. She pushes her parents toward the kitchen and turns back to wink at us. "You too, Chrissy."

"Let's go outside." Axel hops off the bottom step and puts on his slides. I follow him out, feeling all eyes on us.

"Sorry for showing up unannounced like this," I say once he closes the front door.

"Why *did* you show up?" His tone is cold. So is his body language.

"I dropped Ben off after tutoring. Figured I'd try to get you to sign the contract again." I let out a small laugh but he doesn't reciprocate.

"What's the point anymore?" he asks, folding his arms across his chest. "I mean, do you even need my help? Seems you're doing fine without me."

"I am doing fine *because* of you." Axel faces the street and I walk right up to him, placing my hand on his arm. "Do you not want to do this anymore?"

"Guess how many people I've turned down since starting Maple View?"

"People? What people?"

"You haven't noticed other girls checking me out? Guys too. They pretty much undress me with their eyes when we're together, and when you're not around, I have to practically bat them off with a stick."

I shake my head. "I-I didn't know. I guess I'm not always that observant of what's going on around me." I remove my hand from his arm and stare out at the street, side by side with Axel. My stomach clenches as dread makes my chest tight. "Do you want to fake break up?"

"No." His voice is low.

"Well, clearly I'm getting in the way of your love life."

He turns to face me. "Say we met under normal circumstances; would you have given me a second look?"

"That's not a fair question," I say.

"Why?"

"Because I probably wouldn't have." His eyes dart away from mine. I can see I've hurt his feelings, but how can he be surprised? Half the time we're together, we bicker. And we didn't exactly get off to a great start when we met.

"Do you know what it's like to have multiple people chasing after me when the one person's attention I do want is busy chasing after a person who doesn't deserve her?"

"Is this some sort of confession?" I ask, honestly perplexed by Axel's quasi-declaration of . . . something.

"When I saw you and Ben at the library after school, I didn't like it."

"You saw us?" I ask.

"I wanted to tell you something but the two of you were laughing and it seemed like you were having a moment."

Laughing? A moment? "There wasn't a moment. You probably just saw us when Ben was making fun of my inability to do the Macarena."

Axel stifles a laugh. "You really are hopeless, aren't you?"

"I am. And that's why I need you." I exhale and take a step closer, allowing a smile to come through. "I don't want this thing to end. Truthfully, I'm having too much fun. But if feelings are getting in the way and . . ."

"No. Forget I said anything."

He swallows, avoiding my stare. I stand by, tilting my head. His eyes meet with mine slowly.

"Okay," he says with a slight shrug. He pinches his fingers together. "I may have a tiny crush on you."

"Good." I mirror his fingers with my own. "Because I may have a tiny crush on you too. Purely physical."

Axel laughs and it helps break the tension of this weird confessional.

"I'm good with that," he says in that cocky tone I've grown to like.

The sun is about to set. Standing on this porch alongside Axel with a cool breeze blowing between us, I think about lacing my fingers with his. Not for show but because I want to. What if I kissed him? Would he kiss me back? And what if he did? Would it be so bad? Just to see what it's like to kiss someone else. To feel his lips on mine. To press my body up against his. Maybe run my hands through his curls.

I look up to find Axel's eyes on me in a contemplative stare. He slowly bridges the gap between us. Instinctively, I wet my lips before leaning in to meet his.

"Jamie," Axel's mom calls through the doorway, her voice like ice-cold water on a growing fire. I take a step back, a veiled attempt to steady my racing heart. Axel turns away, placing his hands in his pockets. "I know you can't have dinner with us tonight, but Saturday, you come here, we'll feed you. Okay?"

I glance at Axel, whose cheeks are flaming red.

"Okay," I say. "I'll come by."

"Early though," Axel says to his mom. "We have plans that night."

"Okay, busy boy. The early bird special for my lovebirds." His mom smiles at the two of us and Axel raises his brows at his mother. "Sorry, Romeo. I'll leave you alone."

"What plans do we have Saturday?" I ask once his mom is back inside.

"That's what I was coming to tell you at the library. The Red Rodeo concert—"

I nod before correcting him. "Blue Rodeo. Did you get tickets?"

"Don't worry about logistics. I have a plan. Just come by around five."

Saturday night: dinner with my fake boyfriend who I just almost kissed and his Arab family before going to a concert we don't have tickets for. Sounds like a time.

The corners of my lips turn up in a smile. "Can't wait."

CHAPTER ELEVEN

"What're you doing tonight?" Mom asks. We're in the kitchen, piecing together lunch. Amo Eli is at work with Axel. My stomach has been doing flips all day, worrying about having to share a meal with Axel's big Arab family. I know it's just pretend, but I'm for-real nervous.

What if I don't like the food they serve? What if I don't have the right answers to their questions? What if they want to talk politics? What if they discover I'm a horrible Arab? What if they tell Axel I'm not good enough for him? Will that change how he feels about me?

I've never really had another guy confess to liking me before. With Ben, we sort of just fit together like two puzzle pieces. We made sense. Axel, who apparently has his pick of anyone in our school, has a crush on me. But why?

As for me, liking Axel back, even just a little bit, pulls me away from my endgame. It's like Ben is the right answer to the math problem but solving the equation is difficult. Axel may not be on the other end of the equal sign, but everything leading up to the response is a lot more fun. And for some reason, makes me happier.

Mom cuts my salami sandwich in half and I wash a bowl of strawberries for us to share. We sit across from one another at the table.

"I'm having dinner at Axel's and then we're going to the Blue Rodeo concert."

Mom sits up straight, her face slightly scrunched. "Blue Rodeo? I didn't think you were into that kind of music."

"You mean old music?" I smile.

She smiles back. "Yeah. I guess I mean old music."

"I'm not, but Axel is helping me check some items off my bucket list. And one of those items was to watch a concert at Budweiser Stage. This is the last one of the season, so we're taking what we can get."

"I see." She bites into her sandwich and washes it down with water. "Well, just be careful down there. Driving in that part of the city can be kind of tricky."

"I will." Although, I'm not even certain how we're getting there, and oddly, I'm not that worried. Maybe because I have other things occupying my brain.

"So." She pauses. "Dinner with his parents?"

Here we go. I bite into my sandwich and wait for Mom's cynical flood of words to come at me.

"Things must be getting pretty serious," she says, her tone lukewarm. She doesn't want me to be able to read her, except she doesn't seem to know I can read her better than anyone else. We may not share the same viewpoints on a lot of things, but we do share DNA.

"It's nothing formal. I had to turn down their first invite so when his mother asked me again, I said yes because I didn't want to be rude. Anyway, I ate at Ben's all the time."

"That's different. Everything is formal with Arabs." Mom takes another bite while her brown eyes peer into mine, all judgmental like.

Don't take the bait. Don't take the bait.

"So what if it is?" I ask, taking the bait. "Would that be such a bad thing?"

"Would it be such a bad thing if you tried being single for once in your teen years? I thought your generation had moved past all of this."

I roll my eyes. "Don't do that."

"Do what?"

"Mix white feminism with selective Gen Z rhetoric to try to shame me for wanting to experience . . . to want to have . . . to . . . never mind." I hate that she stumped me.

"Let's drop it, okay? I'm the bitter old lady and you're the young, beautiful girl full of potential."

Oh great. The passive-aggressive guilt trip. Been a while since I've been on this ride.

"I'm never going to be good enough for you, am I?" I ask. "I'll always be the reason you didn't get the life you wanted. I could do everything right, and you'll still find something to criticize."

"Jamie."

"It's fine." I rise from the table. "I'm actually not that hungry."

"You're right," Mom says as I walk out of the kitchen. I pause in the doorway, my hands gripping the frame as I wait for her to continue. "Your life is full of so much promise. And I'm afraid you're going to let it all go because of a boy. Like I did."

I turn to face her. "And a baby."

Her face falls. "I don't regret having you. Would I recommend people follow in my footsteps? No. Do I want more for you? Yes."

"Why do you dislike Axel so much?"

Mom stands and brings our plates to the counter. Her thin arms look so delicate in her short-sleeved shirt. Her curls are gathered at the top of her head, out of her face for another full day of work.

"It's not that I dislike him," she says, wiping her hands on her jeans. "It's just when I see Axel, I see everything my parents wanted for me. I've spent half my life running away from all of that only for my daughter to be running toward it."

I walk back into the kitchen and stop so we're almost toe to toe. "Or maybe you're just afraid I might find out the truth: that your parents weren't so bad. That Dad isn't the villain you paint him to be and that the one person in my life, the one who is supposed to want the best for me, is actually the one getting in the way of me having everything I want." I pause and wait for her to look up at me, but she doesn't. "You can get in your own way, but I won't let you get in mine."

Mom keeps her eyes down and eventually just says, "I hope you have fun tonight." She walks past me and opens the door to the basement. Anxiety hums under my skin as Mom heads down the steps to her salon. When music bounces below my feet a moment later—a familiar, sad ballad from Phil Collins—I climb up the stairs to my bedroom and fall to the bed, releasing tears of frustration while lying in fetal position to fend off yet another stomach cramp.

By the time I arrive at Axel's, I'm starving. I've lost track of how many meals have been sacrificed because I was too upset to continue eating after an argument with my mother.

Axel answers the door wearing shorts and a plain white T-shirt. He invites me in and I step inside. His home smells like someone dropped an entire package of allspice on the carpet and rubbed it in. With a couple hundred garlic cloves.

A TV from the family room is seemingly on at full volume, even though no one is sitting in there, while his mother and sisters engage in an intense conversation in the kitchen—intense enough that I can hear them from the foyer. There's a lot going on in terms of decor. A carved wooden statue of Jesus rests on a console table in the foyer, surrounded by two smaller crucifixes and a few wooden camels. Above it, an elaborate tapestry hangs on the wall. It looks similar to one I remember seeing in my maternal grandparents' home. Axel's living room is adorned with photos. Mostly portraits. I walk through, examining the pictures, the happy smiles, the still-intact family.

We enter the kitchen and I ask his mother if she needs any help but she shoos me away. Not rudely, but because I'm a guest and therefore I'm not "allowed to lift a finger." Axel's father is out back cleaning up his vegetable garden and his sisters, who are here without their husbands, are now setting the dining room table. It's all very traditional. Mom would hate it.

"Can I see your room?" I ask Axel once we're back in the foyer.

He looks past me into the kitchen. "Sure," he says quietly before basically tiptoeing up the stairs.

When we arrive, he closes the door gently.

"Are you not allowed to have girls in your room?" I tease.

"Of course not, but they won't say anything. At least while you're here."

"Were your sisters allowed to have boys in their rooms?" I ask while taking in the sight of his meticulous bedroom. I wasn't expecting him to be such a neat freak.

He laughs. "Definitely not."

I sit on his bed, the sheets so smooth I worry about leaving an imprint of my butt. "Do your parents have a different set of rules for you because you're a boy?"

"I wouldn't say that," he says, sitting next to me. "It's because I'm the youngest and they're older and tired." He grins while elbowing my side. "Helps me get away with more."

"Like what?" I ask, turning to face him.

"Like having pretty girls in my room."

My cheeks flush. I suck them in as I get up, inspecting the books on his shelves. "Speaking of, does your mother still make your bed and clean your room for you?"

"No. I do."

"You're the reason this room is so sterile?" I ask, looking back at him.

"Yeah. What's the big deal?" He shrugs.

"My room must have made you cringe," I say, looking away.

"I don't judge how other people choose to live. It's your space. But for me, it's important to have a clean room. For a couple of reasons."

I pull out his desk chair and sit like I'm his therapist. "Go on."

He smiles. "One, if you hadn't already noticed, my house is kind of chaotic. It's sensory overload. This is my safe haven to escape all that. Also, I need room to practice my dances. Which means, no clothes on the floor."

"Fair enough," I say, both respecting and understanding his answer. Except for me, the chaos I keep buried inside comes out in my room.

"Why did you think my mom was still cleaning my room?" he asks, lifting a brow.

"Because *my* mom seems to think Arab sons are treated like kings."

He huffs out a laugh. "That's definitely not the case with me. I've been doing chores since the first grade. And I have to earn an allowance. In some ways, my parents were a lot easier with my sisters than they are with me. Although, I'm sure my sisters would beg to differ."

"I think people sometimes only notice what they want to notice. The things that usually affect them," I say, my eyes meeting with Axel's. "Your dad is kind of tough on you, isn't he?"

Axel exhales as he runs his hands up and down his thighs. "He just expects a lot."

I glance around his room. There's a shelf above his desk lined with soccer trophies and ribbons from swimming classes. I stand again and inspect the gold plaque positioned in the middle of his sports awards. "You were valedictorian of your elementary school?"

"Yeah. Is that so surprising?"

"Yes!" I laugh. "I thought you were... well, I didn't think grades were that important to you."

"Why? Because I like to dance?"

"Pretty much."

"Has anyone ever told you you're pretty judgmental?"

I raise my shoulders. "All the time." Axel shakes his head and laughs. "Maybe it's because I saw you as this rising social media star. And that takes time and effort. Plus, you work with my uncle. I didn't think it left you with the kind of desire or energy to be good at much else. Clearly, I was wrong."

He leans back on his bed, resting his head on his bent arms. "Yeah, it's not easy being perfect."

I grab the pillow out from underneath his head and smack him in the face with it.

"Hey now," he says, securing the pillow safely away from me. He points to his face. "This is a moneymaker. Please treat it with respect."

I roll my eyes and lie next to him. He smells like pine trees and apricots. A weird combination, but on Axel, it works. I like being close to Axel. Even if it makes my heart race sometimes, it's a good racing. A feeling I can't seem to stop chasing. "So, what should I expect from your family at dinner?"

He shifts on his side, propping his head up with his hand. His smile is sweet and the gold chain around his neck falls to the side, drawing my eyes to his bronze skin. "Dad will be mostly silent.

Observing. Mom will smile a lot. Chrissy, she's the middle sister, will ask you a lot of questions. Susannah, the oldest, will find any opportunity to either drag me or talk me up. Depends on what day of her cycle she's on."

"Axel!" I say, matching his pose. "You can't say stuff like that."

"I would never say that to you, my pretend girlfriend, but my sisters are fair game. They had me buying them pads and tampons as soon as I was allowed to ride my bike to the store."

"Sounds like you guys are tight."

"We are," Axel says. "They'll love you. I think my mom already does."

"They love pretend Jamie. The real me, probably not so much."

"Why do you say that?" he asks, his thick brows knitted together.

"Because I come from a broken family. Because my mom raised me without any ties to my culture. Because my uncle is gay."

"Hey." Axel shakes his head. "My parents are accepting of all people."

"I'm sorry. My mom's gotten it in my head over the years that Arabs have prehistoric mindsets when it comes to women and the LGBTQIA+ community. I only recently started pushing back on her own self-hating ways and it's caused a lot of tension between us."

"Is that because of me?" he asks.

"You may have been the catalyst, but the issues have always been there, simmering."

"It's not too late, you know."

"What isn't?" I ask.

Axel sits up and I follow. "To learn about where you come from. To interact with the community. To speak on Palestine. I've been to a couple protests myself. The energy is electric. Everyone makes it out to be like the world is against Arabs, but when we come together, for a cause, like Palestine or Syria, we're fierce. We're strong. We're unstoppable."

"You're amazing," I say aloud, without realizing. I half expect Axel to grin while running his fingers through his hair in an obnoxious way. Instead, he blushes.

"You're not so bad yourself, James."

My mind flashes to his porch when we almost kissed. I think about what would have happened if we had. In a way I'm grateful it didn't happen, because then it might have made things weird and put a stop to all our plans, and to be honest, I'm really looking forward to our plans. It's been a while since I felt excited about non-academic things.

"Come on," he says, patting my thigh. "I can tell by the sound of the dishes hitting the table and the smells infiltrating my room that dinner is just about ready. And don't worry. If there are any awkward silences, I'll fill them. I'm good at taking up space." He winks, and instead of it making me want to roll my eyes or retort sarcastically, it fills me with warmth.

Dinner with Axel's family is perfect. The food is delicious. His mother prepared a spread of homemade falafel, hummus, tahini (which I avoid), baba ghanoush, tabouli, and warm pita. Axel's dad is really sweet, especially with his daughters. His mom can't stop grinning at us. Chrissy does interrogate me, but she seems to be okay with my answers. Susannah teases Axel about his failed attempt to play hockey (finally found something he's not good at), and Axel keeps his promise by filling in the few awkward gaps of silence. There are no questions about if I'm Arab "enough," and nothing to make me feel like I'm not welcome at their table with their family, next to their son.

After dinner, Axel's mom and sisters turn down my attempts to help them clean up. Once we head out, I begin asking Axel questions again about the how-tos behind getting into a sold-out concert, but he refuses to answer.

"You only need to know what you need to know," he says on our bus ride into the city. We're at a bus shelter now, holding onto our transfers. "Here it comes," he says as the streetcar arrives.

"Can you at least tell me where it's taking us?"

"Read the sign." He points.

I look up to see "Harbourfront" on the digital screen.

"Why Harbourfront?" I ask, taking a seat near the back of the streetcar. Axel slides in next to me. It's like he walks around with a constant soundtrack playing in his head. All his movements are lyrical.

"Remember what I said about tonight's plans being on a need-to-know basis?"

I unlock my phone and begin typing into it. "Okay, but Budweiser Stage is still another ten minutes away from Harbourfront and that's not accounting for traffic or construction."

Axel looks down at the phone in my hand, opened to Google Maps.

"Jamie," he says. "Are you mapping this trip?"

"You're not telling me anything."

"So?"

"So, I need to know what I'm getting myself into," I say, clenching my jaw and trying (but failing) to relax.

"Why?"

"So I can prepare myself. I like to be in control of my life and my surroundings. As much as possible, anyway."

"Why do you think that is?" he asks with a smirk.

"For real?" I ask, sitting up. "I have anxiety. I mean, we all have anxiety, but some of us don't know how to manage it." I exhale, looking down at my tight fists. "I was diagnosed with generalized anxiety disorder in ninth grade. My mom made me see a therapist because I wasn't handling my dad's . . ." Clearing my throat, I exhale and try again. "I had a hard time after my father left."

"But that's normal, isn't it? I mean, if my dad walked out on us, I'd probably be a mess too. Not that I'm saying you're a mess," he quickly backtracks.

"No, it's fine." I shake my head and let out a small puff of laughter. "It is normal. But I was developing some unhealthy habits and the panic attacks became a bit more frequent, so we needed to try to find ways to deal with it."

"What kind of unhealthy habits?"

I turn away from him and look out the window. Axel is asking some pretty personal questions, and I can't really fault him because if I were him, I'd want to know too. But I've never really spoken to anyone about this outside of Mom, Amo Eli, and Ben. Ben was the one who was there after every appointment with the therapist. He was the one who took me out for ice cream. Assured me there wasn't a vise around my lungs and that I could breathe. He became my security blanket, and he was a really good one . . . until he wasn't.

Last year, he started to downplay my anxiety. Said I was in control of the way I felt and that I just had to stop listening to the negative voices in my head. Ben thought going for a walk would solve ninety percent of my problems. He said I needed to learn how to cope because life was only going to get harder and if I fed into the anxiety, it would become a monster that would take over my life.

The shared Kill-It Lists were not only a way to keep us focused on our goals, but they were also supposed to keep my anxiety at bay. If I had a plan, if I had goals, if I created a clear path for myself and my future, there'd be less room for the anxiety monster to take over.

And sometimes he was right. But on the days he wasn't, it felt like I couldn't turn to him and that was hard. It's hard feeling like your safe person isn't your safe person anymore.

"A lot of it is just stimming but sometimes in non-healthy ways," I say to Axel. "I used to pick at the skin around my fingernails to the point of bleeding. I wear a mouthguard at night because apparently I grind my teeth in my sleep. I either eat too much or not enough, depending on what kind of stress I'm experiencing. The good news is, I rarely have panic attacks anymore. I've learned the signs and am able to stop them from happening by doing my breathing exercises. However, I haven't been able to gain control over the other thing."

"The other thing?" Axel asks.

I suck in my lips, embarrassment flushing my neck. "Sometimes when I overthink, catastrophize, or get triggered by something upsetting—like fighting with my mom or seeing Ben with Olivia—my stomach starts to hurt a lot and it becomes urgent," I say quickly.

"What becomes urgent?" he asks, looking a little puzzled.

"Like, you know." I expand my eyes, hoping he'll catch on so I don't have to say it.

"No. I don't."

"The bathroom, Axel. My need to go to the bathroom becomes urgent."

"Oh," he responds, his eyes almost as wide as mine, but only for a moment before his face returns to status quo.

"It's why I follow strict routines and try to have my life laid out for me, because if I veer off that path, then I'd have to deal with the side effects that come with my anxiety, and sometimes there isn't an accessible toilet when you need one. Which makes me more anxious and makes the stomach cramps worse and that's why..."

"That's why you're asking me so many questions about how tonight is going to pan out."

"Exactly," I say, feeling a mix between embarrassed and vulnerable and relieved. Relieved that he seems to get it.

"Would it help if I asked you to trust me?"

Okay. Maybe he doesn't get it.

"Look," Axel says, turning his body slightly so he's closing in on me. "I have a plan. A really well-thought-out plan. But if at any point you don't feel safe or you feel like one of your stomachaches might come on, I'll stop everything and find you a toilet. We can even come up with a code word for it. How's 'green apple'?"

I look down at my scraped-up knees with old scars I am sometimes tempted to pick at again and laugh. "It's terrible."

He smiles and takes my hand, rubbing my palms to smooth out the nail indentations. "What you said before about how all people experience anxiety, it's true. Even me. One of my coping mechanisms for stress is dancing, and the other is music." Axel pulls earbuds out of a tiny case. "Here," he says, passing me one.

"What am I supposed to do with this?"

"I mean, it's supposed to go in your ear, but if you'd like, I could suggest other places to stick it in."

"Watch it," I say, before placing the earbud in my left ear. Axel does the same with his. He opens the music app on his phone and hits Play.

"What do you think?" he asks, as the song begins.

"Sounds like country music," I quip.

"Listen to the lyrics," he says, leaning back and closing his eyes. "Most songs tell a story. It's not only the music that's making you feel things. It's the emotion in the singer's voice."

"Who is this?" I ask, resisting the urge to tap my toes in sync with his.

"Blue Rodeo. I listened to their greatest hits last night to prepare for the concert. This one is called 'Til I Am Myself Again.' It reminds me of you," he says, stealing a sideways glance at me.

"Why?" I ask, sitting up straight in my seat.

"Just close your eyes and listen," he says, remaining mostly still, aside from the tapping toes and the strumming of his fingers along his knees.

I slump in my seat, trying to decipher the lyrics. After a couple of verses, my back straightens again and I turn to Axel. "This song is clearly about some lost soul who doesn't know who they are. I know who I am," I say, pointing a finger at my chest before leaning back in my seat. "I guess I should be grateful you didn't tell me to listen to some cheesy love song and say it reminded you of me."

"Because then you'd just laugh in my face, right?" he asks, his expression and body language stiffening.

I open my mouth to say something but can't quite find the right words. Hard to know what to say when you've clearly offended someone but you don't know why.

"We're next," he says, holding out his hand. I place the earbud in his palm and he tucks it away in the case before bolting up. I follow him out of the streetcar.

After we walk for a bit, he points to a sign. *Harbourfront Water Taxi.*

"We're taking a water taxi?" I ask.

"I wanted to go by paddleboat, put those leg muscles of yours to work. I don't need it," he says, running a hand over his muscular thigh. "But apparently the water is too dangerous to go by paddleboat there."

"Careful," I say. "You keep making me roll my eyes, they might end up getting stuck in the back of my head."

"Well, we can't have that." He smiles. "No one else manages to look at me with such adoration and shock at the same time. I'd miss it."

"Whatever." Am I that obvious? Amo Eli does say he can read my face like a book. I've got to get better at hiding my emotions. I wouldn't want Ben to be able to tell I'm faking it with Axel. Although, lately it's been harder to distinguish the moments I am faking it with Axel from the ones I'm not.

It's kind of difficult being fake around someone who brings out the truth in you.

"So, we're taking a water taxi to the amphitheater? Then what?" I ask.

"Is this a green apple moment or do you think you can trust me, at least until the boat ride is over?"

"It's not a green apple moment."

"Good. And I'll ask the captain how long the ride is." Axel smiles. We walk up the dock and Axel chats with the captain for a moment, paying our fare. He extends his hand and helps me on board.

"He says it will take about ten minutes. Once we get to the venue, we'll locate all the bathrooms. Okay?" he says as he takes a seat. I sit across from him and nod.

A boat ride on Lake Ontario wasn't part of any plans I had (it definitely wasn't on the bucket list), but as I take in the fresh lake water, watching how the almost-setting sun glistens while giving the most spectacular view of the quiet Toronto Island on one side, juxtaposed with the bustling city on the other, I think to myself how maybe this should have been on my list. Or maybe going off-plan once in a while is good. Helps me learn to be more spontaneous, like Ben wanted. Deal with the anxiety head-on. Exposure therapy, like my therapist repeatedly mentioned in our sessions.

"How did you know to do this?" I ask, but the breeze and roar of the boat engine drown out my voice. Axel moves closer, placing his arm behind me and leaning his head to mine as I repeat the question.

"I did my research. Not just a pretty face after all." He winks, then glances down at his phone. "The opening act should be finishing their set soon, which means we'll make it in time for the main event."

"Really? You're excited to watch—what did you call them—Red Rodeo?" I ask as the captain revs up the engine. The boat rocks and my body slides closer to Axel. Instead of adjusting myself, I leave my leg pressed up against his.

"Yeah. They've got some good bops."

"What's a bop?" I ask, furrowing my brows.

"Were you born this century or nah?" he asks as the boat heads west. "It means a good song."

"Well, technically it doesn't," I begin. Axel pinches the bridge of his nose and sighs. "The word 'bop' derives from 'bebop,' which is a specific kind of music, early modern jazz. But it's also slang for 'move,' 'go,' or 'proceed.'"

"The Queen of Homographs strikes again."

"Yeah," I say, looking away and studying the water. "Why do I always do that? Sorry."

"Don't be sorry. It's a cute quirk. And I like it."

"Okay. Then I'm not sorry. Speaking of the word 'quirk,' I can think of at least five different homographs for it."

"Fill my brain with your knowledge," he says, scooting himself closer, arm still draped behind me. This time, I lean against it.

"Challenge accepted."

CHAPTER TWELVE

It doesn't take long before the heavy thumping of the music from the amphitheater reverberates to our boat. It's nice being out here, both seemingly in the middle of nowhere and yet in the middle of all the action. The water taxi stops at a marina behind Budweiser Stage. Axel helps me off the boat and his eyes roam around the dock in search of something. I can almost see the wheels spinning in his head.

"First bus. Then streetcar. Then boat. What's our next mode of transportation?" I ask. Axel nods at my feet before his eyes move up my body.

"Now we go by foot. Just need to make our way through those bushes to get to the fence."

"We're hopping a fence?" I ask, stalling in my spot on the dock. "And I'm sorry, did you say bushes?"

"Would you keep it down?" he says, eyebrows raised. "Don't worry. It's not a tall fence. The bushes, on the other hand..."

"Axel, would you please fill me in on what we're about to do? I have the sinking suspicion it's not legal," I say, crossing my arms.

"Sorry." He stands next to me and shoots out an arm and points. "We walk past the dock, through the bushes, and hop the fence. Then ta-da. We're there."

"This is your well-thought-out plan?"

He raises his shoulders. "Yeah."

"And did you bother to consider that we may come across some security guards?"

"Nah. They're busy guarding the artists and the alcohol, not the bushes."

"You think you're pretty clever, don't you?" I ask, biting back a smile.

"My mom tells me I am." He smirks, clearly proud of himself. "Come on, we're going to miss it." He extends his hand and I not-so-reluctantly place mine in his.

Axel's definition of bushes is more like full-grown trees, stacked closely together. The music grows louder and clearer as we weave our way through the dense forest. Once we make it through, we're faced with a fence, but Axel was right; it's not very high. Can't be sure no electrical currents flow through it though.

"See?" he says. "Not a guard in sight." He hops the fence first, then helps me. "The trick is to look natural. Just blend in with the others."

I nod and follow him toward the spectators who legally purchased their lawn seats. Blue Rodeo is already on stage. Axel and I are easily the youngest people here. So much for blending in. We stand side by side and watch the concert under the cerulean sky, and I can't help but admit, at least to myself, how much fun this entire date has been. Ben's never orchestrated something this elaborate for me. I guess it's why I came up with the bucket list. Part of me wanted to branch out and experience more. Maybe that's why Ben really wanted to work that camp job. We both wanted more, but in different ways.

"So?" he asks over the music. "How does it feel to check another item off your bucket list?"

I turn to him. "*Our* bucket list. And it feels good." *Really good.* I smile, while tucking my hands into my sleeves.

"You cold?" he asks.

"A little, but it's fine."

"Do you mind?" He stands behind me and wraps his arms around my waist, holding me against his chest. His body radiates warmth, and I can't help but sink into his embrace. His lips press lightly against my ear. "Warmer?"

"Yeah. Much." It's funny. I didn't think I could feel safe and comfortable in someone else's arms. I always loved how tall Ben was. It gave him this sense of authority, but it's not as if he did anything to earn it. He was just genetically blessed. Axel oozes confidence and isn't afraid to ask for what he wants. With Ben, I had to be the one to initiate our first kiss. I was the one who asked him to be my boyfriend. I guess Ben's height and brawn were just superficial reasons to like him. I had this idea that he was a puzzle piece I fit perfectly with, but as it turns out, a puzzle piece has more than one side.

Axel sways a bit and I sway with him. We're surrounded by a bunch of loud adults drinking beer, which would normally annoy me, but I'm able to tune them out. When the band announces their next song, "Lost Together," the crowd erupts into cheers before going eerily quiet. It's as if someone put a spell over them.

"Must be one of their bigger bops," I say to Axel as the strum of a guitar fills the air.

He lets out a soft laugh. "It is." Axel releases me and steps in front as the singer begins. "Dance?"

"Here?" I ask, glancing around to find other couples slow dancing. The benefit of lawn seats, I guess.

"No one's looking at you. Well, except maybe me. But I don't count." He smiles and I can't help but return it. Axel places his hands on my waist and I rest mine atop his shoulders. There's a decent amount of space between us, like we're in sixth grade or something. It makes me laugh.

"What?" he asks.

"You could stick a ruler between us," I say.

"Let me fix that." Axel palms my lower back, pressing his fingers into my skin and pulling me in closer. "Better?" He's calm. Still. His eyes are on mine and it's as if there is no one else here in this moment but us.

"Better." My heart starts to beat faster and I swallow, finding the strength to speak. "You're wrong, by the way."

He shakes his head. "What am I wrong about now?"

"When you said before that you don't count. You do."

Axel rubs his nose up against my nose before tipping his forehead to mine. We sway slowly with the music. His chest rises and falls in sync with mine. Our breathing a slow rhythm that sounds like a song written just for the two of us. A drop of rain lands on my cheek. Then another. Before I can say *rain*, it pours down, drenching us within seconds, but we remain, bodies entangled, slow dancing while people run around in search of cover.

"Wimps," I say, with Axel's eyes locked in on mine.

His expression grows serious as the song comes to the bridge. He brings his lips to my ear and begins to sing. The warmth of his breath sends a tingle all the way to my toes. We remain moving in sync among some of the other die-hard fans who sing along with the band, and it's probably the most romantic moment of my life.

If this is supposed to be fake, then why does it feel more real than anything I ever experienced with Ben?

The song ends and the rain continues to come down hard. The band announces they have to pause the concert until it's safe to continue.

"Want to get out of here?" Axel asks, his wet T-shirt clinging to his chest.

I nod and follow him out of the venue and past security guards who are none the wiser. He keeps my hand grasped in his tightly. We miraculously get onto a streetcar without having to wait, our clothes completely soaked. We barely say anything on the ride back. I think we're both tired, or maybe avoiding speaking about that moment. The moment we're still sharing while my head rests on his perfectly broad shoulder.

We transfer onto a bus that takes us back to our neighborhood. I walk to Axel's house with him since my car is parked on his street. The rain has let up but we're still drenched, and if I'm being honest, we both kind of stink.

"That was fun," I say as we make it to the end of his driveway. "Thanks for planning that out. Shoot," I say, scrunching my face. "We forgot to take advantage of the location and film a TikTok or take any pictures."

"It *was* fun, and I wouldn't change a thing about it. Sometimes it's better to let a moment be a moment that can only be remembered in your head. That way it's kind of a secret between the people who experienced it. Makes it more special, I think." Axel swallows, while bouncing on his heels. "Besides, next weekend you get to return the favor in a big way."

"Your cousin's wedding," I say with a nod.

"Yeah. You still in?"

"Of course. It's going to be pretty formal, right?"

Axel laughs. "Very. But just wear whatever makes you comfortable."

"How's this going to work?" I ask. "I mean, you're in the wedding party. So, who will I sit with?"

"My family," he says, as if it's no big deal. "And you've already met them."

"Oh."

"Is that not okay?"

"It's fine, I just... you'll be busy and, I don't know, maybe I'll get in the way by being there." My hands turn into fists again. Breathe.

"I want you there," he says, taking my hands and unspooling my fingers. "Jamie, I know we're supposed to be faking all of this, but the thing is..." He pauses, and then glances over my shoulder. He clears his throat and releases my hands. "Ben."

"The thing is, Ben?" I ask.

"He's here," Axel says, looking past me.

I turn to find Ben walking toward us. "What's up, guys?" His tone is less friendly and more asshole-y. He looks us both up and down. "What happened?"

"We fell in a puddle," I say in a deadpan voice. "What do you want, Ben?"

"Just got home from Olivia's. She told me something interesting."

"Can this wait, man? Jamie and I were in the middle of something," Axel says.

"No. It can't wait... man." Ben walks past me and gets in Axel's face. "Olivia told me what you did."

Axel squints at Ben. "What did I do?"

"You tried to get between me and her. When you're supposed to be with Jamie."

Axel shakes his head. "No, I didn't."

"When you were on the ride, at Wonderland. You stole my seat and flirted with her. She told me all about it."

Axel's eyes meet mine. I swallow, looking away from his gaze.

"He did all that to rile you up and it obviously worked," I say, trying to think fast on my feet. "He's not interested in Olivia."

"Open your eyes, Jamie. The guy's a flirt. Whenever you're not around, he's surrounded by girls."

"So what?" I ask, stepping in front of Axel, toe-to-toe with Ben. "I'm confident enough in my relationship with Axel that I don't freak out anytime he speaks to other girls. *He* can control himself."

"You're blinded by his so-called charm. This guy isn't who he pretends to be. He's just using you."

"Excuse me?" I say, trying to ignore the tension growing not only between Ben and Axel but also in my neck.

"Why don't you just go home?" Axel says to Ben.

"What reason would Axel have to use me?" I say, challenging Ben.

"To be his videographer. To drive him to school. To introduce him to people. It's so obvious."

"Jamie doesn't even know anyone!" Axel says in a weird attempt to defend me.

"Go home, Ben. No one wants you here," I say, my voice rising at his false accusations.

"I'm just trying to look out for you," he says, holding out his hands. "The guy's trouble."

"This guy," I say, now standing side by side with Axel, "has been nothing but supportive and encouraging. He makes me laugh. He listens when I speak. He takes me out on fun dates. And," I say, straightening, "he makes me feel things I've never felt before."

"So he's a good lay?"

"Screw you," I reply before pressing my hands up against Ben's chest and pushing him.

Axel wraps an arm around my waist, holding me back from pushing Ben again. "He's not worth it, Jamie. Ignore him."

"Yeah." Ben chuckles. "Ignore me. You've been doing a real good job at it so far." He stumbles backward, pointing a finger at Axel. "There's something shady about that guy, Jamie."

"You're just angry I'm not holed up in my room crying about you breaking my heart. Get over yourself, Ben. I have."

Ben opens his mouth but nothing comes out. He lifts his shoulders, then turns before making the short trek back to his house. I exhale a tired breath before facing Axel.

"Sorry about that."

"You don't need to apologize for him," Axel says.

"Was Ben telling the truth though?" I ask, sucking in my cheeks. "Did you flirt with Olivia on the ride?"

"I was testing her," Axel responds. "I wanted to see how committed she actually was to Ben. Turns out she's pretty committed."

A quiet laugh escapes me. "I'll say."

"So." The corners of Axel's lips turn up. "I make you feel things you've never felt before?"

"Oh." My cheeks burn as I tuck a wet piece of hair behind my ear. "Ben just knows how to get under my skin, so I had to hit him with something that would make him jealous. Anyway, you were saying something before Ben showed up," I remind him.

He shakes his head ever so slightly, his grin fading. "It can wait. I'm tired and am in desperate need of a shower." A strained smile comes out. "We'll talk tomorrow."

"Okay," I say. A sudden and deep sadness knots my chest and I don't know if it's because of Ben or because of how the light that flickered between Axel and me tonight has now dimmed. He watches as I get into my car. From my rearview mirror, I see Ben on the edge of his driveway, glaring at Axel. I don't want to go but I can't stay here. It feels like I'm running away from something real. Something I'm not sure I'm ready for yet.

I'm stuck between who I used to be and who I'm pretending to be.

One thing I know for sure is, I need to find myself. Whoever she is. And fast.

CHAPTER THIRTEEN

This last week has been spent ignoring daily apology texts from Ben. He apparently feels bad about how he approached the "situation," but still stands by what Olivia said. It's not like I can admit to Ben that the only reason Axel stole his seat on the roller coaster was so Ben would be forced to sit with me. That being said, learning that Axel flirted with Olivia has put me and my stomach in a permanent state of unease.

I know I have unhealed trauma from how my relationship with Ben ended, but I don't love that Axel flirted with Olivia, even if it was just to test her. Technically speaking, he is a free agent, but we agreed that he needed to give off the impression we are exclusive. Whatever. I can't control what he does. Clearly, since HE STILL HASN'T SIGNED THE CONTRACT.

Truthfully, I haven't even tried to get Axel to sign the contract in weeks. The closer we get, the weirder it feels to make him sign his name on the dotted line. There was a moment last weekend (lots of them), but I guess they've all faded into oblivion, because we're back to drives to and from school, lunches together, and public displays of affection limited to when we're in public. It feels like we're business partners, not friends. Definitely not more than friends.

What happened?

I keep replaying that moment outside his house with Ben, trying to figure out what turned the setting of our relationship from warm to ice cold.

"Knock, knock," Mom says, standing in my doorway. Her eyes shift around my room. I sit up in bed and place my phone down.

"I know, I know. It's a mess."

She strolls in and opens my closet door. "So?" she says. "Eli tells me you're going to a wedding tomorrow. Axel's cousin?"

"Yeah. Do you have a problem with that?" I ask, struggling to hide the defensiveness in my tone.

"Not at all. Eli and I will be having Thanksgiving dinner with the Camerons, so it actually works out."

"Oh. Maybe you'll get to meet Olivia," I say as a fake smile stretches over my face.

"Jamie."

"It's fine. I really don't care."

"You know, Arab weddings are pretty fun. Do you have anything to wear?" She focuses her attention back on my closet, sliding my mostly empty hangers across the rod and searching through the small percentage of clothing that is hung up.

"I haven't thought about it much," I say, now doodling in my journal.

"The wedding is tomorrow, Jamie. I have an idea," Mom says, rubbing her hands together. "Let's go shopping. I'll treat you to a new dress."

"You hate the mall," I remind her.

"So do you. We can hate it together. And I'll buy you dinner after."

"Why are you being so nice?" I ask, narrowing my eyes at her.

Mom laughs and sits on my bed. "Maybe I was a bit too quick to judge Axel. Eli keeps telling me what a great kid he is, and he seems to make you happy. Would I prefer you stay single? Sure. But it's your life, not mine."

"Wow," I say, squinting at her. "Did Amo Eli spike your coffee this morning?"

"I don't mean to be terrible, Jamie. I just . . ." She pauses and sighs. "I've been through a lot. I look at you and I'm reminded of myself and how we're all just one decision away from changing the course of our lives. I never wanted to be the kind of mom who tells you what to do. It's how I was raised and I won't do that to you, but I also can't seem to help myself from inserting my opinions. Probably doesn't help that I have so many of them." She laughs. "But I'll try to do better."

"I guess I can also try to listen more. And maybe clean my room once in a while."

She grins. "Let's not get ahead of ourselves."

"Yeah. I threw that last one in to be nice but had no real intention of following through."

She playfully pinches my nose before rising. "So, the mall?"

"Sure," I say. "I just need to send someone a message. Be down in a few."

I open Instagram and pull up Olivia's profile as Mom leaves my room. I click Message and start typing furiously.

FYI your boyfriend keeps texting me. I guess karma is my ex-boyfriend.

I hit Send without giving it a second thought.

Shopping with Mom is pretty painless. Parts of it are even kind of fun. She's a lot more stylish than I am. She helps me pick out a short, black, sequined T-shirt dress, although she couldn't seem to help herself from saying the length might lead to some judgmental stares from the more conservative Arabs. After I reminded Mom about her promise to keep those kinds of thoughts to herself, she held her hands up in defeat before apologizing.

Growth.

When it's time to pick out shoes, we struggle to come up with a solution since Axel and I are already the same height. I don't think he's the kind of guy who'd feel emasculated by a taller (or older) woman, but I also don't mind being on his level. Physically speaking.

After amassing a mountain of shoeboxes, we settle on a pair of lace-up Oxfords, which sounds kind of nerdy but look amazing on.

Over dinner in the food court, I show Mom a few of Axel's TikToks. She nods along and even smiles a couple of times.

"He's good," she says.

"He's more than good," I say, taking back my phone. "He's amazing. You should see how the crowd lights up around him. It's a vibe that can't be portrayed through the screen."

"What's his endgame?" she asks, picking up a fry.

"Like with dancing?"

"Yeah. Is it something he wants to do for a living?"

"I don't know," I say, tearing open a ketchup package. "He's sixteen. Pretty sure he doesn't have his whole life mapped out yet."

"You do," she says, raising a brow. "And I thought it was important to you to be with someone who shared the same values and ideologies."

I dip a fry into the ketchup and pop it into my mouth. "Axel's really smart. He's in advance placement at school. Plays soccer and used to swim competitively. He's good at almost everything he does. I'm not too worried about his future." Or ours. I can't exactly tell my mother this is all fake.

"I ran into Ben the other day," she says, wiping the corner of her mouth with a napkin.

"Oh yeah. What's new with that traitor?"

"Jamie." Mom tilts her head. "He says you've cut him out of your life completely. He was upset about you not tutoring him anymore and ignoring his texts. He seemed really hurt."

"Oh," I reply, leaning back in my seat. I suppose I could have responded at some point to his texts, but I'm still so angry with him. For interrupting a private moment with Axel. For accusing Axel of being a womanizer. For betraying my trust and falling in love with someone else over the summer while I was still madly in love with him.

I do kind of miss him sometimes. He was so easy to shock, and I saw it as a personal challenge to come up with inappropriate jokes at the worst times. And he did really push me, in a healthy way, to set goals and meet them. This whole thing with Axel was supposed to bring me and Ben back together, but instead, all it's done is push us further apart.

"Speak of the devil," Mom says, glancing past my shoulder.

Ben strolls up to our table with a sheepish look on his face.

"Hi, Ben." Mom smiles politely. "Would you like to join us?"

He looks down at me for approval. His long hair has been brushed back and tucked behind his ears. A glimpse of who he used to be shines through. I swallow before nodding.

Ben sits to my left and leans his elbows on the table. He's dressed in a green plaid shirt and jeans and looks like a hot lumberjack. "What're you two doing here?" he asks.

"Checking out the local architecture," I say.

"Jamie." Mom shoots me a cut-it-out look.

"I bought a dress." I gesture to the garment bag draped on the chair next to my mother.

"What for?" he asks.

"I'm going to a wedding with Axel tomorrow."

"Oh," he replies, looking down at the table. "So you're not coming over for Thanksgiving dinner then?" His tone is laced with disappointment.

"Shoot," Mom says, glancing at her phone. "Kourtney Dixon just messaged me. Her six-year-old chopped off her hair with a pair of kitchen scissors and wants to know if I can squeeze her in."

"But it's Saturday night and tomorrow is Thanksgiving," I remind her.

"It's hard to turn down business when you're an entrepreneur. Besides, we're all done here, aren't we?"

I look down at our half-eaten meals. "Sort of."

"You go ahead. I'll drive Jamie home," Ben says.

Mom's eyes meet with mine and I shrug an agreeable shrug.

"You're a lifesaver." Mom rises from the table, grabbing her purse and my things.

"You never drive," I say to Ben as Mom walks away.

"I borrowed my mom's car."

"Why? Is Olivia getting eyelash extensions? Or maybe she's volunteering at the food bank again." *Cool it with the not-so-internalized misogyny, James.*

"You're being really judgmental about a person you don't even know," Ben says, all judgmental like.

"I don't need to know her. She's shown me who she really is. Actions speak louder than curated Instagram photos."

Ben doesn't have a comeback, which is weird, because any time I've spoken poorly of his precious girlfriend, he defends her.

"What? You're not going to tell me again how wrong I am?" I ask.

"We're sort of not talking at the moment," Ben says, pulling my mom's tray toward him.

"Lover's quarrel? Let me guess, first one?"

"Yeah," he says with a half-hearted laugh. Ben studies the leftover fries in front of him, picking up a few, but they don't make it into his mouth. He drops them, then looks at me. "She found out about the tutoring and wasn't impressed that I'd kept it from her. Then I called her after I saw you and Axel and she accused me of trying to find excuses to see you. I told her she was being paranoid and insecure and, well, that's apparently all it takes to piss off Olivia."

"It would piss me off too, to be honest."

We laugh.

"It's just weird," he says, sliding the tray away. He leans an elbow on the table and rests his chin in his palm. He turns to me slightly, bumping his knee against mine. "You and I spent almost every day together for three years and now ... nothing. This will be our first Thanksgiving apart since we met."

"Do I need to remind you whose idea that was?"

"No. I know." He shakes his head and sighs. "I guess I just kind of miss you."

Convenient that he misses me when his girlfriend isn't speaking to him. He keeps doing this. He keeps popping up in my life every time I start to think I don't need him anymore. And it's not because he regrets breaking up with me. He just expects me to forget everything that happened to ease his conscience. Well, I won't do that. It's not fair to me. He can't dump me and then expect me to tutor him in math, give him rides home, and accept his new girlfriend. He also doesn't get to interrupt private moments between me and Axel. A moment I'm still thinking about. "If this is about trying to be friends again, I told you, I can't."

"Why not? I don't get it."

"Because, Ben, it hurts too much. Is that what you want to hear? You broke my heart without any regard for our history or my feelings, and the second I feel like I'm putting the pieces back together, you materialize again, all puppy-eyed, trying to insert yourself back into my life. Well I'm sorry. It doesn't work that way." I push out my chair and stand. "At least not for me."

He remains sitting, a look of defeat on his face. "I'm worried about you, Jamie. I don't trust this Axel guy."

"Why? Because your egotistical girlfriend seems to think Axel is obsessed with her?"

"He's not for you, okay? Do I have to say it?" Ben rises and stands so close, his hot breath trickles down to my face.

"What's that supposed to mean?" I ask, breathing out of my nose like an angry bull.

"Come on, do you really see yourself having a future with this guy? He posts videos of himself dancing online. Cringe. Not to mention all the red flags I pointed out before. Why can't you just admit it to yourself?"

"Admit what?" I ask, my heart thumping against my chest, fingernails digging into my palms, mouth dry.

"The only reason you're with Axel is because you're physically attracted to him, but we both know that's not enough for you. You need substance behind the style. Axel can't give you that."

"So what?" I say, placing my hands on my hips. "So what if I'm attracted to him? What does it matter to you?"

"Because I know you and I know how important your future is to you. I just don't see how Axel fits. All he's doing is distracting you."

"You're telling me you're with Olivia because she mentally stimulates you?"

"This isn't about me and Olivia. Axel doesn't understand where you've come from and how hard you've worked to get to where you are."

"Here's the thing, Ben," I say, squaring my shoulders before swallowing. "When you decided I was no longer worth having in your life, it meant you no longer got a say in what I do or who I choose to spend my time with. You might think Axel is using me or isn't good enough or that I just want to jump his bones, but what you think no longer has any bearing on my life or the decisions I make."

"What happened to you?" Ben asks as I toss all the leftover food onto the top tray. "You used to be so much easier to reason with."

"I found my voice." I pick up the tray and my things before glancing up at Ben one last time. "And I'll find my own way home."

CHAPTER FOURTEEN

I come down the stairs to find Amo Eli waiting. "Wow," he says, fanning himself. "You look stunning! Those legs! Are you sure we share the same gene pool?" he asks, looking down at his own with a frown.

"Would you like me to explain genetics?" I ask, in earnest. It would mean I could kill some time before driving myself to Axel's cousin's wedding. I've been filled with dread all day, mostly regretting my decision to be Axel's date. My fight with Ben hasn't helped put me at ease either.

I spent the hour-long walk home from the mall last night re-examining my goal to win Ben back, and I came to the conclusion that I'm not so sure I want to get back together with him anymore. Why would I want to be with someone who clearly doesn't want to be with me? The majority of our interactions since breaking up have been unpleasant, and that's putting it mildly. Most of all, even if we did get back together, I don't think I'd be able to trust him. Then again, the thought of him being completely out of my life forever makes me sad. I just don't see a clear path for us anymore. So where do I go from here?

"I didn't study biology in high school for a reason," Amo Eli says. "But maybe I should have. The teacher was hot! He looked like a young Tom Selleck."

"Who?" I ask, scrunching up my face.

"He played Monica's boyfriend, Richard, on *Friends*," Mom says as she walks into the foyer carrying a pie to bring to the Camerons. "You look gorgeous. And who did your hair? It's fantastic." She winks and grins, clearly proud of herself.

I check myself out in the hallway mirror. I *do* look hot. "My hairstylist talks a lot but she's pretty talented."

"Watch it," she warns, admiring her handiwork. "This crown braid makes you look ethereal."

"And that hemline makes you look dangerous," Eli says. "Have you practiced sitting in that thing?"

"It's not that short!"

"It's not that short, she says, like I can't see the tiny birthmark on her tushy," he teases.

"Stop," I say, instinctively pulling down the dress. "And I don't have a birthmark on my tushy!"

"Take it from someone who changed hundreds of your diapers. You have a birthmark, right here," he says, gesturing to the side of his own butt.

"Oh my god, I'm leaving."

"When will you be back?" Mom asks while Eli giggles to himself.

"I don't know," I say, nervously fiddling with sleeves. "Midnight?"

"Midnight?" Amo Eli folds his arms over his chest. "You'll miss the seafood buffet."

"What do you know about any seafood buffet?" I ask.

"Um, hello. I work with your lover. He tells me everything! I wish I could be there to see his face when you enter the hall. You are going to give him a heart attack. That boy has it bad, Jam-e."

I let out an exasperated sigh. "He's going to be too busy socializing to notice me. I'll just sit at the table and read on my phone. I don't even know why he wants me there."

"Don't be so obtuse," Eli says, before sizing me up again. "And don't forget your purse."

"Why?" I ask, picking it up from the console table. "You want me to fill it up with shrimp?"

"Maybe."

"Okay." Mom chuckles. "Let Jamie go. Be careful, and call if you need anything."

I nod and turn to open the door. Behind me, Eli shouts, "Don't do anything I wouldn't do. Just kidding, do it all!"

"Bye!" I say in an annoyed yet kind of playful tone before heading out.

On my drive to Fantasy Farm, the venue where the reception is being held, I can't stop myself from going over the complexities of my relationship with Axel. It would be easier if I knew where Axel and I stood, both business-wise and . . . not business-wise.

The lines between fiction and reality are getting blurrier the closer Axel and I become. Even though Ben irritated me at the mall last night, I haven't been able to get his words about Axel out of my head. Is Axel just a distraction, and are these feelings swirling around inside me just based on a (mutual?) attraction?

Perhaps I'm falling victim to what so many other teens before me have. Choosing a partner based on physical attraction. But the thing is, if Axel had been in a lineup with eight other guys, I don't think I would have gone for him. His looks didn't jump out at me at first—at least in a good way. The attraction grew over time and continues the more we get to know one another. And is he really a big distraction? Since being with Axel I've checked two big items off my bucket list: Wonderland and a concert at

Budweiser Stage. And both those nights have been the most fun I've ever had.

Fun.

That's what Axel is.

It's also what Ben isn't.

And something I didn't think I was.

I don't understand why things are so confusing. The plan I concocted seemed simple, but nothing is working out the way I expected it to.

When I arrive at the reception hall, I park my car and check my reflection in the rearview mirror. Am I sending mixed signals to Axel by coming here? By wearing this dress? By continuing to play the role of adoring half-Arab girlfriend? Not half Arab. Just half girlfriend.

I step out of my car and take in the sights before me. This place is giving magical, fairy garden vibes. It's the kind of wedding venue where the girliest of girls get married so they can live out their dream of playing princess for a day. But there is something romantic about it. It's like being in the middle of a forest. Tall trees line the path, covered in the bright reds and oranges of autumn leaves. You'd never know this wedding hall was nestled in the city, right off one of the busiest highways.

I walk up some steps and follow the signs leading me to the Dahini wedding. Axel's last name. A pang shoots through me at the thought of Axel marrying another girl one day. I wonder if he's ever dated an Arab girl before. But like, for-real dated. I bet he has and I bet she was a lot more beautiful than I am and probably fit in really well with his family.

He probably only dates girls who love to dance as much as he does. Girls who don't give him mixed messages. Girls who march right up to him and let their intentions be known. Axel already has his choice of almost any girl, but whenever we're together, his attention is always one hundred percent on me. We're not always together, though. And I've seen what can happen when people spend time apart.

I walk into the hall and, to my surprise, it's mostly empty. This is not the loud, Arab reception I was expecting.

Elaborate floral centerpieces in red, orange, and yellow adorn every table, bringing the atmospheric fall-foliage vibes inside. The rust-colored tablecloths match the seat covers. The head table is flanked by gigantic floral displays and large candelabras, set against floor-to-ceiling windows. I stand in the doorway, unsure of what to do or where to go. I'm one of the first to arrive. It's just the DJ playing around in his booth and waitstaff placing bottles of water and wine on the tables. But the invite Axel gave me said to be here for five thirty, and it's quarter to six.

"James," Axel calls from behind me. "You're here."

I turn to find Axel in a three-piece suit and black tie. It's the most clothes I've ever seen him wear. His hair is gelled, which seems to be taming his curls. He looks good. He looks great. But he doesn't look like Axel.

"Hey. Am I early?" I ask, glancing around the mostly empty hall.

"No. Arabs run on different time. Come on, let me show you around. We just got back from taking pictures."

He takes my hand and guides me around the venue.

"Where's the bride?" I ask.

"Fighting with the groom. They're holed up in the bridal suite."

I laugh. "Well that's a promising start."

"It's more like their foreplay. My cousin drank too much in the limo on the way here and couldn't make a straight face for any of the photos." He loosens his tie as we arrive at a large window, overlooking the grounds. "I can't wait to rip this suit off. I've been walking around like a penguin all day."

"You actually look really nice," I say. "Like an Arab Ken doll or something."

"I'm a fool." He steps back to take in the full sight of me. Then takes my hand again and makes me spin for him. "Jamie T-F. You are a fox."

A blush rises through me but I try to find the simmer button. "It's just a basic black dress," I say.

"Maybe on anyone else, but on you, it's fire."

"Thanks, I guess." I look away from Axel, twisting my heel into the shiny tile.

"You're not so good at accepting compliments, are you?"

"I just prefer the ones that have to do with my brain." I smile.

"Okay." He clears his throat. "Your legs look very intelligent in that dress."

We both laugh and it's nice. It's like no one else matters. Just us. I wish it could stay that way. "So, what should I expect tonight?"

"A loud, elaborate entrance by the bride and groom, followed by twenty minutes of nonstop dancing to Arabic music. A lot of the guests join in for that. Then food. Speeches from the wedding party, but most of the Arabs won't pay attention and will likely talk over them. And then entertainment followed by more dancing."

"What kind of entertainment?"

Axel shakes his hips. "A belly dancer."

"Oh. Isn't that kind of old-fashioned?"

"It's pretty typical at Arab weddings. It's not sexist, despite what some people say. Belly dancing is an art. And it's empowering."

"I guess I never saw it that way. Probably just some leftover antiquated rhetoric from my mother. She has me believing every aspect of the Arab culture is embedded in misogyny."

"Well, she's wrong." He takes a step closer as more guests arrive and whispers in my ear, "Will you dance with me tonight or is that too antiquated?"

I swallow, his lips inches away from mine. "I did agree to play the role of adoring girlfriend."

"Or . . ." He pauses. "You could dance with me because you want to." His eyes sear into mine and I get lost in their light-brown hue. The little swoop of curls resting on his forehead. Those very pillowy lips. *Snap out of it, Jamie.*

"Maybe if you sneak some alcohol into my cup," I joke.

"You don't need alcohol. You've got me."

You've got me.

But do I? I want to ask.

"Axel," a groomsman calls from behind.

"I've got to go. I'll come find you once my duties are over." He starts to leave, then comes back and places a kiss on my cheek. "You really do look incredible."

The warmth of his words spreads through me and I can't fight the smile that wants to come out. A moment later, my phone buzzes in my hand. I open it to see a notification from Instagram. Axel tagged me in a photo. Dread fills me as I open it. He snuck a picture when I wasn't looking and captioned it, "My  date."

I wonder if Ben will see this. Just to be sure, I share the photo to my Stories.

Axel wasn't lying when he said the reception would be elaborate. His mother dragged me from my spot at the table to join everyone else on the dance floor to cheer on the bridal party after their introductions. Once I got over the fear that everyone was watching me (they weren't), I clapped along and cheered with his family. About ten minutes into dancing, Axel removed his suit jacket, vest, and tie and rolled the sleeves of his white dress shirt. He kept stealing glances at me, smiling each time. There was a small part of me that wanted him to pull me into the dancing circle to join him (must have been the adrenaline), but I understand he has his own role to play tonight.

Over dinner, Axel and I text back and forth, me at the table with his family and him at the head table with the bridal party. At one point his mother walked right up to him and made him put his tie back on. I took a picture of the interaction and sent it to him. In return, he sent another candid photo of me, this time chatting with his sisters.

The food is never-ending, and I get up halfway through the (second?) main course to use the restroom. Axel's in the foyer with his cousin and his new wife, their heads close together. The bride looks upset. When I come out of the restroom, I find Axel in the foyer alone.

"What's going on?" I ask.

He runs a hand through his now loosened curls.

"The entertainment canceled and the bride is freaking out."

"What? You can't just cancel last minute, especially at a wedding. Your cousin should sue!"

"The belly dancer went into labor." Axel holds back a laugh.

"They hired a pregnant belly dancer?" I ask, feeling my eyes grow.

"Well, they obviously didn't know. Belly dancers are supposed to carry around extra weight in their mid-section. Just not typically an entire human being."

"Okay. Fine. No entertainment. Is it a big deal?" I shrug. "They can just move right to the dancing portion."

"The belly dancer kicks off the party. Engages the guests. It's supposed to be this whole big thing, and Arabs talk. They'll complain my cousin had a boring wedding if there's no performance. Half of them are probably already talking about the fact that my cousin hired a DJ and not an Arab band."

"This has not been a boring wedding," I say. Axel sighs while pacing back and forth. "Why are you letting this bother you so much? It's not *your* wedding."

"They want me to do something," he says, stalling in front of me. "They want me to put together some sort of performance."

"That's great," I say, nodding enthusiastically. "I can film it. We can add it to your account."

"No, Jamie." His eyebrows furrow. "I've never danced in front of my parents before. Much less in front of three hundred Arabs."

"You danced in front of everyone at Wonderland. You have TikToks with over a million views!" I remind him. "What's the difference?"

"The difference is Arabs. And my father. Aren't you listening? What if I embarrass him?"

"The guests will love it. And so will your father."

Axel's arms are crossed over his chest. I place my hands on them and loosen his arms, holding his hands in mine. "Come on. I can help you figure something out. It'll be a bop."

He laughs. "You're such a dork."

I boop his nose with my finger. "Yeah, but you love it."

Axel and I retreat to a quiet corner in the foyer and go over potential ideas and numbers. We debate a long time over the right song and, shock of all shockers, he agrees to go with my choice. I find myself having to play the role of reassurer, reminding him he's got this and will blow everyone away. It's an odd shift in our dynamic. It's always felt like I've needed him more than he needed me, and, in a strange twist of events, I kind of like having him depend on me.

After he does a quick run-through in front of me while I play the song on my phone, Axel's confidence grows. He smiles wider. His shoulders stop slumping. His cocky demeanor has returned.

"Thanks, Jamie," he says, while removing his tie again and rolling up his sleeves.

"No need to thank me, yet, anyway." I grin while helping him unbutton a few snaps of his dress shirt. I run a finger from his neck to the start of his chest. "Give the ladies, and some of the gents, what they want. You ready?"

"Yeah, I'm ready," he says, looking down at my lingering finger. I remove it from his chest, sucking in my lips.

We walk back into the hall together. I speak to the DJ and tell him what song to play once Axel begins. Axel wanted to go with an Arabic song at first, but I thought it would be more surprising to go a different way.

I stand at the end of the dance floor with my phone, ready to film. Axel picks up the mic and takes a deep breath. "Ahlan, everyone." He waits a few minutes for the guests to stop talking. He whistles with his fingers into the mic when that doesn't work. "Thank you all for attending Samir and Reema's wedding. For those who don't know me, I'm Alexander Dahini, the groom's favorite cousin. Unfortunately, I come bearing bad news," he says, nervously raking his fingers through his hair. "The belly dancer they hired can't attend tonight because, well, she's currently giving birth to a little belly dancer."

Silence envelopes the room before a sea of laughter erupts. Axel shoots me a tentative glance, but I know he's going to nail this.

"So instead, you get me," he continues. "Some of you may know dancing is a passion of mine, and I'm not afraid to admit that." His shaky laugh following that statement tells another story. "I hope you're able to enjoy this performance and embrace that people of all genders and ages can and should dance. Regardless of ability." He winks at me, his confidence clearly having returned, before taking a deep breath.

The lights dim and colorful spotlights shine on the parquet dance floor. Axel places the mic on the head table and returns to the center of the room. He runs his hands through his hair again and down his body. A few murmurs and some throat clearing echoes throughout the hall before "Adventure of a Lifetime," by Coldplay begins.

Immediately, Axel moves with the upbeat strings of the intro. His feet pound the dance floor before he bounces on his tiptoes, twisting and sliding all around. His hips move in sync with his feet and it is obvious to everyone that Axel is one hundred percent in his element. People rise from their seats, clapping along and cheering him on, standing in front of me and blocking my view. I give up filming and put my phone down on the table.

Axel's father is the only person still seated. I walk over to him and extend my hand. He starts to shake his head. "It would be rude to say no to your son's girlfriend."

Mr. Dahini sighs before rising, albeit grudgingly. I lead him to the dance floor where Axel is still wowing the crowd. We stand with Axel's mother and sisters, who all have proud smiles plastered on their faces.

"He's good, right?" I say to his father.

He doesn't respond at first, only observes Axel dancing and how much joy it seems to be bringing the whole wedding. The bride and groom are clapping enthusiastically from their perch at the head table.

"He *is* good," his father finally acknowledges. "Hey," he calls out to the man in front of him. "That's my son."

The man gives him a thumbs-up. His father picks up his phone and snaps a bunch of photos, transforming before my eyes into a stage dad. Another drama averted.

Axel approaches us and, for a second, I think he's going to pull one of his family members onto the dance floor, but instead he reaches his arm out to me. Surprising myself, I place my hand in his without hesitation.

He whispers. "You and me are going to start a dabke line. Ever been in one?"

"Um, no," I say.

"Then I'll go easy on you. Just follow the best you can. I've been doing it since I was five. I led a dabke for the first time when I was seven."

"Seven?" I squeeze Axel's hand tight. "We're not all naturals. I don't know how to dance," I remind him.

"Everyone messes up. That's how you learn. Just try to sync the beat of the music in your head and go with that."

A part of me debates ripping my hand away from Axel's, but all eyes are on us. He adjusts his grip, holding my hand, and says, "Always start with the left foot. Watch me: left, left, back, forward."

I study his feet and follow, trying to ignore that the song is now on its second run and that there are hundreds of people observing this very public dance lesson.

"Okay, once you've got that down, pause, and move to the next level of dabke: forward, back, forward, back, tap, tap."

"Wait, why am I pausing?"

"So the rest of the central train can catch on. Think of all of us as one big train. If one cart goes too fast, we crash."

"Who's all of us?" I watch as others begin walking toward Axel and me. An older man holds my right hand, and then Axel's sisters join the line, along with their husbands and the bridal party. The train is literally going off the track and I'm second-in-command.

"Follow me," he says, stroking my hand with his thumb before planting a kiss on my cheek.

I swallow and nod. *Everyone makes mistakes.* I guess I didn't realize up until now that mistakes aren't the end of the world. I tend to hold back on new experiences, afraid I'll crash and burn, so what's the point? But all that leads to is me missing out on fun things. Exciting things. Embarrassing things. Maybe there's beauty in the process, in the mess.

The dabke line grows longer, and it starts off simple enough: left, left, back, forward. We do that for a while, until an older gentleman challenges Axel to do more complicated moves as the leader and passes him a napkin to twirl around. "Don't let go," he says to me as he starts to stomp and kick with more velocity than he had before, waving the napkin in the air with his free hand. Now he's on the ground, one leg out, bouncing on the other, and everyone watches in awe. He rises, facing me now, and grins so wide, it melts me.

Axel passes the napkin, like a torch, to the man next to me and pulls me into the circle. "What do we do now?" I ask, almost breathless.

"Dance like no one's watching."

I nod and just let my body do whatever it wants. Axel laughs and mimics my moves. Soon we're woo-hoo-ing along with the lyrics, moving closer and closer until we're nose to nose, hand in hand. I could kiss him. Right here. I want to kiss him. He wants to kiss me too. I can see it in his eyes. Feel it in how he touches me.

The song comes to an end and we remain standing in the middle of the dance floor, still. The DJ plays an Arabic song that must be popular because everyone cheers. The dabke line continues to grow and encircle us.

"Want to get out of here?" he asks.

"Can you?"

"My job here is done. The dancing will go all night and I'd rather hang with you."

"Really? Don't you want to continue to be the star of the show?" I tease.

"I've made my point. They all know I'm amazing." He smirks like it's a joke, but it's not. He *is* amazing.

"Grab your things, I'll grab mine and meet you in the foyer," he says.

Thankfully, when I return to my table all of Axel's family members are nowhere to be found. Probably lost in the horde of other dancers enjoying the party. I collect my belongings and race to meet Axel. I'm still on a high from that moment, dancing with him, in front of everyone, his family included. Lit from within, I decide that tonight there will be no more rules. No more thoughts of Ben Cameron. *Whatever happens, happens.* At least for one night.

Axel comes out of the hall. He cocks his head to the main door. We head toward it together.

"You drove, right?" he asks.

"Yeah. Wait, are we sneaking out?"

He raises a shoulder innocently. "Kind of. Where's your car?"

"Follow me," I say, heading down the front steps. It's pitch-black out but there are a few light posts dotting the path, circles of light shimmering on the ground. We reach the parking lot and I unlock my car. Axel tosses his suit jacket, vest, and tie into the backseat before taking his seat up front.

"When are you going to get your license?" I ask as I take my spot in the driver's seat.

"I don't need it. I prefer riding my bike."

"And apparently being my passenger prince."

"Yeah, that too." He grins.

I turn the engine, pulling my dress down a bit.

Axel reaches into the backseat and grabs his suit jacket, draping it over my thighs.

I smile. "Thank you." I start to drive, not sure where we're going. "Any place you want to go in particular?"

"Yes." He opens his map app and types in an address but won't let me see. "Just follow Siri's instructions. We're about ten minutes away."

"No problem," I say, following the first directions and turning left out of the venue.

"No problem?" he asks. "No offense, but are you okay?"

"No offense taken. I've decided for tonight, one night only, whatever happens, happens."

And may the consequences of those actions not send me into a spiral I can't get myself out of.

"I like it. Sounds like my daily mantra."

"Perhaps I'm learning something from you after all," I say as I take another left turn.

We drive north on the highway for just over ten minutes before Siri tells me to take the exit at Lawrence Avenue East. After a couple more right turns, Axel tells me to park. He hops out of the car first and comes around to open my door. He helps me out and places his jacket on me before taking my hand.

We walk on a trail for a few minutes and I'm still unsure of where he's taking me. While I hear cars, I don't see them. I know I said whatever happens, happens, but taking a stroll in the middle of nowhere at night wasn't exactly what I had in mind.

Soon we're walking through a tunnel with painted murals. Once we come out the other side, Axel tells me to turn around. Despite the darkness of the night, an arc of colors appears. He brought me to the Rainbow Tunnel.

"I believe this was another item on our bucket list."

My stomach sinks. It *is* on the bucket list, but it was supposed to be "kiss Ben under the Rainbow Tunnel." What could . . . wait. Is this . . . ? Does Axel want to . . . ? *Breathe, Jamie.*

He holds my hand and tucks a piece of hair behind my ear. "I know the name next to this goal wasn't Axel." He bites on his lower lip, then pauses. "I don't want to make you uncomfortable or suggest you do something you don't want to, so if this is a green apple moment, just say so. But I really like you. And I've been fighting the urge to kiss you for a long time now."

I swallow and nod, taking in his words. "I . . . I won't be needing to use the green apple at this time."

He looks down and smiles. "I think there's something special between us," he goes on. "Sure, we came together in an unorthodox way. I mean, who knew I'd fall for the girl who destroyed Betty White."

"You've fallen for me?" I ask, my heart racing a million miles a minute.

"You know what I like most about you?" he asks as his eyes sparkle. "How adorably clueless you can be despite being the smartest person I know." He takes a step closer and stares so deeply into my eyes it's like he's seeing into my soul. "Yes, Jamie. I have fallen for you. Hard. I think about you all the time. I can't wait to go on new adventures together. The reason I've refused to sign the contract is because I don't want to admit to myself or you that any of this is fake. Because it's not. To me."

"It's not to me either. Anymore."

He leans in, then pulls back ever so slightly.

"What's wrong?" I ask.

"If we do this, if we kiss, that means the contract is null. It means Ben is null. And it means . . ." He exhales and runs a hand through his hair. "If you're not ready, I'll wait." He steps up to me so his eyes are level with mine. "I don't want to start something we can't finish, because the truth is"—he looks down for a moment before his eyes meet mine again—"I don't know if I could handle losing you."

My body feels as if it's been hit with an electrical charge so strong I could probably power an entire city. "Hey, Axel," I say, deadpan. "Will you help me check another item off the bucket list, and kiss me under the Rainbow Tunnel?"

The corners of his mouth curl, but they stop before forming a full-blown smile. "What about the original plan?"

I lift my shoulders slightly, cheeks burning. "Plans change."

He releases my hand and snakes his arm around my waist, pulling me closer to him. Our foreheads bump and we laugh. Our eyes meet again and we stare at one another, long past what is comfortable for most people, but with him, it's my safe space. Axel is nothing like I expected. He's brilliant. Funny. Sweet. Confident. And he likes me. The real me.

Our lips inch closer and, just like that, we're kissing. It starts off slow, like we're feeling each other out, which, to be honest, I am. I've never kissed anyone besides Ben, and this kiss is different from all my kisses with Ben. For one, my entire body feels it. I want to kiss him harder, faster. I basically want to absorb him within me. My hands move around his back, bringing him closer. He smells so good. His lips are so soft. This is complete sensory overload, in the best way possible. Under the moonlight with a cool autumn breeze. His warm body against mine. I never want this feeling to end. This is greater than the adrenaline of the roller coaster. More intense than dancing in the rain at the Blue Rodeo concert. More liberating than doing the dabke together at his cousin's wedding. This isn't for show. This is for us.

Axel pulls away slightly, and there's a twinkle in his eye.

"Hey, Jamie?" he asks.

"Yeah?" I answer, studying his lips, wanting to kiss them again.

"I think we should burn that contract."

"I think we should go back to my car and kiss some more," I say.

"That too." He leads me through the path back to my car, where we kiss in the backseat for a really long time.

And there's nothing fake about the way Axel makes me feel.

CHAPTER FIFTEEN

I'm over Ben Cameron.

I really think I am.

I mean, how else would I have been able to make out with Axel in the back of my car for forty-three minutes? And then another thirteen by his front door when we were saying goodbye (over and over). How would I be able to fully let myself get absorbed in Axel's presence if I were still in love with Ben?

Other signs I'm over Ben:

I haven't scrolled through his socials in over a week. Or Olivia's. I continue to ignore him in the halls and barely ever think about him anymore. Except to tell myself I'm over him. Because I am.

And it's all because of Axel.

Axel, who I can't stop thinking about.

Axel, whose mere touch sends pulses of electricity to all my lady parts.

Axel, who makes me laugh and smile and spreads happiness and calm through me.

Axel, whose six(plus)-pack looks even more incredible up close. And feels even better pressed up against my not-quite-one-pack.

It's been one week since the wedding and Axel has taken over my thoughts and my life. When we're not together, we text nonstop. Or FaceTime. There is nothing sweeter than watching his smile grow at something dorky I said through my phone screen, while trying not to get distracted by the small chain around his neck that only serves to accentuate his broad, often bare shoulders. We also seem to have entered the can't-keep-our-hands-off-each-other stage of our relationship.

And it's so much fun.

My phone buzzes on my nightstand. I reach for it from bed and flip it over to see a text from Axel.

> Axel: Ready for tonight?
>
> Me: NO! I have no idea where you're taking me. What am I supposed to wear?
>
> Axel: Something comfortable.
>
> Me: You'll have to feed me first. I'm hungry.
>
> Axel: Are you trying to figure out if there will be food?
>
> Me: You know how I get when I'm unfed.
>
> Axel: There will be food. And music. But no dancing. That's all you're getting. Unless you're feeling super anxious and then I can tell you a tiny bit more but that's a green apple situation!
>
> Me: Fine. I won't be using my green apple card at this time. So, as per usual, I will come and pick you up and you'll tell me where to go?
>
> Axel: It's worked well so far for us. ☺
>
> Me: It has. ☺
>
> Axel: I've got to get back to work! See you at 7.

Axel and I have been dancing around the terms and conditions of our union since our first kiss. I've stopped myself, countless times since the wedding, from bringing it up. The truth is, every time I've attempted to, I either get distracted by his lips on mine or I'm too afraid it will jinx things. Because maybe we don't need a label.

Maybe we could just transition from fake-dating to real-dating without having a whole conversation about it. Everyone else in our lives already believes we've been dating since the end of August. There's really no point in making a big deal out of it.

Who am I kidding?

We definitely need to talk about it.

My gut tells me the reason behind this whole surprise date Axel has planned is so he can officially ask me to be his girlfriend. So, I'll stand by, (im)patiently. Waiting for that moment.

. . .

He has until midnight.

Then I take matters into my own hands.

I sit up and eye the corner of my bedroom, which is piled with Ben's belongings. If Axel and I are going to make things official tonight, then I want to start with a clean palette. That means getting rid of everything that reminds me of Ben. Starting with our message thread. I swipe across his name and, without hesitation, hit Delete. And there goes years' worth of pictures, sweet words, not-so-sweet words, and every conversation we've ever had online. Just like that. Gone with one swipe.

I make my way into Mom's salon feeling ten pounds lighter already. She has Phil Collins blasting and a customer sitting in her chair with layers of foils folded in.

"Jamie!" Mom calls in surprise.

"Do you have a box?" I ask.

"Try the storage room. I should have a couple in there," she says while checking her client's progress.

After riffling through Mom's storage closet, I come out with a decent-sized box marked BioSilk. I stall when I see Olivia standing by Mom's client. She opens her mouth to say something, but before she can, I ask, "What're you doing here?"

She crosses her arms, cocking her head to the woman covered in foils. "This is my mom."

"Ah," I say, nodding between them. "Well, okay, nice seeing you." I turn to make my way back up the stairs and Olivia follows me. She closes the door to Mom's salon so it's just the two of us in the narrow stairwell with echoes of Uncle Phil playing in the background.

"Can I help you?" I ask, stalled halfway up the stairs, still holding the empty box I plan to fill with her boyfriend's crap.

"When are you going to stop inserting yourself into my relationship with Ben?"

"Ben asked me to tutor him. It wasn't my idea."

"That's not what I'm talking about. Ben and I have moved past that."

"Then what are you talking about?" I ask, fingers digging into the cardboard box.

"The DM you sent me about Ben texting you. It worked just like you intended. I confronted him and it started a big fight between us."

"Do you need receipts?" I ask, bluffing, knowing any real proof I have has recently been deleted.

"He showed me the texts, Jamie. He was apologizing to you. Ben has a conscience and can admit when he's wrong."

A huff of air escapes me. "Can he?"

"And I have my own proof," she says, her hands now resting on her hips. "About Axel."

My jaw clenches. I put down the box and meet Olivia at the bottom of the stairs. "You have nothing. The only reason Axel sat next to you on the roller coaster was to get a rise out of Ben. Clearly it worked, since the two of you are still talking about it."

"This isn't about the roller coaster." She pulls her phone out of her back pocket and types furiously before holding it up to my face. There on the screen is a message from Axel, dated a week after Wonderland. The message from him reads: Do you want to grab a coffee sometime?

Before I can read her responses to him, she pulls back her phone.

"Looks like you had a few things to say besides no." I swallow, trying to steady my pulse and not show my hand.

"Yeah. I told him to leave me alone because I have a boyfriend. I thought you should see for yourself what Axel has been up to."

My throat constricts. I can't let Olivia best me, but I don't have any smart retorts. Seeing Axel slide into Olivia's DMs has completely thrown me. Sure, Axel texted Olivia before anything real was happening between us. In Axel's mind, I had my heart set on getting back together with Ben. And I can't exactly tell Olivia that. But also . . . why did he ask out Olivia? And flirt with her. What's his endgame here? Am I just a consolation prize?

"Why don't you focus on your relationship and I'll focus on mine?" I finally say.

"Ben and I are just fine, thank you very much. This is me asking you, girl to girl, to stop with the fake drama and to leave us alone."

I shake my head and begin walking up the stairs. "Actually," I say, pausing and turning to face Olivia. I breathe in and out to slow my heart rate and turn the volume down on my emotions. *Steady. Calm. Breathe.* "Since you're here, I'd love to hear your side of things. For the sake of closure." I sit on a step and exhale again. "What happened with you and Ben this summer?"

Olivia sighs. "Oh my god, Jamie. Let it go."

"Can't you see it from my point of view? Ben tells me he wasn't unfaithful. That things with you didn't happen until after he broke up with me. But I don't believe him. And maybe if you can validate his story, then I can let go of these angry feelings I've been carrying around." I didn't mean to lay my cards on the line. To basically strip naked in front of the girl Ben left me for, but I'm getting tired of being lied to. And I just want to know the truth.

Her eyes dart to the doorway, like she wants to be anywhere in the world but here. "We started off as co-workers who became friends who became soulmates." She takes a hesitant step closer, as my heart hammers in my throat. "I didn't have an elaborate plan to 'steal Ben.' And that's why I wanted to be honest with you about Axel. He's sketch, Jamie. Watch yourself."

I rise and dust off the back of my pants. "Ben isn't perfect either, Olivia. Aren't you upset that he hid the fact that I was tutoring him? And if he was so over things between us, then why did he feel it necessary to obnoxiously interrupt Axel and me when we were saying goodnight to one another? So, yeah, I think it's safe to say as women we both need to watch ourselves."

Olivia's eyes meet with mine as a forced smile stretches tightly over her face. "I've got to go."

I nod and watch her walk back into the salon, a burst of music entering the stairwell as she opens the door and fading quickly behind her once it closes.

I make the familiar trek up Ben's driveway with a half-filled cardboard box in my arms. Luckily, Olivia's baby-blue BMW is nowhere in sight. I can't handle a face-to-face interaction with her twice in one day. Twice in a lifetime is more than enough.

This feels like a monumental step for me. Ending the Ben chapter so that I can move forward with Axel, officially. But standing here in front of his door—the door I used to open without knocking, the door I walked through many times before with Ben, the door where we had our first kiss—I second-guess this grown-up move and decide to just leave the box on his porch and run away, like the seventeen-year-old child I am.

I lower the box to the autumn-themed welcome mat and turn to leave after ringing the doorbell once. The windchime on his porch sounds and I stop to observe it. My mom and I bought it as a gift for the Camerons the first Christmas we spent together. Our first Christmas without Dad. Every time I hear the chimes ring, it takes me back to that Christmas Eve night when I stood out here with Ben, helping him hang it.

It had snowed that afternoon, leaving a fresh layer of powder over everything, creating the perfect setting for a homey Christmas celebration. Ben asked me to come out and help him find a spot for the windchime, but I knew it was just a ruse to get me alone. We'd been inseparable since we'd met in July of that year and had made things official at the winter formal the week before, but hadn't yet sealed it with a kiss.

He was so shy back then. He hadn't come into his own (still hasn't, if you ask me). In a way, I liked it because he seemed to follow my lead. Amo Eli joked about how I had Ben wrapped around my finger, and he didn't know where Ben's personality ended and mine began. Maybe that was true in the early days, but things shifted the longer we were together.

And I guess it ended when he met Olivia and decided to blend with her personality instead of mine.

"Jamie?"

I freeze, clenching my jaw and taking in a deep breath before turning around. "Hi."

"What're you doing here?"

I nod to the box by Ben's feet. "I dropped off a few of your things."

His eyes travel down, and when he looks back up at me, a cloud of sadness surrounds him. The sad cloud is contagious and sends a pang of nostalgia through me.

"Thanks. How was the wedding?" he asks.

"It was great."

A sharp gust of late October wind blows through and the windchime crashes to the ground. We both go to it immediately, crouching down at the same time and bumping our heads.

"Sorry," we say simultaneously, before smiling.

Ben picks up the windchime; the bottoms are all tangled.

"Good luck unraveling that," I say as we stand.

"Twisted wires are better than broken pieces. Easier to fix."

"Sounds like a metaphor or something," I say, tucking my hands into my sleeves as an awkward puff of laughter escapes. "I'm not so good with those."

"You are the Homographs Queen. It's one of the only things you except compliments on."

"Accept," I correct him automatically.

"I know, Jamie. I was just goofing around. We can still do that, can't we?"

I walk to the edge of the porch and grip the railing, looking across the street to Axel's home. It's like I'm stuck in some time loop I can't quite get out of. "I told you. I can't be your friend. Especially when you keep spreading lies about Axel."

"I'm not spreading lies." Ben places the windchime down on the small table perched between two red Adirondack chairs before standing next to me. "Olivia told me about the DM."

I turn to face him. "Did she show it to you?"

"What do you mean?"

"Did she show you a screengrab? Or hold her phone up to show you his message? Or did she just tell you about it?"

Ben's face goes blank as he seems to think over my question. "She just told me about it."

"Interesting," I respond.

"What's interesting?" Ben places his hand on my arm. I look up to find his hazel eyes on mine and I'm transported back to that Christmas Eve night again, standing in the same place, hanging the windchime. Ben grabbed my arm as I was about to go inside. When I turned back to look at him, he froze. It was like he couldn't get the words out. He couldn't be the one to make the first move, so I did. I pressed my lips up against his, making it official. Now here we are, almost three years later, in the same place but further apart than we've ever been. "What's interesting, Jamie?"

"Olivia was at my mom's salon today and showed me the DM. Axel *did* ask her to go for coffee and there were a string of responses from Olivia. Just as I was starting to read them, she pulled her phone away. So if you ask me, that's just as sus. Or wait, what's your favorite word? Shady."

"Why are you with this guy, Jamie?"

"I guess I'm used to being around shady guys," I reply, since I can't admit that technically Axel didn't do anything wrong by messaging Olivia, although I'm not thrilled that he did. I wrap my arms around myself as some sort of shield. I want to leave. I want to storm away dramatically, but my feet betray me, as if the ground is covered in thick glue. "It's so 'funny' how you ran to Olivia the second we were over. Like it was this big, orchestrated plan the two of you devised. You didn't even feel sorry or regretful. There was no grieving period."

"It wasn't like that, Jamie."

"Maybe not. But you still betrayed me and what we had by opening your heart to someone else when your heart was supposed to belong to me."

Ben rakes his fingers through his hair. "You wasted no time moving on with Axel."

"I had to. You dumped me and the next day, she was already at your house, like this new trophy you were showing off to your family. Did they even ask about me? Ask what happened? What did you tell them?"

"I don't understand why you insist on rehashing this over and over," he says, shaking his head and walking away from me.

I follow and step up to him, pointing my finger to his face. "You're a traitor. You sold me lies. Got me to believe you. Love you. Then you left. Just like my father did."

"Why are you bringing your father into this? I'm nothing like him."

"And how would you know?" I say, heat coming off my skin and forming sweat beads along my neck and chest. "You've never met him. Is that why you left me for Olivia?"

"Is what why?" he asks, his eyebrows drawn together.

"She's got the mom and the dad. Going off her car, she lives in a nice house. Her family probably eats dinner together every night. I bet they love you. Tall, handsome, smart. A big protector for their tiny, precious daughter."

"Jamie, are you alright?" Ben asks, lowering his head to mine.

"I have to go," I say, taking clumsy steps back from Ben as I try to ignore the burning in my throat. "You may as well throw out everything in that box. It obviously meant nothing to you." I race down the steps before he has a chance to say anything else and run all the way home without stopping.

If I'm so over Ben, then why did speaking to him just now hurt so much?

CHAPTER SIXTEEN

Once home, I climb up the steps to my bedroom and slam the door shut. Picking up my notebook, I plop down in bed and write Ben and Olivia's names in red marker. Then I create a list of all the reasons why they suck! *Stupid haircut (Ben). Annoying Instagram stories (Olivia). Liar (Ben). Selfish (Olivia). Sucks at calculus (Ben). Doesn't know that there's a helium shortage (Olivia). Barely ever drives (Ben). Ridiculous car (Olivia). TRAITOR (Ben). Boyfriend thief (Olivia).*

Just as I'm about to begin the next, most satisfying step (crossing their names off with a giant X), there's a knock at my door.

"What?" I shout.

The door opens slowly and Amo Eli stands in the frame, pretending to act offended. "Rude!"

"Sorry, I'm just..."

"In a bad mood again?" he asks. "What is it now?" He strolls in, unable to hide his disdain for the mess and clutter. He shoves a couple items off the foot of my bed to make room for himself to sit.

"You ever feel like the world's against you? Or that, like, everyone is in on this big secret, and the secret is about you, but you don't know what it is because no one has the guts to tell you?"

Eli's eyebrows raise, his mouth shaped in an O. "Uh, yeah? I mean, feeling like the world is against you is part of being a young adult. The other thing, you may need to expand on."

I put down my notebook and cross my legs. "It just feels like everyone has their own agenda and they're out to get me."

"Even me?" Eli asks, pressing his hand to his chest.

"You may be the lone outlier."

"What about Axel? He's a fluffy little marshmallow. I don't think there's one evil thought underneath those beautiful curls. He even insisted I go home early and said he'd work until Peter shows up for his shift."

I swallow and release a long breath. "I have to tell you something. Something you have to promise you won't tell Mom. Or anyone else for that matter."

"I'm listening," Eli says, shimmying closer.

"The thing with Axel is . . . was . . . fake. We're not actually a couple. Well, not technically. I mean we definitely weren't at first. Then it started to evolve into something but we haven't put a label on it, and not to mention, he never signed the contract, so maybe that was his plan all along. And then there's that DM Olivia showed me. And Ben constantly getting in my head with his theories about Axel just being one giant distraction based on physical attraction. Ugh," I moan, letting out a dramatic exhale.

"Wait, back up: You and Axel are together or you're not?"

A whiny noise gets lodged in my throat as I bring my gaze up to my uncle and pout. "I need a hug."

"Oh, Jam-e." Amo Eli wraps me in a hug and strokes my hair while I go all the way back to the beginning. The night Ben dumped me. Followed by my plan to get him back. Running over Betty White. Pretending to date Axel. The drives to and from school. Explaining what's in it for Axel. But then it gets more complicated when I tell Eli about the bucket list. Wonderland. The Blue Rodeo concert. The wedding (I leave out the heavy make-out sesh). And I end by telling him what Ben and Olivia have both told me about Axel DMing Olivia behind my back.

"Yumma! You've been busy!"

"What do you think I should do?" I ask as I pry myself off my uncle.

"What does your heart tell you to do?"

The scent of my uncle's cologne lingers. It's the same cologne my grandfather (on my mother's side) wears. "I really like Axel, but I'm not sure if I can fully trust him. And I guess I'd be lying to myself if I said I was completely over Ben. I thought I was. I even dropped off a box of his stuff to him today." I sniffle and wipe away my tears. "How long does it take to truly get over someone?"

Amo Eli holds back a laugh. "Jamie, sometimes I still think about the cute boy I sat next to in tenth-grade religion. There's no timeline for these things, babe. It's kind of like grieving a death. It doesn't ever fully go away. It just becomes part of you, and you learn how to move forward with that experience in your back pocket."

"So you're saying my past relationships will taint all future ones?" Is that what's happening here? I'm using the demise of my relationship with Ben as an excuse not to move forward with Axel?

"'Taint' isn't the word I'd use. For more reasons than one," he says before clearing his throat. "Your past relationships help *inform* your future ones. Unless—"

"Unless what?" I ask, feeling my eyes grow wide.

"Unless you continue to repeat the same pattern. Remember my artist phase?"

"You mean when you dated broke-ass 'artists' who sported man-buns, or beards, or a weird hybrid of both?"

Eli nods. "Yes. That's an example of repeating patterns. Don't do that."

"But it's not like you knew you kept falling for hot, broke-artist types."

"Oh honey, I knew. I just didn't care." We laugh, and it feels good to not take everything so seriously for once. It's why I love being with Axel. We have fun. I don't overanalyze or overthink everything when we're together. At least I didn't until Ben got in my head. "Listen. If you and Axel were really just faking it, the whole charade probably wouldn't have lasted this long. There's something there *and* I think you owe it to both yourself and him to explore that."

"I don't always know how to approach uncomfortable conversations without . . . exploding?" I say, my cheeks burning at the admission.

"I know." He smiles sympathetically. "And it's not your fault. Your parents fought about everything, and you unconsciously picked up on that, but keeping it inside—all it does is give that little thing that's bugging you space to grow and fester. You can break that cycle by forcing yourself to talk about the uncomfortable things."

"Mom doesn't like him," I say, adding that item to my list of worries.

"She's coming around. Your mother is a female chauvinist."

"You mean a misandrist, and I agree."

We laugh again and Eli grabs my hand. "You feel better?"

"Yeah. I do."

"Good. Because Axel couldn't stop talking about how excited he was for your date tonight, and before you even try," Eli says as I open my mouth to interrupt him, "I'm not telling you a thing!"

"You're supposed to be Team Jamie."

Eli leans in and kisses my forehead before rising. "I am. The truth is he didn't tell me much. He knows I have a big mouth." My uncle turns to leave but pauses and faces me again. "I don't know much, but what I do know is there's nothing fake about the way that boy's face lights up when he talks about you. He's a good one."

I smile. He *is* a good one.

CHAPTER SEVENTEEN

"Turn left here," Axel gently prompts, riding shotgun in my car, once again.

I turn into a dark parking lot, per Axel's instructions. "Am I parking?"

"Yes, ma'am."

I pull into a spot and turn off my car. There's a sign in bright pink neon outside the small building. "Kit's Karaoke Dive," I read aloud. "This is the surprise?"

"This place is more than meets the eye," he says, giving me little reassurance. "Kind of like me. Plus, this isn't the only surprise I have in store tonight." He gets out and comes over to my side, opening my door. He extends his hand like some sort of royal butler and I scrunch up my face. "Just play along," he says.

"Fine." I place my hand in his and allow him to guide me through the parking lot.

Once we walk into Kit's, a muscular bouncer asks to see our IDs. He promptly stamps our hands with red ink once he's verified that we are both way underage.

"It's kind of cool that they let younger people in even if they can't serve us drinks," he says.

I follow Axel inside the dark bar. He points to an exit sign to show me that the restrooms are just below it. It's such a small thing, but it means a lot to me.

Kit's is crowded but Axel manages to find us a table by the stage. Loud nineties rock blasts over the speakers. Most of these people look closer to my mom and Eli's age, possibly even older. Axel and I are by far the youngest ones here tonight.

"So," I say, nodding while looking around, "karaoke. You like to sing too?"

"Who doesn't?"

"Me. That's who. I don't like to sing," I say, pulling at my earlobe.

"No pressure. The karaoke is just part of the ambiance." He smiles sweetly and reaches for my hand across the table, entwining his fingers with mine. This is the moment. This is the moment Axel will ask me to be his girlfriend. I will my heart to behave by taking in breaths through my nose and letting them out discreetly. "I wanted to thank you," he begins, "for what you did at the wedding. Encouraging me to get up there in front of my father. It's really changed things between us. It feels like I've finally earned his respect. And it's all because of you."

"And the pregnant belly dancer," I say.

I expect Axel to laugh but his expression remains serious as his thumb strokes my hand. "It's just been nice to not have to tiptoe around my father anymore. I honestly didn't think he'd ever come around. You entering my life, in the bizarre way you did, has made everything so much better. Except my bike." He squeezes my hand and we laugh. "You're unlike anyone I've ever met before. You're so smart and funny. I love how confident you are about some things, and other times, so vulnerable. I don't think you see how special or unique you are. There's only one Jamie Taher-Foster and I feel pretty lucky to know her."

I swallow and study our intertwined fingers. Sometimes when things get too real, too emotional, I struggle to maintain eye contact or I'll change the subject. "I saw Ben today," I say, remaining consistent as ever.

"Oh yeah?" Axel asks without flinching.

"Yeah." I twist my mouth, fighting away a smile. "I went to his house and left a box of his junk at his front door. Want to know why I did that?"

"I do." He smiles.

"Because I wanted to officially close the chapter on Ben Cameron. But I guess that means the end of something else." I reach into my bag and pull out the unsigned contract, sliding it across the table. "Axel Dahini, do you agree to terminate the terms and conditions of this agreement?"

He laughs as he picks it up. "You know, I never did sign this."

"I do know that. And," I continue, looking at the pages in his hands, "you never told me the meaning behind your bike's name."

"It was to honor my grandmother," he finally reveals, as he places the contract on the table. "My dad's mom. She lived with us when I was growing up. She passed away when I was fourteen."

"I'm sorry," I say, seeing the hurt in his eyes. But also the love.

"Thanks. She didn't know much English. The truth is, she couldn't be bothered to learn it." He laughs to himself. "But in hindsight, I'm pretty sure it was her plan all along, because it forced me to learn how to speak Arabic."

"I'm so jealous that you have that," I say. Not only can Axel speak Arabic, but he also got to have a close relationship with his grandmother. "But how does this explain Betty White?"

"I'm getting there. Patience, butterfly." He boops my nose with his finger and winks before continuing. "One day I walked into the family room to find my teta watching *Golden Girls*. I was about eight or nine at the time. She made me sit next to her and translate everything that was happening. And if you've ever watched *Golden Girls*, you can imagine that not everything was"—he clears his throat—"easily translatable. Anyway, it became our thing. We'd watch an episode together at night. I'd practice my Arabic, she'd correct it, and we'd both laugh."

"That's so adorable I could puke," I say, not doing a great job at hiding my envy. "I can't speak Arabic; I barely know my mother's parents; and my grandparents on my father's side are snowbirds and spend half the year in Florida. Not like they're the warm and fuzzy type anyway."

"But you have an Amo Eli, and he's pretty cool."

"He is." I smile. "So I guess Betty White was her favorite Golden Girl then?"

"Rose." He nods. "Yeah. It's kind of funny when you think about it. How my bike brought us together. Maybe my teta had something to do with it."

There's a beat of silence before Axel returns to the contract, looking it over quickly.

"Some of these aren't so terrible, James. I'm not sure I want to terminate the entire contract just yet."

"Which items would you like to revisit, Alexander?"

"Have your lawyer call mine." He grins before putting it down and leaning in to kiss me.

"Ahem! No public displays of affection over rank bar tables," a deep voice says above us.

We pull apart and Axel bolts out of his seat and greets two people with aggressive handshakes turned full body hugs. "Dude! It's been too long," the guy with bleached blond tips says.

"I know. I've been distracted," Axel says, smiling down at me. "Sit down. This is Jamie. Jamie, this is Finn," he says, gesturing at Blond Tips, "and Diesel."

"Hey. I use they/them pronouns," Diesel says. "You?"

"Oh. She/her. I'm straight," I say, suddenly feeling super uncool and out of place. "Wait, sorry. That's not the right way to say it."

I rake my fingers through my hair. My eyes lock with Axel's and he nods encouragingly. I pause and take a deep breath. "I'm a cishet girl," I try again.

Diesel grins. "You don't have to tell us your sexual orientation."

"Right. Because I'm with Axel."

"No." Diesel straightens. "Because you don't owe that information to anyone. For the record, you could be with Axel and be bisexual. Or ace. Or many other things. But I appreciate you feeling comfortable enough to share all of that within thirty seconds of meeting me."

I smile back at Diesel, trying to hide the blush I feel taking over my cheeks. "So, you're Axel's dancing friends?"

They all laugh at my not-so-discreet attempt at changing the subject. "Yes, we're Axel's dancing friends," Finn says. He's super tall and lanky. His nails are painted bright pink and black. They match Diesel's.

"I'm surprised you've heard of us," Diesel says. "We figured Axel forgot about his old life once he moved to the suburbs. Seems to have benefited him though. His TikToks are getting a lot more views since he went solo."

Finn grabs Diesel's arm dramatically. "I told you it was the right decision to let him go."

Diesel nods, painting on a frown. "You were right. But it's been hard. Hold me."

Finn and Diesel fake-cry into each other's arms, then pull apart, laughing.

I lean in to Axel. "So, are these two my second surprise?"

"They are." Axel nods. "I figured in order to get to know the real me, you needed to know a bit more about my other family. Finn and Diesel took me under their wings in ninth-grade gym. They saw I was as hopeless at most team sports as they were and convinced our teacher to let us 'dance' our way to an A. The only catch was we had to perform for the class at the end of the semester."

"That's when some unevolved jerks posted it on TikTok thinking it would go viral, for all the wrong reasons, but instead we went viral for all the right ones," Finn says, leaning back in his chair and crossing his arms.

"Is that when you decided to film dances together and post them?" I ask.

"Eventually," Diesel says. "It took a while to convince Axel. He was a bit more reserved back then. He still is compared to me and Finn."

Axel? Reserved? Not a word I would use to describe him.

"Jamie, are you much of a singer?" Finn asks, nodding to the stage.

"No. This was Axel's idea. Do you enjoy singing in front of strange adults?"

Diesel laughs. "Yeah. We like to sing. Some of us are better at it than others."

I glance over at Axel, who keeps checking his phone. He types something quickly into it, then excuses himself.

"That was weird," I say out loud, without realizing.

"What was?" Finn asks, his blue eyes peering into mine like an old soul.

"Axel's barely ever on his phone, but he's been checking it constantly tonight. If I didn't know any better, I'd be worried he was texting his sidepiece." I laugh but the others don't join.

"Axel wouldn't do that," Diesel says, shaking their head slightly.

"You're his friends. You have to say that," I respond, almost defensively.

"No," Finn interjects. "His last girlfriend, Sky, cheated and it nearly broke him."

"Axel's never spoken about Sky before," I say.

"Yeah, he wouldn't. Once someone breaks his trust, that person is pretty much dead to him." Diesel's eyes bore into mine. I nod to let them know I get their message. Loud and clear.

"I'm the same way, so I get it," I reply. Axel returns and takes a seat next to me. "Everything okay?"

"Yeah. Just wanted to make sure your third surprise was still on track," he says with a wink.

"You know, I don't really love being surprised," I say, before biting on my lower lip.

"I know. But this is a good one." Axel tips his forehead to mine and I rub my nose up against his.

"We heard you're Axel's videographer," Finn says, breaking us out of our love trance. For a second, I almost forgot they were there.

"All I do is hold the tripod thingy. And yes, that is the official word for it." I steal a glance at Axel. He's got a huge smile on his face. I like being here with his friends and seeing a different side of him. And I like that he wanted me to see this side of him.

As the conversation continues, it becomes obvious that Finn and Diesel enjoy ripping on Axel for sport, but I'm pretty sure they'd skin me alive if I ever hurt him. It makes me jealous in a way. I've never experienced that kind of friendship with anyone.

Growing up, I floated around, never really finding "my people." Looking back, I can see part of that was me protecting myself by not letting people in. My parents were teenagers when they had me. They had no idea what they were doing, and I guess that's why I clung to Ben so hard after we met. Ben was stability. Something I'd never had.

Maybe Amo Eli is right. We take something from our past relationships and bring it into our next. If it weren't for Ben, I wouldn't be here now with Axel.

After chatting with Finn and Diesel for a while, over non-alcoholic drinks and greasy appetizers, I get them to spill all of Axel's most embarrassing moments. Finn is in the middle of telling us a story about the time Axel got locked in the janitor's closet with the school principal when the music cuts out. The stage lights turn on and a tall man wearing a red plaid shirt walks up to the mic. He introduces himself as Kit and welcomes everyone. He goes into a seemingly rehearsed bit describing how the karaoke portion of the evening works, then ends it by telling everyone that "Don't Stop Believin'," by Journey is banned from Kit's Karaoke for the foreseeable future. It seems to get a mostly favorable response from the crowd. Although a few people do boo and jeer.

"So?" Diesel says, looking right at me. "Are you getting up there tonight?"

I swallow, shifting nervously in my seat. "Me? No. Definitely not. What about you?"

"Nah," Diesel says. "But Finn should. He's got a wicked set of pipes."

"We'll see," Finn says, chewing on his thumbnail. "Not sure this crowd is my key demographic."

"Right," Axel laughs. "I doubt they have any songs from this century."

"So why'd you bring me here?" I ask, feeling my eyebrows scrunch up. "If none of you plan on singing and this place doesn't hold significance for any of you?"

"Does everything you do have to have deep meaning behind it?" Diesel asks in earnest.

"Yes. But I'm working on it," I reply.

Axel runs a hand up and down my back. He glances at his phone again before tossing another reassuring smile my way.

As the night progresses, something becomes very clear: the people at Kit's Karaoke Dive take their performances pretty seriously. It's as if they're living out some dream to be a rock star they didn't quite get to as teens. Makes me kind of sad, actually. I don't want to live my life with regrets, but I guess I already do in some ways.

Applause breaks me out of my thoughts, as does Axel's face nuzzling my neck. "Having fun?" he asks.

"I always have fun when I'm with you. You're my fun-maker."

"Good. I hope it'll always be that way." He places a soft, gentle kiss on my lips. As we pull apart, I decide to ask Axel about the DM he sent Olivia. Just to clear the air and make sure there are no more lingering doubts, but then the next song begins.

"Oh god," I say, pulling back.

"What is it?" Axel's eyebrows pinch together.

"This song."

"What song is it?" Finn asks.

"'The Flame' by Cheap Trick. It's my parents' 'song,'" I say, barely containing an eyeroll.

"Aww. It's got a nice vibe," Diesel says.

"It's just . . ." The all-too-familiar voice that comes out over the speakers causes a chill to pass through my entire body. It transports me to my childhood home, sitting on the floor of our kitchen with linoleum tiles peeling up at the corners. A yellow halo from the light fixture glows over my parents, who are holding onto one another tightly while they dance. Dad sings into Mom's ear and she blushes, smiling wide. They sway back and forth while I watch this moment I know will be fleeting. So fleeting that instead of it bringing me joy, it fills me with dread. Because I know it can (and will) be over in an instant.

My heart leaps into my throat as I lock eyes with the man on stage. He sings as if this is the most important moment of his life, gripping both hands around the microphone. One corner of his mouth turns up in an apprehensive smile.

Dad.

I sit up straight in my seat, frozen in time and place, watching my father sing to me. My father, who I haven't seen in over three years, haven't spoken to since the day he left, is currently standing a few feet away, almost within arm's reach. It's as if it's just the two of us in this dark bar. Maybe he's not even real. He could be a mirage.

"Jamie. Jamie."

Someone shakes my arm. My name coming from Axel's mouth sounds distant. I rise from my seat as the audience applauds my father's performance. He steps down so he's next to our table, standing across from me.

"Jamie," he says, a pained expression on his face. Pretty sure it matches mine.

"What are you . . . ? How did you . . . ?" My eyes dart around, zigzagging across the table, unable to focus on anyone. "I'm sorry. I can't do this right now." I grab my things and rush out the front door of Kit's, trying desperately to catch my breath. There's a pounding in my head. My heart feels like it may burst from my chest. I bend over, unsure if my legs will support the weight of my body, trying not to throw up. I keep trying to take . . . in . . . deep . . . breaths . . . but . . . they . . . repeatedly . . . get . . . lodged . . . stuck . . . in my throat. In. Out. The vise is back, squeezing my lungs, not allowing any airflow in or out. I float outside my body, head spinning, disconnected from the ground below me.

Just as I feel myself falling backward, someone catches me, saying my name, over and over.

"Jamie. Sweetie, look at me." My dad's hands clasp my cheeks. He's trying to get me to look him in the eye. "Breathe in, come on, you can do it."

I nod and close my eyes, trying to breathe in the crisp night air.

"There you go. Again. Breathe in, then out."

My eyes focus as I slowly come out of my fever dream and return to this living nightmare.

The vibrations of the music from inside thump in sync with my pulse. I stare at my father, his face inches away from mine. He looks the same. But a little different. Older. Scruffier. Leaner.

"Does that happen a lot?" Dad asks, studying me.

"No." I shake my head. "Not anymore, I mean," I say, shrugging off his touch. "Happened all the time after you left." I wipe tears from my eyes with the back of my hand. "I've mostly gotten the panic attacks under control, but I guess when you're met face-to-face with the person who triggered them in the first place, they decide to make an appearance." I let out an unamused laugh.

"I'm sorry. I didn't know."

"Right." I laugh again, the action itself exhausting what's left of my energy. "Why would you? You walked out and never looked back. Hell, I'm surprised you even recognized me," I say, trying to form words as I stand upright, my fingertips still tingling.

Dad covers his mouth with his hand and brings it down his bearded face. "I'd recognize you in a room full of clones. You're my baby. My mirror image. My heart." Tears glaze over his eyes as he takes me in.

"If I'm all those things, then where have you been the last three years? Why haven't you reached out?"

"It's complicated, James. There's so much you don't know." He rakes a hand through his dark hair as a million emotions course through me. Anger. Nervous butterflies. Happiness. Confusion. Sadness. Relief. Exhaustion.

The door to Kit's opens and the bouncer asks my father if there's an extra microphone for a couple who wants to duet. He gives him a quick response before turning his attention back to me.

"Do you work here?" I ask.

"I manage the place."

"You've been in Toronto this whole time?" I turn away and watch as cars pass on the busy road in front of the bar, trying to hide the fact that I need to regulate my breathing again to avoid another panic attack. "I thought maybe you'd moved out of province or even Canada. I had no idea you've been only a few minutes away." I face him again. "I don't understand."

"I wanted to see you. I tried, but your mom wouldn't let me get within ten feet of you."

"Does she know you work here? That you're still in the city?"

Dad nods.

"I can't believe her. She kept you from me?" I step up to him so we're face-to-face. "She made it sound like you left and she had no idea where you were."

"Your mom had her reasons."

"You can't defend her. That's time we can't get back. Milestones missed. Birthdays. Holidays. I'm not the same person I was when you left," I say, hearing the tremble in my voice. "Why didn't you at least email? Or call? Anything to show you still cared."

Dad opens his mouth to speak but is interrupted by Axel, who bursts out of the bar with Finn and Diesel trailing behind him. Axel's eyes are wide as he glances between me and my father. "Is everything okay?"

"Wait a minute," I say, looking at Axel, then my father. "Did you know about this? Is that . . . is that why you brought me here?"

"We're going to take off," Diesel says to Axel.

"Nice meeting you, Jamie," Finn says before he and Diesel head to the bus stop. There's a beat of silence as Axel's friends walk away, leaving an odd trifecta of people behind.

"Maybe I should leave you two alone," Dad says.

"It's what you do best," I say, crossing my arms over my chest.

He reaches into his back pocket and opens his wallet, handing me a small piece of cardstock. "It's a business card," he says, a strained smile on his face. "You can reach me anytime."

"Sure," I say, knowing it's just a hollow gesture. "Whatever."

"Can I have a hug?" Dad asks as Axel stands by.

I swallow and release a breath. "Okay."

My father's arms envelope me in a tight bear hug, but I can't seem to let myself unclench my shoulders from my neck long enough to return the sentiment.

Dad steps back and extends a hand out to Axel. Axel accepts it with apprehension.

My father heads inside the bar and I watch as the door closes behind him. Axel comes into my line of vision but doesn't speak.

"So, that was my third surprise," I say, my tone devoid of emotion. "The big one, I assume."

"I just wanted to do something nice for you," he says, exhaling a deep breath. "Especially after what you did for me and my dad. I wanted to repay the favor."

"You thought hunting down the man I haven't seen or spoken to in over three years was 'repaying the favor'?" I ask, my eyes wide. "You can't compare your relationship with your father to mine. Your dad lives with you. He didn't abandon you. All I did was bring your father to the dance floor and tell him to look up. This is completely different. You had no right inserting your nose into my business."

He frowns. "I just thought if you could see him again, then maybe it would . . . I don't know."

"What? Fix me?"

"You hold back, Jamie. Even with me. And I guess I believed part of that was because of your dad. Maybe I did overstep. But I wanted to bring you two together again to at least open the lines of communication. All this time has passed and it's going to keep passing. And the problem with that is, the scars will never heal."

"No. They won't. Especially if someone you thought you trusted goes behind your back and picks at the scab."

Axel looks down, his feet still. "I thought it would make you happy."

"Clearly you don't know me as well as you seem to think you do. But then again, why am I surprised? This was never meant to be something real."

"Jamie, don't do this," Axel says, taking a cautious step toward me. "I made a mistake and I'm sorry. But it doesn't erase everything else."

"Doesn't it?" I ask, sucking in my cheeks. "I mean, really, everything about us was based on a lie. And someone who claims to know me, the real me, wouldn't make this kind of decision. Face it, Axel. Our 'relationship' is as deep as a puddle."

"You're just trying to push me away by saying mean things. It won't work. I'm not walking away from us. You're not your mother and I'm not your father."

"Right. My father didn't send DMs behind my mother's back."

"What DMs?" Axel shakes his head. "What're you talking about?"

"Olivia showed me proof of you sliding into her DMs and asking her out after Wonderland."

He brings his fingers to the bridge of his nose and pinches it, releasing a deep sigh. "It's not what you think."

"Ben was right about you. And me."

"What did Ben say about me?" Axel asks, eyebrows furrowed.

"He said you were shady. Which you've proven yourself to be. And that ultimately all you were to me was a distraction. Well guess what? My eyes are open now. I can see clearly again. Find your own way home." I head to my car, slamming the door shut behind me. I want to cry. I want to scream. Every single person

I've ever trusted has broken that trust in some shape or form. At a certain point I have to face the truth I've been trying to push away for years.

I'm unlikeable *and* unlovable.

And no number of lists or accomplishments will ever change that.

CHAPTER EIGHTEEN

I've been sitting parked in my car in the driveway for almost half an hour, waiting for my mom's bedroom light to go off. I don't want to see her. Because if I do, I won't be able to hold back the deluge of emotions boiling inside of me. She's responsible for all of this.

A loud thud on the passenger-side window causes me to scream and maybe pee myself a little.

"Jam-e? What're you doing?" Amo Eli asks, thick brows pinched together. An annoyed sigh escapes before I open my door and step outside. He's with Eric because of course he is. That's what couples in a healthy relationship do on Saturday nights. They hang out together.

"I was just listening to music," I lie.

"I didn't hear any music. Did you hear music?" Eli asks Eric.

"Your niece is entitled to privacy, Eli. Let's not pry," Eric says. I want to shout "thank you," but all I manage is a half-hearted smile.

"Fine, but have your entitled privacy inside the house. It's cold," Eli says, shivering. "I'll make you hot chocolate. Or wait, it's pumpkin spice season, isn't it? Would you rather have that as your sad autumn girl drink?"

"I apologize on his behalf," Eric says, guiding Eli toward the front door while I drag my feet behind them.

Eli fumbles with the keys before he unlocks the door. We all walk through the threshold and I hold in my breath, praying *she* doesn't come down.

"Where's Axel?" Eli asks. "I thought he was taking you to karaoke. Oops. I'm not supposed to know that," he says, covering his mouth. I'm starting to wonder if Eli has had one too many gins and tonics tonight.

"Karaoke? Now that's some straight-up white-people shit." Eric laughs. "I can say that because my mom's white. Just know neither my white nor Black side approves."

"Wait," I say, grabbing Eli's arm. "You knew I was going to a karaoke bar? Did you know why?"

Eli shakes his head. "No. Well, he did tell me he wanted you to meet his friends. Flipper and Petrol? That's all I got out of him."

"Finn and Diesel," I mutter under my breath.

Eli and Eric remove their shoes and head to the kitchen. "Come on," Eli says, looking back at me. "I'll make you that basic-girl drink. Eric loves it."

"*I* love it? You're the most basic bitch I know," he teases.

"I'll be right there," I say, sitting on the bench and untying my boots. My phone keeps lighting up. Texts and calls from Axel. Surprised he cares enough to keep trying. Or maybe he just wants to make sure I pay him back for Betty White. Which I intend to do ASAP. No more new books. For real. And I guess this also means no more drives to and from school. I'll have to avoid Shawarma Sitty too. And Varley Crescent. And Maple View High. I wonder: If I start digging a hole now, how long will it take before it's big enough for me to crawl into?

"Jamie?"

Shit.

"I wasn't expecting you home for another hour at least. Everything okay?" Mom asks, standing on the lower landing of the staircase, dressed in a fluffy pink robe. Eli bought it for her ironically and she wears it all the time.

I rise from the bench, gripping my phone. "No. Everything isn't okay."

She comes down the last three steps so she's in front of me, the top of her head at my chin. How could someone this tiny be such a destructive force in my life?

"I saw him tonight," I say, expecting her to read my mind. Truth is, I'm so angry it's hard to formulate coherent sentences.

"Axel? Yeah. You told me you were going out with him."

"Not the *him* I was talking about." I swallow as my heart drums against my chest.

"Ben?" she asks, like this is some sort of guessing game.

"No, Mom. Not Ben. Not Axel. Dad. I saw Dad tonight."

Her face drops and she looks away. "Oh."

"Is that all you have to say? Oh?" My chest heaves as my voice rises. My anger is an airborne disease, leaving no one safe in its presence.

"Uh, where? Um . . ." She keeps pausing and stuttering. She's been found out and she knows it.

"Kit's Karaoke Dive. Turns out he's the manager there. Gave me his business card and everything."

"So you, um, you talked to him?" she asks, folding her arms across her chest. She still isn't making eye contact.

"Yeah. I talked to him for the first time in over three years. And you want to know what I found out? The reason he hasn't reached out is because of you. *You* won't let him."

She shakes her head almost dizzyingly. Eli comes out of the kitchen to find me and Mom still in the foyer. Mom holds her hand out and gestures for Eli to stay where he is. He ignores her and comes to us. "I can explain," Mom says.

"Then do it," I demand, before searching my uncle's eyes for answers. "Did you know?"

"Habibi, it's not my business. I can't . . . your mother has her reasons."

"Then you did know she was purposely keeping me from him?" I focus my glare back on her. "I lost out on a relationship with my father for three years. Three years," I shout. "Time I will never be able to get back. Don't you understand that? Who are you? Who are you to control both my life and his? How could you be so selfish?"

"Hey, Jamie, come on," Eli says, placing a hand on my arm. "Let her speak."

She just stands there, swallowing, eyes glistening, like I'm the bad guy. There's a lot of things I'm not sure about in life, but I know I am not the one in the wrong here.

"Your father chose to walk out on us, Jamie. He left both you and me behind. I stayed and picked up the pieces," she says, shakily pointing a finger to her chest. "And when I couldn't do that anymore, I brought us here. That man chose to leave. I begged him to stay. I pleaded with him to get help."

"Help? Why? Because he couldn't live up to your expectations? You wanted him to work in a job that was creatively stifling. You expected him to provide. When he decided he couldn't handle living by your rules, he left. *You* pushed him away," I say. "Like you pushed away your parents."

"That's not what happened. You're creating your own version of events and it's not accurate. I take part of the blame for not telling you the full story, but this isn't all on me."

"*Part* of the blame? I . . . can't even with you. This isn't just about Dad. It's about how you try to control me. You're so afraid I'm going to end up like you or, even worse, be way more successful, that you insert yourself into every facet of my life."

She closes her eyes and sighs, like my mere presence annoys her. "You're doing that thing again where you don't listen and you let your anxiety take over. If you would just pause for a second, breathe, and give me a chance to speak—"

"Let's go into the living room and sit, okay?" Eli suggests, his big eyes full of hope.

"Just tell me one thing," I say, ignoring my uncle's plea. "Did you keep me from working at the camp this summer because you wanted me and Ben to break up?"

"No. That's not why I kept you apart."

"Then you admit you did purposely keep us apart?"

She exhales. "I made that decision so you could get some distance and maybe find out who you were outside of Ben. I didn't want you, in a moment of freedom and passion, screwing up your life by sleeping with him and getting pregnant."

Silence possesses the house like a ghost as the truth comes to the surface. When Mom looks at me, all she sees is a huge mistake. She's so worried I'm going to copy and paste her own past that she actually thinks she has the right to play puppet master of my life.

"How could you even think . . . ? That's not why we wanted to work together."

"Things happen, Jamie. And as your mother, I couldn't continue to sit by and watch you grow more and more attached to Ben. I just wanted you to take a breather for a second. Focus on yourself. But all you did while Ben was away was mope around, and when he decided to break up with you, on his own volition, not through anything I said or did, you started dating another guy in 2.3 seconds."

I shake my head, processing all the lies and half-truths coming out of my mother's mouth. "You don't know what you're talking about."

"What were you even doing at a bar?" she asks, hiking her arms up her chest as Eli continues to dart his eyes between us like a ping-pong ball in an intense match.

I show her the stamp on my hand. "They let minors in. It was Axel's idea. He orchestrated the big reunion between me and Dad. He probably thought it would make great material for a thirty-second TikTok," I say, full of spite. Axel doesn't get how screwed up our family is. And why would he?

"Jamie, you can't possibly believe that. It was a sweet gesture," Eli says. "That boy cares deeply for you, and he wanted to reunite you with your father. He probably thought it would make you happy. Please tell me you didn't get angry at him."

"Of course I got angry at him. It's what I do. I don't know how to be in a normal, healthy relationship because I've never been around one," I say, glaring at Mom.

"Drinks are ready," Eric calls from the kitchen entryway, seemingly oblivious to the drama unfolding out here. Or maybe he's giving Eli an out. Okay. So maybe I've seen one healthy relationship in my lifetime.

Eli turns to face the kitchen and shakes his head slightly at Eric, who opens his mouth and nods slowly before walking backward into the kitchen. "Where is Axel now?" Eli asks.

"I left him in the parking lot of Kit's and came home."

"Jamie," Eli says. "How could you do that to him?"

I shrug in response as my eyes meet Mom's. "I guess I learn from the best." Squeezing past my mother, I race up the steps to my bedroom and slam my door shut.

I hate her!

She kept me from my father.

She tore me and Ben apart.

She planted seeds of doubt in my head about Axel.

I grab my notebook off my nightstand, plop down in bed, and turn to a fresh page. *New life goal: get as far away from Nadia Taher as possible—both in distance and personality!!!*

CHAPTER NINETEEN

It's Halloween. Maybe I should go to school dressed as a notable woman from history who's been wronged by her lover. Problem is, my classmates wouldn't get the joke if I dressed up as Princess Di in her black revenge dress.

Instead, I'll go as myself.

Nothing scarier than that.

It's been two days since my fight with Mom and Axel. Eli has tried multiple times to get me to speak to them, like it's my job to be the one to "fix" things. But I'm not the one who went behind my back!

I'll just go to school, keep my head down, focus on my classes, and come home. It's probably what I should have been doing all along. Mom *was* right about one thing: I don't need a man in my life. Especially not a man-child who charms you with his million-dollar smile, convinces you to dance in front of other people, introduces you to his family and friends, and then backstabs you in the same breath.

Losing Axel as a fake boyfriend is one thing. But losing him as a friend has been a whole other beast. A beast that's been sitting on my chest, crushing me, making every breath I try to take nearly impossible.

I didn't realize a person I've only known for two months could be everywhere. And I don't mean his actual presence. He's in that spot in my room, where he tried to teach me how to dance for the first time. He's on my bed, where we drew up our contract officially. He's in my car, his scent still lingering. By my locker. The lunch table. The halls. My Instagram account. He's there when I close my eyes. When I listen to music. When I cry.

I was with Ben for three years, and the main emotion I felt after getting dumped was anger. Sure, I shed some tears. My stomach twisted in knots the first few times I saw him with Olivia. But it was different. It wasn't this constant ache. This yucky absence. This huge void. And the worst thing is, I don't know what to do about it.

With Ben, I had a plan: Axel.

With Axel, I have nothing.

The school day goes quickly. Thankfully, I didn't run into Olivia or Ben, and I even managed to avoid Axel. But for how long?

On the way to my car at the end of the day, I spot a familiar figure leaning up against the passenger-side door. Guess I spoke too soon. I don't really have it in me to deal with Ben, but at least he's alone.

"Hey," he says as a hesitant smile appears. "How're you holding up?"

"What do you mean by that?" I ask, unlocking my car and tossing my bag to the backseat.

Ben scrunches up his face as if he's said the wrong thing. "Sorry. I shouldn't have." He pauses and then sighs, running a hand through his hair. "My mom told me you saw your dad this weekend. And the look on your face makes me think it went about as well as I would have predicted."

I study the ground. "Yeah. It was pretty terrible. I was caught completely off guard."

"It must have felt like seeing a ghost or something."

"That's exactly what it felt like. At least it gave our parents something to gossip about." I shake my head as I twist my heel into the hard pavement.

"I don't think they were gossiping, Jamie. My parents still care about you. We all do."

I exhale a deep breath while meeting Ben's eyes, feeling slightly comforted by his presence.

"How is he?"

"Alive. You want a ride home?" I ask.

Ben nods and I appreciate that he's not pressing for a deeper response, because right now, I don't have one. He gets in the passenger seat while I get in the driver's side and turn the engine. My radio blares on, playing some annoying song Axel loves.

"Sorry," I say, reaching for the knob to turn down the volume. "Was drowning out my thoughts on the drive to school this morning. So where's Olivia? Surprised the two of you aren't dressed in some matching couple's costume."

Ben barks out a laugh. "Yeah. If she'd had her way, we would have been. I mean, that was the plan, but things kind of took a turn this weekend for us."

I pull out of the parking lot and glance at Ben. "I thought you made up after the whole tutoring and text message debacle."

"I thought so too," he says, his head tilted down. "We broke up."

"Must be something in the air. Axel and I have also decided to end things," I state simply, while continuing to drive.

"Oh," Ben responds.

When I turn onto Ben and Axel's street a few minutes later, my heart aches. A flashback of the night I met Axel flickers through my mind like an old black-and-white movie. I make a sharp turn onto Ben's driveway and park.

"Want to talk about it?" Ben asks. "Share war stories?"

"Not really," I say, staring straight ahead.

"Can I talk about it then?" Ben asks. I guess with Olivia gone, I'm the only quasi-friend he has left. So much for all that enlightenment he'd achieved working at the camp over the summer. He seems to be back to where he was before he left me. Nothing to show for two months in the inner circle with Olivia Chen. Because of course her friends would choose her over Ben.

I unbuckle my seatbelt and turn to face him. "Go ahead."

He matches my pose, all excited, like he's been waiting all day to talk to someone—me—about this. "She brought up the fact that I'd lied about you tutoring me. Again. It spiraled from there."

I guess my words got through to Olivia after all. "Spiraled how?"

He lifts his shoulders. "I asked her to show me Axel's text. I wanted to see how she replied to it."

"And?"

"She got defensive. Claimed she'd deleted their exchange and didn't understand why I wanted to see her responses anyway. She accused me of not trusting her. Which is just so ironic I could puke. But if my enemy is DMing my girlfriend, I think I have a right to see the messages."

"Enemy?" I ask, side-eyeing Ben. Axel is a lot of things, but I wouldn't consider him anyone's enemy. Even now. I don't hate Axel. I'm just disappointed. And hurt. Maybe I'm pushing him away as an act of self-preservation. I guess I'm more like my mother than I care to admit.

Ben continues. "The guy is dating my ex-girlfriend and trying to get with my new girlfriend. I think it's fair to call him an enemy. I'm sure you don't have warm and fuzzy feelings for Olivia."

"No. I don't. But, at a certain point, you have to decide whether or not to trust someone. And as far as I can see, Olivia hasn't given you any reason not to trust her."

Ben thumps his head against the headrest, exhaling a loud breath. "I've really screwed things up."

"Just say you're sorry."

"It's not that easy. I said some things. Things I can't take back. Things I'm not sure I need to take back."

"What did you say, Ben?" I ask, running a hand over my stomach, as a baby cramp pulses.

"You know how some people have a tell? Like when my mom makes brussels sprouts for dinner, she pulls at her earlobe, and how my dad swallows a lot when he's about to tell my mom he has to go on another business trip?"

"Sure," I say with a shrug, trying to ignore the memory of when Ben and I discovered his mom's earlobe quirk. We laughed about it and then went to his room. We made out and it got pretty intense. It's why we had to come up with that winter formal plan. Ben didn't want us to lose focus and have our first time be rushed and unmemorable. He was always so adamant about not getting lost in the moment.

Lost together.

Like me and Axel.

"Olivia rolls her eyes. A lot. Especially when she's trying to hide something." Ben shifts closer to me, his left arm leaning on the center console. "I think Olivia and Axel are messing around behind our backs. In fact, I accused her of it."

"No." I shake my head. "Definitely not."

"Why else would she erase the messages?"

"Lots of reasons. It actually would have been weirder for her to keep them," I say. "There's no way Axel and Olivia were hooking up. All his free time was spent with me."

"Then why aren't you two together anymore?" Ben asks, a sharp edge to his voice. He hates being told he's wrong. He hates *being* wrong.

"It's complicated. But it has nothing to do with Olivia." Both our phones ding and we immediately pick them up. "New message from the social committee," I say.

Ben nods and opens the message. I freeze, completely confused at how I ended up here. With Ben. In my car. On his driveway.

"They've announced the location for the winter formal," he says. "The CN Tower. December 19."

"Well, that just solidifies the fact that I will not be going to the formal," I say, facing forward.

"Why not?" Ben asks. "I mean, we're both single now." He traces a finger along the top of my hand. "It's not too late to meet the goal we'd set. We can go together, make an appearance, and then . . . disappear. Like we'd planned all along."

Ben's touch is a sharp pang to my skin. He wants to forget everything we've been through. Pretend the last two months (and then some) haven't happened. He wants to be my date to the winter formal. He wants to . . . He couldn't possibly be that dense.

He continues to drag his finger along my skin while I sit still. Processing.

I have Ben where I want him. My father is just a phone call away. Axel is out of my life.

All things I wanted.

Some of them were goals I had been working toward.

And none of it feels right.

It's all hollow. Fancy packaging but nothing on the inside.

"I know you're afraid, Jamie, but I'll be there. I'll hold your hand on the ride up."

"Sorry?" I ask, turning to face him again.

"Your claustrophobia," he says. "The elevator. It won't be so bad if I'm there with you. I promise." His eyes are kind. His grip on my hand firm but caring.

He actually remembered.

"Sure," I say, nodding along. "We can go together." The words slip out of my mouth before I can stop them.

"And then we'll come back here?" he says, leaning in slightly.

I pull away, not ready to feel his lips on mine again. "Just because I agreed to go as your date to the formal doesn't mean we're back together. And it doesn't . . . well it definitely doesn't mean the other thing."

"I get it. You need time."

I need peace.

Maybe in seven weeks, I will have come around to the idea of me and Ben again. After all, he was my endgame. Or was supposed to be. I just need to get Axel out of my system first. It shouldn't take too long. Studies say it takes about half the time you were with a person to get over them, which means a month from now I'll likely have forgotten all about Axel Dahini.

His existence will be nothing more than a glitch in the timeline of my life when I look back ten years from now.

He'll just be some boy I used to know.

CHAPTER TWENTY

When I pull into my driveway, there's a pickup truck parked on the side of the road by our house. Probably one of Mom's customers, except her salon is closed on Mondays. Maybe it's a friend of Eli's.

I stay in my car for a few minutes before going inside. Something about my interaction with Ben isn't sitting well with me. It was choppy. Awkward. Presumptuous. Does he think after all this time and everything that happened, I'd still consider being with him?

Just because something was once part of a plan doesn't make it a canon event. When he leaned in to kiss me, the only thought I had was *No. Get me out of here.* But then why did I accept his invite to the formal? And why didn't I tell him to eff off when he suggested going back to his house *after* the formal?

I just sat there like an injured deer on the side of the road.

What is wrong with me?

I went from wanting to do whatever it takes to get Ben Cameron back to sliding away from his attempt to get close to me. He's single. I'm single. *We're* single, and yet, I had zero desire to kiss him. When he told me about breaking up with Olivia, he may as well have been telling me there was a chance of rain in tomorrow's forecast. There were no pulses of excitement coursing through my body when he asked me to the formal. Zero sparks flew when he touched my hand. How could I be getting everything I want and still be so unhappy? Empty. Blah.

Axel.

I miss him.

It's only been two days, but I miss him so much.

Axel saw in me something no one else ever has. Me included.

Someone who deserves to take up space.

Couples fight and make up all the time. Not every fight needs to lead to the demise of a relationship. This must be how healthy relationships span decades! No need to cancel someone the second they mess up. No one is perfect. And really, what Axel did wasn't actually that bad. He had good intentions. His heart was in the right place. He couldn't have possibly known how I'd react.

Speaking with Ben today, him trying to hit Resume on where we left things off before he went to camp, was exactly what I needed to help me see that my feelings for Axel are real. And they're not going anywhere. I need to text Ben and tell him the formal is off.

But first, Axel.

I pick up my phone and scroll through the messages Axel sent Saturday night. It's not too late. I can fix this.

Axel: I'm sorry.

I didn't mean to hurt you.

I thought I was giving you something you wanted. Like you'd given me. But I was wrong.

I should have asked you first.

I feel terrible.

I get that I broke your trust and I'm really sorry.

If you ever want to talk, I'm here. Jamie, I really like you. A lot.

I hope I didn't screw things up between us.

And finally, the last message he sent me, which was at 9:45 Sunday morning.

> I guess I'll stop texting. But I'm here if you want to talk. I really am sorry.

I start typing a reply into my phone.

> It's okay.

Then I delete it.

> I get what you were trying to do. I can even understand it. But

I delete again.

> I miss you.

Delete.

> I really like you, too.
> Maybe even more than like?

Delete. Delete.

Ugh. I don't know what to say. How do you open the lines of communication with someone when you're still hurting?

Ben and I rarely argued. If one of us was upset, the other would speak calmly and explain their position. And that was that. Even if I didn't "get" Ben's position, even when I thought his reasoning was full of it, I accepted his explanation and moved on because that's what we did. Conflict made Ben uncomfortable and, to be honest, it made me uncomfortable too. I didn't want to end up like my mom and dad. I wanted to be in a healthy relationship. But I'm not sure what Ben and I had was healthy either.

Instead of coming to me earlier with his feelings about wanting to spread his wings and fly with Olivia, he dragged it out over the summer and then blindsided me. Even if he's telling me the truth about what happened, that nothing did go down between him and Olivia until he broke up with me, because of the way he went about it, my trust in him is forever broken.

Maybe my trust in all humans.

All this drama is making me hungry. I need food and maybe a good cry session. Then I can work on drafting the perfect response to Axel.

I grab my things and make my way inside the house. When I open the door, there's a pair of runners on the rug, not neatly tucked away like Eli demands. It can't be one of Mom's customers, since they come in through the basement entryway, and they're definitely not Eric's shoes. For one, they're huge, and second, he'd never wear shoes with as much of a scuff on them. These look like they've been dragged through the mud and back again.

"Jamie, is that you?" Mom calls from the kitchen. Her tone is even-keeled. Not icy like it's been the last couple of days when we've been forced to address one another. "Come into the kitchen. There's someone here to see you."

I take in a breath and exhale as I remove my coat and boots. My steps are laced with apprehension as I walk to the kitchen. Mom is seated at the table with a man. Dad. He turns as I come in and smiles. Dad rises from the table, shifting his stance like he's deciding what to do. Run away, maybe? He's good at that. Instead, he extends his arms. My gaze moves away from his and onto Mom, who's still seated. A tight smile paints her face. It's like she's giving me permission to hug my father. He seems to read my hesitation though and pulls out a chair for me instead.

"Can we talk?" he asks.

I nod and sit. It's quiet as the three of us seemingly acclimate to being seated at a table together for the first time in over three years.

"No Halloween costume?" Dad asks.

"Nope. This moment is scary enough," I say, and they both let out a quiet chuckle.

"Your dad called me this morning and asked if he could come over and speak to us. I was a bit hesitant at first, but after we chatted awhile, it felt like the right thing to do," Mom says, looking at me.

"Why do you always get to be the one who makes decisions for all of us?" I ask, digging my fingernails into my knees under the table.

"Don't be upset at your mother, James. It's me who you should be mad at."

"But she kept you away from me for years."

"She did. But she did it for good reason," Dad says, unable to meet my eyes.

"Maybe this conversation should be between the two of you." Mom stands. "I'll be in my salon if anyone needs me." As she passes us, she places a hand on my shoulder and grips it slightly before leaving.

My stomach growls, breaking the awkward silence. "Skipped lunch," I say. "Want a snack?"

"Sure," Dad says, his large hands wrapped around Eli's rainbow-colored mug with the words *I WAS PETTY TODAY* written in all caps.

I riffle through the cupboards and fridge, making a plate of cheese, crackers, and grapes. I bring it to the table and sit next to my father, picking at the vine, plucking the grapes but not eating any.

"So, you were going to tell me the million reasons why you walked away," I say with a bit more edge to my voice than I'd intended.

"Not a million reasons, James. Just one real reason. Something your mother and I have kept from you." He slides the mug away and takes in a deep breath before exhaling slowly. "When I left, I told you it was because it felt like my life was slipping away. While there was truth behind that sentiment, it was really just an excuse."

"What are you talking about?" I ask, rolling a grape around my fingers.

"This isn't easy for me to admit, even after all this time. Especially to you, my baby girl." His eyes turn red and glossy. He keeps swallowing, seemingly moments away from breaking down. "I'm an alcoholic, Jamie."

A chill passes through me as the grape slips out of my fingers and rolls across the table. Alcoholic? My father? I had no idea. "I had no idea," I say.

"That's because I was pretty good at hiding it and I'd begged your mom not to tell you. I didn't want you to look at me the way you're looking at me now."

"How am I looking at you now?" I ask.

"Like you're disappointed. I get it. I would be too." He hangs his head low and I bring my chair closer to his, tapping my knee with his.

"I'm not disappointed that you're an alcoholic. I'm disappointed you felt like you couldn't tell me."

He raises his eyes to meet mine. "Your mother and I were so young when we ran off together, and despite that, or maybe even because of that, we thought we had all the answers. Turns out we knew nothing. About raising a baby. Being married. About ourselves. But we both loved you so much. You're the reason we stayed together for so long, because we couldn't fathom being without you." He pauses and sighs. "It was hard living in the middle of nowhere, away from all my family and friends. I used to be an adventurous guy and I felt so . . . stuck. Eventually, the high

I'd kept searching for led to a battle with some inner demons. Enter alcohol. It got to the point where I was no longer just a danger to myself but to you as well."

"What do you mean?" I ask, tucking my hands under my thighs.

"Your mother pleaded with me to get help. She cleaned up my messes. Gave me more chances than I could count. But after she learned I'd driven you home from the baseball game drunk, it was game over."

"Oh." I remember that day. I was thirteen and a half. Dad had taken me into the city to watch the Blue Jays play. We had hot dogs. He let me drink soda (which Mom never did), and he had a beer. Maybe more than one. Every time I looked at him his cup was either full or empty. I never thought to question it. He was my father and I trusted him.

"It was reckless and dangerous and every time I think about that moment it makes me want to punch a wall or, even worse, hurt myself. So I ended up hurting myself more and more. Drinking to erase the shame. To erase all the mistakes I'd made. To pretend none of it was true." He drags the mug back and a puff of laughter escapes as he seemingly reads the words for the first time. He brings it to his lips and takes a sip. "I've been sober for ten months. I'm ashamed it took me so long to get my life together. Every time I tried to reach out to see you, your mother wouldn't let me when she learned I was still drinking. I couldn't seem to hide it from her. She's too smart for her own good," he says around a smile. "But this last January, after I missed your seventeenth birthday, it finally clicked. All this time was passing. Time I'd never get back. And for what? A drink?"

"Alcoholism is a disease. She shouldn't have kept you from me," I say.

"You're right, it is a disease, and maybe it wasn't the right decision to keep us apart, but it was her decision and I respect that.

Knowing I'd driven home drunk with her baby in the car. I'd never trust me again either if I were her."

"Plus, she's stubborn," I say.

"Not that you'd know anything about that," Dad responds, and we both laugh. There's a smile on his face. A smile I haven't seen in years, and it fills me with warmth. And a bit of sadness. How many smiles I've missed. Hugs. Tender moments.

"My one year of sobriety will be on your eighteenth birthday. You were the reason I got clean, but I've learned another person can't be the reason why you stay clean. So now I wake up every morning and decide I'm doing this for myself."

"I'm happy for you," I say weakly as tears fill my eyes.

"I regret so much, Jamie. Most of all that I missed out on watching you turn into this beautiful young adult. If you'll allow it, I'd love to be invited back into your life again. But you call the shots. Your mother and I have agreed that you're old enough to decide for yourself."

I swallow before turning to face my father. "I've missed you every single day you've been gone. Your absence had a pretty devastating effect on my life. It made the divide between Mom and me even wider. I tried to mask the pain by kicking butt in school and parading around with Ben, but inside, I was broken. Until . . ." I pause and close my eyes. Axel's face appears and my stomach sinks.

"Your mother isn't perfect, but she did her best. I believe that. She was trying to protect you. She begged me to get help. Eventually, she gave me an ultimatum: get sober or leave. When I left, she had to figure things out alone. She's done well for herself and you. You're healthy and thriving at school. And that boy, Axel, seems like a good friend. I remember how much you always wanted to have a best friend, and it looks like you have that now."

"Yeah," I say, breathing out some of the weight of this moment. "He's pretty great."

"I don't know how he tracked me down, but when he did, he was so excited. Just like a golden retriever puppy. I didn't want to go along with his plan at first, but, well, he can be pretty persistent and charming."

I smile, swiping away a few tears that have sprung loose. "Yeah. He is."

"Is he maybe more than a friend?" Dad asks with a raise of his brow.

"It's complicated."

"You know," Dad grins. "'Complicate' is a tricky homograph. The differences between the multiple meanings are so slight, it really takes a sharp mind to see them."

"Did you know the word 'complicate' comes from the word 'complicit' and the Latin word 'complicare,' which translates to 'fold together'?" I ask, sniffling slightly.

"And?" Dad asks with a soft smile.

"And when you think about it, Axel thought bringing you back into my life would be as easy as folding a piece of paper in half, but what he forgot to take into account were all the previous existing creases on the page, which made making a perfect fold . . . impossible."

"Does that mean you're upset with him?"

I exhale and try to answer my father's question, but the truth is, I don't really have an answer because I don't know. I'm both grateful and upset.

"Hey," he says, placing a hand on my thumping knee. "Maybe you can tell me about it later. Once you've had a bit more time to process. Your mother invited me to dinner next weekend."

"She did?" I ask, sitting up straight.

Mom comes through the kitchen carrying a bunch of empty mugs. Dad shoots up to help her bring them to the sink.

"She did," Mom says with a hesitant smile. "Is that okay?"

"Yeah." I nod. "That's okay. Speaking of food, I'm starved. Can we get some burgers?"

"The usual?" Dad asks, a familiar sparkle in his eye.

"The usual," Mom and I respond.

"I have a question," Dad says, looking between us. "I met Axel. But who's Ben?"

I let out a groan at the same time as my mother.

"Sorry I asked," Dad responds, holding up his hands.

"I'll catch you up while Jamie picks up dinner?" Mom says, shooting me an "I got you" look. I smile as I release an appreciative sigh. Dad's gaze flits to Mom, a slight flush visible in his cheeks.

I have no grand delusions of my parents getting back together. They're not right for each other, romantically, and I can see that now, but maybe the three of us can find a new way to be a healthy, maybe even happy, family unit.

One day at a time.

"Can you call in the order?" I ask Mom as Dad helps her with the mountain of dirty mugs. "I'll run out now to get it." It'll give me an excuse to go to Axel's first. Because what I want to say to him can't be done over texts. We need to see each other in person.

Back in my car, I make the short drive to Axel's, but as I pull up to Varley Crescent it appears I'm not the only one who decided to pay him a visit. Olivia's car is parked outside his house. I'm not going to jump to any conclusions. There must be a reason why she's here. Before I can get out of my car to ask Axel himself, Olivia steps outside his front door and hugs Axel goodbye. He hugs her back and my heart breaks like glass, shattering into a million tiny little pieces.

My throat closes in on me as a flash of heat rushes up my face. I try to breathe, even just short breaths, but I can't. I can't get them out. As soon as the tingles start in my fingertips, I know it's only a matter of time before I lose complete control.

I need to get out of here and fast.

I can't believe this is happening again.

CHAPTER TWENTY-ONE

Step one in getting over Axel: give Ben a second chance. Second chances. Seems to be the theme lately, so why not? It *is* what I wanted, according to my notebook. Written down, in ink, and so it must be true.

Right?

Right?

I guess.

In order to get the ball rolling on this whole getting over Axel thing, I need to tie up all loose ends, like paying Axel the money I owe him to repair Betty White.

I managed to make sixty dollars tutoring Ben. That combined with the hundred and twenty dollars I have left in my bank account still leaves me short seventy-five dollars. I glance at my beautiful bookshelf. Expensive hardcovers. Special editions. Signed author copies. I know what I have to do.

I take photos of two of my most prized possessions and post them to our school's "Buy and Sell" Discord group. If I can get fifty dollars for each book, I'll be able to e-transfer Axel the money and close the chapter on us.

Instead of staring at my phone, waiting for someone to buy my book babies, I decide to tackle something I've been putting off for far too long: cleaning my bedroom. Now that Ben and I are trying to make things work between us, I figure I should put in the effort to create a more inviting space for him. A clean slate. A fresh start.

We can't move forward if I follow the same patterns as before.

Anxiety whirs under my skin as I glance around my room and see how much work it needs. The clothes on the floor alone overwhelm me. I'll just do what the organization TikToker Eli follows suggested. Make one pile for laundry. One for donations. The rest I'll fold and/or hang up in my closet. After that, I'll clear all surfaces and wipe them down. Clutter. It just distracts you. Makes it hard to focus. The TikTok person said clutter makes anxiety worse. I never saw it that way personally, but maybe I'll try their method out, since whatever it is I'm doing doesn't seem to be working.

Why is this so hard?

I can find the derivative of any given function in calculus, but the sight of dirty laundry and stacks of books paralyzes me.

I must push through.

With holey socks in one hand and old notebooks in the other, I take a deep breath and put them both down. Music. That's what I need.

My music app is pathetically sparse. I haven't ever curated any playlists. That's never been my thing. I like music but I don't worship it like Axel does. For him, music is a religious experience. I lie in bed on some propped-up pillows and decide to create a playlist to help me clean. It takes longer than I thought, since I don't always know the names of the songs or artists and I end up having to google the lyrics I do remember. By the time I'm done, I have a playlist of twenty-three songs.

Most of which Axel introduced me to.

All of which remind me of him.

I turn on my Bluetooth speaker and hit Play.

The first song comes on. "Baby" by Justin Bieber. This is the song Axel chose for his Wonderland performance under the rainbow. The first time I truly noticed how talented he was. By the time the song is over, I've sorted through all the clothes on my floor.

As I alphabetize my novels, "New Rules" by Dua Lipa plays. This is the song he chose for our first dance lesson, right here in my room.

Beauty products. I bet these brushes could use a wash. I raise the volume so I can hear the music while I clean the brushes in the bathroom down the hall. "Treat You Better" by Shawn Mendes comes on, and without realizing, I bop my head along with the song as I rub cleanser into my brushes. Butterflies flip around in my stomach as I think about the intense eye contact Axel served me while dancing to this song in front of the fountains and the entire senior class.

Back in my room with Windex and paper towels, "Adventure of a Lifetime" plays. With a bare bedroom floor, I do the dabke alone, laughing on the outside at how terrible I am and aching on the inside because that moment seems like it was so long ago. I was so happy that night. Free. I danced in front of other people and didn't even care.

Then "Lost Together" by Blue Rodeo comes on and that's when I lose it completely. I fall into bed. Tears prick through my eyes and I cry remembering how safe I felt in Axel's arms at the concert. How the cool rain danced on our warm bodies. How important and special it felt being on the receiving end of his eyes. Those eyes. Sometimes intense. Sometimes silly. But whenever his eyes were on me, nothing else mattered. With one look, he made me feel like the most important person in his world. That's not something I get to experience often. Or ever.

Axel—even though we were technically fake-dating—made me feel like I was his entire universe and his best friend.

What did I do? I pushed him away and into the arms of my nemesis.

I sit up and glance around my almost sterile bedroom. This isn't me. This isn't the person I was when I was with Axel. I was messy. Chaotic. Emotional. I was me. And Axel liked that person. A lot.

Screw it. I'm going to text Axel and ask if we can talk. We're good at talking. Communication has never been our issue. I need to stop getting in the way of us. Just as I'm about to start typing my message to him, I receive a notification from the "Buy and Sell" Discord. Someone wants to buy my books, and they're willing to transfer me the money now.

I message back and forth with MartyMcFlyWishes, who is pretty elusive but quickly transfers the money into my account. When I reply asking where I should drop the books off, they tell me they'll get back to me later with a date and time.

Weird but whatever.

I place the two sold books on my desk, running a hand over the covers. Regardless of what is going on with Axel and me, I should pay him back now that I have all the money. I open my bank app and transfer Axel the entire two hundred and twenty-five dollars.

Maybe when he sees the alert, he'll call or text me. I lay back in bed and stare at my phone, waiting to see a message come through. A few minutes later I receive a text alert: Alexander Dahini accepted your money transfer.

My stomach twists as I wait for another alert.

Seconds pass.

Then minutes.

I'm doing that thing where I pick at my fingernails and chew my lips. I'm only made aware of this because I taste blood. Instead of letting the anxiety monster take over, I decide to kill time by crossing off the last items on my cleaning to-do list.

But then an hour passes and still nothing from Axel.

It's too late.

He's already started to move on.

No second chance for us.

Instead, I'll settle on being someone else's second choice.

It's surprisingly easy to revert to old routines. Instead of picking Axel up for school, I pick up Ben. Instead of having lunch with Axel, I have lunch with Ben. Instead of spending all my free time with Axel, I spend it with Ben. We do our homework together—like old times. Watch TV on Amo Eli's couch—like we used to. Ben talks about our future. Unlike old times, I just listen. When he tries to hold my hand, I resist. I'm not there yet.

Maybe it isn't so easy reverting to *all* old habits.

We're two weeks into November and the winter formal is just over a month away. Every night I promise myself I'll tell Ben I don't want to go to the formal with him (or do anything else with him), but selfishly, when the sun rises, I can't bring myself to do it. Because the truth is, being with Ben is easier than being alone. If I'm alone, I'll have to face the grief of losing Axel. It's like I'm stuck inside the same episode of a TV show that keeps repeating itself and the only way out is if I make a decision: commit or go. But I can't seem to do either. So I just hit Play again at the end of the episode, hoping that the situation will figure itself out.

It doesn't.

It's Friday night and I'm heading out to pick Ben up for another date. Dinner and a movie. I'm on the front bench tying my boots when the door opens. Eli walks in and leaves the door wide open, clearly not seeing me behind it.

"Come in. She's not here," he says.

"Nah. I'm good."

Axel.

"Just for a minute. I want to show you something," Eli insists.

I sit frozen on the bench, with one boot on, as Axel steps inside. He closes the door and they both spot me.

"Oh. Jamie. I didn't think you'd be home," my uncle says, a little quirk in his lips.

"My car is outside. Where did you think I'd be?" I ask, my eyes darting between his and Axel's.

"I thought maybe you were on a run or something." Amo Eli winks at me, then nods his head back at Axel. He seems to think he's being slick but he's as smooth as a porcupine's butt.

"You wanted to show me something?" Axel asks, his voice low. I study his hands, wanting so badly to hold them in mine. His lips. Wanting so badly to press mine up against his. His eyes. Wanting so badly for him to look at me and make me feel like the most important person in his universe one more time. But he doesn't.

"Ah. Yes. I'll be right back." Amo Eli slides off his shoes and heads up the steps to his bedroom. He shuts the door behind him, leaving me and Axel in the quiet and empty foyer.

"I don't think he's coming back," I say as I rise from the bench, a little lopsided with just the one boot on. I swallow to muster up the nerve to keep going. "How have you been?"

He shrugs. "Fine."

He still won't look at me.

"I wanted to tell you," I say, getting in front of Axel, "my dad came by after that night at Kit's. We talked. For a while actually. Hashed things out. Laid everything on the table. He came over last weekend too. The three of us had dinner together. There was a lot I didn't know about the situation. We're working toward rebuilding our relationship, and it's all thanks to you." I try again to make eye contact after getting out my rambling updates. "Things with my mom have even been pretty good too."

Axel nods. "I'm happy for you."

My jaw clenches and I struggle to get out my next words. "I'm sorry for losing it on you and ditching you at Kit's. And for not taking your calls or answering your texts. I'm sorry for all of it." When he still won't meet my gaze, I grab both his hands and practically shake him. "Would you look at me?"

"No, Jamie. I won't look at you."

"Why not?"

"I screwed up. I admit that and I apologized. I thought after some time and space you'd come and speak to me when you were ready. But instead, you ran right back to Ben and I had to hear about it from Olivia." He peels his hands away from mine.

"No. That's not true." Light heart palpitations make the room spin. He's got it wrong. I need to explain myself better but I don't know where to start or what to say.

"I've got to go. I have plans."

"You have plans?" I ask, my stomach lurching as the image of Olivia leaving Axel's home plays in my mind. "With who? Olivia?"

"Yeah." He pauses and his eyes meet with mine for a fleeting moment, confirming my worst fears.

My mouth opens but I remain silent as Axel walks out the front door.

And out of my life.

CHAPTER TWENTY-TWO

"Jamie, we need to talk," Ben says. We're parked on his street after watching a terrible movie he suggested and having a subpar dinner (also his recommendation). "Let's go for a walk, get some fresh air."

"It's the middle of November and freezing," I remind him.

"Just for a few minutes. We can walk off those garlic breadsticks," he says with a sincere smile.

"Fine." I unbuckle the seatbelt and step out of my car. As Ben comes around, I hike up the zipper to my coat and throw on my hood. He extends his hand but I shrug to show him mine are in my jacket pockets. "What's up?" I ask as we begin walking.

"You were really quiet over dinner."

"It was loud in the restaurant," I say, even though the truth is I couldn't get the image of Olivia and Axel out of my head.

"Then is there a reason you cowered every time I tried to touch you?"

"I didn't cower."

"You cower *every* time I try to touch you." Ben stands in front of me. We're stopped in the middle of the road. Scattered streetlights dot the ground with halos of light. "What're we doing here, Jamie?"

I shrug again, picking at the inseams of my pockets.

"I thought we were trying to give our relationship another chance," he says. "But it feels like I'm the only one trying."

"I don't know what you expect from me. You dumped me for another girl, and then when that relationship ended, you came crawling back—and what? You thought I would just run into your arms and be so grateful?"

Ben runs a hand over his face and sighs. "You have a relationship with your dad. We're going to the formal together. It's everything you wanted and you're still not happy."

He's right. I do have everything I thought I wanted. But that was before. Before I ran over Axel's bike. Before he held my hand. Before he rubbed the tip of his nose against mine. Before the dancing, the kissing, the laughing, the talks. Before Axel, I was asleep, but he woke me up. And now? I'm in some sort of weird purgatory where I just exist. I can't go back to how things were because I don't want to and I can't move forward because I don't know how.

A car horn sounds and we jump. Ben pulls me to the side of the road as a baby-blue BMW speeds past us and stops abruptly in front of Axel's house, breaks squeaking.

"You've got to be kidding me," Ben says. He stampedes over to Axel's. I follow behind with a bit more reluctance.

Olivia gets out of her car and slams her door, eyes searing into Ben's. "What?"

"What?" Ben practically shouts. "You're hanging out with this guy now? After you promised me there was nothing going on?" Axel gets out of the car and spots me on the street. We share a moment of solidarity as we stand on the receiving ends of this awkward encounter between exes.

"I can hang out with whoever I want. Interesting you seem to think you get a say, seeing as you ran right back to *her*," Olivia says.

She doesn't even look at me when she says it. Like I'm not worth the effort. "Heard you're going to the formal together." She crosses her arms over her chest.

"We're not . . ." I interject. "I mean we are, but we're not officially back together or anything," I say, fumbling my words.

"Looks like you're back together," Olivia says. "At least that's what Ben is telling everyone."

"Ben?" I ask, feeling my face tighten.

He turns to me. "I don't understand why you're acting so surprised. What exactly do you think we've been doing the last two weeks?"

"We're just hanging out. We haven't been"—I pause, searching for the right word—"intimate."

I glance over at Axel. His expression softens at my TMI reveal.

Olivia barks out a laugh. "Hilarious."

"At least I can trust Jamie," Ben says to Olivia. "She doesn't DM other guys secretly behind my back."

"That's rich. No, seriously," Olivia says, getting in Ben's face. "Like you're in any position to talk about secrets."

As soon as Olivia finishes the sentence, Ben reaches for me, ignoring the brick wall I've been building in my mind. "Let's go."

"Wait," Axel says. I stand still, looking between Ben and Axel, Olivia just outside my line of vision. "I think it's time Jamie finally learns the truth."

"Come on, Jamie, we don't need to hear this," Ben says, his hand now wrapped around my wrist. My feet stay planted where they are.

"No." I twist my arm free from Ben's grasp. "I want to hear what Axel has to say."

Silence descends on the four of us. My eyes meet Axel's, pleading with him to say something. He bites on his lower lip, his gaze moving between everyone. "I did slide into Olivia's DMs after Wonderland, but it wasn't so I could get with her. I was digging for information."

Olivia squints her eyes at Axel. "What information?"

Axel focuses his attention on me. "I knew you wouldn't be able to fully move on until you got the closure you needed from your relationship with Ben. And I knew you'd only get that closure once you learned the truth about what happened between him and Olivia at camp."

"Jamie knows what happened. Nothing," Ben interrupts.

"Let him speak," I say to Ben, while keeping my eyes locked on Axel.

"I wanted an opportunity to speak to Olivia face-to-face, so I asked her to grab a coffee. But she basically told me to screw off and that she was with Ben. When I tried to explain that I wasn't actually asking her out, she said she didn't believe me and told me to stop messaging her. So I did."

"Told you I didn't do anything wrong," Olivia says, glaring at Ben.

"Okay. But what's this about?" I ask, waving my hand between Axel and Olivia. "Are you with Olivia now?"

"No!" Axel and Olivia say in unison.

A knifelike pain pierces through my stomach. I rub my hand over my lower abdomen and Axel's eyes meet mine.

"Green apple?" he asks.

"Green apple," I respond quietly.

"You can come inside if you need to," Axel offers.

"Why are you and Olivia hanging out?" I ask again, ignoring my stomach cramp. "I saw her leaving your house a couple weeks ago, so this clearly isn't just a one-time thing."

"Wounded birds nest together," Olivia says, crossing her arms over her chest. "We both needed someone to talk to. Someone who would understand what we're going through. I didn't realize Axel was just using me." She glares at Axel, who is still looking at me.

"You talked to Olivia about me? About us?" I ask, feeling my face scrunch up. Another piercing pain shoots through my stomach.

"She told me the truth," Axel says. "Ben kissed her *before* he broke up with you."

"Is that true?" I ask Ben, this interaction giving me whiplash. He bows his head low and I step right up to him. "Answer me."

"It was a mistake and I told Olivia we couldn't do anything else until I spoke to you."

"I knew it," I say, shaking my head.

"I stopped it from going any further," Ben says, probably thinking that it makes what happened okay. "I slipped up."

"And then you lied about it. Repeatedly."

"I didn't want to hurt you," he says.

A stunted laugh escapes me. "Is that why you unceremoniously dumped me the day you came back from camp?"

"I'm not sure what you think I should have done instead. At least I didn't ghost you."

"Oh. At least," I say, repeating Ben's words back. "The fact that you thought we could get back together without telling me the truth first . . . Is that how little you respect me? After three years of being my boyfriend, you didn't think I deserved to know the truth?"

"No. It's not like that. I just knew you were hurting over Axel and I was hurting over Olivia and thought it might be . . . I don't know what I thought," Ben says, raking both hands through his hair.

"Apparently," Olivia says, hurt radiating in her voice. "You can't just ping-pong back and forth between girls, messing with their emotions, Ben. It's not fair."

I run my hands over my face. "So what's this?" I ask Axel, nodding to Olivia. "You two are besties now? Divulging secrets? Sharing war stories? Trash-talking me?"

"No." Axel remains still, his voice shaky. "We're just hanging out."

"Out of all the people you could hang out with, you choose Olivia?" I study him, trying to read his face as he rubs the back of his neck. "You did it to get me to react. Admit it."

"I wanted to find out the truth, for you. But yeah." He sighs, his shoulders slumped. "I guess I kept hanging out with her because I thought you were back with Ben and I wanted to . . ."

"Hurt me." I finish the sentence for him. "Did you tell her the truth about us?"

"What truth?" Ben asks, stepping closer.

Axel gives me a pleading look but I ignore it. "Axel and I faked our entire relationship," I say, a forced laugh coming out. "All of it. I needed someone to help me get you back and Axel had his own reasons for playing along. None of it was real."

Ben shakes his head in validation. "I knew you could never go for a guy like him."

Olivia's mouth falls open. "Axel didn't tell me that."

"No." Axel looks me square in the eye, ignoring the others. "It may have started that way, but it was real. You can't deny that." He swallows before taking a cautious step toward me. "Can we talk? Alone?"

"I wanted to talk to you earlier tonight, but clearly I wasn't worth your time. You had better places to be. I feel so stupid."

"I should get going," Olivia says, walking back to her car. She looks at Ben once more before getting in and driving away. Ben comes up to me but I put my hand out to stop him.

"I can't right now," I say. "You need to go home."

His shoulders lower in defeat and he sighs dramatically before walking past me on his way to his house.

And then there were two.

"I'm sorry, Jamie. I misread the situation. I reacted emotionally." Axel covers his face with both hands like he's masking a scream. He takes in a deep breath and looks at me. "You stopped talking to me. And then I thought you were with Ben. I admit that I tried to make you jealous. It was dumb. But I never said a bad word about you to Olivia. I was just hurt."

"Hurt people hurt people," I say quietly, almost to myself.

"You have to believe that the only reason I sent Olivia that DM was to get the truth. For you. For us."

"There is no us." I shut my eyes and take in a deep breath before releasing it. "It's gotten too messy. We've both said and done things we regret, things we can't take back. It's probably best we just cut ties." When Axel doesn't respond, I say the first thing that comes to mind. "Do you still have the contract I gave you at Kit's?"

"It's in my room."

"Could you please go and get it?" I ask, struggling to maintain eye contact. He nods and heads inside his house. I walk back to Ben's, get in my car, and drive it to Axel's. I park in front of his home. The exact same spot I ran over his bike on the night we met.

Axel returns with the contract in hand. I grab a pen from my glove compartment and meet Axel at the front of my car. "You received the money for Betty White?"

He nods as I check that item off the list.

"I helped you film multiple TikToks and I lived up to playing the role of supportive Arab girlfriend, even attending your cousin's wedding."

"You did."

More checks.

"And I helped you get a job with Eli. The only part of this contract I didn't completely live up to was providing you with rides to school until Christmas break, but I think you can understand the circumstances behind me being unable to fulfil that."

Axel exhales. His lips part but I speak before he can.

"As for you," I continue, "you have lived up to all the terms and agreements on your end of the contract... and then some." I place the contract on the hood of my car and hand the pen to Axel, pointing to the line that has been left unsigned for nearly three months. "Please sign here."

He takes the pen but hesitates. "What about item number four? The bucket list. We were supposed to go to those places together," he says, with what appears to be hope in his eyes.

"I will no longer be needing your company." I point my chin to the contract, keeping my tough exterior as Axel's vulnerability is on full display. He nods before finally signing the contract. Once he does, I pick it up and tear it in half.

"Our relationship, fake and otherwise, is now terminated. Thank you for your help. I can take it from here."

The torn pages slip from my hand and fall slowly to the road. I get back into my car and immediately drive away. I am done with relationships. And boys. And people. All I need to get by in life is myself.

All this time, Mom was right.

Next goal: learn how to do life alone and get to a toilet, ASAP.

CHAPTER TWENTY-THREE

The next morning, I ditch breakfast to lie in bed so I can ruminate over the previous night's events. Ben kissed Olivia before breaking up with me. Even though I'd strongly suspected he'd crossed the line with her, having confirmation hits in a way I wasn't expecting it to. But the biggest bombshell of all last night, one I didn't see coming, was learning that Axel turned to Olivia when he thought I'd gone back to Ben.

"Jamie," Mom calls from behind my door. "You decent?"

I sit up and run a hand through my tousled hair. It does nothing to help the severe case of bedhead and tangles I'm sporting. "Yeah. Come in."

She opens the door and stops dead in her tracks. Placing her hand on her chest, she calls Eli frantically. He comes bolting up the stairs.

"Mashallah," he exclaims, hand to heart.

"What's the matter with you two?" I ask.

Their eyes are wide as they walk through my room, observing the neat stacks of books and folded clothes.

"Nothing." Mom shakes her head. "I just never thought I'd see these floors again until you moved out."

"Jam-e," Amo Eli says before sitting on my bed. "What is the reason behind this?"

"I was bored," I lie.

Mom pulls out my desk chair to sit and it feels as if I'm about to have some sort of emotional intervention. "Your dad called. He wants to know if he can take you out today. Are you free?"

"Yes," Eli says. "*Are* you free? Did you and Axel talk last night after I left the two of you alone?"

I clear my throat. "Oh, we talked. But it's not what you're thinking. It's over with us. Completely."

"Because of Ben?" Mom rests her elbows on her knees, leaning in.

"No. It's completely over with Ben too."

"Then I guess you are free," she says, offering me a sympathetic smile. "Want to talk about it?"

I look between them.

"Yeah. We didn't think so," Eli says, tucking a piece of hair behind my ear.

"Why didn't Dad call me to ask if I wanted to hang out?" I ask.

Mom forces a smile. "I guess he still thinks he needs to go through me first."

"Well he doesn't," I snap back. "We already discussed this. Doesn't anyone ever listen to the words I say? Does my opinion mean nothing?"

"*Now* do you want to talk about it?" Eli asks, grabbing my ankle and shaking it.

"I'm not going to the formal with Ben anymore, or anyone else for that matter. I received confirmation that Ben kissed Olivia while we were still together, and if that isn't enough suckage for one night, Axel has been spending time with Olivia."

"I have a question. Are there any other girls in this town besides you and Olivia?" Eli quips.

"It's not funny," I say. "My life is a giant mess."

"At least your room isn't. Kind of ironic, right?" Eli says. He sucks in his lips before I can shoot him a glare.

"What if you try talking to Axel?" Mom asks. "Maybe if you speak to one another now that some of the dust has settled, you can figure out how to fix things."

"There's nothing left to figure out. It's over." I rip my covers off and get out of bed. "I've decided to take your advice and spend some time alone. I need to stop relying on others to make me feel complete. I'm my own best friend." Maybe if I say it enough times, I'll start to believe it.

"So you're just going to close yourself off to friends and romantic relationships?" Eli asks, crossing his arms over his chest.

"Yes." My bucket list comes into view and I pick it up. "And I'm going to start by completing the rest of these goals. Alone."

"Hey. I'm all for spending time alone and learning some independence, but don't do it to make a point. Do it because you want to. Can I see that list?" Mom asks. I pass my notebook to her and her eyes move through the pages quickly. "Maybe you and your father can go to one of these places together."

"That is a fantastic idea," I say to my mother before leaning over to plant a kiss on her cheek. The notebook slips from her lap and onto the floor, landing with the contract facing up. Before I can grab it, it's back in my mother's hands. The room falls quiet as she reads through it.

"I . . . I don't understand. Why did you and Axel have a dating contract?" Mom asks.

I bite on my lip, trying to think of a simple way to explain everything. My eyes plead with Amo Eli to step in. Thankfully, he does.

"You know Jamie loves to read and well, sometimes life imitates art," he says, looking back and forth between me and my mother. I smile at my uncle before mouthing the words "tell her." He takes my hand and squeezes it. And then he tells my mother everything, while I sit by, embarrassed and heartbroken.

"That certainly explains a few things." Mom nods. "You'll get through this, Jamie," she says, placing her hand on my knee. "You're probably the smartest, most resilient person I know. To be honest, I hate how resilient you've had to be, but I'm completely on board with this journey to self-discovery. And quite frankly, I'm impressed with the whole fake-dating scheme. You had me fooled."

A small laugh escapes me. "Maybe there's an item on the list I could do with the two of you," I say, allowing myself to continue being vulnerable.

"Let me see that list," Eli says, snatching the notebook from my mother's lap. "Watch a hockey game, eh? That's on my bucket list too. Maybe we can swindle a bro into buying us a couple tickets. Those things don't come cheap," Amo says while poking my side with his finger.

"And I know just the bro," Mom replies.

Later that day, I take the streetcar downtown to meet my father. I thought it would be too weird to sit in a car alone with him. Especially with how unpredictable and crappy Toronto traffic is. Besides, I don't think we're at that level of comfort yet. After my chat with Mom and Eli, I sent Dad a photo of my bucket list and told him to choose an activity. He went off-script and suggested skating at Nathan Phillips Square, since it just opened this weekend. Kind of old-school but I thought it could be fun.

The ice rink at Nathan Phillips Square is situated in the heart of Toronto, just in front of City Hall. We used to come here every winter and admire the Christmas window displays at the Hudson's Bay Company, then take goofy photos by the three-dimensional

Toronto sign. After that, Mom and I would rent skates (Dad would bring his own) and we'd try not to kill ourselves on the ice.

I agree to meet Dad by the Tim Hortons across the street from the rink. He's already there when I arrive, hands in his pockets, trying to keep warm.

"Dad," I say, observing him in a flannel coat and wet hair. "Seriously?"

"What?" His eyes twinkle.

"I know you're all about being cool, and excuse me for sounding like an old Arab lady, but you're going to catch a cold dressed like that. With wet hair to boot."

"Ah. Said just like a Canadian teta." He laughs, running a hand through his hair. "Winter kind of snuck up on me this year."

"Let's go to the Eaton Centre and get you a hat. Maybe some gloves."

"Hot chocolate too?" he asks, his eyebrows wiggling.

"Sure. It'll have to be your treat though. I'm broke."

We smile before we head to the mall on foot. The sidewalks are packed full of pedestrians: young families, twenty-somethings on their own paths of independence, and older couples, strolling slowly and enjoying the view.

"Ever notice that couples these days dress alike?" Dad asks. He nods his head to the thirty-somethings walking toward us. I glance down at their matching Blundstones, cuffed jeans, and military-like coats.

"Those two even have the same haircut," I scoff.

"Speaking of funny haircuts," Dad says as we wait to cross the street, "how's Axel?"

I shrug, watching the crosswalk countdown. The light switches and we make our way to the other side of the street. Neither of us speak as we come to the mall entrance. Dad opens the door and

I'm instantly slapped in the face with loud Christmas music and huge decorations dangling from the ceiling.

"A little early for this, don't you think?" I ask.

"It's almost December. Besides, people love it. Gives them something to look forward to."

"I guess," I say, wishing I had something to look forward to. "Let's go to Roots. They'll have lots of warm hats and gloves to choose from."

"Okay, Teta." Dad laughs.

"Hey, Dad," I say as we walk through the mall. "How well do you know Mom's parents?"

He shakes his head. "Not very. We spent most of our courtship sneaking around, and after we eloped, she kept her distance from them."

"Why?"

"I think because she thought they were ashamed of her. For getting pregnant. And when they tried to reconnect, she'd meet each attempt by pushing them away. Said it wasn't worth it. When I asked why, she'd explain that every time they got together, she couldn't shake the feeling that they were disappointed in her."

"But don't you think it isn't fair that I have no relationship with them? I mean, your parents I at least see a couple times a year. That is until you left," I say, quietly. "I used to go visit Teta and Sedo with Amo Eli when I was younger, but then it felt like Mom was starting to resent me for having a relationship with them. She had this big fight with Eli once about it and told him he couldn't take me over there anymore. And now so much time has passed, it feels weird to reach out."

"It's complicated, James."

"What isn't?" I ask with a dismissive roll of the eyes.

"You're almost an adult now. If you want a relationship with your grandparents, you should have one."

"What about Mom?"

"No one could tell your mother what to do when she was seventeen."

"Eighteen in January," I remind him. "So you're saying I should outright go against her wishes?"

"Do you know how she feels about this topic? I mean, have you sat down with her to discuss it or are you building this up all in your head to be bigger than it is?"

"She's not the easiest person to talk to," I say simply.

"Believe me, I know." Dad smiles. "She wouldn't even accept money from me after I left. The few times we communicated it was only to make sure that I'd sign the divorce papers. She asked for full custody, which I of course granted, and she refused any child support. She insisted on doing it alone." A prolonged silence stretches between us as we continue to walk. I didn't know any of that. There's still so much I don't know about those three years Dad was gone. "We made it," Dad says as we come to the storefront.

"We did," I respond, my throat tight.

After Dad buys a red toque and gloves, we leave the busy mall and grab some hot chocolate at Tims before admiring the holiday window displays. I haven't done this in years, and while it's nice to be with my father again, reliving some childhood memories, it's also pretty bittersweet. All those years lost. Moments that could have been memories. Instead, it's just a black hole of time.

We head back to Nathan Phillips and rent our skates. We bring them to a bench and, just like when I was a kid, Dad gets on bended knee to tie my laces for me.

"It feels nice to be needed for something," he says in a way that's supposed to be a joke, but I can tell he means it.

"I've always needed you," I say softly, my fingernails pressing into the cold metal bench.

He looks up at me. "I'm here now. And I don't plan on leaving again."

"Good. Because I haven't skated in years, so I'm really going to need you in about two minutes." We laugh as Dad finishes tying my laces. He helps me up and guides me to the rink.

"Just hold onto me. I'll keep you upright."

"And if I fall?" I ask.

"Then I'll help you get back up."

My throat tightens again and my eyes well up. Dad releases one hand and strokes my face. "I missed you so much, James."

"I missed you too."

"I'm so sorry I screwed up."

I cry, and then Dad cries and we hug each other, crying on the ice in front of hundreds of people. "I screwed up too."

He pulls away slightly, wiping my tears before holding my face in his hands. "You didn't do anything. None of this was your fault."

"No. Not with you," I say, shaking my head, my lower lip quivering so hard it's playing its own beat. "With Axel."

"Oh." He sighs as he brings his hands down. "Well, take it from me. It's not too late. You can fix things with him," Dad says like a dad.

"I don't think that's true," I say. "We're probably beyond help."

"That kid cares deeply for you. Just give it a little time. And while you're giving each other space, use that distance to figure out what it is you both need to move forward."

"You make it sound so easy."

"It is and it isn't. You'll see. One day, it'll just come to you."

"What will?" I ask.

"A plan."

"I think I'm all out of plans," I say, smothering a grin.

"According to what your mother tells me, I find that hard to believe." He chuckles. "Anyway, this one will be different. It won't come from here," he says, pointing to my head. "It'll come from here." He places a hand over his heart. "And that's how you'll know."

"I hope you're right."

"I usually am. When I'm sober." He winks. "Come on. I've got you," he says, wrapping an arm around me. "And this time, I'm not letting go."

I put my trust in my father and allow him to guide me farther into the ice rink. My legs keep wanting to spread away from me, either side to side or front to back, like a baby elephant, but Dad keeps propping me up and saves me from falling. After about half an hour, I'm skating upright, while still holding on tightly to my father's arm. It's kind of magical once I get out of my head to take in the moment. Skating downtown with my dad while music plays in the background, surrounded by people from all walks of life. Somehow, we all started our days apart and ended up at the same place. There's something really beautiful about that.

My therapist, Dr. Mueller, calls this mindfulness. She said staying in the moment and focusing on what is right in front of us, by giving it our full attention, stops our brains from fixating on the future and the what-if scenarios we have no control over.

Maybe Mom's right. Maybe I should meet with Dr. Mueller occasionally to check in and discuss some new ways to manage my anxiety as life ebbs and flows. I can't depend on another person to be the solution. Nor can I rely on lists and plans. And with Dad being back in our lives and trying to heal and move forward, I think talking to a therapist again might help.

Mom is going to be so thrilled when I tell her.

After I request a time-out, Dad uses it as an opportunity to skate laps around me, showing off his skills. He trips on a bump and falls on his butt. We both crack up: one, because when a six-foot-five man falls hard on the ice, the only way to fall is comically;

and two, because I refuse to move from my safe spot on the ice to help him up.

Dad manages to get up and dust the ice shavings off. He leads me around the rink, arm in arm and, shockingly, I finally start to get the hang of it. I nod for Dad to release his grip and I begin skating on my own. Wobbly and slowly, while lacking direction, but still, I'm doing it.

I might not know where I'm headed or what's in front of me, but instead of being terrified of the unknown, right now, in this moment, I'm hopeful.

CHAPTER TWENTY-FOUR

The rest of November speeds by, and December is moving just as quickly. Probably because I've decided to keep myself busy. I've been checking more items off my bucket list by taking myself on dates and sometimes even inviting members of my family to come with me. Not because I need the company, but because I want to share the experience with people I love and care about. That's something I learned from hanging out with Axel. Looking back, I can see now that spending time with him was never about checking items off a list. It was about the memories we made. Together.

Last week, Mom and I went to the Royal Ontario Museum. She told me how she used to go every year on school trips as an art student. She even showed me where she had her first kiss. Surprisingly, it wasn't with Dad. Rather, it was with some guy named Angelo in the Gallery of Ancient Egypt section, right by the bust of Cleopatra VII. They got caught by their teacher and were forced to sit on opposite ends of the bus on the ride back to school. They never spoke again, but he ended up running the grocery store in the small town where we lived when I was growing up, and she had to pretend every week that she didn't know who he was.

Another day, I bundled up and took the streetcar into the city alone. I ended up at Ripley's Aquarium. There weren't any lines and I was able to walk right in. It was such a peaceful experience strolling around at my own leisure with my headphones on, tuning out the world around me. At certain points, it felt like I was underwater and just another sea creature. There was one fish that looked like it had a mop of hair on its head. At first, I laughed because it reminded me of Axel, and then I cried, standing there alone, as the fish with the bad toupee swam away from me.

Tonight, Amo Eli and I are at a hockey game with Dad at Scotiabank Arena. Dad has to explain how hockey works to both Eli and me. Turns out it's a pretty simple sport: puck in net equals goal, but Eli has more questions. Lots of them, like: Why did the play stop? What does "offside" mean? Why did this person just get a penalty? What's a power play?

I can't bring myself to care enough to listen to the long (LONG) explanations.

I'm trying to enjoy the experience of being at a game with my dad and uncle, while simultaneously checking another item off my list, but the arena keeps playing songs that remind me of Axel. Which leads me to checking his Instagram page obsessively. And then his TikTok account. He hasn't posted a new TikTok since we stopped talking. Or a new picture, for that matter. Every time I land on his Insta I hold in a breath, afraid that this will be the moment I notice he's removed the pictures of me and him. But he hasn't yet. It's like I'm playing this cruel game with myself each time I go on there and I don't know why.

Definitely something to bring up with Dr. Mueller at our first appointment next week.

Mom greets us at the door when we return from the game. "You're home earlier than expected," she says as Eli rushes straight for the bathroom. He uncharacteristically drops all his things to the floor. He may have overindulged in nachos and hot dogs.

"You know Eli. He refuses to use public restrooms," I say as I remove my boots.

"Besides, the Leafs were getting destroyed. It's not like we're missing much," Dad says, heaving a defeated sigh.

"It's still early in the season." Mom smiles, trying to give Dad a sliver of hope.

Even though it's late, Mom invites Dad in for coffee. Just as they're about to take their first sip at the kitchen table, Eli's phone rings.

Mom answers. "Hello?" There's silence for a moment as Mom's face scrunches up. Dad glances at me and I shrug. "Let me see how he's feeling."

"What's wrong?" I ask as she rises from the table.

"Shawarma Sitty is slammed with customers and Axel's there alone. He wants to know if Eli can come in."

"What about Peter?" I ask.

"He called in sick," Mom replies, still holding the phone. She leaves the kitchen to check in with Eli. When she returns a moment later, she shakes her head. "I don't think he's coming out of that bathroom for a while."

"I can go," I say, standing.

"I'll come too," Mom says. "There should be an adult there."

Mom brings the phone up to her ear and tells Axel we're on our way.

Dad offers to stick around for Eli. Mom shows Dad where the chamomile tea is and asks him to make it for Eli once he's out of the shower. "I bet he forgot to take his Lactaid today. And on cheat day? He should know better," she says.

In the foyer, Mom places a hand on my arm as we're getting our coats on. "Are you sure you want to go?"

"Yeah. Axel needs us."

"I thought the two of you weren't on speaking terms."

"We're not," I say, looking away.

"Will this be a problem?"

"No." I shake my head. "We'll go in. Help. Then leave."

"Okay," she says, sizing me up as if she's trying to determine how full of it I actually am. "We better get going then."

∿

Axel wasn't kidding. There's a line outside Shawarma Sitty that spills into the parking lot. Apparently, some guy's house party down the block got busted and we're the only food joint still open. Customers give me and Mom side-eye as we cut to the front of the line. Mom forges ahead, straight to the cash register, and I remain frozen, watching Axel try to keep this small operation afloat. He's got his baseball cap on backward, keeping his curls away from his face, a grease-stained apron on, and a look of relief on his adorable face when he sees Mom.

And then it happens. His eyes lock on mine. I swallow, unsure of what to do. He gives me a casual nod and smile. I mirror his actions before heading behind the counter. I tie back my hair, wash my hands, and throw on an apron.

"How can I help?"

"Fill the next order," he says, putting together a takeaway of chicken shawarma and salad.

For the next two hours, Mom takes orders and payments while Axel and I put together the meals. When I notice we're almost out of meat, I make the announcement to the remaining customers and turn the sign on the door to "Closed."

Luckily, we have just enough to serve the last customer a huge chicken shawarma sandwich with poutine. Our Arab ancestors would be proud . . . or perplexed at this weird Arab Canadian fusion meal.

When the last customer walks out it's close to midnight. Mom locks the door before leaning up against it and sighs. "That was a lot," she says. "I better balance the registers. You two clean up."

I glance at Axel quickly, then swallow. "What should I do?"

"Um." He stalls, unable to look me in the eye either. For a while there, we were a smooth duo, pumping out meal after meal. We even exchanged multiple smiles, and Axel sang and moved along with the music once things were under control. But now that it's just us and my mom, it's back to Awkward City.

"I'll clean out front. I'll even do the bathrooms," I say, like a martyr. Or someone who feels guilty. But I'm not sure why.

"Sure." Axel nods, without even tossing a glance my way.

I hate this. I hate that we can't talk to each other anymore. That being around him feels so good but hurts so much. Probably because it does feel so good, but it's fleeting. And it's not real.

He turned to Olivia. He could have gone to anyone else in the world. But he purposefully chose her to hurt me. The annoying thing is, I get why he did it. And I'm no better.

I tune everything out and focus on the tasks at hand. Sweeping. Wiping. Mopping. Scrubbing toilets (ugh). I gather all the trash and go out back to toss it. It's freezing but the sky is clear and a few stars are visible, which is pretty rare. I look up and breathe in and out. I smell like garlic and onions. Or maybe that's the trash bin to my left.

I miss him.

Even though he's right inside this building, I miss him.

Maybe I should tell him, or at least initiate a conversation. Get a dialogue going. It used to be so easy to talk to him and now it's like I'm afraid to do or say the wrong thing. The last few times we've been around each other, our words get twisted up in our raw emotions and everything gets messier. The truth is, we've both hurt one another. Intentional or not, pain was inflicted and the trust between us has been compromised.

I come back in from outside to grab the last bag. The music is off and Mom and Axel are engaged in conversation. I stay hidden in the bathroom hallway, listening. I can't help it. I'm thirsty for intel. For insight. Maybe a lead on how I can fix things. If we're fixable at all.

"It's fine," Axel says to Mom. "I sometimes come off a bit too strong when meeting people."

"It's not that," Mom replies. "I judged you for all the wrong reasons. For being a male. An Arab male. For being confident. For embracing who you are and where you come from. It scared me."

"Why?" he asks.

"Because you're everything I'm not. I didn't grow up feeling proud of who I was or where I came from. And I kept my Arab side from Jamie, denying her an opportunity to learn about her culture and roots. Then here you come, showing her how great it can be to be part of a loving Arab family. I knew she'd call me out, and I needed to be called out, but I was afraid of that moment happening. I'd been afraid for years. Because I think deep down, I knew I was wrong. Adults . . . we're just adolescents with a few more wrinkles and bad knees."

Axel laughs. "I get it. I wasn't always so confident. I'm *not* always so confident. But I learned to be proud of my culture from an early age. My dad taught me not to try to hide anything about myself because people would see it as a weakness and prey on it. So instead, I'm loud and proud and sometimes . . . obnoxious. It kind of backfired on my dad though. He wasn't really into my passion for dancing at first."

"And now?" Mom asks.

"Jamie helped him see how important it is to me. Figures, I finally get my dad on my side and I've lost my drive to dance or perform."

"Why's that?" Silence follows Mom's question. When Axel still doesn't answer, Mom presses on. "What happened with you and Jamie?"

"We're not right for each other. We're too different. She wants something safe and quiet and I want to be with someone who will shout their feelings about me to the world. Take risks. Put down the lists. And that's not Jamie."

I lean up against the hallway wall and squeeze my eyes shut. I thought maybe we had just misunderstood each other. I didn't realize there was more to it.

"Differences aren't all that bad, Axel. Jamie thinks she wants something safe, but at the end of the day, none of us knows what we really want. We just know how we feel. And when I see my daughter around you, I can tell."

"You can tell what?" he asks.

I grab the last bag of garbage and toss it in the bin before slamming the door shut behind me. I can't bear to hear them talk about me for another second. It's too weird.

"All done," I say, coming out of the hall all nonchalant-like a few minutes later.

"We're all done in here too," Mom says, smothering a grin. "Do you need a ride home, Axel?"

"No, thank you." He removes his apron. "I rode my bike."

"You fixed Betty?" I ask.

"Yeah." He nods. "She's as good as new."

"I'm glad," I say, nodding back.

"Same. Was worried she wouldn't recover," he says before swallowing.

"I didn't think I took her to the point of no return." I fight the smile that wants to come out.

"Not quite. But almost."

Mom clears her throat as she stands by the front door. "It's late, kids. We should head out." She pushes open the door, making a beeline for her car, leaving me and Axel behind.

"Hey, Axel," I say, feigning bravery by allowing myself to stare deep into his eyes. My heart rate immediately quickens.

"Yeah?" he asks, hope sparking in his voice.

"I know we've both done things to hurt each other, things we can't take back, but when we walked the halls at school hand in hand, I was proud to be by your side. When we danced at your cousin's wedding, I was proud to be your date. I've always been proud of you and proud to be with you. I just wanted you to know that."

"Okay," Axel replies. He doesn't smile. He doesn't say anything else. He just nods repeatedly and readjusts his baseball cap.

"Okay?" I repeat. "That's it? Axel, I like you. A lot. So much it scares me. The way I feel about you . . . it's unlike anything else I've experienced."

"I don't know what you want me to say, Jamie. If it makes you feel better to tell me those things, then fine. But I'm not just some item you can cross off your list. I fell hard for you. I even . . ." He pauses and shakes his head. "Here's the thing about telling someone you love them: there's only one way to say it, but there's a million ways to show it. And you, Jamie Taher-Foster, have a funny way of showing your feelings."

Axel opens the door and I follow him out. I watch as he locks up, waiting, hoping he'll say something else, but all he does is get on his bike and ride away, without looking back.

Maybe we aren't fixable after all.

CHAPTER TWENTY-FIVE

For so long, all I wanted was my dad back in my life. And now he is.

For the last few years, my relationship with Mom has been super strained, to the point where there were times, especially lately, when I didn't think there was any hope left for us. And now, we're slowly building to something that feels nice and comfortable.

When Ben dumped me, the only thing I wanted was to get him back in time for winter formal. And then I did. Except I didn't want it anymore. Because I don't want Ben. I don't want the life we planned out together. I don't want any of it.

So here I am, seemingly with everything I thought I wanted, and somehow the dopamine rush I expected got lost in the mail.

I've tried to focus on being independent, and sure, that's been good for me. But it's not enough. On some level, I've always been pretty independent. I'm an only child. We don't have relationships with much of our extended family. I've never had a big group of friends. So I'm well-versed in what it's like to be alone, and I've been okay with it most of my life.

Checking some items off my bucket list by myself was a good reminder that I could spend time alone and enjoy it, but it also showed me that sharing experiences with someone by my side was just as great.

I want a partner. A best friend. Someone who makes me laugh. Someone who makes me think. Someone who challenges me to step outside my bubble and live in the moment.

I had this person.

Someone who was all those things and more. And I let him go.

But Axel made mistakes too.

"What's on tap today?" Eli asks from the kitchen sink. He's wearing bright yellow rubber gloves while scrubbing the soap dispenser clean.

"Not cleaning cleaning products," I say, waiting for my uncle to shoot me one of his unimpressed looks.

He pauses and looks down at what he's doing. "I deserve that. Anyway, I thought you turned a new leaf," he says, looking back at me. "With the clean room and all."

"Oh, yeah," I say, bringing a spoonful of cereal to my mouth. "It's not that clean anymore."

"Good." He shuts off the water and peels off his gloves.

"Good?" I ask, setting down my spoon.

"Yeah, good. I found the whole thing kind of... disconcerting."

"You found my having a clean room disconcerting?"

He pulls out a chair and sits across from me. "Are we just going to continue repeating each other or will we actually move toward having a real conversation at some point?"

"A real conversation about what?" Mom asks, entering the kitchen. Amo Eli and I both bang our heads down on the table. "What did I interrupt?"

"Nothing," I say, sitting up. "Nothing at all."

"I was just asking Jamie what she had planned today. What are the remaining items on your bucket list?"

"Just one item left," I say, "and it will probably remain unchecked forever."

"Which one?" Mom asks.

"The CN Tower."

"Isn't your formal being held there next weekend?" Eli asks, studying the soggy bowl of cereal in front of me. His face scrunches up in disgust as I ingest another spoonful of it.

"Yep. But I'm not going."

"You're not going?" Mom asks. And we're back to the echoes.

"I know you want me to be independent, and I get that, but I also really don't want to go to the winter formal alone."

"That might be for the best," Eli says, straightening the napkins. "Since Axel will be there."

"He will?" Axel is in eleventh grade, so the only reason he'd be at the formal is if he were someone else's date. Probably Olivia's. Maybe that's why he was so cold to me at Shawarma Sitty. Why he barely responded when I stood there opening my heart up to him.

And just like that, I've lost my appetite. "I've got to go," I say, pushing out my chair and rising.

"Where to?" Mom asks, looking up at me.

"I . . . I don't know. Out." I bring my bowl and glass to the sink.

"Will you be back for dinner?" Mom asks, glancing between me and Eli.

"I think so."

"Okay good." She nods.

"Why? Is Dad coming over again?"

"No. But we are having guests."

"Who?" I ask. *Please don't say it's Ben and his parents.*

Mom swallows before stealing another glance at Eli. He reaches across the table and squeezes her arm. The room is quiet as they continue to exchange glances. "Your grandparents are coming over for dinner."

"My grandparents, as in, your parents?" I ask, standing frozen by the sink. They both nod. "Since when?"

"Seeing you and your father rebuild your relationship inspired me to reach out. So did Eli's constant nagging." She smiles and her eyes crinkle. "I don't want to pressure you or anything, but I'm sure they'd love it if . . ."

"I'll be there. I can't wait," I say, hugging my mom, then my uncle. "I'm proud of you two. You're finally growing up."

They laugh before taking turns pinching my cheeks.

"Make sure to be back by six," Mom says.

"Will do."

If Mom in all her stubborn glory can take the big step of reaching out to her parents after years of silence, then I can cross the finish line on my bucket list by checking off the final item: riding the elevator up the CN Tower at the winter formal.

If I'm going to the formal, I need a dress. A really great dress that will make me feel super confident. Maybe then I won't care so much about seeing Axel and Olivia there together. And if I focus instead on all the things I need to do in order to get to the formal, I'll spend less time freaking out about the other big thing I need to do . . . or ride.

Look at me, practicing mindfulness. Both Mom and Dr. Mueller would be so proud.

First stop: the Eaton Centre. If I can't find a dress there, then I'm more hopeless than I thought. I take the streetcar downtown, trying in earnest to stop thinking about Axel. I imagine him giving Olivia a corsage. Riding in Olivia's BMW to the formal. Holding her hand in the elevator. Dancing with Olivia all night while everyone takes pictures of them.

Even though thinking of Axel with another girl hurts more than words can express, I don't regret letting him into my life. I'll take the pain of losing Axel over never having known him.

I walk into the first store. It's loud. And bright. This is when having a friend who is into fashion would help. Or a friend at all. I don't even know what's "in" or "out," or if we've all just given up on the rules of fashion and see it more as a construct, choosing to wear what we want. Or maybe that's wishful thinking, since I have zero personal style.

I must be really pathetic, because none of the salespeople will even look at me. I'll just grab a few dresses off the rack and try them on. It's not rocket science. But it kind of feels like it is.

If I were to describe Axel's style, I'd call it loud (and sometimes kind of hot). Ben is definitely preppy (with a side of asshole). Olivia, hmm. What *is* Olivia's style? I know! Princess Insta-Ho...ly shit. *Olivia.* She's here because of course she is. And I can't exactly hide. My arms full of bright dresses attached to my five-foot-ten frame make that kind of hard to do.

"Jamie?" she says, turning from the mirror. She's standing on a round pedestal and her eyes move up and down my body, stopping at my arms. She stifles a laugh. "That's a lot of dresses."

"I haven't decided what look I'm going for," I say, feigning confidence. What I really want to say is, *I don't know what the hell I'm doing and you look perfect standing there in that tight, baby-blue dress.* Another image of Axel and Olivia together at the formal flashes before my eyes, and my stomach sinks.

A salesperson grabs the dresses from my arms and counts them before hanging them up inside a changeroom. I wince every time I hear the plastic hanger clang against the metal hook.

I stuff myself inside the changeroom once they're done and pull the curtain closed. Maybe if I wait here long enough, Olivia will be gone by the time I come out and I can just forget all about this stupid idea. Feeling the nerves starting to take over, I sit and practice my breathing exercises, but the changeroom starts to close in on me. The wall span is so narrow and the dresses hung on the two hooks to both my left and right feel as if they're going to suffocate me. Why do they make the lights so bright? Why is it so hot in here? I stand quickly and rip open the curtain. I bend over, hands on my knees, trying to breathe.

Olivia steps off the pedestal, eyes wide. "Jamie." She approaches me slowly, bending to meet my eyes. "Are you okay?"

I shake my head.

Olivia leads me to a chair and sits next to me, taking my hand in hers. "Breathe, okay? It's all good. Just breathe."

I nod and try to follow her lead, breathing in and out as my free hand runs up and down my thigh. In . . . and . . . out. A salesperson comes to the back and before they can speak, Olivia demands they bring me water. A moment later, Olivia is twisting off the cap on the bottle delivered by the nervous salesperson and lifting it to my mouth. I take a sip of the lukewarm water.

"See? If the water goes in, that means the air can come out. You're fine," she reassures me.

She strokes my back, and my breathing begins to return to its normal rhythm. I open my eyes, my cheeks completely flushed as I realize what just happened. Olivia Chen witnessed me having a full-blown panic attack.

"Feeling better?" she asks, her big brown eyes on me.

"Yeah. Thanks," I say, wiping away the tears. "How did you know what to do?"

She smiles as she takes the bottle of water from my shaky hand. "My mom suffers from pretty debilitating panic attacks. She got into a bad car accident when I was a baby. I was in the car with her and got trapped in my car seat. It took a while for the rescue team to release me. It was pretty traumatic obviously. She'll be fine for months and then out of nowhere something will trigger the memory and it's like the entire world stops spinning."

"I'm sorry. That must be really scary."

She offers me a kind smile, but then it falls. "Did *I* trigger this panic attack?"

I shake my head. "Not entirely. I just... I've made such a mess out of things, and I came here thinking if I found a dress that I felt good in, then maybe I could go to the formal, but then I saw you looking perfect and I got into the changeroom and just got hot and overwhelmed and..."

"Hey. It's fine. Let me help you."

"You already did," I remind her.

"No." She smiles. "With finding a dress. I'm good at shopping. It's my special talent." She laughs. "So... you needing a dress for the formal." Olivia pauses, tucking a piece of hair behind her ear. "Does that mean you're going with Ben?"

"*If* I go to the formal, I'll be going alone." I exhale and lift my head to meet Olivia's gaze. "It's completely over with Ben. *I'm completely over Ben.*"

"Wish I could say the same thing," she says, placing my water bottle on the empty chair next to her.

"So then you and Axel aren't...?"

"Axel?" She lets out a soft laugh. "No. Axel and I are nothing. He did apologize, though, for using me. But I guess we were both using each other to get back at you and Ben. People act in strange ways when they're hurting."

"I guess it didn't help that Ben and I made it look like we were back together."

She offers me a small smile. "I don't blame you for putting up walls around me. I'd do the same if I were in your place. But I'm not who you think I am. I'm just a girl who connected with a guy who happened to already have a girlfriend. For what it's worth,

Ben was honest with me from the beginning about you. We tried to keep our distance, but it wasn't easy since we worked side by side." She sighs and looks down before her eyes lock with mine. "Did you mean it when you said you and Ben hadn't done anything after he and I broke up?"

"We didn't even kiss. I didn't want to."

"But he tried?" she asks.

I bite down on my lip before exhaling a breath. "Ben probably believed if we got back together it would somehow erase all the pain he'd caused me and maybe also help him forget about you. But if we had kissed, he would have realized right away that our story is over. It's been over. I just wish he hadn't lied to me about what happened between you two at camp."

Olivia nods. Her eyes meet with mine in a sincere way. "It was a moment of weakness, for both of us, and after it happened, he felt really bad. So did I."

"Not bad enough to be honest with me about it," I say.

"I think he thought he was protecting you. And maybe part of him was in denial and ashamed that *he* of all people let that happen. I love him, but he can be pretty dense."

"You love him?" I never really considered if Olivia's feelings for Ben were real, and that's probably because I never really considered Olivia's feelings. Like, at all.

"Unfortunately, yes," she deadpans. "And for what it's worth, I'm really sorry I kissed him while he was still your boyfriend. It was wrong. No excuses."

"I appreciate that. So," I say, breathing out a sigh, "are you going to the formal alone?"

"Unfortunately, yes," she says again, looking down at the floor.

"I see no reason why you should. If you love Ben, you should tell him. He was furious when he saw you with Axel. He wouldn't have acted that way if he stopped caring about you." She shrugs as a small smile sneaks onto her face. "Wait," I say. "My uncle told me Axel was going to the formal. If he's not going with you then who's he going with?"

"As far as I know, he's not going with anyone. He's performing."

"Performing?"

"Yeah. The social committee asked if he'd kick off the formal by doing a few dances. Do you, like, pay any attention at all to what's going on outside the classroom?"

I shake my head. "No."

Olivia laughs and it makes me laugh a bit in return. "Do you want my help?" she asks, her eyes on the dresses hanging in the changeroom behind me.

"Maybe," I say, sucking in my cheeks.

"Okay. Let me change back into my clothes and we'll find you something that'll wow Axel." She pauses. "That's what you want, right? To get him back?"

"I don't know what I want, to be honest."

"I'll tell you a secret," she says, her lips curved upward. "Most of us don't. We fake it. And half of faking it successfully is looking the part. Speaking of looking the part," she begins. "Were you and Axel really just fake-dating?"

"At first. But then..."

"You caught feels?" She smiles.

I nod. "I caught feels."

"Do you love him?" she asks.

I think about her question.

"You don't have to answer me. Let's start with finding you a dress, and maybe after some forced time together, you'll see that I'm really not so bad."

"Thanks," I respond, and because I'm nervous and need to say something to fill the silence, I go on. "Did you know *Webster's Dictionary* has ten different definitions for 'bad' as an adjective, and the tenth includes the slang version? It dates back to the nineteenth century, and no, I don't mean the 1900s and Michael Jackson's *Bad* album, because first of all the nineteenth century began January 1, 1801, I mean . . ."

"Jamie." Olivia cuts me off. "You're rambling."

"My bad," I say. After a moment of silence, we both break into laughter.

"Wait here," she says. "I'll be right back. Just going to change."

I check my phone. No messages from anyone. "Hey, Olivia?" I call from my seat outside her changeroom. "Do you have any fears?"

"Sure. Who doesn't?"

"I'm claustrophobic," I say. "Mostly when it comes to elevators. And the thing is, I'm not sure if I can actually attend the formal because of the elevator ride up the CN Tower."

Olivia slides open the curtain and appears in front of me in her street clothes, holding onto her dress. A salesperson approaches as if out of nowhere and takes it from her, saying they'll hold it at the cash register. Clearly, we're not all treated as equals in the world of retail.

"It's a one-minute ride," she says with a casual shrug.

"But what if we get stuck? Like, halfway up? How do you get out? Will it take hours to get rescued? And what if it's crowded and hard to breathe? What if I have to pee?" *Or worse.*

"A meteor could hit Earth right now and wipe us all out."

I squint my eyes at her. "What's your point?"

"Isn't it obvious?" She lifts her shoulders, and I respond with a slight head shake. "Stop asking yourself what if something bad happens because . . . what if something great happens? Not to mention, it feels pretty kick-ass when you face a fear. There's no better elevator to challenge your claustrophobia in than the one at the CN Tower. And all it takes is sixty seconds. In sixty seconds, your life could change—for the better!"

"You're right," I say, thinking about how many times in these last few months my life has changed in sixty seconds or less. Usually when I was least expecting it. I know there's no cure for anxiety, but sometimes I get so frustrated by how unpredictable it is. I've been trying to practice mindfulness. I do my breathing exercises. I journal. I'm seeing my therapist again. And still, the panic attacks can come out of nowhere and the catastrophic thinking rears its head at the worst times, often resulting in painful stomachaches. Dr. Mueller tells me to be patient with myself, and that it is possible for me to live a full, balanced life.

"Ready?" Olivia asks.

I take in a deep breath and let it out slowly before standing. Olivia reviews my choices and shakes her head at the dresses I haphazardly selected. She walks back into the store and examines the options. Moments later, she's smiling as she shows me the dress in her hands.

"This," she says, holding it out, "is the dress."

The gold sequined dress in Olivia's hands is beautiful. A surefire knockout, but I'm not as confident I can pull it off as she seems to be. "It looks expensive."

"It's half off. Under a hundred bucks. You can't go wrong. Just try it on," she says, handing it to me.

I take the dress and force a smile. Behind the curtain, I begin to undress. As I'm slipping it on, it occurs to me that I am not wearing the right kind of bra for this neckline. "Um, Olivia. I don't have on the right undergarments."

She laughs. "You're seventeen. Go braless."

"I will not," I say.

"Just do it now so we can see how it fits. If you need chicken cutlets, we'll buy some."

I have no idea what she's talking about but I follow her orders and remove my bra. "I need help," I say, backing out of the changeroom, my hands cupping my chest. Olivia zips me in and then forces me to turn around.

"Do I have taste or do I have taste?" she says, nodding approvingly. "See for yourself."

I step onto the pedestal and face the mirror. The crisscross straps and pleated skirt look perfect for dancing in all night, but it's not quite me. As I try to find a way to break it to Olivia, a familiar song comes out over the speakers. It's the Dua Lipa song Axel played in my room when he tried to teach me how to dance. The memory brings a smile to my face.

"Thinking about Axel?" Olivia asks. "And how he'll twirl you around in that fierce dress? To be honest, I don't know why I'm encouraging you to buy it. I think I'm in love with it myself."

As Olivia goes on about cut and fit, I focus my attention on the lyrics of the song and they make me laugh. And smile again. They also make me want to dance. Right here. In front of Olivia and everyone else. Something I never thought I'd be able to do or want to do. But Axel changed all that.

He changed so many things. He showed me the world through his eyes. He taught me to stop taking myself so seriously. He encouraged me to embrace who I am and dared me to take risks. And he showed me how to love again.

Axel made me feel like I was the main character in his life.

For a time, he was mine.

I love him.

I love Axel Dahini.

And I know exactly how I'm going to show him. Because words aren't enough.

"Then you buy it," I say, nodding enthusiastically. "I'm going to need something shorter. And easier to move in. Also something I can wear with a normal bra."

"What? Why?"

"I'll tell you over hot chocolate. But first, get me something short, that'll work with Converse sneakers," I say as I step off the pedestal.

"Okay," she says, eyeing me up and down. "Whatever you say. You don't mind if I try that on, do you? In my size of course. Not all of us were born with legs up to our necks."

"Go ahead. And thanks," I say. "Not for the leg compliment—I have nothing to do with my genetics—but for helping."

"Confession," she says, her cheeks pink and rosy. "I texted Ben when you were changing. You were right. He still loves me. Never stopped. We're going to the formal together."

"Hashtag-bolivia lives to see another day," I say with a grin.

"It's so terrible, isn't it?" She laughs.

"The worst."

Olivia helps me find a perfect dress for winter formal: a long-sleeve crushed velvet mini. I charge it to my credit card, which I only use in case of emergencies, but this feels like an emergency. Afterward, I treat her to hot chocolate while telling her about my big plan, and I can't tell who's more excited about it—me, or her. She even has a few ideas of her own.

I love a good plan, but sometimes going off-script can result in pleasant surprises and, dare I say, new friendships?

Or at the very least, one less nemesis.

CHAPTER TWENTY-SIX

After our hot chocolates, Olivia drives me home from the mall. It's surreal being inside the car that has become synonymous with someone I thought I had strong feelings of dislike for.

"Oh no," she says as she drives onto Ben's driveway and parks. "I wasn't thinking and drove to Ben's before dropping you off. I'll take you home," she says, her hand on the gear shift.

"It's okay," I say, glancing at Axel's house. "I can walk from here. It's not that cold today."

"You sure?"

I nod and toss her a genuine smile. "Yeah. I appreciate the help with the dress and the ride and bouncing ideas around with me and . . . the other thing."

"My pleasure. And see?" she says, grinning. "It pays to have friends in high places. Or at least the social committee." The word *friend* hangs in the air between us like my uncle's scent after he returns home from a shift at Shawarma Sitty in July. "I mean, acquaintance. If friends is too strong a word?" Olivia asks with hesitation.

"Actually," I say, sitting up. "The word 'friend' has multiple meanings. There's the obvious definition: a person you like who you enjoy being with. Or a person who helps or supports you in a cause. And then there's 'Friend,' capital F. A member of a Christian sect that stresses Inner Light and rejects sacraments and opposes war. Also known as a Quaker."

Olivia scrunches up her perfect brows before basically snorting. "Maybe just the first two?" she says.

"You enjoy spending time with me?" I ask.

"So far," she replies. "I was kind of threatened by you when I was with Ben. I think it's because I only saw how different we were and figured if he spent three years with you, then he'd learn quickly I wasn't the right fit for him."

"I was kind of hoping that too for a time," I say, feeling a blush rise.

She laughs again. "I like how honest you are. And yeah, I think we do qualify as friends. At least two of three definitions. I'm Catholic," she says, a smile tugging at her lips.

"Then it's settled. We're friends." I nod. "I guess I'll DM you when I hear back from the others?"

"Give me your phone," she says, and I oblige by placing it in her manicured hand. She adds her number and name under Contacts and then sends a text from my phone to hers. "There. Now we're in each other's phones."

"Is this today's equivalent to blood brothers . . . or shall I say sisters?"

"You have an interesting way of seeing things, you know that?" she asks as we get out of her car.

"Yes. It's why you're my only friend." Olivia snorts and I snort back in solidarity as I head down Ben's driveway.

"Good luck. I know they'll say yes," she hollers from Ben's porch.

"Thanks." I put down my bag and pull out my phone, implementing part two of my plan to get Axel back. I always feel creepy sliding into people's DMs, but it's all for the greater good.

"Jamie?" Ben calls from behind just as I finish typing my message. I hit Send and turn around. Ben jogs over to meet me at the end of his driveway, Olivia already inside.

"What's up?" I ask. "Oh my god. You finally cut your hair."

He blushes as he runs his fingers over his short tresses.

"Yeah. I did it as an act of protest after everything blew up." His eyes find mine, and with his hair short again, he looks like the old Ben. But he doesn't feel like him. "You really didn't like the longer hair?" he asks, squinting at me.

"On you, short is better. In my opinion. Which," I chuckle, "clearly bears no weight anymore." An awkward silence stretches between us as we struggle to make eye contact. "I . . . I didn't mean that in a snarky way. Just that I've finally accepted that it's over between us."

He nods, tucking his hands into his pockets, and I can't quite read his eyes. Are they relieved? A little sad? Maybe both? "Hey, we had a pretty good run."

"We did," I say.

He opens his mouth to say something and closes it about three times before the words finally come out. "I should have been upfront with you from the start. Instead of telling you about my growing feelings for Olivia, I spent more time with her behind your back hoping it was just a small crush and that by the time summer was over, I'd be over her. But then I slipped up. That's not who I am," he says, his eyebrows in a sad little frown. "I'm not someone who cheats. Or at least, I wasn't. And I think the reason I didn't want you to find out is because then it would be like admitting that yeah, I am that guy."

"I'm more upset that you lied to me about it than anything," I tell him. "You made me feel like I was making it all up in my head, but I couldn't ignore my gut. It also made me doubt everything else. Our whole relationship. And that's kind of a crappy feeling, you know? To think that our time together wasn't real."

He shakes his head. "The three years we spent together were great. Amazing." It's quiet again. I don't really know what to say back to that, so I just look at Ben and nod. "I really did love you, Jamie. You were my first love. My first kiss. I didn't set out to be with Olivia. She's so different but it just . . ."

"Happened. Believe me, I get it." We both smile, then look away. "So you guys are back together?"

His eyes shine. "Yeah. Wait, is that hard for you to hear? I can stop talking about it."

"No. It's fine. Olivia's not that bad," I say, scraping my shoe against the curb. "In fact, she's pretty great."

"Is that your seal of approval?"

"Does it matter what I think?" I ask.

"Yeah. It does. You're the smartest person I know."

I poke his chest. "And don't you forget it."

Ben drags a foot over the ground before looking up at me. "Even if we'd never met Olivia or Axel, I think eventually we would have broken up. I saw you with Axel, Jamie. You legit looked lit from within when you were together. I couldn't give you that."

My throat starts to constrict, but I swallow down the burn. "I think I might be ready to try being friends with you."

"Honestly, nothing would make me happier. Can we . . . hug it out?" he asks, eyebrows raised in hope.

"Sure. We can hug it out."

Ben and I exchange our first hug in months and it feels good, but different. Kind of like putting on an old comfortable sweater I like but would never wear in public.

We release one another, each taking a tentative step back. "I guess I'll head back inside so you can go see Axel. Your 'fake' boyfriend," he says teasingly.

I want to retort that I have no plans to see Axel but that would be a lie, so I just say thanks before picking up my things and continuing on my way. I don't even know why I'm walking to Axel's house. It's not like I have anything to say. I just want to see him. Maybe I'm hoping that will be enough and then I won't have to follow through on this plan that could potentially blow up in my face and ruin me socially.

No big deal.

I walk up the steps to his front door and take in a deep breath before knocking. The door opens a few seconds later. Axel stands in the doorway dressed in a blue hoodie and gray sweats. He looks so warm and cozy. I imagine an alternate timeline where I'm here to watch a movie but instead all we do is make out. The most heartbreaking thing about this fantasy is it could have been true if I hadn't gone and screwed it all up with my fiery temper and predisposed inclination to be a stubborn ass.

"Hey," I say. "I was just in the neighborhood." God. Is that the best I could come up with?

"Visiting Ben?"

"Ben? No." I shake my head. "That's long over."

"Then why did I see the two of you hugging on his driveway a few minutes ago?"

Okay, this is not off to a good start. "We were making up," I say, the words coming out quickly. "But as friends. He and Olivia are back on."

Axel doesn't respond.

"No seriously," I say, nodding with wide eyes. "They're going to the formal together. Which, by the way, I hear you're performing at."

Axel sighs and runs a hand through his curls. "The social committee begged me to. I eventually caved, but to be honest, I'm not really feeling it."

"I've noticed you haven't posted any new TikToks lately," I say, trying to keep my shaky hands still.

He shrugs, looking past my shoulder. "Haven't felt inspired to."

"Maybe you can talk Finn and Diesel into performing with you at the formal. It might help to have some friends on stage."

"That's actually not a bad idea," he says with an approving nod, warming up ever so slightly. "So, will you be there?"

I look down at the shopping bag in my hand and slide it out of view. "I haven't decided. I don't have a date and, well, the venue itself leaves much to be desired."

When the silence between us drags on, I take a step closer and go on. "I really liked you, Axel."

"Yeah. I really liked you too."

"I guess I need to make this clearer." I put my bag down and take a deep breath, letting it out slowly. "I think I was falling in love with you and it scared me. I'd been down that road before and it ended in heartache. It always seems to end in heartache when I open myself up to someone. When you orchestrated that reunion with my father, I felt blindsided, like I did when Ben dumped me. I know it's not the same but it's how I felt, and the way I reacted was wrong. I think I was just trying to protect myself."

"Okay," Axel says, nodding.

"And when I thought you and Olivia were getting close it felt like the ultimate betrayal."

"It's not what you think," he replies.

"I know. I spoke with Olivia. She explained everything."

"Huh," Axel says, taking a step back. "You listened to Olivia, but you wouldn't listen to me when I tried to explain?"

"I was too angry and hurt to hear you. It's one of my worst habits. Letting my emotions override clear thinking. I say and do things I shouldn't. And I'm sorry. I'm really trying to work on it."

"Do you know what it's like to always feel as if I come in last place with you?"

I scratch at my temple, then rake my fingers through my hair. "What do you mean?"

"Whenever we were together it was about how much you hated your mom and Olivia. How annoying your uncle was. How much you missed Ben, and your dad. I was never a priority, Jamie. Even worse, you felt the need to remind me time and time again that we were just a business arrangement, constantly dangling the contract in front of me. And just now, you took the time to listen to your sworn enemy over someone you claim to be falling in love with. I've never been enough for you."

"No. You've got it all wrong, Axel."

"And now you're invalidating my feelings. When we were together, fake or not, I tried to bring you into my life by introducing you to my family and my friends. I put you above everyone else. And you couldn't do the same for me. Not even a little. Relationships are supposed to be give and take. The truth is, we were never balanced. I always liked you more than you liked me."

"That's not true. I was just afraid."

"Of what?"

Of letting you in. Of facing heartbreak again. Of experiencing the greatest love. A love I never thought I would get to experience. A love I didn't think I deserved. I don't say the words out loud because I don't want to make this about me. It's about us. Why can't we get it right?

"I understand why you felt the way you did. *Do.* I'm not discounting that," I say. "But you're all I think about now. I miss you. I want to be with you." I take a step toward him, breathing in his scent, wanting so badly for him to hold my hands. "I love . . ."

"No." He shakes his head. "Don't say it. Don't say it if you don't mean it."

My phone buzzes in my back pocket. I grab it to a see a message from Mom asking where I am. "I have to go," I say, hearing the defeat in my voice. "My grandparents are over for dinner. For the first time ever."

"That's great," Axel says, his smile small and reserved.

"If I don't get to see you perform next weekend, break a leg. I'm sure you'll be great. You always are when you're doing what you love."

"Thanks," he says, his eyes meeting with mine briefly.

"Take care, Axel," I say before picking up my bag and turning to leave.

"You can keep your books."

I turn back. "My books?"

"Yeah." He grins. "Marty McFly doesn't need them."

My mouth falls open as I process this reveal. "It was you?" I ask.

He raises his shoulders slightly. "I didn't like the idea of you selling your books just so you could pay me back. They mean too much to you."

"Thank you," I say.

"You're welcome." Our eyes meet and I wait for Axel to say something else. When he doesn't, I turn back around to leave.

"Later, James."

I pause at the end of his porch, warmth spreading through me as a secret smile dances on my lips.

Maybe we aren't completely broken.

"So?" I ask Mom. We're at the kitchen sink. She's washing, I'm drying. "How do you feel?"

"So?" Eli asks, coming into the kitchen, carrying dirty espresso cups. "How do you feel?"

"I think it went well," I say, nodding at my uncle.

"I think so too," he says, placing the cups in the sink.

"Are either of you going to give me a chance to answer?" Mom asks, turning off the water. "I think it went well."

We all laugh, and I return to drying dishes as Mom and Eli each pull up a seat at the table.

"They seemed really proud of you. And," I say, looking back at Eli, "they even asked about Eric. That was nice."

"And surprising," Eli says, raising his brows.

"Very. Maybe they've grown more liberal in their old age," Mom replies.

"Or maybe," I say, putting away the last dish, "they've come to realize life is too short to spend it being angry at people just because they decide to live their life in a way that you might not understand. A lesson for all of us," I say, looking at them smugly as I join them at the table. "I'm glad you came around. Because even if you hadn't, I'd planned to reach out. They're my family, too, and I deserve a chance to get to know them and where I come from."

Mom nods and reaches across the table for my hand. "You're right."

"Maybe I should create a Teta and Sedo bucket list and add a bunch of things we can do together. Did you know your mom is the one who made the Palestinian tapestries that hang in their home? It's called tatreez. And no, I don't have a homograph for that word."

"I knew that," Amo Eli says. "Maybe Mom can do a lesson for all of us when we visit on Christmas Eve."

Mom's eyes grow glossy as she swallows repeatedly. "I can't believe how many Christmas Eve dinners we've missed with them," she says, shaking her head. "I regret so many of the decisions I've made. It's kind of embarrassing how much and how often I've screwed up our lives."

"You did what you thought you had to," I reply with a shrug. "I'm guilty of the same. Besides, you didn't turn Dad into an alcoholic. As for Teta and Sedo, let's just be happy that they're still here and we have time to get to know each other—again and for the first time. Don't be too hard on yourself," I say, looking at Mom, who is now blinking back tears. "You brought us to Amo's. You weren't too stubborn to ask for help when you needed it. And Amo, you helped us both rebuild. Even if I don't always show it, I love living here."

"Aww." Amo Eli brings a hand to his heart and tilts his head. "And I love having you spicy gals here. Even though one of you leaves hair clippings everywhere she goes and the other one's room looks like a tsunami rolled through, having you both here has forced me to stop being such a lone wolf and embrace the chaos. If I hadn't, I never would have agreed to go on that first date with Eric. I needed an excuse to leave this estrogen-filled home."

"Ooooooh, Eric," Mom and I say in unison.

"Oh, shut up or I'll start making you pay rent!"

"Okay, okay." Mom laughs. "I do have a serious question, though. For Jamie. How would you feel about inviting Dad over here for Christmas dinner?"

Amo Eli and I lock eyes in surprise.

"Go for it," I say. "May as well invite the Camerons while you're at it. Eric, too, of course."

"The Camerons?" Mom asks.

"I thought Benjamin was canceled," Amo Eli says.

"He was. Now he isn't. We're going to try to do the friend thing."

"Look at the two of you ladies," Eli says. "Continuing to evolve. I didn't think it was possible, seeing how hard-headed you both are."

"Hey, Mom," I say, raising a brow. "It's been a while since Amo had his hair cut. Why don't you grab your scissors while I hold him down?"

"Who needs hairdressing scissors. I'll just use the kitchen shears."

Amo Eli pushes back his chair and jolts up, stretching his arms out in defense. "Don't you dare. You know I only trust Alejandro."

"Okay, now you're definitely in for it," I say.

"You've been seeing Alejandro behind my back?" Mom asks, pretending to be offended.

Amo Eli runs out of the room and Mom chases after him. Just as I'm about to follow and see which geriatric millennial wins the battle, my phone lights up.

I pick it up to see a response from both Finn and Diesel. We're in.

I bite down on my lip, heart racing, blood rushing—but in a good way. Guess there's no turning back now.

CHAPTER TWENTY-SEVEN

Six days until the winter formal and I've set a goal so high, it rivals the CN Tower. But Axel needs me to show how much I love him. Words are not enough. So that's why I'm here, waiting outside my dad's work for Finn and Diesel to arrive.

A TTC bus pulls up to the stop in front of Kit's Karaoke Dive and I wait with bated breath for Axel's two best friends to come out. It was bold of me to reach out to them after having met them only the one time, but I needed to go big, and I needed them on my team. They step off the bus and nod when they see me waiting out front.

"Hey," I say, smothering a nervous grin. The last time we were here together it ended terribly. Who knows what Axel has said to them about me or what they think themselves based on the horrible first impression I made.

"What up?" Diesel asks, hands tucked into their pockets.

"It's cold," I say. "Let's go in."

Finn tosses me a polite but strained smile before nodding.

We step inside the club. It's empty, except for my dad, who's sitting at a table balancing the books. Kit's doesn't open until after five on Sundays.

"Hey, Dad. We're all here now."

He looks up from the table and nods a hello to Finn and Diesel. "Feel free to use the stage or whatever else you need."

I clear my throat and approach my father at the table as Finn and Diesel check out the stereo system. "Is there, like, an office in the back where you can work?"

He laughs. "Why?"

"Because." I sigh and try to still my thumping nerves. "Finn and Diesel are going to teach me how to dance, and I really, *really* don't need an audience. Even if it's just my father."

"Just my father," he scoffs before closing his books and standing. "I get it. I'll be in the back if you need anything. The speakers and mic are on, and I sent you the file with the song you asked for this morning."

"Thanks," I say, heart drumming in my chest. Dad grabs his things before heading to the back. When I asked my dad if we could use Kit's to rehearse, I ended up telling him the truth about my entire relationship with Axel. He was so understanding. Almost too understanding. I forgot how nonjudgmental and easy to talk to he is. It's been really nice having him back in my life.

"So," I say, removing my jacket. Finn and Diesel have already removed theirs and are waiting by the front of the stage. "Where do we begin?"

They exchange glances and I mentally prepare myself to be let down, gently.

"Can we talk first?" Finn asks.

"Sure." I swallow before clenching my jaw. *Relax, Jamie.* They said talk. They haven't walked out. *Yet.*

The three of us sit at a table. The same one we sat at the night we met. They continue to exchange glances and I continue to wait for someone to say something, tapping my fingers quickly and obnoxiously on the table. I force myself to stop and, instantly, my knee begins to thump.

"The thing is," Diesel begins. "We're Axel's friends, and I know this is something you're doing *for* Axel, and we respect that, but it also feels like we're going behind his back a bit."

"He asked us if we wanted to perform at the winter formal with him and we said yes, obviously, not only because we're always down to perform together but because we're already going to be there—for you. But then . . ." Finn's words trail off and he sighs, like he doesn't want to say the next thing. "When he asked to rehearse today, we had to lie and say we couldn't meet up until later. And it felt really shitty lying to him."

I suck in my lips before releasing a nervous breath. "I'm sorry if you feel like I've put you in a difficult position. But I promise I won't take up too much of your time. I'll work really, really hard today and then I'll rehearse on my own. I just really need your help. Like, really bad."

"Really?" Diesel asks. Diesel and Finn laugh, and it's clear they're laughing with me, not at me, so I allow myself to join in.

"I screwed up with Axel," I continue. "Repeatedly. And in so many ways. It's not enough for me to say I'm sorry. It's not even enough for me to tell him I love him. I need to show him how I feel, and it needs to be this big, public gesture because I don't just want Axel to know how I feel, I want everyone to know."

"We get it," Finn says. "We're just not sure if we can choreograph an entire dance in one afternoon. Especially since . . ."

"We're working with a novice," Diesel says, diplomatically.

"I may be a novice but I'm a really good student. I take direction well and I really want this."

They look at one another again and smile. "Okay," Finn says. "Did you pick a song?"

"I did," I say, nodding enthusiastically. "One that holds great meaning. My dad already mixed it for us."

"What do you mean by mixed it?" Diesel asks, their dark eyebrows scrunched.

"The idea is that you and Finn will begin the performance, and when the first chorus comes on, I'll get on stage and sing my own version of the chorus. Which will be a declaration of love." Finn and Diesel look at one another a bit apprehensively. "My dad manages this place and has access to karaoke versions of almost every song, plus he's sort of like a low-key sound engineer. He faded out Dua Lipa's voice and blended it with the karaoke version just in time for the chorus so that I could be heard loud and clear."

"What happens after you sing your version of the chorus?" Finn asks, studying me like I'm a person who is clearly in over their head.

"The song will return to status quo and I'll dance with you or—and this is what I'm hoping for—Axel will pull me off stage and we'll kiss and make up."

"She's been drinking the delulu potion," Diesel says, smothering another laugh.

"I have been. But I believe a little bit of delusion is necessary to make things happen."

"So, let me get this straight," Finn interjects. "We're going to choreograph a dance that you may or may not join us on stage for? But you're definitely going to sing your own chorus that we're supposed to just pretend is normal and dance through?"

"Exactly." I nod, plastering on a confident smile.

"Clearly she meant big when she said big," Diesel says to Finn.

"It's . . . different." Finn shakes his head slightly.

"This has to be perfect . . . for Axel. So, you still in?" I ask, biting on my lower lip. "I know it's a bit more than I'd originally pitched, but it's really, *really* important to me."

"Yeah. We're in," Finn says. "Not only for you, but because we *really* want to see Axel happy again."

"Alright." Diesel rises from the table and rolls up their sleeves. "Let's get started. We don't have much time."

"Awesome," I say, allowing a relieved smile to come out. "I'll cue the music."

We rehearse for three hours before we take our first break. We've chest-pumped and body-rolled so many times, I am going to feel it in my bones tomorrow. But it's important I get all the moves down perfectly on the off chance I do have to follow through and perform the entire routine. We have less than an hour before Dad opens the club up to the public. Diesel's seated, listening to the song on repeat, closing their eyes and tapping on the table, and Finn is chewing on his fingernail while staring down at his phone.

"What's wrong?" I ask, bringing over the bottles of water that Dad left for us on the bar.

"Axel isn't responding to any of my texts. I told him we're running a bit late."

"Did you try calling?" I ask, sitting at the table with them. "He sometimes picks up."

Finn nods and calls Axel with the speaker on. My pulse quickens as the first ring comes through the phone—followed by another ring, and then a third before his voicemail plays. "Am I screening this call? Probably. Either way, no one leaves voicemail anymore. Don't be that person."

Finn laughs at Axel's recording, but all it does is make me question if everything I'm doing is a huge mistake. "Do you think he's onto us? Do you think he knows you're with me and that's why he's not answering? Would he be pissed?" I ask.

"Jamie, you need to chill. Sometimes Axel doesn't reply to our texts for days. He's not obsessed with his phone," Diesel says.

"He always responded to my texts immediately," I say.

"That's because he's in love with you," Finn replies.

"Did he tell you that?" I ask, hearing both the hope and desperation in my voice.

"It was pretty obvious the night we all met," Finn says, tucking his phone away.

"You two know Axel better than anyone. Do you think this will work, or am I just wasting your time?"

Diesel looks up from their phone. "He's hurting, and when he's hurt, it's hard for him to see outside those feelings sometimes. So yeah, there's a chance this might not work. But there's also a chance it might."

"Axel's worth taking the risk, right?" Finn asks.

"One hundred percent." One million percent. "The clock's ticking. We should get back to it."

"You're such a little keener." Finn smiles.

"Funny thing about the word 'keener,'" I say before taking a sip of water. "It originates from the word 'keen,' which in adjective form has more than a handful of homographs."

"Jamie," Diesel says, nodding their head to the stage. "If you want Axel to be *keen* on you, I suggest we focus on the performance."

"I'm keenly aware of what you did there," I say, biting back a smile.

"No wonder Axel likes you so much. You're almost as corny as he is," Diesel says. We laugh as the three of us make our way back to the stage.

CHAPTER TWENTY-EIGHT

It's Saturday. December 19. The day of winter formal, and a huge amount of snow fell last night. Toronto has practically shut down since there aren't enough plows to deal with the amount of snow that dumped on our city, and even when they do manage to plow the roads, there's nowhere to put it all.

Olivia calls. She's freaking out because she's head of the social committee and people keep messaging her, wanting her to reschedule the formal, as if it's that simple. As she puts it, it's "effing impossible." For one, we'd lose our deposit. And secondly, the CN Tower is all booked up for the rest of the season. The fact that we got it at all, according to Olivia, was a miracle.

"It's still early in the day. I'm sure by the evening they'll have most of the main roads cleared off," I say, trying to reassure her over the phone. But the news station playing in the background in a constant loop paints a completely different picture.

"Even still, how am I going to get my hair and makeup done?"

"Can you come here?" I ask. "All my mom's customers canceled. I'm sure she'd be thrilled to help doll us up for the formal."

"Oh my god. Yes!" Olivia basically shouts into the phone. "I don't care how long it takes me to dig out my car, I'll be there."

"Be careful," I say.

"And what about you?" she asks. "Are you ready for tonight?"

Am I ready for tonight?

"Let's just worry about getting there first. Then I can worry about the performance. What if Axel doesn't show up?"

"His friends will make sure of it. But you better check with them," she says, a bit less reassuringly.

"Right," I say. "Okay, I'm going to practice a few more times and then take a shower. When should I expect you?"

"I'll text you updates. Too bad Ben isn't here to help me shovel. What good is having a big, strong boyfriend when you can't use him in emergencies?"

"I'm sure if you asked, Ben would shovel a path to your house."

She laughs. "Probably. Okay, wish me luck! And hopefully I'll see you soon."

"Good luck!"

I end the call and tell my mom that Olivia is attempting to come over and will require her services. Mom's strained smile isn't exactly comforting. I know what she's thinking. We're all thinking it. I go to my room to try to take my mind off everything by rehearsing. After running through the song ten times, I take a much-needed shower. My stomach growls while I throw on clean sweats (I mean, I think they're clean—they weren't on my floor). Remembering there's leftover Chinese in the fridge, I head downstairs excitedly, the thought of day-old chow mein making my mouth water. The front door opens and I'm met with a snow-covered uncle and...

"Axel?" I say, blinking in surprise. Axel's cheeks are all red. His curls are tucked in a toque, a few tendrils peeking out as he closes the door behind him. "What's going on?"

"I need to get into the garage for a second shovel," Eli says, opening the console in search of the spare garage door remote. "The remote in my car is dead and the keypad is frozen."

Axel rubs his hands together, trying to get warm.

"Why? Where are you going?" I ask, still on the landing of the stairs.

"Work," Amo says, like I'm clueless. "With this kind of weather, we could get a lot of walk-in customers. Peter will need extra hands."

"You're working tonight?" I ask Axel.

"Sure." He shrugs. "What else have I got to do?"

"The formal," I spit out before turning to my uncle. "He's performing at the formal. He can't work tonight."

Axel shakes his head. "Jamie, there's no way the formal is going to happen. The roads are a mess. It took me half an hour just to walk here. As it stands, getting to Shawarma Sitty is going to be nearly impossible."

"No," I practically shout. "You have to be there."

"Why?" he asks, his eyes narrowed at me.

"Because," I say, stalling, begging my uncle to read my face, but he's completely out to lunch. "Because everyone is expecting you to kick off the party."

"I think the three people that show up will be fine without me." His voice is dry and devoid of emotion.

"Amo, can I speak to you, please?" I ask, cocking my head to the family room.

"I have my boots on," he whines, grasping onto the spare garage remote.

I roll my eyes. "Fine. Axel, do you mind waiting outside for just a minute?"

"Whatever." He sighs as he steps outside.

I take the final few steps down the stairs and close the door behind Axel. "Amo!"

"What?"

"Tonight is the formal. Axel is supposed to perform. He *has* to be there." My words come out sharp as I over-enunciate each syllable.

"He said he didn't want to go anymore." My uncle clicks his tongue, like he's annoyed with me.

I click my tongue right back. "Tell him you don't need him. Peter will be more than enough help."

"Jesus, woman. If your eyes get any bigger, they're going to bulge out of your head."

"Please. It's important."

"Sorry, babe. He asked if he could work. I already told him yes."

"You're so stubborn!" I whip open the door and Axel turns to face me. "You can't miss the formal."

"Jamie, the formal isn't happening. Face it!"

"Oh, it's happening," Olivia says, rounding the corner. "If I got my little Beamer to make it over here, the senior class will find a way to make it downtown. Come hell or high—what's the saying?" She pauses to ask me.

"Water," I answer.

"Right. Come hell or high water, the formal is a go! And I expect you to hold up your end of the agreement," Olivia says, eyes on Axel.

"Verbal agreement. I didn't sign anything," Axel says before looking back at my uncle. "You ready?"

I exhale loudly at my uncle as he passes me with a shrug. "I'll work on him," he whispers, but I know it's a lost cause. The whole thing is.

"Artists are so temperamental. We have bigger problems anyway," she says, rolling her eyes. She proceeds to remove her coat and boots. "There are one hundred and fifty-two full-time students in the senior class."

"Okay," I reply stoically, watching the front door close with a thud.

Olivia types furiously into her phone. "I have an idea." Before I can ask what that idea is, she pulls my arm, leading me up the staircase.

Once we get to the top, she stalls.

"Which one is yours?" she asks.

"Follow the mess," I say, nodding to my bedroom. The floor is mostly cleared off because I needed space to rehearse my performance, but the rest of my room is probably in the worst shape it's ever been in.

"My room is ten times messier," she says with a laugh. "It drives Ben crazy."

"He hated my room too!"

"He's so uptight." She flops down on my bed, and for a moment I think to myself how strange it is that Olivia Chen is in my room.

I pull up my desk chair and sit across from her. "So, what's your idea?"

"One sec." She holds up a finger before typing into her phone again. I glance around my room to see my formal dress hanging in the closet and sigh. What if Axel doesn't change his mind? Is there even a point in hoping anymore?

"Okay," Olivia says, bringing her attention back to me. "One hundred and twenty-one students are attending the formal."

"One hundred and twenty-three, if you add Axel's friends. One hundred and twenty-four, if you count Axel," I say.

"Here's my idea. We charter two buses! All of us live close enough to the school to make it there, even if by foot. And then from the school we'll take the bus to the CN Tower. It's the best way to ensure the most people come."

I cock my head at Olivia.

"What?" she asks, oblivious.

I breathe out an exhale, feeling like a mean parent who's about to burst the bubble of my child's ridiculous dream. "First of all, how are we going to charter two buses this late in the day? It's almost three o'clock. Secondly, how do you expect to pay for these buses? Thirdly," I say, while throwing an arm to my bedroom window, "did you forget Frosty and all of his descendants exploded all over the city last night?"

Olivia straightens while crossing one leg over the other. "The snow stopped hours ago. Plows have been working overtime. I have no doubt that Front Street is clear. In terms of cost, the social committee's accountant just messaged me that we have a surplus. We were going to use it for senior prom, but we'll just find another way to raise money before then. As for booking two buses, I'm already on it. Don't worry so much. I've got this," she says, giving me one of her signature smiles. I can't imagine being that confident. It's probably one of the reasons I was so envious of Olivia in the first place. She doesn't question everything like I do. She just goes for it.

"You are really good under pressure," I say.

"Yeah, I'm totally faking it. Goes with the hair extensions, nails, and"—she opens her mouth wide and points—"these two teeth."

We both laugh.

"I'm so glad we got past our differences, because I like hanging out with you," I say. "And I'm pretty sure Ben loves that we hang out now too."

"Aww, Jamie. That's the nicest thing anyone has ever said to me. I'd hug you if you looked like a hugger, but I can tell you're not."

"You would be correct." I nod. "I'm going downstairs to tell my mom you're here and heat up some leftovers. Meet me in her salon when you've got the bus situation all sorted out."

"Will do," she says, bringing the phone up to her ear. "And Jamie?" she calls out. "Can you heat some food up for me too?"

"You got it!" I smile.

Olivia spends most of the time on her phone while Mom does her hair. She's working really hard to pull everything together last minute, and I can't help but feel useless because all I'm doing is stewing in my own drama.

I snuck off to my room for a bit while Mom worked on Olivia, practicing my routine again and texting Diesel and Finn relentlessly. They keep telling me not to worry and that Axel will be there, but my confidence is waning.

In everything.

Once we're dressed, Olivia and I, both in boots, head out to her car. She drives us to the school (which is a terrifying experience) and parks.

"Oh no!" she says. "You forgot to bring your shoes."

"Oh!" I look down at my combat boots. "It's fine. I can dance in these. I'm sure it's fashionable . . . to someone."

"You can totally rock it. As for me"—she reaches into her backseat—"I'll be bringing these strappy things to change into on the bus. You ready?" she asks, holding onto her shoes and purse.

"No." I shake my head while reading my latest message. "I'm not. My uncle just texted. He said Axel is still at work. I'm worried his friends won't be able to convince him to come, and even if they do, the roads will be a challenge. It's just . . ." I slam my phone face down on my lap and rub at my temples. "Nothing is coming together the way I expected it to."

"Look at us," Olivia says, pulling one of my hands away from my head and forcing eye contact. "Never in a million years did I think I'd be going to winter formal with you. But here we are. Life can surprise you."

"I'm tired of the surprises. I just want to know if this will all work out."

She squints at me and smiles. "Are you? Haven't the surprises been the best part of the last few months? Axel. *Me*." She grins. "Your own metamorphosis."

I sigh and frown at Olivia, still unsure.

"You've got this, and even if you don't, I've got your back. So does Ben."

She's right. Even if things with Axel don't go as planned tonight, I am walking into that formal a new, better version of myself, with friends.

"Okay. Let's do this," I say, exhaling another sharp breath.

CHAPTER TWENTY-NINE

It's quarter to seven. The formal officially starts in fifteen minutes and I haven't heard from Finn or Diesel in almost an hour. My uncle isn't answering my texts either. The drive into the city is slow-going but steady. The only buses available at such short notice were the most expensive ones, so while we are definitely riding in style, the social committee completely drained their resources to make sure this event wasn't a bust. Despite all the snow, what we do have going for us is no traffic. Which in Toronto is pretty much a miracle.

The energy on the bus is like a simmering pot. People are excited but afraid to show it in case we don't make it. We've passed many stalled cars and even a stalled city bus. I'm seated in the row next to Ben and Olivia, who keep looking over at me like worried parents. I can't seem to let myself sit back and relax, especially when I don't know if we'll make it there (in one piece) or if Axel will show. This whole thing hinges on Axel being there. Without him, there's no point.

The logical side of my brain is telling me Axel won't be there. There are too many obstacles stopping him, but my heart . . . my heart holds on to hope and the belief that the connection we shared was real. *Is* real.

My phone pings and I jump slightly in my seat.

Diesel: We finally made it to Shawarma Sitty and he's not here.
Me: What did my uncle say?
Finn: He's swamped. He said something about Axel running an errand.

An errand? In this weather?

Me: Is Axel answering your texts?
Diesel: No. But he might answer yours. Text him Jamie. Confess. Tell him what we're doing. It might work.
Me: There's no point. It's too late.
Finn: It's not. Just try. We're on our way to the cn tower now.
Me: What's your ETA?
Diesel: About twenty minutes, give or take a stalled car. TEXT HIM!

I breathe out a loud sigh and Olivia pushes her way into my seat. "What's wrong?" she asks, placing her hand on my jittery knee.

"Axel wasn't at work when Finn and Diesel showed up. They don't know where he is. He won't answer their texts."

"Then you text him," Ben says, his body turned to our seat.

"He's not answering his best friends. He definitely won't answer the girl who broke his heart."

"Yes, he will," Ben affirms. "Text him. Or I will, and I'm not bluffing. You deserve to be happy. Stop getting in your own way."

Ben's words echo in my ear. *Stop getting in your own way.* It's something I've said to my mother. Repeatedly. I love my mom but she's lost years and experiences to holding grudges and closing herself off to relationships, old and new. I don't want to make that same mistake. I don't want to live with regrets. Axel has to be there, and I'll do everything in my power to make sure he is.

Me: Olivia figured it out! She chartered two buses and we're all headed to the formal. I know you're not really talking to me right now, but it's important you come. For one, Finn and Diesel need you there for the performance. The whole senior class is expecting you, and the thing is, I want you there. I need you to be there. Please Axel. Don't pull a Jamie and let your stubbornness get in the way of a really good time. Just come to the formal. You won't regret it. I promise!

"Okay," I say after hitting Send. "I texted Axel. Now we wait and see."

"He'll be there." Ben smiles.

"He'll be there," Olivia repeats.

"He'll be there," I parrot, hoping if we say it three times, it'll come true.

People on the bus start to cheer as the CN Tower comes into view. It's happening. It's actually happening. In a few minutes, I'm going to check off the final item on my bucket list by riding the elevator up the CN Tower. And I'm going to celebrate by making a fool of myself in front of the entire senior class.

Once again, I'm left wondering, *How did I get here?*

The bus pulls up to Front Street and parks. The simmering pot boils over and everyone rises, talking over one another in excitement. I remain seated, allowing the others to get off the bus first.

"Nope," Ben says, sliding in next to me. We're the only two students left on the bus. "You're not doing this loner-Jamie act. Let's go."

I shake my head while staring into Ben's sympathetic eyes. "I'm scared."

"Good."

"Good?"

"Yes, good. Be scared. Be uncomfortable. It means you're challenging yourself. You can't put fear on a checklist, Jamie. You can't write it down and cross it off. You have to live through it. You have to experience it. You have to take that risk."

"And if I fail?" I ask.

"At least you tried. You won't look back twenty years from now with regrets."

I swallow and nod, looking at the boy I loved for three years. I still love him, but in a different way. "I know things were kind of messy between us for a while, but you were a really good first boyfriend and I have no regrets about that."

Ben smiles as he rises, extending a hand. "Look at us. We did end up at the winter formal together after all."

I stand, taking his hand. "Yeah. You, me, and your girlfriend."

Once we step off the bus, we find Olivia in her gold dress waiting for us, shivering as she stands on the only spot on the sidewalk that isn't covered in snow. The others have gone ahead. Ben, like some sort of prince, carries Olivia up the snow-covered steps so she doesn't get her feet wet. I follow them toward the CN Tower. A Blue Rodeo song plays over the speakers and it stops me in my tracks. It's a sign. It must be. The lyrics make my heart swell until I look up . . .

and up . . .

and up.

Holy shit.

What was I thinking? There's no way I'm getting in that elevator. I want to turn back, with everything inside me, the fear having fully taken over, but I know Ben and Olivia won't let that happen.

They wait by the glass doors and wave me over. "Come on, Jamie. It's freezing," Ben shouts.

I nod and step inside with tremendous buckets of hesitation. The walk is long and quiet as we make our way to the elevators.

A few groups are ahead of us. As we wait our turn, I check my phone, hoping to see a text from Axel, but there isn't one.

"Jamie! Jamie!" a deep voice calls out. I turn around to see Finn and Diesel running toward me. The elevator doors open and I tell Ben and Olivia to go ahead.

"You promise you won't back out?" Olivia asks, her brown eyes wide.

"I'll be there," I assure her, even though I'm not confident I will. The elevator doors close as Finn and Diesel approach.

"Any word from Axel?" Diesel asks.

"No. You?"

"No," Finn replies. He looks down at his phone. "What time are we supposed to go on?"

"Seven thirty," I answer. "They're not doing a formal dinner. Just finger foods and drinks. Olivia wanted it to be an all-night party."

"This is sweet," Finn says, looking around.

"So, we should head up, right?" Diesel asks.

"You two go without me," I say.

"Axel may already be inside, for all we know," Finn says in a tight but hopeful voice. "Let's go see."

"Here's the thing," I say, stalling to let out another shaky breath. "I am extremely claustrophobic, like more than you can even imagine, and the idea of riding in that elevator terrifies me. But I have to do it. And I have to do it alone."

"I feel you," Diesel says with a nod. "Being here is doing things to my fear of heights. For real."

"And Jamie, if we get up there and Axel isn't there, it'll be okay. We don't need him to put on a good show," Finn says. "You've put in the work."

"But he's the reason I'm even doing the performance."

"Umm, hello? Everyone with a phone will be recording us. It'll be up all over the gram, Snapchat, and TikTok by the end of the night. The message can still get to Axel whether he's here or not," Finn says.

"I never thought of that," I say, my pulse quickening. The idea of being immortalized on the internet, for more than just our senior class to see, is not something I signed up for. But then again, none of this is.

"Whatever you do, don't chicken out!" Finn says. "And if you do, I'll come back down and ride up with you. Just text if you decide you need someone by your side. It's okay to ask for help."

"That's sweet," I say.

The elevator doors open and the CN Tower employee ushers in Finn and Diesel. The metal doors close and I take in another deep breath.

"You planning on going up?" the employee running the elevators asks.

"Um. Yeah." I swallow and nod at them. "I'm going up." After another minute of waiting, the doors open and I pause. "Wait. What do I press when I'm in there?"

"I control the elevator from out here. All you have to do is enjoy the ride and view."

"Right. Okay." Realizing I can't stall any longer, I step inside. My heart starts to run a marathon. Already I feel the walls closing in on me. Half the floor is made of glass and the elevator itself is comprised mostly of windows. I'm sure the view would be amazing if I didn't want to piss myself. But hey, I did it. I'm inside. And in sixty seconds I will have officially killed the Kill-It List.

The doors begin to close and I lean back against one wall, my feet on solid ground, when the doors slowly reopen. My stomach sinks, the first cramp making its annoying appearance. Technical issues already? This can't be a good sign. But then the scent of chicken shawarma fills the elevator, and Axel steps inside.

"Mind if I ride up with you?" he asks, his cheeks red, hair a mess. "Or is this something you wanted to do alone?"

I glance past Axel's shoulder to see if the CN Tower employee is annoyed, but they couldn't look less interested in what's going on.

"Sure. I mean, I don't want you to think I need you here but—" My breath catches. Axel blinks and his gaze meets with mine. "I want you here."

Axel smothers a grin before stepping in farther. The doors finally close and the ride up the tower begins. My hands are balled into tight fists, my breathing steady but quick. Axel leans up against the wall opposite me, the glass floor between us.

It's quiet and I want to ask him a million questions, but my mind is in overdrive. Minutes from now I'm supposed to get up in front of my entire senior class and . . . dance? What the hell made me think this was a good idea? I was so focused on Axel being here, and now that he is, it's all wrong. It's not at all—

A screeching noise pulls me out of my thoughts as my eyes meet with Axel's. His deer-in-the-headlights' expression does not bring me the comfort I'm seeking. The elevator stops, but there's one problem—the view of Toronto is still in front of us. We're suspended halfway up. We're . . . "Are we stuck?" I ask, on the verge of hyperventilating.

Axel shakes his head. "No. There's no way." He straightens and eyes the panel.

"Hello?" A voice comes out over the speaker.

"We're stuck!" I yell back.

"I understand that," the CN Tower employee responds calmly. "This happens occasionally on windy or cold days. I've dispatched for help. Just stay still and remain calm."

"How long?" I blurt out, now standing under the speaker, as if that will make a difference.

"Approximately fifteen minutes. Half an hour, tops."

"Half an hour?" I silently mouth, frozen in place.

"If you need anything, press the red call button. I'm just below you, and you're on camera, so we're keeping an eye on everything. It will be over before you know it."

"Easy for you to say with all that space and air surrounding you," I say, my arms flying up.

"Miss, are you going to be okay in there?"

"Yes," Axel says, his voice directly behind me. "I'll make sure she is."

"How?" I ask, nodding my head up and down. I know I'm losing it. I can feel myself losing it, and I know that losing it will not help with ... any ... thing ... I ... can't ... breathe.

My head drops and my knees weaken. My vision starts to blur as Axel's arm wraps around my waist.

"Let's sit, okay?" he says, his eyes big and trying their best to be reassuring, but how can I be reassured when I am currently living through my biggest nightmare? Except, I never imagined it happening with Axel next to me. Thank god he is. If I were in here alone, stuck ... I don't even want to let my mind go there.

I nod slightly while my breathing continues to intensify. We slide down the wall together until we're both seated on the floor. I tuck my knees to my chest, too afraid for any part of my body to touch the glass floor.

"We could watch some TikToks," Axel says. "To pass the time."

"Okay," I say, nodding again and trying very hard not to cry. I know this is a mental game, but the sharp pangs piercing through my lower stomach are very real.

He lifts his butt slightly to pull out his phone. His screen lights up to show a photo of the two of us, taken at Wonderland. He clears his throat. "I keep forgetting to change that."

I open my purse and pull out my phone to show him my background photo. A picture of the two of us, taken at his cousin's wedding. "Same."

Our eyes lock and I want to tell him everything, so many things, but it's like I can't think straight. Not with him sitting so close. Every mistake I've made flashes through my mind. I've been so foolish. I let this person slip out of my fingers. And here he is, literally stuck with me for the next god knows how long and I can't find the words. Again.

"Did I ah . . ." He exhales and runs a hand through his curls. "Did I ever, um." He clears his throat and I study him quizzically. I've never seen Axel so stuck for words before. "I'm terrified of heights."

"No, you're not," I say, emphatically.

"Would you like to feel my racing heart as proof?" he asks, eyebrows raised ever so slightly.

"But all the rides we went on at Wonderland. And you've never mentioned it before."

"There's varying levels of my fear and, well, being stuck halfway up the CN Tower qualifies." He swallows and his Adam's apple bobs up and down his throat as his eyes shift to the windows.

"Then why would you agree to perform here tonight?" I ask.

He looks down at his hands in his lap. Those hands I miss so much. I think about unspooling my sweaty fists to hold his hands in mine, but something stops me.

Something always stops me.

"I had this plan," I say, almost abruptly.

"*You* had a plan?" He manages a half-hearted laugh.

"This one was different though because it wasn't about me," I say, my legs now outstretched, phone tucked away in my purse. "Or for me. Okay, it was a little bit for me, but only because I wanted to make things right between us. I've been so miserable since we stopped speaking, and I've tried different ways to tell you how I feel but it was never about the words. Like you told my mom."

He shakes his head, turning his body slightly toward mine. "What did I tell your mom?"

"That night we both came in to Shawarma Sitty to help you. I was taking out the trash, and when I came in, I overheard you tell her how you needed to be with someone who would shout their feelings for you to the world. Someone who would take risks. So when words weren't enough, I hatched this plan with Finn and Diesel."

"Hello." The same disgruntled employee's voice comes out over the speaker. We both look up. "Help is on site. New estimated time is twenty minutes."

"Finn and Diesel?" he says to me, ignoring the update.

I suck in my lips, trying to level my breathing. Twenty minutes. I can do twenty minutes. I've got Axel and enough air—I think. I run a hand over my stomach. I haven't had a cramp in a few minutes. Maybe it's passed.

"Yeah. We met up and they helped me choreograph a dance, and the plan was for me to get up on the little stage tonight and perform with them to that Dua Lipa song. You know, the one you played in my room when you were trying to teach me how to dance? The one with numbers," I say, shaking my head as the words come out fast and on the verge of nonsensically.

"'New Rules,'" he confirms.

"Yes!" I snap. "That's the one."

Swirling noises sound below us as the elevator rattles slightly with the battering December winds. I squeeze my eyes shut, breathing in and out, in and out.

"I was going to get up there and dance with them, or I was going to let them dance and then I was going to get up there, I forget now," I say, running my sweaty hands up and down my thighs. "And I was going to get a mic and I'm not sure from where but I mean, there had to be one, right? It's not like we had a dress rehearsal. But the plan was for me to step up and start singing my own, rewritten chorus and, you know . . ." I nod, willing him to fill in the gaps of my rambles.

"No." Axel leans in, trying to make me meet his gaze. "I don't know."

I exhale not once, not twice, but three times. "I was going to profess my love for you in front of everyone. Because that's what you deserve. Someone who tells the world how they feel. And shows you and takes risks." I stand quickly and open my purse to pull out the song lyrics I changed from the Dua Lipa song. My hands shake as I decide to read out the lyrics. Singing seems highly unnecessary in this moment.

"One, fake-dating plan, long drives, hold hands, official on the gram.
Two, keep seeing him, you'll eventually fall in love again.
Three, don't be friends with Ben, you know you're gonna fall back into old habits . . .
and if you're back with him, you'll never find happiness.
I love Axel Da-hi-ni.

"And then I was supposed to repeat that last line three times to the tune of the song, but that feels a little awkward to do in this moment."

I swallow, staring down at my jittery hands. Axel rises and stands so his nose almost touches mine. His familiar scent overtakes every single one of my senses and I feel my body start to relax. My shoulders lower. My heart slows. I lift my eyes to meet with his as the terrible song lyrics I wrote fall to our feet.

We're standing on the glass floor.

"You love me?" he asks.

My throat burns as I watch his brown eyes glisten. "So much. I mean, I was willing to get on stage and sing and dance in front of people I know. For you! Not to mention . . ." I say, looking around the elevator and pointing down to the floor.

He laughs. "I love . . . that you were willing to do that, Jamie. But you don't have to. You never had to. When I said those things to your mom, I was hurting and probably just trying to convince myself that we weren't meant to be together. Knowing that you reached out to my best friends and somehow convinced them to teach you a dance all so you could win me back? I mean, I don't want to compare," he says, squaring his shoulders, "but I think this beats any plan you had to win back Ben."

"You win, Axel. You win a million times over Ben. The way I feel about you is so different from what I felt for him. Ben made sense. With Ben I could see our entire future. I knew exactly what to expect with him and it was everything I thought I wanted. Or needed. The plans, the lists, it was all so I could have control over my life in some small way, since that had been ripped away from me at such a young age. But it was all fabricated. It was like following a script. For a while, the safety in knowing what lay ahead helped heal parts of me, enough that when you came into my life, I was ready for the real thing. The messiness of love. The fun. The 'I have no idea what this guy is going to say or do next,' and I love that." I swallow and find Axel's hands, interlocking his fingers with mine. "The thing is, I do feel calm with you. Serenity. Peace. Because you accept me for exactly who I am. And," I say, smiling to myself, "while I may not know what our future holds or what might happen when we step off this elevator, when I'm with you, the anxiety that lives within me is a whisper."

Axel's grip tightens as his chest rises and falls with my words.

"Jamie, I—" The lights flicker off and on and the elevator shakes before resuming. Our bodies jolt apart as we lean against opposite walls.

Seconds later, the doors open and loud music pours into the elevator. Axel nods for me to exit first. I do, and then I inhale a large breath of air, but when I turn back to find Axel, he's gone.

"Jamie!" Olivia calls out. "Are you okay? We heard there was an elevator that was stuck. Was that the one you were on?"

"Yes," I say, like it was no big deal. "Where did he go?"

"Who?" she asks, looking past me.

"Axel. He was with me. We were . . . stuck together."

She tilts her head and smiles. "Aww. That's so romantic. Did you guys kiss and make up?"

"Not exactly," I say, still searching for him.

"Ben!" Olivia yells over the music.

"For a tiny person, you're very loud," I say, peering down at her.

"Sorry. I'm just so excited. Are you still going to do the thing?" she asks, eyebrows raised.

"No. I don't have to."

"Ben," Olivia says, pulling him into our huddle. "Jamie isn't going to do the thing anymore."

"You rode up the elevator," he says, seemingly surprised to see me.

There is just way too much going on right now. Ben is beaming. Olivia is chiding. Axel has disappeared. I'm sweating under my coat. Ben must notice because he helps me remove it and Olivia brings it to the coat check person and then rejoins us.

"Have you seen Axel?" I ask him.

"Yeah. He's by the stage with his friends."

"Right. He's performing," I say, completely having forgotten that he was here for his own reasons.

"You coming in?" Olivia asks, clasping Ben's hand.

"Yeah, I just need a minute," I say, staying behind.

They smile as they walk away from the elevators and into the party. After a few steadying breaths, I force myself to do the same.

The CN Tower observation level is circular and surrounded by floor-to-ceiling windows and mirrored ceilings. The view of Toronto is breathtaking. Especially at night. Especially covered in snow. Especially now that I'm not seeing it trapped inside an elevator.

I stand at a window, staring out. It's a sea of different shades of blue, from the sky to the lake. Yellow lights from the highways and the structures dot the view, and tonight, the water glistens like diamonds. The buildings look like they're part of Santa's village (if Santa lived in a city), and the horizon is a beautiful indigo.

I remain taking in the sights, thinking about how I spent the last four months not only getting to know myself but also getting to know this amazing city.

"Toronto is beautiful at night," Axel says, coming up next to me.

I turn to him in surprise. "I thought you had to get ready for your performance."

"It can wait." He smiles, and warmth spreads through me.

"Wait," I say, studying Axel as he stands close to the floor-to-ceiling windows. "Your fear of heights."

He looks down and laughs. "I made that up. I was just trying to distract you from your own fears. It worked. Got you talking. And talking."

A huff of air escapes me. "What could be scarier than being stuck in an elevator with your fake ex-girlfriend who decided to declare her love for you in a terribly written song?"

"I loved it," he says, holding up the small piece of paper with the song lyrics.

"But?" I ask, nervously waiting for Axel to tell me it's all too little, too late.

"Do you know why I love performing so much? Because until recently, it was the only time I ever felt free. Fearless. I don't even get afraid of messing up anymore because it's so easy to shake it off and pretend it's all part of the act. The adrenaline, I imagine, is like being high. You know what else feels that way?"

"No?" I ask before sucking in my lips.

"You." His lips curl into the most beautiful smile I've ever seen. "Being with you is all those things and more. When we're together it's like my feet don't even touch the ground. I get this dopey-ass grin on my face, and I keep trying to force myself to wipe it off but it won't go away. Not whenever you're nearby. Not when I can see your eyes sparkling back at me. A sparkle I know I helped put there. Watching you transform into the person you were always meant to be has been amazing, and soul-crushing, because I haven't gotten to be part of it for the last few weeks."

"How about now?" I ask, my voice quiet but drowning in hope. "Is the sparkle there now?"

"You tell me." His mouth curves up in a half-smile/half-smirk. The way it always does before he kisses me. The electricity between us is fierce. Fierce enough to stop elevators.

"What up, Maple View?" Olivia's voice booms over the speakers. I turn to see her on the small stage holding a mic. Everyone cheers back, but she holds up a finger to her lips to silence them. "We got off to a late start tonight with the snow and our star performer getting stuck in an elevator, but now that we're all here, it's time to get the party started! Axel!" Olivia yells. "Get that Arab booty up here and shake that thang."

"Oh my god!" I say, cringing at her words, but of course, the whole class is under her spell. I don't blame them. She's almost as charming as Axel is.

"I guess I'm needed," he says in that cocky way I've learned to love. Axel slips away, and I watch as he huddles with Finn and Diesel for a moment before speaking to the DJ.

My eyes meet with both Finn's and Diesel's as I approach the stage. They smile and Finn leans down to me. "You joining us?"

"No," I say, shaking my head and pulling at my earlobe. "I, uh, did my part earlier. The stage belongs to the three of you."

Finn nods with a wide grin as he steps into place.

The music begins and Axel, Finn, and Diesel dance together. They have the entire senior class enraptured by their performance. Seeing Axel doing what he loves again, this time with his friends at his side, fills me with so much pride and happiness, my face hurts. In a way, I'm glad I got stuck in that elevator. It saved me from getting up there tonight and taking the spotlight away from him. Dancing is his thing, and I don't have to make it mine. But it isn't lost on me that I did tell Axel I loved him, more than once, and he has yet to directly respond.

Maybe he won't. And maybe that's okay.

Maybe—

Axel hops off the stage and stands face-to-face with me.

"You're incredible," I say, grinning like a fool in love. Axel starts speaking, but the clapping and hollering around us drowns out his words. I shake my head, pointing to my ears, mouthing, "I can't hear you."

The music cuts out at the exact moment Axel shouts, "I love you too!"

Silence follows for a moment before a collective *aww* sweeps the area. The next song begins, and the attention that was on us floats back to the stage as Finn and Diesel perform without Axel.

My mouth opens slightly as I stand in place, unsure of what to do or say next, sweaty bodies bumping against us.

"Jamie," Axel says, snapping his fingers in front of my face. "You high again?"

I smile. "Maybe a little. Could you repeat yourself?"

Axel laughs and stands so we're nose to nose. He tips his forehead to mine, staring right into my eyes. Finn and Diesel continue to dance on stage behind us while the party resumes around us. But Axel and I may as well be in our own world.

"Jamie T-F, I love you more than I love shawarma sandwiches. More than I love Betty White. More than I love dancing."

"Does this mean you'll be my real boyfriend?" I ask, holding back the very strong urge to kiss him right here.

Axel rubs the tip of his nose with mine, smiling that irresistible smile, and I'm a goner. There's no holding back. I bring my lips to his and kiss him with everything inside me. All the doubt, pain, fear, love, joy, hope I've been holding onto for the last four months, for my entire life, is released with what is probably the best kiss of my life . . . well, maybe it ties with the kiss under the rainbow, and all the ones that followed.

Because every kiss with Axel has been the best kiss of my life.

Feeling his arms around me, the warmth of his body, his scent, fills me back up. This moment is not something I could have ever put on a list. It's not something that can be contrived. It's spontaneous. It's unpredictable. It's real. It's now.

It's love.

And no check mark can compete with that feeling.

We pull apart and Axel grins. "You have a funny way of showing your feelings."

"Someone said that to me once," I say, rubbing the tip of my nose with his again.

"Do we need to sit down and discuss the terms and conditions of our union?" Axel asks.

"To be quite honest with you, I've had it with contracts, rules, and stipulations."

"Does that make you a free agent? Because I may have a problem with that," he says, squinting at me.

"I guess there's room to negotiate," I say.

"I'm very good at negotiating."

"Axel," Finn shouts from the stage as a new song begins.

"My people are demanding to see me," he says, before planting a fast kiss on my lips and getting on stage with his friends. They dance to "How Dare You Want More" by Bleachers and the entire senior class hops up and down, singing along, except me.

As the chorus plays, the lyrics speak to me in a way they probably wouldn't have months ago. When a song was just a song. Then Axel forced me to slow down and really listen to the words. I did dare to want more. But the "more" I was after was all about checking items off a list without stopping to enjoy any of the experiences. It was constantly moving goal posts. Being with Axel taught me to enjoy all the moments—big and small—in real time. The roller coasters, the dancing, the falling in love, forgiveness, and moving forward without leaving others behind.

"Jamie," Axel calls from the stage, his arm extended. He has the most adorable look on his face. I take his hand and pull him off the stage to where I'm standing. He stumbles slightly and wraps his arms around me to ground himself. Finn and Diesel continue dancing on stage, no apparent choreography anymore. Just freestyling it like everyone else.

"I changed my mind," I say, shouting over the music again.

"About what?" Axel asks.

"I think we do need some new rules."

"Hit me," he says, as the stage fills up with people dancing and filming themselves and one another.

"Rule one," I say, fighting back a smile. "You need to call me out when I'm being hard-headed."

"I can do that." He crosses his arms over this chest. "Next."

"Rule two: you must also embrace my chaotic energy. And yes, that means you will sometimes have to cancel out rule one."

"Got it." He nods, trying but failing to keep a serious expression.

"Rule three—and this is a big one: if you can't agree to this then I don't think we have a future," I say, sucking in my lips to fight a grin. "No matter how terrible or embarrassing I am, I get to be your number-one dance partner."

Axel shakes his head and then nods. "I don't only agree to that rule," he says, before uncrossing his arms and pulling me toward him, "I insist on it."

We kiss with the music blasting above us, our entire senior class dancing around us, and the most spectacular view of Toronto surrounding us.

"Last rule," I say, pulling apart slightly from Axel. "You have to always kiss me like that."

"Hey, did you know 'kiss' means to touch with the lips as a sign of love, and also, in billiards it means a slight touch of a ball against another ball?"

I narrow my eyes at him. "Stop talking about balls and kiss me."

"You drive a hard bargain, James," Axel says, before leaning in.

"I want a picture," Olivia shouts, breaking up our very public display of affection.

We turn to face Olivia, and Axel slips his arm around my waist. Butterflies. Millions of them.

"Say Betty White!" Olivia commands with a knowing wink.

"May I?" Ben asks Olivia, holding out his hand. She lifts her shoulders slightly before passing him her phone.

"Smile," Ben says, positioning the phone to capture the moment. Instead of facing the camera, Axel and I stare at one another, but we do hold up one end of Ben's request. We are most certainly smiling. In fact, I'm pretty sure my eyes are tiny slits from grinning so widely, but my eyes will still be big enough to know. Big enough to know, when I stare back at this photo a month from now—or years from now—exactly how I felt and what I was thinking.

Jamie and ~~Ben's~~ Axel's Bucket List Playlist

1. **STAY**—*The Kid LAROI & Justin Bieber*
2. **Cruel Summer**—*Taylor Swift*
3. **I Wish It Would Rain Down**—*Phil Collins*
4. **drivers license**—*Olivia Rodrigo*
5. **traitor**—*Olivia Rodrigo*
6. **get him back!**—*Olivia Rodrigo*
7. **New Rules**—*Dua Lipa*
8. **Baby (feat. Ludacris)**—*Justin Bieber*
9. **Treat You Better**—*Shawn Mendes*
10. **we can't be friends (wait for your love)**—*Ariana Grande*
11. **Til I Am Myself Again**—*Blue Rodeo*
12. **Lost Together**—*Blue Rodeo*
13. **Adventure of a Lifetime**—*Coldplay*
14. **Teenage Dream**—*Katy Perry*
15. **The Flame**—*Cheap Trick*
16. **Against All Odds (Take a Look at Me Now)**—*Phil Collins*
17. **pretty isn't pretty**—*Olivia Rodrigo*
18. **Fix You**—*Coldplay*
19. **Daylight**—*Taylor Swift*
20. **Levitating (feat. DaBaby)**—*Dua Lipa*
21. **How Dare You Want More**—*Bleachers*
22. **Anyone**—*Justin Bieber*
23. **Life Is a Highway**—*Tom Cochrane*

ACKNOWLEDGMENTS

The idea to write *You Started It* came to me not in one moment but a series of moments. It was 2021 and we were in the height of the COVID-19 pandemic and sheltering at home. I had learned that although I had a bachelor of education, I was, in fact, a terrible teacher to my daughters. I also learned that even though I am a homebody, I have my limits.

I started to daydream about leaving my house and having new experiences. I needed some FUN! This, combined with listening to Olivia Rodrigo's *Sour* album on repeat, allowed an idea to start piecing together in my mind. A book that would start off with a breakup, throw in some fake-dating, and feature a main character that would be very different from my first, Jessie Kassis. Also, wouldn't it be fun if my characters got to explore the city of Toronto and do all the things I was daydreaming about doing myself?

I knew that this would be a more mature book than *Something More*, and as such, it was important for me to address some heavier themes. An absent parent. A main character with diagnosed anxiety (like myself). A Palestinian mother who struggles with her identity, and her mixed-race daughter who also has questions about where she belongs. And a love interest unlike any I'd written before.

I wrote this novel with an Arab teenaged boy love interest for many reasons. Most significantly because I had been so brainwashed by Western media as a Palestinian Canadian that I never questioned why all the love interests in the media I consumed were white. In the rare instances when they weren't white, they definitely were not Arab men.

It was really only when my two Arab nephews became teenagers that I started to deconstruct all those years of internalized discrimination. Here were two smart, funny, charming, and adorable boys—why were people like them almost never featured as the love interest?

Then there's my father, who, at the time of writing these acknowledgments, had passed away only months before. A man I admired and adored and who was hilarious, strong, insanely talented, and loving. A deserving hero in any story.

Western media often portrays a one-dimensional, stereotypical, and false (and tired) take on Arab men. Writing this book felt like my opportunity to help change the narrative.

I hope Axel Dahini and Amo Eli show how truly amazing Arab boys and men can be. That they deserve to fall in love and take up space on the shelves too.

To my father, Nicola Khalilieh: You were so proud of me and my first book, *Something More*. I will never forget standing by your hospital bed in your last days while you told our family doctor, with a big smile on your face, that I had written a book. You were telling him how I'd faced a lot of criticism for it, especially because I was Palestinian. This conversation took place in November 2023, and so, especially then, my existence as a Palestinian author put a spotlight on me that I hadn't been prepared to stand in. It wasn't a huge spotlight, and I don't have a large platform, but I did and continue to do with it what I can. Not only to make you proud, but because I was somehow put in this position, and like you, I will do everything in my power to be a positive voice for Palestinians. Even if that means facing backlash, harassment, one-star review

Alena Bruzas—you are such a talented author and amazing listener. I feel honored to be on this journey with you (again). Thanks also to my SP writing group, for continuing to be there through everything. You're all my favorite writers.

To my little family, Rob (thank you for keeping me hydrated), Elsie (thank you for the random office drop-ins and even more random stories), and Emma (there's no one else I would have wanted to go to both the Guts concert and Era's Tour with. Best nights ever!)—I love you!

To my mom, family, and friends, who I'm not fully convinced understand what I do, how all of this works, and the hours (and tears) that go into this—that's okay. You can continue to show your support by buying my books. You don't even need to read them!

To my nephews Nicolas and Joey, thank you for helping me change the narrative.

And to my readers!

I didn't get to thank my readers with my first book because, at that time, I didn't have any. And now, I am so honored to be building a community of readers from around the world (!!!) who root for both me and my books. Readers who see themselves in my characters. Readers who post and share my books. (The insightful TikToks! The beautiful Instagram posts! The cover reveal you helped make a success!) Maybe I'm biased, but I happen to think I have some of the best readers!

Thank you so much!

You Started It is set in Toronto. As a Palestinian in the diaspora with complicated feelings about my own settler status, I wanted to acknowledge that Toronto is the traditional territory of nations including the Mississaugas of the Credit, the Anishnabeg, the Chippewa, the Haudenosaunee, and the Wendat peoples. It is now home to many diverse First Nations, Inuit, and Métis peoples. Toronto is covered by Treaty 13 with the Mississaugas of the Credit. I am very grateful to work on these lands, and I encourage you to join me in reflecting and learning about the lands that we inhabit. You can visit Native-Land.ca to find more information, and if you'd like to donate, please consider an organization such as Indigenous Youth Roots (indigenousyouthroots.ca).

I used to think in absolutes. Probably a product of my autistic mind. But with the gift of age, I've learned that nothing is all good or all bad. There is beauty in the mess, in the sadness, and in the process.

Jamie experiences her anxiety very similarly to how I experience mine, just like Jessie's autism very much mirrors my own. If my characters' experiences don't align with yours, it does not invalidate your experience with anxiety or autism, nor does it invalidate mine.

The beautiful thing about reading widely and diversely is that we get to see the world through the eyes of multiple people: sometimes people who are a lot like us and sometimes people who are not.

Thank you to everyone who took a chance on *You Started It* and to the friends who returned after reading *Something More*. I hope you'll stick around for my third YA book, *Everything Comes Back to You*. And if you haven't yet gotten to meet Jessie, she's a pretty fun time, in my humble opinion.